CC

LIGHT-HEARTED LOOK AT MURDER

Mark Watson is one of the UK's most talked-about stand-up comedians. He has won and been nominated for many awards, including *Time Out Critics' Choice* (2006), the if.comeddies Panel Prize for the Edinburgh Fringe (2006), and the Perrier Best Newcomer Award (2005). Mark is renowned in comedy circles for having performed three marathon stand-up shows lasting 24, 33 and 36 hours. His fiction debut, *Bullet Points*, was published in 2004.

ALSO BY MARK WATSON

Bullet Points

MARK WATSON

A Light-hearted Look at Murder

VINTAGE BOOKS
London

Published by Vintage 2008

2 4 6 8 10 9 7 5 3

First published in Great Britain in 2007 by
Chatto & Windus
Random House, 20 Vauxhall Bridge Road,
London SW1V 2SA
www.vintage-books.co.uk

Addresses for companies within The Random House Group Limited can be found at: www.randomhouse.co.uk/offices.htm

The Random House Group Limited Reg. No. 954009

A CIP catalogue record for this book is available from the British Library

ISBN 9780099460862

The Random House Group Limited supports the Forest Stewardship Council (FSC®), the leading international forest certification organisation. Our books carrying the FSC label are printed on FSC® certified paper. FSC is the only forest certification scheme endorsed by the leading environmental organisations, including Greenpeace. Our paper procurement policy can be found at www.randomhouse.co.uk/environment

Printed and bound by CPI Group (UK) Ltd, Croydon, CR0 4YY

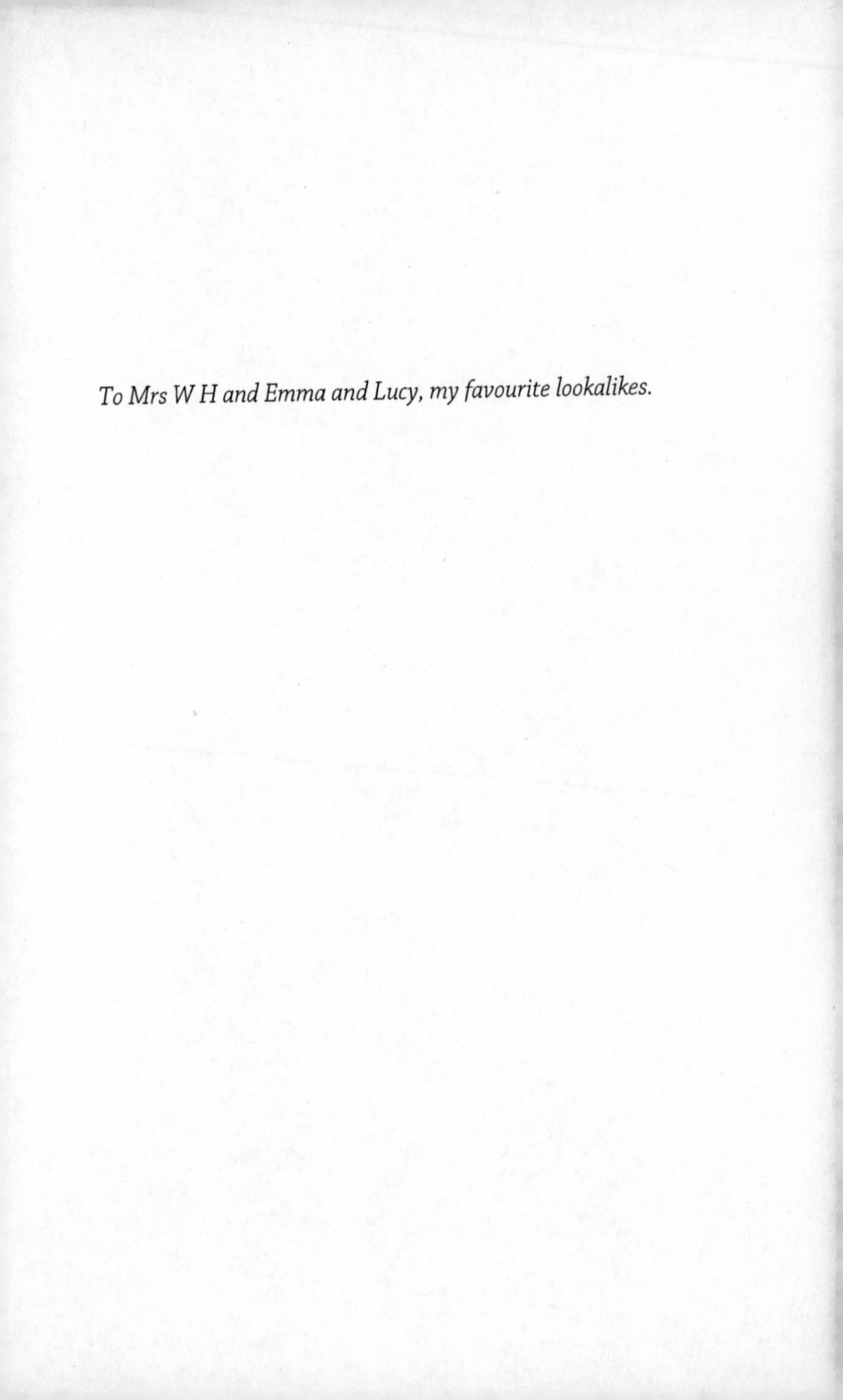

To Mrs W H and Emma and Lucy, my favourite lookalikes.

» Alexandra

They usually left before I was even up in the morning. I would hear the shower running, stopping, running again, the fussy sounds of male preening – little bottles being opened, scents being sprayed – and conversations with most of the words left out.

During the summer of 2003 there were a lot of wet mornings. Up on the twenty-sixth floor, rain never hammered on the windows, it just sort of drifted past, no matter how heavy it was. Lying in bed, I found I could tell if it was raining by a sort of silence which rose up from the streets below. Even on bright days you never saw many people around where we lived, even though there were three hundred apartments in the complex. It seemed everyone was always in their flat, or at work, but never anywhere in between.

Dan and Gareth were out of the building by eight o'clock and would be making money by half past. I waited to hear the faint ting of the lift down the corridor before I got up. Most likely, they would still be out when I came home from work. Sometimes they stayed out all night and came crashing in about six in the morning; often there would be female voices I didn't recognise.

Just a couple of years ago, I lived in a small house with a group of friends so tight knit that it was impossible to cough without someone banging you on the back. Here, I could go whole days without seeing my flatmates.

Standing in the shower always gave me a real feeling of futility if I knew I was going to get soaked again on the way to work. I didn't like umbrellas: the fiddly business of folding them away and popping them open, the way you had to stand them in a corner and let them shed water like an animal. Also, when I did get one, I invariably lost it straight away. Probably half of London had an umbrella that had once belonged to me. Every time it happened – last week, for example, when I'd left a tiger-striped umbrella in the cinema – I would get rained on the next morning, and spend the whole day with people telling me that I should get an umbrella, as if I might not have heard of the invention before.

Taking the shampoo out of the bathroom cabinet, I got the usual feeling of foreboding at the sight of a small bag of white powder nestling between two aftershaves with masculine names, Advantage, Predator. Next to the coke was a gym membership card. DANIEL KEELE, my brother, had recently become a GOLD MEMBER. Gareth had had a couple of things to say about that name. Nonetheless, he'd upgraded his own membership.

A Gold Member meant you could lift weights that other people didn't even know about, swim in the pool after hours, and get discounted protein drinks. For a person with such a big coke habit Dan was mad on health and fitness. He spent almost as much money reversing the effects of drugs as on the drugs themselves. Gareth did less drugs, as far as I could tell, but it might just have been that he was less conspicuous about it.

For breakfast I ate some crackers and jam. It was too much hassle to go down twenty-six floors to buy a loaf of bread. There was rarely much food in our flat because the other two spent so little of their lives there. There were empty pizza boxes and sushi cartons stacked by the bin. We had a family bag of crisps; Dan would sometimes get through five or six packets in the early hours while out of his head.

The sky above the Thames was low and grey, just as I had imagined in bed. Our flat was normally chilly in the morning, because the flashy design meant the radiators were tucked away so well they gave out virtually no heat. The feeling of cold was intensified by the little metal gadgets everywhere, the stripped pine, the glass-topped tables, the smooth black furniture. There was a tower of DVDs which were rarely watched.

We were one of the first households in London to have a wireless connection, if you called this a household. This allowed me to spend a lot of time on the internet without emerging from my room. I checked my email before leaving, more from habit than anything. There was one message, from Helen, about her birthday party which was still two months away. Her parties were legendary, and planned up to half a year in advance so that it was practically impossible to escape. But, unthinkable as it would once have been, since moving out of her house I'd missed two in a row.

Helen had been the ringleader of our group, in the old house; she was the friend we all had in common. She suggested that I should go out with another of the group, Craig, which we did, successfully, for two years. Then she warned against proposing marriage to him, a piece of advice which I chose not to take. She had an opinion on everything. I missed this, where I was living now. Opinions, here, were always expressed in the most ironic way possible. I hardly ever knew what Dan or Gareth were actually thinking.

My computer had belonged to Gareth, before his work gave him a much better one. He had left a couple of old files on it, including a CV which stated that he was Young Businessman of the Year in 2001, that he 'had' eight languages to conversational standard, and that his other interests included juggling and composing music. His linguistic skills had come in handy recently when he saved a multi-million-pound deal by negotiating for half an hour in Japanese. Dan still teased him about this success. People in their line of work never owned up to making an effort. You had to give the impression that if you were a success, it was just that you'd exploited the stupidity of everyone in the world; if you were a failure, you were a victim of the same stupidity.

The longest conversation I'd had with Gareth, one on one, was about three minutes long. It was the afternoon I completed the miserable job of moving all my stuff across London from my old home to this apartment. Gareth, because he happened to be in, helped me with a couple of boxes without saying anything. There was something about seeing all my possessions spread out in eight or nine boxes that made me feel very self-conscious, though the most embarrassing things were the odd non-boxed items that stuck out here and there. I cringed as he picked up a poster of *Singin' in the Rain* which had come partly unrolled during the demoralising £34 taxi ride from my old home.

'I don't, um, I don't like that film,' I said. 'I just collect . . . well, I used to collect film and music posters.'

'Isn't it going to be odd?' asked Gareth suddenly.

'Odd? What?'

'Having your brother as your landlord,' he muttered, looking at Gene Kelly. He was always muttering.

The thought of the rent jumping from my account into his was very unpleasant to me, and so was my mother's delight that I was now sharing Dan's 'snazzy pad' in London, as she described it to her friends, and so were many other aspects of it, but I didn't want to concede any of that. 'It's just a stopgap,' I said.

'And what about seeing your friend at work? The one with the—'

'With the breasts? Helen?'

'Yeah. Won't it be odd seeing her, now you've moved out?'

'Well, again,' I said, 'the job is . . . a stopgap too, really.'

'Right,' said Gareth, 'and how long do you think these gaps are going to be?'

The question threw me; I don't think it was meant as a challenge but it certainly sounded like one. Before I'd thought of a reply, Dan came in. 'What are we talking about?'

'Helen,' I said.

'Oh, the one with the—'

'The resplendent breasts, yes,' said Gareth. Dan started talking about a 'Hundred Fittest Women' feature in a magazine and I left quietly.

That remark of Gareth's continued to come into my head from time to time, two years on. The gaps had already been longer than expected.

*

I left the flat with the strong feeling that I'd forgotten something. Thanks to my email habit, I was slightly behind schedule. In front of our apartment was a sort of cobbled boulevard with a couple of fancy wine bars which were only ever busy at weekends. The station was three minutes' walk away, along the river. The rain matted my hair on the way and my coat kept dripping onto the hand of the woman next to me. I always had an optimistic idea when I went down into an underground station, or a cinema or other windowless place, that it would have stopped raining when I came out again. This faith was rarely justified. I splashed my way through Soho and swiped my card in the little metal box outside our office block. Sometimes I felt I could measure out my week by the little clicks of this card and the other one which let me back into the apartment block in the evening.

Helen had bought me an apple. She never let up insisting that I was undernourished, especially now we lived apart. 'Did you get my email about the party?'

'Yes,' I said. 'I'll . . . I'll have to think.'

There was a pause. 'What are you up to tonight? We're going to see this band that Greg's mate plays bass in, if you fancy it.'

'I think I'm . . .' I said, and then the phone rang and spared me.

Helen had got us the jobs when we left university: a friend of her uncle's owned the media group. It was the kind of friendship we had that if one of us got a job, the other would follow. What I'd said to Gareth was more or less true: the job was always meant as a stopgap. 'What else are we going to do with a history degree?' Helen asked. 'Get paid to think about the past?' The job title had been 'researcher', but it was even less glamorous than it sounded.

Fifty per cent of my job was redirecting calls. Twenty-five per cent was writing letters, or emails, to say no. There were different types of no. 'Not at the moment' to people asking for work experience. 'Unfortunately, not yet' to writers trying to chase up money we owed them. 'Never' to members of the public who'd sent in programme ideas. We only made historical documentaries and docu-dramas, yet almost every day we received sitcom scripts, proposals for animated series, unsolicited theme music. Albert, who worked on the front desk – he was a receptionist, but of the slow-old-man, security-guard type, rather than the blonde-telephoning type – brought the whole pile in first thing, and at the same time collected most of yesterday's postbag for recycling. 'All this to go?' he would ask, every single day, as if each time he'd really expected this to be the day we got a bumper crop of wonderful post. The remaining twenty-five per cent was divided between going out to fetch drinks, arranging transport, and then, bottom of the list, doing whatever research there was that someone else hadn't done while I was buying the coffee.

At the moment we were between two shows, or 'projects'. We had just finished a series on the Restoration for a digital channel. It was presented by an ex-Olympic athlete who'd made the quite common leap from sportsman to TV presenter, and there was a spin-off book planned for Christmas. We were about to do something on the French Revolution and we already had a commission for next year, about the Romans.

Jeremy, our boss, often said that history was an inexhaustible subject because the same topics could be covered again and again without anyone seeming to notice. Jeremy had a porn calendar in his office, with a different girl for every month, and a quotation from a famous historical figure – 'I have a dream' and so on – in a speech bubble as if attributed to the model. His ambition was to be a movie director.

At the moment I was meant to be researching prison museums we could film in for the Revolution show. They wanted some shots of actors huddled in chains and so on. We always used 'real' locations rather than studios; it was normally far cheaper. Next month a small party was going to Paris to look for locations. These trips were always popular. Helen and I had put our names down; they should be choosing the team in the next couple of weeks.

'Have you heard about Paris?'

'No. Have you?'

Helen and I had a conversation like that every day.

I was hoping that we would both get it, because our relationship benefited a lot from jaunts like that. We saw each other every day, of course, and we did sometimes go out on our own together, but it was still too much for me to see the rest of the old group, and far too much to see Craig. As a result, I spent a lot of time inventing reasons why I couldn't go out, and she spent a lot of effort pretending to believe them.

I have a passion for history and desperately want to work in this area.

I am conscientious, hard-working, with good literacy and numeracy skills.

I believe I would contribute . . .

Quite often, I came across application forms from recent graduates, that were almost word for word the same as the one I'd written two and a bit years ago. For reasons I could not exactly identify, this always depressed me.

Around three in the afternoon, Jeremy paid a visit to my desk. 'Alex, was it you who found the thing about holding the hair?'

In the Restoration documentary there was a charming detail about Charles II: he used to hold the hair of his wife, Catherine, while she was being sick. This was something I remembered from reading a biography at school. Little 'human' nuances like this were exactly what our shows were popular for.

'Yes,' I said, proudly, 'that was mine.'

'Where did it come from?'

'I read this book a few years ago.'

'What was it?'

'I don't remember now,' I said. 'Some biography.'

'Well, can you find out?' asked Jeremy. 'We need it for the book. I don't want to put it in, then find out it's some dream you had or something.'

'So it was OK to put a possible lie in the show, but not in the book?'

'People pay attention to books,' said Jeremy.

'And you don't trust my memory to be right?'

'Frankly, no,' said Jeremy, disappearing around a corner. I watched him go, muttering to myself, but before I had got very far with my indignant thoughts, I realised I had come out without a key.

Dan and Gareth and their workmates were drinking in a pub by the river. I saw with a sinking heart Dan's new girlfriend perched on his knee. She had one of those names like Dixie or Trixie, couldn't have been older than sixteen, was already a model, and seemed to think it was a fantastic adventure to be going out with my brother.

I could never walk through this part of the Docklands without remembering the occasion I trudged through here at five in the morning, after the proposal. Not everyone has a definite 'worst day of their lives' but it was definitely mine; the only problem was whether it was 1 or 2 September, as it happened in the early hours. In fact, the proposal was about half past midnight; I knew that, because it was read out on the radio. So 2 September. It was the night of a big football match which England won, anyway, and I knew Dan would still be out celebrating. That was why I rang him to ask if I could stay at his. At that point I had no idea I would end up living there, though I pretty much did know that I wouldn't be able to live with Craig and my friends any more.

Not really knowing the area well – I'd only been to visit Dan a couple of times – I'd got off the night bus too early and had to walk about half a mile. On the bus someone already had tomorrow's paper and was reading a report of the football: IT DOESN'T GET MUCH BETTER THAN THIS! said the headline. My hair was all over the place, though at least I hadn't been crying; I was too stunned. I remembered walking in a daze, feeling that nothing was quite real or solid. I kept having to dodge packs of drunk men who came past singing. Once I nearly ran into a cyclist and he screamed at me: 'Dozy bitch!' I saw the apartment building and was so relieved that I hugged my brother when he buzzed me in. It was probably the last hug we'd had, that, and the previous one was probably the night our father left, so perhaps some good had come out of both things, though it was a bit of an optimistic way of looking at it.

I tried to push these memories out of my mind as I approached the group. There was whistling and applause. A colleague of theirs was walking backwards along the wall overlooking the river, downing a pint of beer at the same time.

This was a forfeit their office imposed on whoever made the most money that month. Gareth had done it a couple of times. Dan never had, yet. He tended to be the one who thought up the forfeits and the nicknames for others. He'd coined the name 'Noddy' for Gareth, because of his tendency to go red, and it was a big hit. Dan was very popular at work.

The guy tipped his head back, finished the pint and lobbed the plastic glass over his shoulder into the Thames. Everyone applauded. He hopped off the wall and landed with a little flourish like a gymnast.

Dan gave me the key. 'Stay for a pint if you want,' he said.

'Yeah stay, it would be cool? We're going to have a couple more?' said Dixie/Trixie, who had that voice-lilting-like-a-question tic which is meant to have been transmitted through Australian soaps.

It was half past seven, the night was young, but I was tired and my hair felt wet and straggly. I knew they'd be talking about the office.

'I'm going to head home,' I said. 'Lots on . . .'

'Lots on,' said Dan, semi-mockingly. 'Oh, well then. Sounds important.' Gareth was smirking to himself, I would have quite liked to punch him in the face. I promised to leave the key out if they came back too late for me. There was an obvious feeling among the three of them that I would probably be in bed by ten.

'You should get an umbrella?' said Dixie/Trixie, as I got up to leave.

I was on the internet doing a search for 'prison museum' and along the side of the page popped up, as usual, a series of mostly irrelevant pages: 'Buy prison memorabilia from $9.99', 'Find any prison instantly'. Then at the bottom I spotted

'Write to a prisoner!' 'Brighten someone's day . . . or someone's year!' it said. That might be nice, I thought, clicking on the link. I did this sort of thing all the time; I couldn't search for something on the web without having my head turned by something else.

I left the page open and forgot about it while reading about the Clink, a prison museum on the South Bank with 'an excellent collection of torture implements'. I made some dinner. It was a good couple of hours before I came back to the page and started reading about the prisoner correspondence course run by a company called WriteToAConvict.

Lots of people became 'pen pals' with Death Row convicts in the USA, the site said, but what about the thousands of prisoners in this country who had no post, no visitors? There was a form to fill out; after that, you had to go for an informal interview.

'Think about it,' the site said. 'Do you have an extra hour or two in the evening once a week to write a letter? Maybe you feel you are a good listener or a good talker and you could be a friend to someone? Maybe you're in need of a refreshing new challenge or opportunity to do good in the community?'

I pondered. At least two of these things were probably true of me. I filled out the form online and sent it. What harm can this do, I thought, most likely I won't even hear back. Within half an hour, though, I'd had an email from someone called Claire asking me to 'come in for a chat'. Their offices were in Soho, ten minutes' walk from ours.

I went and watched TV, wondering whether I really wanted to get involved in anything like this. I'd always had a tendency to make bad decisions: buying an exercise bike, going on a terrible last-minute holiday to Turkey, proposing at the age of twenty-four – though I couldn't blame that one on the internet.

Still, it couldn't hurt to go for a chat. And I suppose I liked the idea of doing some good. Who doesn't like that idea?

The first surprise was that Claire was only about my age. I had pictured a middle-aged, busybody sort of woman from the tone of her emails and perhaps from my general preconceptions about people who did this sort of work. She made me a cup of coffee so strong I would still be able to taste it on my way home, and said she hoped I hadn't been caught in the rain. The coffee came in a novelty mug with the words 'WAKE ME WHEN IT'S HOME-TIME!' and a picture of a yawning lion. On her desk was a half-done crossword and a box of Disney tissues.

Helen and I often had lunch together, normally a hearty lunch if she got her way, but today I'd told her that I was going to the shops for 'a few things'. I wasn't sure that she believed me, but she was hungover after the previous night's drunken adventures with the gang.

It was, as advertised, very informal. For quite a lot of the half-hour Claire told me about herself. Her own mug said 'ELEVENSES'. She worked as a prisoner welfare officer and went round five jails, one a day, sorting out 'issues'. She'd set this pen-pal scheme up herself, a couple of years ago. 'You know, a lot of the guys don't see anyone at all, all week long, and there's not a lot to look forward to.' After a pause I realised that 'guys' was her name for the prisoners. 'So Bob and I – my fella – began a little company to put people in touch with folks in jail.'

There was a long digression about Bob. He was a consultant of some kind. They were childhood sweethearts and I got the impression they would be together until death. By now I felt as if I was, after all, younger than Claire, but I wasn't sure if that was a good thing or not.

'Have you worked in the community before?' Claire asked. She had a way of mentioning 'the community' as something she had no real relation to, but had taken it upon herself to help.

'Not really,' I said, and added hastily, 'I mean, I'm not really interested in working . . . I'm just here about the writing-to-a-prisoner thing . . .'

'Oh, absolutely,' Claire said, 'but writing to a prisoner is caring for someone, and caring is work, isn't it?'

'I suppose so,' I said.

'I shouldn't be having this,' Claire muttered, and emptied about a quarter of a spoonful of sugar into her tea.

She then started talking about the things you should, and shouldn't, put in a letter to a prisoner. You should talk about your routine, the little things. 'Even if you think it's trivial, to them it probably isn't, because there's so little variety in their lives.' You should be bright, optimistic, cheery. 'The last thing they need is to hear about a load of problems. But you don't seem the depressive type!' You should be careful sending photos, or saying anything which might give them false expectations of the relationship. 'Some of the guys haven't had a proper chat with a woman for years. Well, unless you count me!'

You shouldn't ask what a prisoner's crime was, till they felt ready to tell you.

'And I will never be able to tell you any details,' said Claire, 'because all that is completely confo.' After a short pause I realised that she meant 'confidential'. It wasn't clear whether it was part of established prison jargon, or something she had made up.

'A lot of the guys get so used to telling a – an untrue version of events, they sort of believe that it's true,' Claire said.

'But there must be times when someone really is innocent and there's a mistake?'

'Well, all sorts of things can happen, I suppose.' She gave me a rather sceptical look as if to say that in her experience, the world tended to go pretty much as planned. She sipped her tea, got a tissue out of the box, dabbed her nose, and apologised for being 'a bit snuffly'. I gathered that that subject wasn't going to be pursued.

The last guideline was that you should avoid using your own address, at least at first. Initial letters always went via their office. 'After that, it's up to you,' she said.

She gave me a file of prisoners' details; there was a photo of each one and a brief autobiographical note. 'There are some absolute corkers in there,' she said. 'Some of the loveliest people.' I had to choose one, let her know, and then write. It suddenly seemed that I'd actually agreed to do this. On the outside of her door, I noticed on my way out, was a poster of a lion that matched the mug.

It was impossible to look through the file at work – one of the annoying things about the job was that, although most of it was completely unchallenging, you could never quite get away with something completely different. At least, I couldn't. Helen had once taken eleven cigarette breaks in a morning, but then, it was her uncle's friend who owned the whole company.

As soon as I got home, I opened the file. I was surprised at how many prisoners there were looking for a pen pal: more than a hundred in total, spread over the five jails that came under Claire's jurisdiction. A note at the top of the front page said: 'N.B. There are NO FEMALE prisoners in this file. There is a waiting list for those wishing to write to a female prisoner. Why not try a male prisoner instead?' It reminded me a bit of Battersea Dogs' Home, where the cuter ones got all the attention. I thought maybe I'd pick one of the less attractive photos.

Rodney, 23. LIFE. *I'm a compassionate, nice, interesting guy who would love to hear about your life.*

Shax, 27. Parole decision: 2011. Into my music, born-again Christian.

Darren, 48. LIFE. *You've tried the rest now try the best! Only kidding but I am a thoughtful, intelligent guy who's totally changed during my time in here. Would like to hear from* WOMEN.

Craig, 21. . . .

The name immediately jarred me and at the same moment the door to the lounge opened and Dan, Trixie/Dixie and Gareth all appeared. Gareth was fiddling with some palm-top gadget of his which could send emails, advise motorway routes and probably cure sickness. Dan bundled his tiny girlfriend onto my sofa so that I had to move up to accommodate her. She tucked her knees under her chin like the schoolgirl she, to be fair, more or less was. She had taken her shoes off and was giggling as Dan tickled her cute little feet, with the freshly painted toe nails. It was hard for me to imagine walking around someone else's flat in bare feet.

They put the TV on and Dan began to roll a joint, producing a little packet of weed from his jacket pocket. Obviously this was going to be the kind of night when they spent some time hanging around the flat preparing for the excesses to come. I preferred the other kind. Sweet smoke trailed up towards the ceiling. The place had the permanent smell of a student flat as it was. If there ever was a drug bust around here, it wouldn't take them long to convict.

The host of a quiz show asked a question of a middle-aged woman with large frightened eyes. Dan and Gareth snorted at the question and then jeered the woman's ignorance as it became clear she didn't know the answer. I tried to remain immersed in the prisoner files.

'My God,' said Dan.

'Should people this stupid be allowed on TV, I wonder?' Gareth asked. 'What if it inspires young viewers to become idiots themselves?'

The camera cut to the woman's husband in the audience, chewing his nails. 'I don't know what he's worried about,' said my brother. 'He's already lost, he's married to her.'

'Shut up? You two are terrible?' Trixie/Dixie laughed, jokily slapping Dan on the back of his hand.

Ronald, 31. Release: 2008. I should never have been locked up in the first place. I'm itching to get out and make a difference.

'D'you want . . . ?'

Gareth was offering me the joint in his outstretched hand. His tone was so flat that it took me several seconds to realise I was being addressed.

'I'm all right, thanks,' I said.

'Not smoking tonight?' asked Gareth, and the other two laughed. Smoking made my lungs hurt, but we'd had the conversation before; to them, I was just perverse.

Andreas, 33. Release: 2005. German-born, university-educated, introspective, melancholic, erudite. Jailed after a series of events too freakish and appalling to recount. I have never been interested before in correspondence schemes such as this, since I have had no interest in connecting with, let alone rejoining, society. As I approach the latter part of my time in prison, however, I would be pleased to correspond with people, of either sex, who may be able to help me re-engage a little with the world as it is today.

I got up, engrossed in this strange paragraph, and stubbed my toe on a floorboard in my eagerness to get out. As I closed the door behind me, I could hear their laughter.

The picture of 'Andreas' was a black-and-white passport photo which could well have been taken a few years ago. It showed a young, serious man with a neat, slightly old-fashioned-looking hairstyle: what my mother would have called the 'undertaker's assistant' look, the hair divided into a very careful parting. He was wearing a light-coloured top and seemed to be quite slight. That was all you could tell. There was no expression whatsoever on his face. He didn't look at all like a criminal to me, but then, that was often the way when you saw one on the news. He was in St John's, a medium-security jail in Kent. The website said that prisoners were often moved at very little notice, and that added to their sense of alienation.

'Andy is a funny one!' said Claire when I phoned her about it the next day. 'The thing with him . . .' She lowered her voice, as if she was going to let me in on a shocking secret. 'The thing with him is he's really smart.'

'But he hasn't got a pen pal?'

'People tend to be a bit put off,' said Claire, 'by the . . . cleverness.' I heard her sip a drink. 'People tend to prefer . . . not too demanding prisoners. Andy'll be thrilled if you write to him! Good luck!'

Beginning a letter was harder than I expected. I kept glancing at Andreas's photo and wondering whether I had anything worth saying to him. My own life wasn't what you would call thrilling. The most exciting things ever to happen to me were bad: the break-up of our parents' marriage, and the humiliation of the proposal. Still – surely he would be pleased to get any letter at all. The guidelines recommended writing a very brief note of introduction as a first step. I said I was called Alexandra (I thought the long version of my name might appeal to him), worked in television (half true), and was interested in hearing his story. I then changed the end to 'interested in hearing from you'. Then, 'I would love to hear from you', and finally, 'very much like'. I was quite tired by the time I sent it.

I'd been warned by Claire that prisoners could only send one letter a week, so I shouldn't expect anything till next Thursday, when I could go to the office to see if a return letter had been sent. At this point, this seemed a better arrangement than corresponding directly. I could imagine what life would be like if Dan found out that I had a 'prison pen pal'. I would almost be better off in jail myself.

The week passed slowly. Each day was much the same, as it always was. Helen and I had lunch together. There was a new type of doughnut, cinnamon, in the shop around the corner. Helen found a dead bird on her way home one night. Another evening, we went to see a film. These are the more exciting bits.

The Paris visit was put back by a month for 'administrative reasons'. Helen, with her insider knowledge, said it was because someone had booked tickets for the wrong month. I couldn't find anything to corroborate the Charles II hair-holding story, but the editors decided to include it in the book with the word 'reportedly'. It meant I would get a credit, which was nice; after the TV show my mother had rung to say that she'd seen my name. I didn't hear from Dad – we hadn't spoken for three years or so – but I could always pretend that something might have possessed him and his new wife to watch a documentary on the Restoration.

On the Thursday I made an excuse and went casually off to Claire's office. It surprised me that my heart speeded up as I entered; was this really that exciting? 'Let's see what we've got in the lucky dip . . .' said Claire, delving in a drawer. She brought out an A4 envelope. ALEXANDRA KEELE (MISS), and the words C/O 'WriteToAConvict' SCHEME, were written in extremely neat capitals, all exactly the same size. Claire began to say something, then her phone started to jump around on the table. I saw purple hearts dancing across the screen and she picked it up and crooned her husband's name. She gave me a distracted wave and wink as I left.

I ripped the envelope open as soon as I was out on the street. There was a single sheet of Basildon Bond writing paper and, on it, just a few lines in the same scrupulous handwriting.

Dear Alexandra,

Thank you for taking the trouble to initiate a correspondence with me. I was very pleased to receive your letter and hope to hear from you again in the coming weeks.

Yours faithfully

Andreas Hönig

Naturally, I was disappointed. It was so brief and formulaic, it reminded me of the letters I used to get back when I wrote to film stars. Surely if he was really so bored he could do better than that? I folded the letter up and put it in my bag.

A couple of days went by. I declined a dozen requests for work experience, the new doughnut flavour was recalled by the manufacturers because a shard of glass had been found in one, and Helen and I discussed whether we might be able to retire if we sued them successfully. On the Friday night, I told Helen I had a 'commitment' which would stop me from going for tapas with the rest of the gang.

As a matter of fact I did have a plan – I was going to the National Gallery, where there was an exhibition of medieval religious art which was on loan from an American museum. The faint part of me still connected to my student self was keen to see it. Religious art had always appealed to me for some reason: that and movie posters were my two favourite themes for an exhibition. You couldn't really call it a 'commitment', though: it was going to be there for another five months.

It wasn't as if I had never seen Craig since it all went wrong; we had been thrown together a few times and we were more than capable of being civil to one another. But it cost me a big effort, not to mention a lot of wasted time, thinking about it afterwards.

I was walking down St Martin's Lane when my phone went off. It was Claire. 'Just ringing to find out how it went with Andreas,' she said. 'Are you going to keep the correspondence going?'

'How it went' made it sound like more of an event than it had been, I thought. 'Well . . .' I said. 'His reply was really short. I'm not completely sure if he wants to be, um, pen pals.'

'Oh, of course he does, sweets,' said Claire. 'You have to remember, it's very hard for prisoners to trust anyone.

They've had no proper contact for so long. Trust me, he was over the moon when you wrote.'

'Really?'

'Honestly. Give it another try. The thing about Andy . . . well, I shouldn't tell you, really.' She paused. I felt like the potential victim of a clever saleswoman. Still, it was impossible not to be interested. My day-to-day life threw up very few situations which people 'ought not to tell me' about.

'Yes?' I prompted her.

She sighed. 'One of the things about Andy – I mentioned he was bright. He's been a bit too bright for his own good, at times. A bit too sensitive. He would have been out by now, except he was involved in a . . . a serious incident with another prisoner,' she said. 'Someone really wound him up. He over-reacted. He's one of these quiet people who have – you know, the potential for violence.' She paused, and I imagined she was reflecting, as I was, that this wasn't really 'selling' Andreas to me. 'So do give him another chance, it'll be great!' she said, finally, straining to make it sound like an invitation and not a threat.

In spite of Claire's slightly counter-productive encouragement, I decided it was only fair to write again. All right, he hadn't shown much excitement, but then my opening letter was hardly a classic, and I could see that it was probably down to me to take the lead. I bought some fancy paper from the gallery's gift shop, with a famous painting in the corner of each sheet, and sat down in a pizza place on the Strand to write.

This time I managed four pages. I told him that I was mid-twenties, single; a little about my job. In the last page I admitted that I didn't particularly like living with my brother, but hadn't quite found it in myself to move into a place on my own, because I had got so used to communal living in the past few years. I explained that I had put all my eggs in one basket by being in a closed-off group of friends, and then spent a bit of time explaining the phrase in case he was unfamiliar with it. It was hard to get the tone right. Still, it was a proper letter and I had to admit to myself I'd enjoyed writing it.

A week later came another reply, about the same length as my letter, and slightly less formal in tone. Andreas said that it was 'refreshing' to hear about someone else's life. He said that I shouldn't worry about being boring – it would reassure him in some ways, he said, to know that not everyone in the outside world was 'forever in a party or a celebration'. It was lucky he wasn't writing to Dan. He then mused for a bit on English phrases that made him laugh and some other trivia. Towards the end he wrote, 'I would be curious to hear how you came to be in this rather unlucky domestic arrangement.' There was still absolutely nothing about his life, out of prison or inside. But we were making progress. The trouble was that I was already nearly out of things to say about my life.

There had been a further two emails reminding us that Helen's party was getting closer, and revealing more and more details about the plan for the night. Each one made me uneasy. Finally, Helen raised the subject.

'So are you coming this year?'

'I don't know if I'll make it . . .'

'It's always a bit of an unlucky time of year for you, isn't it,' she said, chewing a pen and looking at her screen, 'what with the mystery illness two years ago, and the – what was it? – funeral last year?'

I sighed. 'Look, you know it's difficult for me to see Craig and the rest of them. I think it's better for everyone if I stay out of the way.'

'It's not better for everyone. What you mean is, it's better for you. Everyone else wants to see you.'

'I'm just not sure if I'm ready.'

'Ready,' said Helen impatiently. 'It's been – what, nearly two years since . . .?'

'It'll be two years next week.'

'OK. That is too long for it still to be affecting your life now. I mean, if you look at—' She stopped dead.

'How can it not affect my life? I used to live with all of you, now I live with two people who I don't get on with. I used to be in love . . .'

'Oh, stop it. If it had been love it would have all worked out,' said Helen. Before I could answer her, Albert had come for the recycling. Away went someone's twenty-nine-page proposal for a show about the history of the bicycle.

Helen's answer to pretty much any misfortune was to say that things 'just weren't meant to be' and so on. I knew she was trying to make me feel better. But the conversation had had the opposite effect. I went home feeling very weary, despite Helen's attempts to patch things up by buying me a tub of ice cream on the way back to the station.

The flat was cold and sterile as ever, and neither the TV nor even the internet seemed able to distract me. In the lounge, with lights just beginning to go on over London, I pulled out the pad and began writing to Andreas. I didn't make a conscious decision to tell him the whole story: I began with the basics. Craig and I were part of a group of friends at university and thereafter. I thought our relationship had come of age and decided, at someone else's wedding in fact, that I wanted to make it permanent; I was pretty sure he had been dropping hints to the same effect. I had a proposal read out on the radio, during a late-night show we always listened to. He was dumbfounded, said on the contrary he was thinking the relationship had 'run its course'. That phrase, I never forgot. What 'course' I asked, but he couldn't really answer that.

Every half an hour I would glance out of the window, looking at the sky getting darker, the city lighting up, and feel I was in the right place. Each time I read back I was surprised at myself for being so candid, but then, there was always the chance I would never send this.

Pages went by and I began to elaborate on the story. I mentioned the long, empty moment when – after the conversation had gone so very badly wrong, and after we'd sat there in this numb, inescapable silence for about a quarter of an hour – Craig apologetically said he was 'going out' and left me sitting, looking at nothing. I remembered in the letter a detail that had almost gone from my memory: the fact that I sat in the lounge counting my change, ten and twenty pence pieces, from one hand slowly into the other, and back again. I also included more memorable details, like the way Helen came back with a bun she'd bought me from an all-night supermarket, and the two of us stared at it blankly in its paper bag, as it came some way short of making up for the fact that my life was ruined.

There were other particularly jarring memories, which, as I began to enjoy the feeling of disclosure, I chucked in for my invisible pen pal to enjoy. The thought of text messages zipping between the other people in the house discussing the situation. The voicemails left on my phone by other friends who'd heard the proposal live on air (read by radio 'love guru' Graham Boston) and wanted to congratulate me. Understandably, because who the hell ever *failed* with a marriage proposal? How many conversations over the next few months would begin with me having to explain this humiliation?

I'd forgotten how long it took to write things without a computer. At ten o'clock I got a takeaway; by this time the letter had taken on its own momentum, and felt like a project. I described how I'd said to Helen that I would have to leave – she finished the bun off for me – and how she'd replied, 'I think you might be right.' And I replied, 'I mean, leave the house. Move out. Not . . . live here.' And a pause before she said, 'Yes. That's what I thought you meant.' No attempt to persuade me this could all be brushed aside and forgotten about. If he had just said no to marrying, then maybe. But not now he wanted to end the whole thing. I went to Dan's that night, pretending it was an emergency measure, but with a terrible feeling I was going to end up being there for a long time.

At midnight, I retired to my room, still writing. By now I was becoming lyrical on the subject of that awful night. Even if you are jilted at the altar, I wrote, at least people sympathise. If you propose – especially when you're young – and it goes wrong, people just think you are a fool. I finished with an apology for having gone on so much and then said, 'Top that if you can!' It occurred to me, as I was putting the pen down, that he probably could – he was in jail after all – but whether he would care to write as much as that, I very much doubted.

I finally got to bed just in time to be woken up by the three of them barging their way in, Trixie/Dixie making loud and repetitive comments about a bouncer they'd had a run-in with.

In the morning, I lay in bed listening to the shower and their croaky voices laughing about last night, and thought about what I'd written. I felt somehow exhilarated. You often hear how nice it is to confide in a total stranger, but it was not something I'd ever envisaged doing, because heart-to-heart chats had not tended to be my forte. This seemed a good compromise.

Without reading back through the letter I put it in an A4 envelope and addressed it. During the lunch-break I went to the post office, weighed and sent it. I saw the man behind the counter glance at the prison address for a short moment, then push his glasses up his nose as if he hadn't seen it.

Claire rang me during work on the Monday; I took my phone out of the office. I could feel Helen's inquisitive eyes on my back as I went out into reception, where there was only Albert, immersed in his newspaper.

'Just checking in,' said Claire, 'wondering how things have been with Andy? Promise I won't keep pestering you.'

'It's going well, thanks,' I told her. 'I've sent him a nice long letter. I told him he was welcome to use my home address, by the way, so I won't need to collect it from you this time.'

'OK, sweets,' said Claire. Her voice tightened a little. 'Just to say, we do normally recommend you correspond via us for the first few weeks at least.'

'I thought you just said the first couple of letters,' I replied. 'I think we're fine trusting each other.' Helen came out with a lighter and a packet of cigarettes and slunk past me, half-heartedly pretending not to be listening.

'That's great, babe,' said Claire. 'Just . . . we always tell people to be careful. You know, it's easy to get too involved and perhaps misjudge how well you know someone.'

'I think I'll be OK,' I said, a little bit impatiently. 'I don't imagine I know him.'

'Well, that's brilliant,' Claire said. 'I'll see Andy tomorrow and I know he'll be made up to have heard from you again. Oh – listen, babe, I've got to go. Thanks!'

'You don't imagine you know who?' asked Helen, coming back into the office.

'Nothing,' I said, 'it's nothing.' I slipped the phone back into my bag. Helen looked at me for a moment, plumped herself down on the swivel chair and went back to work, whistling to herself.

When Thursday came around, I told myself not to expect a letter today necessarily, because it might take longer than usual now that he was writing to me directly. There was no real logic to this. Because we were in a high rise apartment, our post didn't come to our door, but was put in little pigeon-holes by the concierge, so it wasn't until I was on the way to work that I checked it. There was nothing with my name on apart from a loyalty card from a clothes shop I'd never been to. I realised I had been protecting myself from disappointment, and it hadn't worked.

The next morning, I woke up with Andreas on the brain – it was one of those situations, like waiting for a phone call, where not thinking about it just makes you think about it. Two or three times during breakfast (crackers with butter) I considered going down straight away, rather than on the way to work. I resisted, it seemed like building it up too much. Nonetheless, to give the post as much time as possible to arrive, I dawdled over leaving, wondering if I could wear a baseball cap to keep the rain off. I left it and went downstairs. There was nothing at all in the pigeon-hole, but other ones were full. Tomorrow was Saturday and our post at the weekends was very erratic, as if the postman thought this part of London vanished outside office hours.

Feeling like an idiot, I trudged to the station in light rain. On the stairs, someone trod on my trouser leg as they shoved past, briefcase in hand, and I stumbled and missed a step, landing awkwardly on my ankle. I sat on the train staring at the muddy mark on my jeans.

All day, I wondered what had possessed me to reveal so much of myself with so little provocation. I suppose, looking back, there was a vacancy for a listener of some kind. Helen was my major confidante and the two of us had nothing new to say about it. My other former best friends still lived with Craig; my less close friends knew too little about the situation to understand. My mother, well, the last thing I wanted was to discuss my love life, past or present, with her – she was too full of ideas, like speed dating, and TV shows called things like *Desperate Singles*. And my flatmates were people I wouldn't confide in if I was suicidal.

I thought of Andreas, this person I didn't know, reading my long, chatty, confessional letter with polite bafflement, and the thought made me squirm. I felt as if I'd hugged someone who didn't think it was appropriate. I made a resolution to be more guarded in future. Helen made me eat two-thirds of a pasta salad for her; she was on a fashionable diet.

I got back to the apartment block and swiped my card in the door. The metallic doors clicked their welcome. Dan and Gareth would be out from tonight until Sunday morning, maybe solidly; I wondered if I'd get through the weekend without seeing the girlfriend. My footsteps echoed on the floor. Maybe I was the only one who hung about here at the weekend. Maybe the other two hundred and ninety-nine apartments sat empty. I'd had these sorts of thoughts before.

Outside our front door was a thick manila envelope. 'This came for you' someone had written, on the reverse side. I flipped it over in my hands; my name was on it, and a special HM Prison postmark. I shoved open the door, tore open the package. Inside was a heavy sheaf of papers. I dumped it on the kitchen table. There were probably two hundred or two hundred and fifty pages, I guessed, because the reams we had at work were five hundred. My hands were shaking slightly. I removed the blank cover sheet and my heart dropped. The first page was in German. Everything was in German.

For the whole weekend, the pile of papers sat next to my laptop, as if I was hoping the computer would cave in and start translating it for me. I looked through the whole envelope, and through all the pages, but there was no explanatory note; nothing. Just line after line after line of tight little characters all done in blue biro. The funny double-S letters and dots over vowels made me feel slightly like a spy, but a pretty helpless one.

The front page said 'ANDREAS HÖNIG – MEINE GESCHICHTE', which seemed pretty likely to mean 'my story' or 'my thoughts' or something similar. I tried for a bit to pick out a word here and there. There were some English people's names – Cambridge popped up a few times, then London – but it was hopeless. I tried feeding sentences into a translation program on the internet, but the results were extremely stilted. 'Hitler moustaches were never comically possible in Germany, but this is the first place,' announced the computer proudly. I ran a search for German night-school classes and was a few clicks away from signing up for one, before I realised it was ridiculous.

On the Saturday afternoon Dan and Gareth went to watch Arsenal; their company had an executive box. I'd planned quite a busy weekend – my mother was coming to London tonight and we were going to a musical, then on Sunday morning I was going to Spitalfields Market with Helen. I forgot about Andreas's manuscript for a while, while we were in the theatre. I watched the chorus members in their gaudy colours, wailing and gesticulating, and wondered what it would be like to do that for a living. Probably more fun than my job. At the end, my mother stood up and applauded, so I had to. We went to an Italian restaurant, she asked if there was any news. I said there wasn't, really. It was a perfectly nice and normal evening.

I got home just before midnight, riding the Docklands light railway through glass towers, multi-storey car parks and little streets that looked like film sets. We had drunk a carafe of wine with the meal, which Mum said had made her 'pretty tipsy'; I wished we had had a bottle at least. I went to my room. Andreas's heap of paper was sitting there. I picked it up and rested it in my lap, stretched out on the bed. Was this the only copy? How could it not be the only copy, but if it was, why had he entrusted the whole thing to someone he had never met?

I was about to get into bed when there was a knock on the door. The sound made me jump; I'd thought I was on my own in the flat, as usual.

'Hang on, hang on, hang on,' I shouted. The manuscript was spread out in front of me on the bed. 'All right,' I said. The door opened a crack and Gareth leaned in. A wave of pleasant, artificial smells drifted into my room. His meagre hair was stuck up with gel and he had a crisp white shirt on. He was holding the kettle.

'D'you want . . . ?' he asked, nodding at the kettle.

'Oh. Thanks.' I was disconcerted. 'Are you not – out?'

'On the contrary,' said Gareth, gesturing with his hands to show that he was real. 'I'm literally standing here.' He coughed. 'Got a presentation on Monday. Working.'

He took a moment to register the papers. 'What's that?'

'Oh, it's nothing,' I said. 'Just something from work – they're thinking of making a film of it.' This was a flimsy lie but, luckily, neither of them took any interest in my job, so I could claim that pretty much anything was 'from the office'.

Gareth's eye had been caught by the foreign text; he slipped inside the door, which closed gently behind him. My peripheral vision scanned the place for anything embarrassing. 'But you don't speak German, do you?'

'No.' I could see an opportunity. 'And they're too stingy to get a translator.'

'Hitler moustaches are not popular in Germany as novelty items,' Gareth read, picking up the first page, 'but nonetheless it is with one of these articles that everything started.'

I murmured admiringly.

'Not exactly difficult German,' he said in the voice some people use to describe cars or guns.

'Well, there's loads of it,' I said. 'It'd take someone until Christmas to do it.'

Gareth took it in his hands as if it were a baby about to be weighed. 'Not if they knew what they were doing.'

I looked at him.

Gareth gave another half-shrug and hefted the papers again. 'Make a change from most of the crap I get given at work,' he said. 'If you want . . .'

'I'd be . . . are you sure?' I said.

The conversation had returned to its default level, almost non-conversation. He tucked the papers under his arm and went out. I heard him go quietly into the kitchen. It was odd how quiet he always was, when Dan wasn't there. Things had worked out quite well, I felt.

Five minutes later he tapped lightly on the door and handed me a mug of tea. It was made the way I liked it, strong, with one sugar; he always remembered that, even though he often scarcely seemed to know who I was.

*

There was bright sunshine on the Sunday morning; weak rays even made it through to our lounge. I walked past Gareth's room, wondering if he'd read any of the manuscript yet. Dan's door was shut; he and the adolescent would probably sleep most of the afternoon. I went out in a good mood.

By the time I got to Spitalfields, Helen had already bought a hat, ten candles, some Indian cheese, a T-shirt with a cat on it, a vase, incense sticks, and a large bag of pastries which we ate as we walked around.

'Your diet's over, then?'

'It's on hold.'

'Listen, about your party,' I said. 'I'm going to come.'

She squeezed my arm. 'Are you sure?'

'I can't keep missing important events because of all this stuff that happened in the past,' I said, grandly. We were standing in front of a bookstall. 'I've got to get over it. The best thing would be if I saw Craig more and we just became friends again.'

Helen was looking at me with something almost like admiration. 'It would mean a lot to me to have you there,' she said. 'It's never going to be a perfect party unless you're there.'

'Excuse me for interrupting this love-in,' said a grey-haired man in a scarf, leaning over our shoulders, 'but I am trying to get at a book.' We apologised and moved out of his way. He picked up a copy of *Tintin in Tibet* and handed it to the stallholder, giving us a contemptuous look. We went on our way arm in arm, laughing. I was surprised that I'd come to this resolution. I hadn't been planning to say any of it.

That night, I wrote to Andreas to thank him for sending the mysterious package. It was harder than ever to phrase myself in these odd circumstances. 'I have taken steps to get it translated,' I wrote, then changed it to 'I have given it to someone who speaks German,' then – in case that sounded like a betrayal of confidentiality – settled for 'I am working on it.' But then, what confidentiality? Surely he didn't send it expecting me to be bilingual? I couldn't imagine what had possessed him. Perhaps it was just as simple as loneliness, but how lonely did you have to be before you sent something like this to a complete stranger? But then how lonely did you have to be to write to one in the first place?

Midway through the next week, I was on my own at home watching a documentary on Rome by a rival production company. It was being repeated after a successful broadcast last year. I'd been given the job of taking notes on their series to see what we could 'learn from it', or steal. Their shows were presented by a celebrity historian, rather than, like ours, a celebrity pretending to be a historian. Their guy had a creamy, university-educated voice and my colleagues were always making fun of him and doing impressions. Personally, I would rather have had a qualified expert than a sportsperson reading a script, but then I would have done a lot of things differently.

'Caligula was one of the most decadent emperors,' the professor said with a little smile and twitch of his nose. 'He is supposed to have made one of his horses into a senator . . . and some contemporary accounts suggest the relationship was even closer than that!' Another twitch.

'Is this one of yours?' asked Gareth. I jumped in surprise. He had entered the room without making a sound and was right behind me. His breath was mint-fresh as usual.

'What?'

'Is this by your company, this horse-fucking documentary?'

'No, no,' I said, fumbling for the remote control, 'this is . . .

well, it's nothing to do with me. It's by someone else.'

'OK, I believe you,' said Gareth, with a wry look. While I was searching for something to say, he dumped a sheaf of papers in my lap. There, typed neatly out, was a translation of Andreas's work. I didn't know what to say.

'All I could do for the moment,' Gareth muttered.

'This is . . . thank you!' I said.

'Obviously I'm hindered by the – by not knowing what it actually is,' Gareth said. 'He's pretty long-winded, whoever he is. I've tried to sort of keep the, um. Keep the tone. Over-the-top sort of vocabulary and. Yeah.'

I thought about letting him into the secret, but by the time I had considered how I might be able to do it, he had turned his back and was halfway out of the room again.

'Hey, I'm really . . . thanks for doing this!' I called after him.

'See you around,' he muttered. It was probably impossible for him to acknowledge my thanks without admitting to himself that he'd done something nice for me. I looked through the pages, which had previously been scrap paper from his workplace; on the reverse side of each sheet were incomprehensible charts and figures showing 'growth'. I retired to my room, lay on my bed and began reading.

☞ ANDREAS

Hitler moustaches are not popular in Germany as novelty items, but it is nonetheless with one of these articles that everything started. It was my first week as a postgraduate student in Cambridge and a fancy-dress party was being held to allow us to meet each other. To my mind it was perverse to accomplish this by making us dress as other people, but, being new in this country as well as at the university, it did not seem advisable to raise objections, nor to miss the event. Barely had it begun to be advertised when one of the students on my corridor came into the kitchen triumphant, having obtained a pair of Elton John glasses and a flamboyant shirt. This was how I came to pay what was probably the first visit to a joke and fancy-dress shop of my life.

The establishment was about halfway up the hill that led up from the centre of town, just past a bridge which I stood on for some time, watching tourists being conveyed down the river in long boats. The boatmen twirled the giant punt-poles in the river and rattled off statistics about how old everything was. Autumn did not seem to have started yet, or perhaps it had already gone; anyway, it was cold and dark early in the afternoon and the city felt as if it had been standing still for a very long time.

A bell rang as I entered the shop and the owner nodded politely. There were no costumes immediately visible and, since I had no specific notion of what I wished to dress as, I felt diffident about beginning a conversation with the proprietor. Rustling around between the displays of miniature amusing items, I soon came across an interesting thing: a 'Hitler moustache' in a plastic packet. BE AN EVIL GENIUS! it said on the wrapper. These were two words I had not previously seen as likely bedfellows.

'Are these popular?' I asked the proprietor, who, detecting the accent, immediately realised that a very funny situation was brewing. There was no malice, however, in his manner.

'Would you be German, sir?' he asked.

'That's right,' I said. 'As of this week, not West German, just German,' I added proudly. The man blinked in confusion and I was reminded that reunification was not so big a piece of news here as in Germany.

'Studying at the university?'

'Yes,' I said, 'an M.Phil. in American literature.'

'I see,' said the shopkeeper. 'And what American literature is there?'

This question disconcerted me, as I was not sure if it was meant to be a joke. Soon, however, it seemed the shop owner had something else on his mind. He slid the little sliver of hair from its container and invited me to try it on. I pressed it to my lip, resisting the urge to sneeze as a stray hair tickled my nostril.

'Very nice, very nice,' said the man. 'Go on, sir, give us a *Sieg Heil!*'

Well, I thought, why not, Hitler means nothing to me, or to this guy; it's only a joke. '*Sieg Heil!*' I said obediently, with a little salute. The proprietor chuckled appreciatively and called a spotty youth from the stockroom to see an encore of my performance. They gave me the moustache free and even included some novelty balloons as a gratuity. The bell chimed again as I opened the shop door and cold air blew in. I waved at the man through the window as I walked down the hill, feeling that I had negotiated some small rite of passage.

In general, however, my first weeks in Cambridge were marked by an inkling that I was always missing something. I stayed at parties where I was failing to have any fun, for fear of fun breaking out if I should leave: including the fancy-dress affair, which I eventually attended as a sea captain, without great success. I heard my neighbours laughing and joking in the corridor and felt alienated from their new-blossoming friendships. My room was situated very close to both the college bar and the hall where discos and the like were held, which meant that at almost any time of any evening, I could hear people who were happier than myself. I do not wish to exaggerate the sadness I felt at all this – in my previous student career I had always been a solitary sort of person, by choice – but it may make it easier to understand why I later became so eagerly involved with the people I did.

More of a problem than my general solitude was the cold, which, unfortunately, everyone had warned me about so often that I stopped paying attention. I spent nine pounds on a fleece jacket from the market, and was quickly given the nickname 'Fleecy' by one of my neighbours, a first-year engineer. He was the one who had the Elton John costume, and was the sort to dish nicknames out to avoid getting one himself.

Most of the people living near me were undergraduates. On the other side of me from the engineer was a girl named Nina with blonde, slightly frizzy hair which she sometimes wore in pigtails, but which usually hung loose around her face. She was in her final year. She and the engineer soon became intimate friends after some sort of incident in our communal kitchen. After this, she too began to call me 'Fleecy'. I was indifferent to it; it was better than an abusive epithet of some kind. To put it into perspective, in the next corridor was a fellow who had come to be known as Fat John before the first night was over.

One time, when we were washing up together in the kitchen, they each told me an uninteresting story about a visit to Germany. The engineer made a remark about the football World Cup the summer just gone, which, in his view, Germany had been fortunate to win, partly at England's expense. He then commented on the many varieties of sausage on sale in my country and the two of them laughed for some time. Moments like this were awkward because I could not tell precisely where the amusement emanated from, let alone share in it myself.

I hung one of the novelty balloons, shaped like a penis, outside my door for a while, to show that I did have a sense of humour. But after a few days it had outstayed its welcome somewhat, and I removed it without ceremony. The engineer had a picture of a naked woman on his door and the insignia of some football team. Nina also had a woman upon her door: a picture of the actress, Kim Basinger, torn from a magazine article about 'Ten People Who Will Shape the 1990s'.

At first I thought it curious that Nina should display a female pin-up so proudly. Then, as a result of someone playfully calling her 'Kim', I realised that Nina looked a certain amount like the actress – her hair was a similar blonde, her face was not so different a shape – and by displaying the picture she was attempting to comment upon this similarity. Basinger was at the time very popular because of a recent appearance in *Batman*, the film sensation, which was the main subject of a four-hour conversation I attended during my first week. I say 'attended' because it soon transpired that I was the only person not thoroughly familiar with the movie, and my participation in the chat was limited to a series of elliptical remarks meant to conceal my ignorance.

The resemblance between my neighbour and Kim Basinger was of course not really so striking. Nina was more heavily built than the model-turned-actress, and inevitably lacked, for instance, the gloss and pearly teeth which gave Basinger her famous smile. Besides, Basinger was well into her thirties while Nina was barely twenty. All the same, Nina tacitly encouraged people to compare her with the star. She did this by reacting with conspicuous modesty when anyone brought it up, saying, 'Do you think I look like her? I'm not sure I do, really . . . I'll never be as thin as that . . . I suppose there's something there but I can't really see it . . .' and so on until the notion was firmly in the listener's head.

She also won a 'talent competition' in the college bar, purely by dint of appearing in an erotic costume and making sexual remarks to the mostly male, universally drunk onlookers. The whole affair was less than serious, yet when I saw Nina coming back to her room with the cheap trophy (which had been used in previous years for the college pool championship, discontinued this year because someone spilt orange juice on the table) there was unmistakable pleasure on her face. I felt glad for her. She was an aspiring actress and I would sometimes hear her describing auditions she had done for university productions. She secured a part as a screaming woman in *The Crucible* but missed out on *42nd Street* because they tried to make her sing.

Every few days I would collect my change together and go to call my brother Ralf and father at home. There was another student, an Icelander, in a similar situation, and we would always exchange a sheepish smile before entering our respective booths, our similar lives somehow not quite resulting in a friendship.

My brother Ralf and I were tremendously close, and had really always been so, with none of the hatred sometimes seen between siblings. He drove me to the airport the day I left for Cambridge and we were both taken a little by surprise by the sadness of the occasion, a sort of coming of age: it would be the first time we had ever lived apart and, moreover, he was about to do a year of military service. We had played tennis the night before. Ralf thrashed me as always: I had taught him to play when he was little and then watched as his talent for the game far outstripped mine. During the *Autobahn* trip, Ralf papered over the awkward sense of melancholy by pretending to fall asleep at the wheel until I shouted at him to watch the road. This was an extension of a traditional prank in which he feigned death by lying astoundingly still and holding his breath. More than one aunt and grandmother had been ready to call an ambulance as a result of this talent of his.

At the airport, when the flight was called, I dug him in the ribs until he squealed for mercy. 'You'd better call me every day, bro,' he said – he was just beginning to get a taste for American slang and I had promised to send him any good examples I came across. For myself, I was in the business of collecting as many little English idioms as I could; it was that sort of thing which allowed one not to stand out as a foreigner.

Now, when I phoned from the cold phone booth opposite the college gates, watching the dark river and in the next box the Icelander talking animatedly, Ralf's voice sounded different, gruffer, older already. Ralf seemed to have been serious about calling him every night; he was indignant if I left it more than a couple of days. 'I'll call you, man,' he once offered. 'The old man won't care. Just give me a mate's number and use their phone.' Instead of telling him I had really acquired no such 'mates' yet, I asked to speak to my father. This began well, but the exchange descended into our customary silences, and we felt every one of the several hundred miles apart; I told him the pips were going before it was really the case.

I had arrived with a very small fund, and unexpected holes kept opening in the budget. Fat John left the college after only a few weeks; though I didn't know him, I contributed to a yukka plant which was purchased as a leaving present. Then I was invited to a birthday party which turned out to be in a curry house with a minimum spend of £10, enforced in a spirited manner by frightening staff. There was an English students' trip to Tintern Abbey and

Stonehenge for which I put down the deposit before realising I could not afford the trip itself. (My fellow postgraduates returned from the outing with a repertoire of in-jokes and anecdotes which they would refer to for the remainder of our time together.) I never accepted the offer of a drink for fear of having to reciprocate. I shaved with cheap razors which cut red nicks in my face; a shadow of hair built shiftily on my lip. To avoid social awkwardness, I studied nearly all the time.

One day I returned from my pigeon-hole with two leaflets. The first gave notice of a professional comedy show to be held at the college. The second advertised the chance to earn 'DECENT MONEY' by donating sperm. Straight away I was tempted. My sperm was among the only things I had which anyone might need, except blood, and you were not paid for donating that, except with a cup of tea and a biscuit.

In the largest of the college's courts, a few people were hastening about, not noticing each other – people always walked quickly here, it seemed to me. It was a typical cold, dark evening. I looked at the leaflet from the sperm place. The sum of £30 was offered for a short spell of masturbation. This seemed a large amount for doing something relatively easy, and the threat of becoming a progenitor was remote enough to ignore. In my eagerness to peruse the small print I did not notice the engineer and Nina stealing up behind me.

'Going to donate your spunk, Fleecy?' asked the joker very loudly, making me flinch in shock. Both of them laughed.

'Actually, I was thinking about . . . the comedy show,' I said, looking to the other piece of paper for rescue.

'You should come, have a laugh,' said the engineer. 'You like a laugh, don't you, mate?' There was a definite sarcasm but it was hard to respond without confirming the lack of humour he was alleging. I looked out of the window again and saw, below in the courtyard, the most astonishing human being I had ever seen or will ever see.

She was extraordinarily, dumbfoundingly tall; the fifth tallest woman in Great Britain at the time, I was later to learn. Even people who were used to her could hardly comprehend the sight. Her hair looked golden at the time, though I later saw it was darker, the colour of honey. It bobbed and swayed energetically as she strode down the path, several books under her arm. She moved with a certain ease, as if her amazing dimensions facilitated, rather than hindered, movement. I saw her stop to greet someone as they crossed, and felt a bizarre envy of this other party.

'Who the hell is that?' I found myself saying.

Nina, surprised at my initiating a conversation, glanced out of the window. 'The giraffe? It's Rose Ravenhill. You must have seen her before.'

'Maybe she sneaked past him,' suggested the wise-cracking engineer, and they laughed.

'Who is she?' I asked, lamely.

They told me she was in her final year, studying law, and had become a celebrated figure for obvious reasons. She was heavily involved in organising college events. There were many rumours about her: that her height was caused by a medical condition; that she had been seen talking to an even taller man in the town centre, to the astonishment of passers-by. I swallowed these small pieces of information with an awe which my listeners found highly amusing.

'What an interesting sort of person,' I said.

'I think Andreas is in love!' said Nina.

I went back to my room and tried to concentrate on my

studies. American literature was the core of my M.Phil. I had first become interested in it when reading *Slaughterhouse-Five*, by Kurt Vonnegut, which describes the Allied bombing of Dresden. I happened upon this book in my teenage years; it was the first time I had heard the war described from a victor's standpoint. My English courses at school and university had only briefly visited American writings, so I was now filling in a large gap in my reading.

I worked very assiduously, in common with all the other international students. Often, the Icelander and I would be the last two people studying in the library when the septuagenarian librarian switched the lights off and made signs with his eyebrows to show that it was time to leave. I was motivated by fear of failure, by a desire to justify my decision in coming here and their decision in having me, and probably by whatever it was that also motivated my father to work as remorselessly as he always had.

That evening, however, I could not convince myself to read more than half a page at a time without my mind flicking back to the giant girl I had seen striding across the court: the prodigious yet elegant length of her legs, the way her hair bobbed about, the books under her arm, the unanswerable questions of where she was at this moment, and what she was doing.

I dreamed about her twice. The first time, she knocked on the door and asked to use my telephone; not having one, I was greatly flustered. The second dream came on the night of the comedy, when, exhausted after staying up to finish an essay, I flopped down on my bed and fell sound asleep at teatime. By the time I woke up, feeling queasy and disorientated, the comedy show was about to start. From the hall below I could hear thunderous applause as things kicked off. Swearing at myself, I threw on a shirt, smoothed my hair and raced down to join the audience, arriving two minutes after the start.

It was a gross blunder. The first comedian spotted a chance to mock my lateness and get the laughs off to a start. 'Welcome, sir, nice of you to join us!' he said, or some other ironic pleasantry. The feeling of three hundred pairs of eyes swinging to see me was like an intense and hot light. I could just see Nina and the engineer sniggering, and even my fellow loner the Icelander, who was sitting with some computing students. And in the corner of the room, to my utter misery, was the very tall girl. If I could have traded places with anyone living I would in all likelihood have done so.

'What's your name, mate?' asked the comedian, looking for material.

'Andreas.'

'Andreas,' he echoed. 'Sounds a bit German to me!'

'That's because I am German,' I said. In my head, it was something of a smart reply, but the ominous guffaws around me told me that I had invited disaster. Sure enough, the comedian launched into a rapid series of jokes about Germany. The main theme seemed to be that I had 'invaded' the show and so on, in the manner expected of my countrymen. Desperately I tried to make myself unseen, almost sitting in someone's lap in my haste.

'You can run,' said the comic, 'but ve vill find you!' What this was meant to parody I did not and do not know, but it was again popularly received. 'Anyway,' the funnyman went on, 'you're welcome here. Everyone, say *heil* to Andreas. I mean hi!' This was the coup de grace and there was a measure of applause. I could see some people shaking their heads, but no one seemed seriously offended. Even I was not exactly offended; I was just desperate to disappear. I found a vacant seat at last and sat, feeling as if my skin were luminous. The comedian moved on, aiming remarks at various others, but nobody else was made to suffer. At one time he spotted Nina and said flirtatiously that she reminded him of someone. 'Kim Basinger,' someone suggested loudly, and Nina blushed and looked around at everyone to make sure they had registered it.

As the show wore on, some of my composure returned, though I still felt hugely embarrassed, and when the lights were turned up at the interval I examined my palms and waited, like some shuffling nocturnal creature, for darkness to fall again. People went about their business around me, wandering to the bar and returning with clusters of plastic pint glasses, beer spilling over the sides onto the floor. I heard people repeating some of their favourite jokes to each other. The very tall girl was nowhere to be seen – she was probably having fun backstage with the comics.

When the lights went out and the entertainer strode out to begin the second half, I felt the pit of my stomach twist, almost resigned to more humiliation. To my relief, however, his eyes scanned the room for another target. I experienced a surge of guilty delight as he pointed to Nina, who was munching on a packet of potato crisps. 'If you want to look like Kim Basinger, you might have to cut out the snacks . . .' he said.

So delighted was I to avoid being the victim that I cackled loudly at this tasteless jibe, expecting to be just one among many. But this time there were disapproving breaths and sighs, a couple of people even jeered, and my solitary laugh was like a klaxon. The comedian apologised hastily for his remark, for fear of becoming unpopular. In the fake light, I met Nina's accusing eyes for a moment. And as other people glanced at me I felt stupid for the second time in under two hours: silent during the laughter, and now laughing in the silence.

I would have liked to leave the comedy night immediately after that second error, but it was clear that to depart prematurely would make me as much of what the English call 'a sitting duck' as my late arrival had done. I was forced to sit with a game smile upon my face as the remaining two comedians delivered observations about the poor taste of kebabs (to judge from the reaction, I was the only person alive not to have eaten one), and gave impressions of how James Bond might speak if he were from Manchester. I had never seen a James Bond movie nor visited Manchester, and so, again, I did not have to hold my sides together after these remarks. As applause broke out at the end, I felt weighed down with the feeling of not being in the right place – not just in this show, but in general. Overall the comedy show had been somewhat less than the invigorating dose of entertainment I had counted upon.

Back in my room, as I listened to most of the crowd noisily dispersing into the bar, my sense of failure intensified. I sat on the edge of the bed and tried in vain to find a consoling thought. It was too late at night to phone Ralf – he would certainly be out at some party – and nobody else would understand.

I looked in the mirror with contempt. All the silly economies, the non-shaving, the poor eating, had left my face with a bedraggled, fuzzy appearance. On an impulse I leapt to my feet, took hold of one of the impotent orange razors lying in a pack of one hundred by the basin, and began to attack my upper lip, to annihilate the absurd little hedge of hair. My hand trembling, I carved tiny flecks of flesh out with every sweep of the blunt instrument, but the pain seemed normal. Only when the first adrenalin wore away did I realise suddenly that I was streaming blood from a clumsy cut; it was falling in great globs on the tiles of the sink and beginning to stain my fleece jacket. I groped around feebly, I hadn't even so much as a tissue. Furious and abject at the same time, I tore out of the door and bolted to the corridor bathroom.

Arriving there, I remembered that there were no paper towels in the dispenser; the college had confiscated them after a recent vogue for wetting them and throwing them at things. There was still paper in the toilet cubicle, but this was occupied; I shrank back from the locked door in speechless frustration. There was blood in six different places, I was dripping into the sink and onto the floor in a shocking red trail; it was a ridiculous sight, completely without dignity. A tiny cough confirmed that it was Nina in the cubicle. There was no question, after what had happened earlier, of asking her to pass some paper under the door. I went out, wondering if I could make a raid on another corridor's bathroom without being seen.

'Hey, are you all right?' someone asked in the corridor. I ignored it, moved on with my head down, then stopped as some quality of the voice, the soft, twinkling humour of it, made me freeze and turn. There was the giant girl. The ingredients of humiliation were complete.

'I've had a slight problem,' I said, looking anywhere but up at her face, which was both amused and concerned. 'I didn't intend it to go this far,' I added, not very revealingly.

'God,' she said, 'what a mess!' She delved into a small shoulder bag and stooped to hand me a bundle of tissues. Feeling too silly even to thank her, I pressed it to my face and watched as it turned a soggy red.

'Listen,' she said, 'you're Andreas, aren't you?' My last chance of escaping this night with anonymity disappeared in – as I had heard someone say – a puff of smoke. 'I just came to apologise for that moron,' she said. After a pause I decided that she meant the comedian.

'I thought it was I who looked like the moron, I mean, I thought it was me,' I said, struggling to make my grammar casual as I met her eyes for the first time. They were large and brown; a strand of hair trickled into one eye and she blew it out of the way with a humorous puff.

'Not at all,' she said. 'It's my fault, I booked him, he shouldn't have been so offensive. I'm on my way to find Nina because she deserves an apology as well.'

It was a chance to help her. 'She's in the WC,' I said. 'And I am Andreas Hönig.'

'Two useful facts,' she said, with a slight smile. 'I'm Rose Ravenhill.'

'I'll wait here, I suppose.' She said after a pause.

There was a silence which I would have dearly liked to fill with a worthwhile action or word of some kind. Come into my room to wait, I thought, in fact to hell with Nina, just come with me, we can find out all the things we have in common. I imagined her dipping her head under the door frame, sitting down on the edge of my bed, asking about the photo of the Berlin Wall, admiring my collection of Kiss and Iron Maiden cassettes. It was while mentally showing her my room, all tidy and prissy with the cassettes in alphabetical order and my clothes neatly folded and ironed, that I glanced into an imaginary mirror and it became clear to me just how improbable this was.

There was the muffled sound of the toilet flushing and this acted as the impetus for me to go away. I said I hoped to see Rose again. As this sentence emerged from my mouth I felt as if I had been contemptibly eager: it was almost akin to asking her out on a date. On the other hand perhaps I had not been bold enough. Probably neither was true, I thought, closing the door to my room as she smiled genially down at me; probably, the whole episode would escape her mind in a little time, especially with all the things that must jostle for the attention of such an unusual person.

Home at Christmas time, I told Ralf of the joking I had received from the comedian, and he was indignant. He had cut his hair short to fit with his army comrades, his physique had improved markedly in the past couple of months, and he could probably now lift me off my feet. He was unforthcoming about military life itself. 'It's just a job,' he shrugged. I myself had worked in a home for the elderly rather than do military duty. Still, in most other ways he was unchanged. He asked me how many English girls I had 'done'. I humoured him by supplying a cagey answer that suggested prowess too great to bother boasting about. Probably he saw through it.

My father asked me, a few days before I returned to Cambridge, 'Any thoughts yet about what might happen afterwards?'

'Afterwards . . .?'

'When you leave university.'

'I am thinking about various branches of academia . . .' I said vaguely. 'Or translation work . . .'

'*Ach so*,' muttered my father. When he said this, it could

mean almost anything from disgust to admiration. In this instance it was perhaps closer to the former. It was clear enough to both of us that I was not sure which direction my life was going at present.

'Perhaps there might be opportunities with theatre companies producing American work,' I said, hoping to reignite the discussion, 'or . . . other things to do with American literature.'

My father nodded slowly. He worked in construction and had done so for many, many years; in fact he worked on the Berlin Wall. He had never taken a day off sick in his career. Ralf, having a view of the world that was heavily influenced by anti-establishment rock music and youthful idealism, said he was a slave to work. In my view, he simply preferred it to the other business of life. He enjoyed having a clear set of things to accomplish.

'A good thing about the Cambridge degree is its versatility,' I said, paraphrasing the prospectus.

I could hear the clock ticking on the mantelpiece and some drunk shouting outside. It was always pretty quiet around Christmas, my mother having died giving birth to Ralf on 20 December, when I was four. My father had done his best with some decorations this year, and my aunt cooked a goose on Christmas Eve, but it was invariably a slow time of year. It was not that anyone became sombre about my mother; that might, in fact, have been better. There was just no talk about her at all.

My father was disinclined to discuss important subjects if he could avoid it, and he had a way of killing off conversations by simply letting whatever you said flutter, as it were, out of the window. He would grip the arm of his chair very hard and whistle a tune, sometimes something pertinent to the topic it was replacing, for example Gilbert and Sullivan if I mentioned England. Ralf and I had therefore always had a relationship with him which, for all the love on each side, was punctuated by long, long moments where nobody was saying anything.

Indeed, I was the one who told the four-year-old Ralf that Mother had gone to heaven and explained how he would see her there. But we were not a religious family; my father didn't believe in God, or at least he never said anything to show that he did. Ralf cottoned on to this soon enough and realised he would, in all likelihood, not meet his mother.

We shared a room throughout our childhood. At one point my father spent a considerable time knocking down a wall between two little storage rooms to create a new bedroom. He bought a new bed and decorated the room with pictures of trains and other things a boy might like. He put Ralf proudly to bed at eight o'clock, turned off the lights, and it was as if the whole street, the whole suburb were waiting with bated breath for Ralf to nod off to the greatest sleep of his life. Of course, within an hour he was back in my room, and that was where he stayed from then on. '*Ach so*,' said my father, 'very well,' and turned it back into two storage rooms.

Ralf always used to sleep with a scrap of blanket and a bear, and – being button-nosed and with hair that was blond almost to the point of whiteness – looked something like a bear himself. When I thought of Ralf it was still this Ralf first, and the muscular, stridently masculine new model afterwards, which I conjured up in my mind.

I went back to Cambridge for my second term thinking that, whatever else, I needed a plan for my future before I went home again. Perhaps there was an urgency, a desperation almost, in my thinking this, because I had no more cards of procrastination to play once this second student career had passed. This might in some way explain how I became drawn into the things I am about to describe.

>> Alexandra

And that was where the translation stopped. The feeling at the end was a bit like when the projector goes wrong in the cinema and the lights come up suddenly. It was quiet in the flat when I finished reading; I made a cup of tea and read through it again. What I would have liked was to talk to someone about it, but there were only two of us watching this film, and not together.

I thought about it for the whole of the next couple of days, trying to imagine it all – the young Andreas at university, the momentously tall girl, the irritating neighbours. These images filled up my imagination and provided a welcome break from thinking about the present moment. Gareth had done an amazing job of the translation, not that I had the chance to thank him: for the next three days I didn't see him at all. His presentation had been a success and there was now talk of him going to America. From what I could take from their early-morning conversations, this was pretty impressive;

impressive enough for Dan to needle him about it and for Gareth to get annoyed.

One evening, I forgot my ID card and had to stand outside the apartment block waiting for someone to let me into my home. It was about eight – I had been for a drink with Helen after work – and getting chilly. I pressed the red button to summon the concierge, but no luck; he was probably dealing with a maintenance problem in one of the other flats. I buzzed our flat, but there was no answer. Irritated now, I rang my brother, but it went through to his answerphone, which invited you to leave a message after a catchphrase from a TV series, which he had downloaded from a premium phone line. As I was standing, shivering, in the shadow of our ugly block, I saw a familiar figure flip-flopping her way towards me. It was Trixie – I was pretty sure now that was her name. She had on a beanie hat, purple tights, green shoes, designer shades pushed to the top of her head. What does she look like? my mother would have asked, except that because she was Dan's girlfriend, she would probably have raved about her.

We exchanged a fake greeting. 'I've forgotten my . . .' I said.

'Oh, nightmare,' said Trixie. 'Hang on a second let me just I've been at a shoot?'

She sat down on a concrete step and began to burrow around in her bag, which was about the size of a Swiss roll, yet seemed to contain more or less everything she had accumulated in her life so far. 'I've tried calling,' I said, thinking she was looking for her phone, 'but he's not answering . . .'

'I know, Dan is such a mentalist,' said Trixie, gesturing at her head. Out of the bag she brought lip salve, foundation, a keyring, a membership card to a club, a credit card, anti-ageing cream, a tub of 'body butter', a ticket to something or other, a badge. Finally, with her belongings laid out over the step like gifts in a shop window, she produced an ID card.

'Is that Dan's?'

'No, it's mine?' said Trixie. 'He got me one?' She swiped the card in the slot, pushed the door open at the click. I watched her. It was strictly forbidden to give a key card to anyone who wasn't a resident. Perhaps she was a resident, perhaps she was going to move in with us. What could I do, I was a lodger myself. The two of us stood in the lift, in silence, all the way up to the twenty-sixth floor, reflected on both sides in the unflattering mirrors on the lift walls, so it looked as though there were hundreds of pairs of us. At floor fifteen, she got out a pocket mirror and examined herself until twenty-three.

There was a little gathering in progress in our lounge, which was thick with the herby smell of weed; I coughed involuntarily and a couple of people glanced peevishly at me, thinking I was being difficult. About eight men were perched on the furniture with their eyes on the TV. Dan and another guy were sitting on giant cushions on the floor. The little men on the screen dashed this way and that; the real men ooh-ed and aah-ed and shouted things. The commentator was very excitable. Someone's hand knocked over a beer can which fizzed foam onto the carpet.

'Who's playing?' I asked no one in particular.

Three or four people smirked at each other and at me, but no one answered. I was backing out of the room when Dan turned his head.

'Hey, Alex, there's mail for you on the table,' he said, 'from the prison.'

'Oh, right, thanks,' I said, not breaking step.

'From the prison,' Dan repeated, so everyone could hear.

'Yes yes, it's something for work,' I said, in retreat.

'I did this shoot for a like urban label and we did it at a prison?' said Trixie. 'And we actually went in the prison? It was weird.' Everyone immediately began fussing around her. I shut the door feeling hot and bothered. I heard, muffled, Dan making some remark – I was almost sure my name was there – and Trixie's blaring laugh: 'You can't say things like that!'

I went into the kitchen to collect my letter. Gareth had just returned from the gym and was fishing a pack of beers out of the fridge. He looked surprised to see me. He was still wearing his gym clothes: shorts – which made his legs look very long – and a blue T-shirt which said: MY TASTES ARE SIMPLE, I LIKE THE BEST.

'A'right,' he muttered. 'Do you want . . . ?' He snapped a beer off the pack.

'I'm all right, thanks.' He glanced at the beer, looking vexed that he'd gone to the trouble.

'I like your T-shirt,' I said.

'Oh, it's . . . my sister gave it to me,' he said, dismissively. 'Love letter?'

'What?' I looked guiltily at the envelope. 'No, no, it's . . . it's nothing. It's not a love letter.'

'I was joking,' said Gareth, quietly. He eased his long body past me.

'Who – who's playing?' He looked at me, puzzled. 'In the football.'

'It's a computer game,' he said. 'It's not real.'

'Ah . . .' I said, remembering the smirks when I'd asked the question in the lounge. There was a pause. 'That's embarrassing.'

'It's a very realistic game,' said Gareth, kindly, as he left.

The letter was, again, about four pages long. 'I must thank you,' it said, 'both for taking the trouble both to translate, or have translated, my lengthy memoirs, and also for revealing something of your life.' Later on in the letter he wrote, 'Given that I receive no visitors, you have become the closest thing to a friend that I possess.' This was such a big statement to make, I read it four or five times, trying to imagine someone writing it. We weren't friends – we hadn't even met. If the sentence was true, he must be lonely beyond what I had previously imagined.

I emailed Claire to ask if 'pen pals' like me ever visited prisoners in person. Within half an hour, she had replied. I wondered how someone with such a happy home life could also be such a prolific emailer. 'While we are happy to arrange such visits, we warn very strongly against forming close attachments which may lead prisoners to have groundless hopes.' This was a recap of what she'd already said to me, and it seemed to be phrased with a strange formality – as if she had cut and pasted it from something else. The last sentence, however, said, 'See you soon, sweets!!' And 'groundless hopes' of what? I sent a message back asking her to arrange a meeting.

Albert came trundling in with an extra-thick bundle of mail: the sight of it made me weep inwardly. 'All this to go?' he asked, picking up yesterday's rejects for recycling. Every day, when he said this, it made me think of my most embarrassing work moment. It was when I was quite new in the office. Albert had asked, 'All this to go?' 'Yep,' I said, handing the pile to him, 'all absolute crap.' Or something offhand like that. The submissions were no worse than usual, but my mood was. 'Crap,' he repeated thoughtfully, flicking through the papers with his old eyes scanning the words one by one. 'My daughter sent one of these in.'

'Oh . . .' I said, and then stupidly, rather than immediately washing my hands of my comment, I said, 'Are you sure?'

'Here it is,' said Albert, 'this idea for a travel show. She's looking to get into presenting and what not. Well, anyway.' He turned to go.

'I don't remember that one, I didn't read them all that carefully, I'm sure that one was really good,' I said hurriedly, but it was too late. He walked away and I sat with burning cheeks and, at the end of the day, made Helen summon him into the office on some feeble premise or other, so I could sneak out and go home.

The lucky thing was that Albert seemed to be one of these people who lived each day as if the previous one hadn't happened: he used the same joke ten mornings running, he never remembered anyone's name, and quite often you would see him reading a paper from several days ago.

'Heard about Paris yet?' Helen asked, as he went on his way.

'No. Have you?'

'I haven't even thought about it,' said Helen, 'because I've got bigger things to worry about!' She gestured triumphantly at her desk, which was already covered in cards and birthday merchandise. The big day wasn't until Sunday, but the party was tonight.

I had bought her a large, tacky helium balloon, in keeping with a tradition of ours.

'You are still coming, aren't you?'

'Of course,' I said. The Andreas manuscript had successfully prevented me from worrying about seeing Craig and the others. I had, however, carefully bought an outfit – a shortish skirt and knee-length boots – and tested it on Helen who said it looked beautiful. It was an important endorsement as Helen had, at least once, made someone cry by being truthful about their clothing purchases.

Helen's utter frankness had been what attracted me, and also repelled me, when I first met her. It was a game of spin-the-bottle in our first week at university. I'd got some question like 'your worst memory' (of course, this was pre-proposal, indeed Craig was just another student around the bottle). I told the story of the night our father left, more or less at the orders of our mother, after a week of nothing but screaming in our house. It was one of those very studenty, earnest performances; I talked about how my brother's bullying tendencies had probably been shaped by that night, how I had always been introverted since then, and so on. I was looking at the ground and passing my room keys between my hands as if it was too painful even to look at people. I think if I could see it now, I would be embarrassed. A girl I didn't know, and never really spoke to again, was nearly in tears on my right. All in all I was quite enjoying myself. At the end, there was a reverent silence and then Helen – whom I hadn't met – said, 'Yeah, well. Worse things happen at sea.'

'I'm sorry?' I said, offended.

'I'm just saying,' she said. Later I would find out that she'd had a worse family life; it isn't until you meet a lot of new people that you find out how banal your problems have been. But at the time, I hated her. One good-looking bloke, with long hair, made everyone laugh when he got the question, 'What are you most afraid of?' and, pointing at us, said, 'Those two having a fight'. We both glared at him. The boy was Craig and it was one of those quirks of student life that the three of us ended up living together as best friends.

Tonight, Helen was going drinking with Craig and the

others before the party began, but I didn't quite feel up to that sort of intimacy; my plan was to go home, prepare myself and go back into town. It started to go wrong straight away, because Gareth was in the living room, where the best mirror was; also, just having him around made me inhibited.

Still, I spent an uncharacteristically long time getting ready. The bag of powder in the bathroom cabinet had been severely depleted the other night, after the computer football championships; it now fitted neatly behind my conditioner. I read the letter from Andreas once more before I went out. I had borrowed an umbrella, for once, from someone at work, but it was a clear night.

'Off out?' asked Gareth, sticking his head around the door, just as I had steeled myself for it.

'Yes, it's Helen's party,' I said. 'The one with, um, with the . . .'

'The mountain-range chest,' said Gareth. 'Well, have a good time.'

'Are you not going out?'

'Yes,' he said, 'later. I've got . . . I've got a . . . an appointment.' He looked ill at ease suddenly. I had no idea if he had a girlfriend, but he quite often took a phone call in a confidential manner and you could hear him late at night – on the nights they weren't out on a binge – talking in a low voice. If there was a girl, he never brought her here. He could probably get married without me finding out, though.

The train got stuck in a tunnel for about five minutes without any explanation being offered. People glanced at each other as if the culprit was among us. Although it was only a short delay, I was beginning to feel restless; I was going to get there after everyone else. Out on the street at last, I phoned Helen. 'No worries!' she shouted over background noise. 'Just whenever you can!' I think I'd been hoping she would be worried.

My heart sank a little when I found the place. It was one of these aggressively 'urban' bars with a name that meant nothing but sounded clever, menus printed in a font that hurt your eyes to read (and no pound signs; £11.50, for example, just appeared as 11.5); toilets marked 'XX' and 'XY', and an in-house DJ playing 'a fusion of minimalist jazz and Eastern-inspired hip-hop'. There was a very loud group on a mezzanine level overlooking the rest of the restaurant, and their noise filled what was left of the air after the music. Still, it meant a lot to her that I was there.

No sooner had I begun saying that I was looking for a group under the name of . . . than the woman gave me a contemptuous look and pointed towards the mezzanine. With severe misgivings I walked up the half-staircase. An enclave of about ten tables had been created for the party and there were at least eighty people there. I waved at Helen and she waved back, with a little extra shrug/smile/grimace to acknowledge that she was rather busy. Craig, in a black shirt with his hair quite long, was sitting near her; he looked up from a conversation with a blonde girl and gave me a smile, then went back to it. I was forced to take the only seat I could see, so far away from the people I knew that awkward eye contact with Craig was now literally impossible. I'd forgotten how enormous Helen's database of friends was. It wasn't going to be my sort of night.

To my left was a woman who kept going out for cigarettes and saying things like 'God I'm totally going to get cancer'; to my right was a man with a laugh so loud and breathy it could truly be called a guffaw. The random seating plan of a party was exactly the sort of way I might meet my next boyfriend, but it wasn't to be tonight. I got my first guffaw by reluctantly ordering a cocktail called 'panties on the floor' – the entire list had names ranging from cheeky to outright disturbing – and the second came when there was an awkward silence, or what passed for a silence. He was a very friendly, talkative person and that made it a lot worse.

We went on to a bar, with diminished numbers, and there I got to talk to Helen, at least, but the music was too loud to hear anything. 'Having a good time?' she yelled. I gave her a thumbs-up. 'I know you're not,' she shouted, 'but try and go with the flow for me.' I squeezed her shoulder and went over to talk to Lauren, one of my old housemates. We discussed her job and mine. It struck me that if you let a friendship go for a certain length of time, it was nearly impossible to reignite it; the length of time varies from one friendship to another, but Lauren and I seemed to have gone past ours. Craig said a muffled hello on his way past with an armful of drinks. On the occasions we did meet, we both acted as if it was the most natural thing that we had once been in the habit of seeing each other naked and yet were now talking like people who vaguely knew each other through a third party.

By the club, more people had drifted away, but that still left about thirty. We queued outside the place with a bouncer looking at us as if he would rather we were all dead. One of Helen's friends was being supported as she threw up into a drain. Two people from work with a very long, tedious on-off relationship switched back to 'on'. It was getting cold, but, of course, in the club it was hot as hell. Here there wasn't even the option of ignoring the music. I danced for as long as was polite, then sat around for a bit, then satisfied myself that Helen was too drunk to mind if I went home. Craig had already left, and that, I supposed, was a very small victory.

When I got on the night bus I realised I'd left the umbrella somewhere.

After all the hype it had been a forgettable night. I was an idiot to have ever expected anything else. The fact was, Helen and I were very different people at heart. She had always been very sociable, into drinking and dancing, whereas I had borrowed the traits from her and these days was struggling to make them fit. One of the things Craig said which hurt me most, in the weeks after the break-up which saw a fraught series of calls and emotive text messages, was that he had never quite been 'convinced' by our relationship. He'd never explained the remark but I occasionally felt I knew what he meant. I could have asked him tonight, had we not spent the entire night glimpsing each other between a hundred other bodies. I had the beginnings of a headache without any real feeling of intoxication to make up for it.

The ID card slid into the door, my boots click-clacked on the shiny floor. The concierge raised his eyebrows in greeting. The lift took a long time to come. There was a notice up about a recent spate of thefts. Our flat was silent, with its usual trace of cannabis and male perfume in the air.

I went into my room and caught my breath. There was a pile of papers on the bed: again about twenty pages, typed out on that company paper. He must be spending half of his office time doing it, I thought with a surge of satisfaction. But there was no covering note, nothing. I looked with some regret around the room as Gareth had found it, still recovering from my party preparations and rushed departure. The bed was unmade, there were tights slung over the chair, and all sorts of clothes and knick-knacks on the floor, including underwear, in a sad echo of the cocktail I'd consumed hours earlier. The wardrobe was open. I saw it all through his sardonic eyes. It was some minutes before I realised that I was wasting time thinking about this, when the story lay there ready for me to rejoin it.

☞ ANDREAS

I had thought about Rose Ravenhill more than I realised while I was away, but a week after returning to Cambridge, I had not caught sight of her at all. She never seemed to work in the library, where I sat up late with my head in books of American history, while the Icelander pored over computing problems and the old librarian waited to go to bed. I did not spy her in the canteen, but then I rarely was there myself as it was cheaper to patronise the supermarket. I had no idea where in the college's maze-like courts her room might be found. But, it occurred to me one day, I did know where her pigeon-hole was (they were in alphabetical order) and that was one place she was certain to visit. Once this had entered my head, I took to dawdling when collecting my correspondence, in case she should appear. This evolved into making the odd detour to the pigeon-holes when I was in the area.

It was only a matter of time before I took this too far and

it happened very late one night. I had gone for a walk around the college to clear my head for a challenging essay. There was no one else about. In the cold pigeon-hole room, there were posters for plays, college societies and so on. Some pigeon-holes were stuffed with mail, but in RAVENHILL, R. there was just one thing, a little yellow note. Of course, there was no way I could read the note. Yet suddenly this truth turned itself inside out: I could hardly bear not to read it. The next hand to touch it would be hers, I thought, stealthily removing the note – I hardly knew I was doing it – reading it and immediately replacing it and moving away.

It said, COCO CLUB. TOMORROW (23rd). DO COME. ROBERT.

My first reaction was mild disappointment – I could make nothing of this – then relief: it could have been a love letter. Soon I settled upon what was probably the most natural feeling, puzzlement that I had invaded someone's privacy, and unprovoked. True, it was not motiveless; I had done it because I wanted to involve myself in Rose's life somehow; but was this how normal people behaved? Still, wriggling under a suffocating extra blanket that night, I reflected that, if I did not try to quench this thirst soon, perhaps it would push me to even more peculiar measures. I would, therefore, go to the Coco Club.

I got the address easily enough. As the day wore on, I asked myself repeatedly whether I had gone completely mad. The place could be anything, a fetish club, a hangout for Freemasons, or, for that matter, exclusively for people well over six feet five. But the truth was that I had had no adventures for a long time, and walking through the streets with the night air stinging my face was rather exhilarating.

I passed the club twice before having the good fortune to sight it. It was situated at the bottom of a staircase, partly hidden by a row of tethered bicycles. There was a churning in my bowels as I descended. Down I went until there was a double door with a bouncer posted outside.

'Member of Collett Security?' he asked.

I said an assured yes.

'ID?' asked the man.

'Shit,' I said, 'didn't bring it!' This was done very spontaneously and sounded convincing; I was impressed with myself. The bouncer shrugged and cocked a thumb to show I could go past.

Initially it seemed nothing more than a wine bar, dimly lit with nondescript music, and people in smart clothes milling about everywhere. From eavesdropping on the shouted conversations I gleaned gradually that it was some kind of recreational night laid on by a firm for its workers. In time I noticed that there was a makeshift stage at the front of the room with a spotlight rigged up at a suitable angle to illuminate it. But there was no sign of Rose, and besides, I was beginning to wonder what my excuse would be if she did appear. I purchased an unbelievably expensive drink from the bar – I would have asked the barman to repeat the price, but was fearful of speaking too much – and waited.

After fifteen minutes or so of this, the lights were dimmed still further. It was announced that the entertainment would commence in five minutes and there was a little whooping and light applause. I found a seat for myself. The five minutes became seven, then ten; I felt more and more that I was probably wasting my evening, and for very questionable reasons. At last, a fake drum-roll announced the start of the show. An amplified voice from somewhere said that we were about to meet some of the world's leading personalities.

'Without further ado,' said the voice, 'ladies and gentlemen, I give you Margaret Thatcher!'

There was rousing applause and onto the stage came the Prime Minister of Great Britain. The permed hair and ghastly smile were as I had seen in the newspapers and other media. 'Thenk you, thenk you,' she said in an upper-class voice. I looked around; people were laughing and clapping. 'It is a privilege,' said Thatcher slowly, 'to meet the people of Collett Security.' I was watching my first professional lookalike.

When Thatcher had spoken for a few minutes, her place was taken by someone who resembled Kim Basinger, seductively dressed like her *Batman* character, I imagined; I was beginning to feel I had seen the film. This woman, with her shimmering fair hair and pert breasts, was a great deal more like the actress than my college neighbour was; I was glad Nina was not there as she might have found it rather chastening. The lookalike Kim singled out a cackling member of the audience and made a number of bawdy suggestions.

Act after act went by, a fake Jon Bon Jovi, a lookalike of someone from an Australian show I had never seen. Most of the onlookers were enjoying themselves greatly, all the more so because there were frequent jokes about burglar alarms and security systems. These remarks served to remind me periodically that I had no right to be here, but by and large I was beginning to relax; the oddness of the situation had swept me along. At length we reached the finale. The disembodied voice returned. 'Ladies and gentlemen, Robert, the world's tallest man!'

Onto the stage came a man so tall, it was almost impossible to believe. For the second time in a couple of months I experienced the jolt of setting eyes on a person whose dimensions seemed to defy logic. There were gasps and shocked laughs. 'Stilts, has to be,' someone muttered, but Robert immediately defused this idea, showing various portions of his leg to establish that his fantastic height was no trickery.

'Jesus, that's impossible!' someone whispered. The laughter around me had a nervous quality. He was, I fancied, even taller than Rose. It was incredible.

He leaned over to say hello to the audience and then straightened up, seemingly one vertebra at a time, like an ancient scroll unfolding. He was wearing what looked like a straitjacket, as if to suggest that he might, otherwise, run amok like an animal. 'I know what you're thinking,' said the giant in a caricatured southern American twang. 'What a freak! And y'all got that right. My eyes sure are very close together.' There was a roar of laughter. Though the joke of course was that his eyes were hardly the major issue, I studied them nonetheless: they were watery and lugubrious. 'Well, you're right, this here is a freak show,' continued the towering individual. 'Y'all should see my pops. He calls me Shorty.' More laughter. He went on in this parodic vein for a while.

'Hey, look – that must be his girlfriend,' whispered someone to his friend behind me. I looked over my shoulder and then snapped back guiltily; there she was, at the back of the room, as inconspicuous as possible, her shoulders hunched. She had her hands knotted together and seemed to be looking slightly downwards rather than concentrating on the act. My heart was, as I had heard someone say in college, in my boots. Of course it made sense that these exceptional people were drawn together in a friendship, probably a love affair. What was I doing in this environment I did not fully understand? I felt a real dejection that grew each time the giant wrung another laugh from the assembled employees. It was as if our respective heights were a metaphor for his superiority. I would have liked to leave, but there was no way to accomplish this without being seen by Rose.

The 'freak' went off with applause ringing around the basement room, and there were clamorous appeals for an encore. But the lights snapped on rather untheatrically, and my only thought was to get out. I apologised and squeezed past a dozen people and made for the doors, running almost instantly into Rose Ravenhill.

'Andreas!'

'This must seem peculiar to you,' I said, feebly.

'Not at all,' she said mischievously. 'I suppose you're an employee of this security firm?'

'It's a tall story why I am here . . .' I said, meaning a long story. I then thought it looked as if I had deliberately satirised her height and added, 'Not so much tall as . . . difficult. Anyway, I guess you have to see the star.'

'Oh, he won't be out for a while,' she said, 'and besides, I'm more interested in this coincidence. Come on, what are you doing here?'

I was tongue-tied. I certainly did not have the courage to say, quite simply, that I had wanted to see her. My hands were buried in my pockets and one of them, my left, brushed against hair. It gave me an odd, but just workable idea.

'I'm . . . thinking of becoming a lookalike,' I lied. 'I wanted to research the area.'

'A lookalike!' said Rose. 'Of whom?' Her eyes were warm on my face. There was already no getting away from this situation. I fumbled in my pocket and brought out, saggy and rumpled but still serviceable, the Hitler moustache. I gummed it to my top lip and forced my shaky arm into a salute. '*Sieg Heil!*'

'Hitler!' said Rose. She chewed on her lip. 'Well, that's interesting. That could be a real . . . Speak some German.' I did as I was told, and threw in some Hitler-like scowling for good measure. A couple of businessmen passed, ties slung back over their shoulders, and gave me understandably odd looks.

'Listen,' said Rose, 'if you're serious, you really should meet Robert. He knows the business inside out.'

I could wait no longer. 'Is he your boyfriend?'

She laughed. 'No, no. Just a friend.'

The weight rose from my shoulders and I felt a couple of inches taller, though in the present company that was no great accomplishment.

'He won't be ready for a while,' she said. 'It takes him five minutes just to get out of that straitjacket. Shall we go outside?' She laid her hand flat on the ceiling. 'I prefer the sky to this.'

I followed her up the stairs, narrowing my eyes to focus on the reality of this and blot out the many peculiar features. She was wearing a very long black skirt which swished around her feet; her large shoes clacked rhythmically on the steps. I admired the poise of her body, which she held upright somehow despite having to bend and sway away from light fittings and arches.

'So how did you find out about this?' Rose asked. This was a question I had anticipated with some dread. It was a corporate thing, after all, not open to the public, certainly not open to me.

'I . . . slightly know one of the lookalikes,' I lied.

A couple of the performers were within earshot, lighting cigarettes whose smoke curled up into the sky, mingling with cold breath. I caught the eye of the Jon Bon Jovi impersonator, who had removed his hairpiece and was completely bald; it made me think that comparatively little natural resemblance was needed to do this job. Behind him, Margaret Thatcher climbed into the back of a taxi, waving to her colleagues as she opened a packet of sandwiches. It was important that Rose did not ask me whom it was that I knew, so I moved things on. 'Are there many professional lookalikes on the . . . circuit?'

'What you saw tonight was just the tip of the iceberg,' Rose said. I looked up into her face, the moonlight playing across it; dark blue clouds were rushing across the sky. I thought her phrase a neat one, though it was later revealed to me as a cliché. 'There are dozens of lookalikes out there. I mean, the ones tonight were all from one agency.'

'Agency?'

'Yeah, all these people have managers,' Rose said, 'to look after bookings, you know.'

'But who books them, who hires them to . . . look alike?'

'Oh, all sorts,' Rose said. 'A lot of stuff like this, corporate entertainment. And of course stags and hens.' I nodded, feigning understanding of the words in this context. 'Then there's TV stuff,' she continued. 'Adverts especially. And then there's a whole load of other things, public appearances. There are people who get excited just seeing someone who looks like someone famous.'

'This is what I was going to say to you in there,' she went on, grabbing my sleeve: I felt myself stiffen at her touch. 'Robert knows a guy who's looking for a Hitler lookalike for next month. It's similar to this, an office party.'

'An office party,' I repeated, thinking that I was getting in deeper than anticipated already. The only Hitler lookalikes I had ever heard of were the unfortunate 'ringers' employed to risk assassination by posing as the Führer in public. In truth, though, I was not thinking of my situation so much as of her eyes.

'It's being done agency-free,' Rose said, 'in other words, arranged privately, so . . . look, Robert will speak to you about it.'

Back in the basement bar I was introduced to Robert at last. He was now dressed in jeans and an extra-large T-shirt which was almost grotesque in its dimensions, the sort of thing people would try on for a joke if they found it in a second-hand shop.

'What do you think, as a Hitler?' Rose asked. Robert surveyed me critically, looking deep into my eyes as he crunched my bones in a handshake. I was unsure how to assume the look of a Hitler-to-be. It was surprising, the seriousness with which all this was evidently taken.

'OK, come round to Rose's on Wednesday,' he said. 'Bring the Hitler moustache.'

I had been invited to her room, albeit not by her. I swallowed and nodded solemnly as if this was the very least I could expect.

It did cross my mind to ask if Rose wanted to walk back to college with me, but I sensed I might gain more points in the end with a show of nonchalance. I wished them goodnight, said that I would see them on Wednesday and walked up the stairs a second time, my head fogged with many emotions I could not name.

I could scarcely believe the direction events had turned in. People always said that if you went looking for adventure it sought you out in turn, but I had never tested this out before. It was also widely held knowledge that if one told a lie, more lies were often necessary to sustain it. How far I would pursue this lie of being an aspirant lookalike depended on whether I could wean myself off thinking about Rose. The thrill of our second-ever conversation suggested there was little likelihood of that. For the moment, the chance to be in her orbit justified even the extraordinary prospect of volunteering to do something I ought not, and perhaps would not be able, to do.

I wanted to tell my brother what had happened, but it was nearly impossible to know where to start. We discussed his military exploits instead. He had a new buddy called Uli and had beaten his time for the obstacle course that week.

I was immediately struck by the spaciousness of her room, in the old part of college. It wound itself around into a sort of five-pointed star, with all sorts of nooks and corners. There was a very high ceiling: it was almost like being in church. The room smelt sweetly and faintly of incense and femininity. There were prints of artistic works. Each object – a teapot, a large strip of lustrous orange material draped across a chair – inspired my jealousy, representing a history of Rose which I wanted to be able to write myself into somehow.

Robert was sitting stiffly at a small dining table in the centre of the room. Rose indicated that I was to sit on her bed, which was huge, covered in an immense pink-and-white bedspread, and hard as iron.

'You're lucky to have such a great bed!' I said, meaning a compliment.

'Yes, thank God for my awful back pains!' said Rose with

bright sarcasm. I straight away set about apologising, but she waved it away. 'Don't worry, Adolf.'

'Shall we get to business?' said Robert coldly.

A Hitler imitator was required for a function in Peterborough. 'It's easy stuff,' he said. 'You'll have to present some awards – they give you all the info – and maybe mingle.'

'Mingle . . .?'

'With the other guests.' Robert opened and closed his hand to signify mindless chatting. 'Standard stuff. It's a hundred and fifty, cash.'

Some moments passed before I grasped that this figure was my potential fee. When the realisation had dawned, I tried to assume the pose of someone who was always spending such sums. My heart had speeded up.

'Cash . . .' I repeated faintly.

'Yeah,' Robert said, 'that's why it's less than you'd normally expect. An agent would probably get you two-fifty but you'd have to sign up and everything.'

'And . . . will they definitely have me?' I asked.

'They like the sound of you,' Robert said. 'The German stuff is a good angle. We'll need a photo, though, and I'll send a CV. You haven't worked as a lookalike before?'

'Absolutely not . . .' I said, and then, to avoid looking like a charlatan, added, 'But I have performance abilities.'

Rose reached up to a shelf I had not even noticed, well above usual head height, and brought down a Polaroid camera. Robert raised his eyebrows at me and ran his finger along his lip. Feeling extremely self-conscious I gummed my false moustache into place and stared in a menacing way at the robot-like camera, my arm raised in a grim salute. Robert placed the result on the table and the three of us watched, in silence, as it developed, and my outline turned into Hitler.

'I think they'll go for it,' Robert said, satisfied. 'They trust me.'

'I could go with him,' Rose said suddenly. I clenched myself against the surface of the bed to avoid leaping up in excitement.

'Cool,' Robert shrugged. 'Listen, Andreas, I'll give you more details next week, and I'll need to know by the start of March if you're definitely in.' Rose gave me a wink and rubbed two fingers together in a gesture meaning that I couldn't decline the money. But of course the money, though astounding, was not the crux of the thing at all. I would be going to Peterborough with her.

It was as if my life, after plodding along in a straight line, had accidentally stepped onto a trampoline and been pitched skywards. But when I glanced down at the ground I wondered whether I would land and bounce up again, or crash straight into the floor. Naturally, this thing I was taking on raised some puzzling questions.

If I went through with this, did it mean that I was saying the war, and all the shame of Germany's past, was a joke? I spent a night or two sleeping badly, looking up at the ceiling and thinking about my relatives, and the pictures of the Holocaust everyone had seen many times. But it seemed more progressive to think that, by showing Germans could laugh at themselves, I was contributing to the process of repairing relations between the countries, which had been going on ever since the hostilities ended.

After all, young Germans like me were not 'the Nazis'. It had shocked me when, for example, on a camping trip to Italy in our youth, someone shouted 'Nazi!' at us after spotting our car licence plate; not so much because of the bad taste (though our father thumped the steering wheel and swore in a highly uncharacteristic display of anger) as the improbability of anyone seriously thinking we were somehow connected with what had happened in the 1940s. I had no personal debt to pay. My family had suffered enough, with my father's father being killed at Dresden and my father growing up in a ravaged, depressed Germany. There should not be any onus on me to be apologetic, after all this time.

Besides, this was already common ground for comedy. The English always seemed to be making Nazi jokes against Germans; why couldn't I, possessing more knowledge of the difficult subject? And anyway it was a party, a nonsense, who cared? But there were more basic justifications that had little to do with ethics. I needed the money, for one thing. I wanted to feel less of an outsider. And beyond everything else there was Rose, Rose, Rose. Certainly, this was an unconventional way to woo somebody, but she was, to understate the matter, an unconventional woman.

'Did you see that massive lady!' gasped a little boy, pointing in awe at Rose's legs which, sticking into the aisle like a couple of pipes, had nearly pole-axed him. A red-faced mother, wearing a headscarf, scolded the child for impertinence. Rose shifted her legs a few degrees and waved away the woman's apologies with a smile. Her arched left leg rubbed against mine. She put up the armrest and slid towards me so our thighs, too, were in contact. I had been sexually aroused without a pause for the past forty minutes; it was tiring.

'I'm from the planet Zog,' she said, rolling her eyes at the child, who gawped in delight.

'People get self-conscious, they don't know where to look,' she told me, as scenery rushed by. 'It's like being really obese. You can be in a changing room and people walk through completely naked, and they look at *me* like *I'm* the one that should be embarrassed!'

This talk of nakedness was not what I needed at all. To make things worse, the train announcer mentioned Peterborough and I felt tension building in clods in my gut.

'Surely it isn't like being obese, though,' I said. 'There is no . . . shame in tallness.'

'You might think,' she said. 'But it's the same problem; difference is, you know, threatening. My last – um – three relationships have ended because my boyfriends got sick of people's comments.'

'Then your boyfriends were stupid!' I said rashly. There was a pause. 'I don't mean . . .' I said. 'They must have been intelligent, also.'

She laughed. Disaster had been averted.

'I just try and be positive about it,' she said, 'without being too much like Robert and banging on: *look at me folks! I'm a freak!*'

'But that's an act, isn't it?'

'Nothing's completely an act,' she said.

'My Hitler will be, I hope!' I objected. She giggled again; well, that is not quite the right word for her laugh, it was girlish but also rather sensual, as if one could imagine a sound corresponding to melting chocolate, and I associated her laugh and the crisp smile and the fresh smell of her room and her graceful walk and teasing voice all together.

We talked some more about her great height. I did not want there to be any moment of silence, in case the improbability of our being together suddenly caught up with us. 'There was one time,' she said, as the inspector stamped our tickets and passed, glancing back over his shoulder for another look, 'when my dad actually called me an "aberration" in an argument.'

'My father doesn't care about many things,' I said, hoping to create fellow-feeling. 'My mother is dead,' I added, rather overplaying my hand.

Her hand brushed against mine. 'Well, this is a cosy chat, isn't it!'

'I have one brother and we're great friends, if that helps,' I added, hastily, to remove the gloom. 'And I am in good health,' I added for a wisecrack. To my great satisfaction it went off with some fireworks. She laughed her sweet-tasting laugh again and sighed afterwards. 'Ah, you make me laugh a lot,' she said, almost wistfully. 'Most people are so fucking dull.'

I noticed that she pronounced the word 'laugh' in much the same way as the comic who had done impressions of James Bond. 'So you hail from Manchester?' I asked. 'Yes, I do "hail from" there,' she said, grinning. 'See, even when you're not trying to be funny, you use funny words. I don't often go back there though. One of the other top five tallest women lives not far from my parents. She's six foot nine. She's really boring and I always seem to run into her.'

Anxious to avoid making a faux pas on the subject of her lankiness – even though she was so relaxed about it – I moved the conversation on to the task in hand.

'Without wanting to undermine your confidence,' I said carefully, 'I am feeling rather . . .'

'You've got the heeby-jeebies?' she suggested.

'What are the heeby-jeebies?' I asked. This, once again, amused her greatly and she made me say it once or twice more. 'You know,' she said, 'the butterflies. The yips.' She went through a few more, seemingly enjoying my curiosity to learn idioms, and the rather tentative way I repeated them. I was surprised that the supposedly stoical and composed English had so many words for nerves.

'Well, yes,' I said, 'all of those things. I am not used to . . . well, to pretending to be Hitler. Few people are,' I added; my confidence as a humorist was rising, thanks to her laughs.

'Relax,' she said, squeezing my elbow. 'You'll be fine. It's not like there's any pressure, it's not like you have an agent depending on you.'

I had thought of artists as depending upon agents, rather than the other way around. 'Well, it works both ways. If you get it right, management is a licence to print money. You just need a few bankers like Elvis and Marilyn, and a couple of trump cards. I mean, a Hitler . . .' she raised her eyebrows. 'You could be real hot property.'

'And if it's a disaster?'

'Then it's our secret,' she said firmly. I like the idea of our having a secret, but first, there was one I need to disabuse myself of.

'Listen,' I said, 'can I take you into my confidence?'

'I'm very discreet,' she said, cocking her head on one side. 'Actually I'm thinking about being a spy.' I laughed for slightly too long a time.

'I thought you were doing law?'

'I hate law,' she said. 'That's the main thing my Law degree has taught me. They should have said in the first lecture: before we start, you are going to absolutely hate this.'

'So what do you aspire to in the future?' This was rather a large question to ask, but it was one of my conversational strategies to induce people to speak about themselves at length; I was more comfortable in a methodical exchange of ideas than in what the English call 'small talk'.

Rose seemed to ponder the question, or at least, the phrasing of her reply. 'The short answer,' she said, 'is that whatever I do, I want to be a success. I mean – a real, big success.'

There was a lull in the chat as I wondered whether to attempt another joke or pass comment upon her hunger for success. In the end it was she who spoke next.

'So, take me into your confidence . . .' she said.

'Yes,' I said, 'well, the fact is that when I came to the Coco Club, it was in fact, largely a – a ploy, a . . . a special journey to see you.'

'I knew that, idiot,' she said, laughing. 'Following me to an invite-only event for a bloody security firm and trying to act all innocent! With subterfuge like that I can see how you people lost the war.'

I made some retort to the effect that, if all the English had been as tall as her, we might have bombed them more easily. Halfway through, it struck me that this might well be a witticism too far, but she had already grasped the comic idea and finished my sentence with an indignant cackle. Our time together was going rather well. I would have been perfectly happy had I not agreed to spend the evening doing something very peculiar, and quite incompetently in all likelihood, in front of her. I began to wish we could have got to know each other without this trip to Peterborough.

We were rolling into the station, past a lot of low-roofed buildings, clusters of small houses, the stands of a football stadium, a church. 'Peterborough!' she said ironically, spreading her hands as if it were Hollywood, but the undermining was wasted on me. Sweat was building up on my palms, my stomach was tight and I would have gone to relieve myself if she had not been present.

The train stopped. People waiting to get on stared frankly through the windows at Rose as she got to her feet. I walked with her, past the inquisitive boy, out onto the platform and into a taxi.

'Got stilts on back there, have you?' the cabbie asked with a theatrical look at Rose, and the joke satisfied him so much that he used his radio to relay it to someone else. 'Got one from the circus here!'

'Just drive us there, please,' I said. It came out sounding less authoritative than I hoped, even petty, but Rose gave me a grin that was part gratitude, part mockery. I had to try not to think about her too much, however, from now on. We pulled up outside the Victorian civic building where, bizarre as it still seemed, I would shortly be impersonating Adolf Hitler.

'Do this full-time, do you?' asked the event's organiser, unlocking a cold dressing room. There was a full-length mirror, a sink and a kettle. Rose, as my 'partner' for the night, was enjoying a drink in some private room; the organiser had made a great show of not commenting upon her size. I was left to prepare.

I had bought a fresh moustache from the costume place, to the great amusement of the proprietor; and when I also put in a request for a full Nazi costume, he seemed to believe it was Christmas. 'Mind you, you're lucky to get this, sir,' he told me. 'Last week we hired out all our Nazi stuff for a themed ball.' Examining myself in the mirror, I applied cream to my hands and manipulated my hair into the dictator's sloping fringe.

The door swung open and the organiser surveyed me with satisfaction.

'Well, you look the part!' he said. 'Let's hear some German!' I obliged him with a few guttural sounds.

No sooner had I entered the hall than people began to notice me. As instructed, I started talking to a few of the guests, who were mostly dressed in cheap suits and chutching flutes of champagne. I had to do no more than rasp the occasional '*Heil*' to provoke great laughter. Someone – the first of many – asked me to pose for a photograph and we stood, five in a line, with Nazi salutes outstretched. I reprimanded one man for the poor angle of his arm, and there was plenty of mirth; more ensued when I commanded silence.

The main event of the evening was the prize-giving, which came after dinner. Somewhat to my surprise I was given a meal. Rose was content to stay upstairs, out of sight.

'Is it odd for you, as a German, impersonating Hitler?' asked one official.

'Well,' I said, 'it's important for us as a nation to recognise our past, and humour is one way of responding to it.' I was pleased with this answer, and moreover, I was really starting to believe it.

I had been given cards inscribed with the awards: all were frivolous accolades such as 'Biggest Flirt' or 'Most Embarrassing Piss-Head'. Speaking into a microphone, I was treated to silence at first, but as the festivities went on, this wore away. Many of the prizes were comic objects like joke breasts or underwear, which made everyone restless with amusement for some time.

After a while the room was so lively that I could hardly muster any interest for the award of 'Biggest Balls-Up'. I asked myself ironically what Hitler would do in such a situation. '*Ruhe!*' I yelled in a hoarse voice. Quiet! The shock factor was considerable and silence reigned for a while. From then on, I began to scream German monosyllables at each disruption: sometimes a legitimate word, sometimes whatever came into my head, like the words for various toiletries – it was all the same to them. Before long people began misbehaving on purpose, to bait me, so in a certain way, my response was counter-productive. I was not sure how well things were going, but it was my first try, and we were getting through the evening at least.

The last award was 'Biggest Hitler' and it had been designed especially for the manager. The audience chanted, 'Hitler, Hitler!' and offered a forest of Nazi salutes as the boss made his way up from the back. Even in the present setting I found this an unnerving and very peculiar sight. The boss was grinning indulgently: he seemed to relish the abuse. Saluting stiffly, I handed over the boss's prize, which was gift-wrapped. It was, perhaps not surprisingly, a Nazi outfit like my own; he put it on and there was a rash of camera flashes. I tried to announce into the microphone that the entertainment was now finished, but it was impossible: having provoked the excitement I could not, as they say, put the genie back into the bottle. I said a hasty goodnight and left the stage.

Rose was lying on the floor of my dressing room. She was a confounding sight, her hair behind her head, her chest rising and falling lightly.

'That was brilliant!' she said, getting slowly to her feet. Her shawl fell from her shoulders; she did not bend to pick it up.

'You saw it?'

'I watched the whole thing,' she said proudly, 'and you did a great job.'

'I'm not sure,' I said. 'I thought at times it wasn't easy to get heard.' The words were coming rather quickly and I realised that my heart was thrashing against my ribs.

'That's because they were idiots, but who cares!' said Rose. 'Give it time, you'll be doing your own act. Except, I forgot . . .' She made an ironic face. 'You don't even want to be a lookalike, do you?'

She put her arms out and I was within them, my face level with her breasts. She bent towards me, her hair fell on my face, and we kissed. A fraction of a second before the kiss, it still seemed impossible, but at some point in my recent life, the impossible had given way to reality. I savoured the taste of her, warm and sweet. The kiss went on. There was a knock at the door and we sprang apart, Rose chewing her lip. A man came in holding an envelope full of money and it seemed, suddenly, that I had everything in life I wanted.

» Alexandra

There were more festivities coming up. Gareth's birthday was 21 September. He was keen to make sure there would be no fuss about it, so Dan was equally keen to make sure there was. He set to work planning a surprise party.

'You're coming, aren't you, sis?' he asked me midway through the week. It seemed everyone saw me as a valuable asset at a party, even if I didn't speak all night. 'And bring that friend of yours, you know . . .' He mimed her breasts. 'And anyone else,' he added. 'The theme is G.'

'G . . .?'

'G for Gareth. Dress as something or someone beginning with a G.'

'G . . .' I muttered.

'You could be a goose, no one's doing a goose yet,' said Dan helpfully.

'What are you coming as?'

'God,' said Dan with a smirk.

In the aftermath of Helen's party, someone had emailed the whole list of guests to say what a great night it had been, someone else replied agreeing, and on it went. The correspondence had now reached about fifty emails.

I had written to Andreas proposing a visit. 'This may seem very forward of me,' I said, 'but since you mentioned that you never receive any visitors . . .'

He wrote back after the customary gap of a few days. 'I would be honoured to meet you,' he said, 'though be warned that I may be a somewhat dull companion.' I arranged a date with Claire when she would be at Andreas's prison, so I could go and see her afterwards and tell her how it went. I just needed to arrange the day off work. Helen, an experienced truant, had once given me some tuition on this, one night when we were forced to wait around for some phone call or other, until we were the only people there apart from Albert.

She told me that a stomach bug was the best type of 'illness' for a single day off. 'With a cold or sore throat or something, people can question it, but if you mention throwing up, people leave you alone very fast. Also, stomach bugs disappear very quickly so you don't need to worry about making out you're still a bit croaky when you come back. And it's easier to sound convincing on the phone. No fake coughing. You just have to sound weak.'

I had duly laid the foundations last night by mentioning that I was feeling 'a bit queasy' as I left work, making sure it was within earshot of at least three people. Sure enough, Jeremy swallowed the lie easily. 'Get better!' he said, sympathetically. The feeling was like hearing, on a snowy morning, that school is closed. I wallowed in relaxation too much, dawdled in the bath and had to shovel breakfast down to make sure I would make the jail appointment.

I had to get down to London Bridge on the tube and then take an overland train to Kent. Sitting between a businessman reading the free paper and a kid with a noisy hissing stereo, I noticed that I had genuinely started to feel slightly unwell. I could feel my breakfast being churned around my stomach. It was probably just nerves. It was starting to dawn on me that I was about to meet someone I didn't really know at all, and for no reason other than impulsiveness. Pretty much everyone else on the train was chewing. I wondered what kind of conversation I could expect with someone who'd had virtually no human contact for years, then told myself not to be melodramatic; it was only a prison, he hadn't been found in a cave or something. An old black woman got on the train with a radio turned up very loud, on which a preacher yelled about damnation. I could see the red brick of the jail, and the high, wire-topped walls. Very few other people got off at the station. It was littered with empty fried-chicken boxes and there were shadows of urine up the walls.

As I reached the prison, other people began to fall in alongside me, and somewhat to my relief, the car park was quite busy. There were a lot of tired-looking women who could have been either wives or daughters, with hair tied back and tracksuit bottoms on. They stubbed out cigarettes on the ground before going in, grinding them under their feet; some of them led little children by the arm. One tiny boy was yelling and screaming frantically and trying in vain to dig his heels into the ground: he seemed to think he was going to prison himself. A tattooed woman spat out a piece of gum almost onto my shoes as she passed, without seeming to see me at all. There were also some family-sized groups, making an attempt at cheer, one person perhaps cracking a token joke about forgetting where they'd parked the car. My stomach still felt over-full and I thought what an irony it would be if I did get ill.

I was searched by a short, angry-looking female guard who rubbed me up and down and ran a little machine like a microphone over my pockets and bag. A man whose badge said 'DEAN' ran his eyes over a list and ticked my name off. As we streamed into the room, my main impression was that it was like a school hall. Men sat at tables, staring straight ahead, or at their hands. It occurred to me that I did not know the face I was looking for. Then in the corner of the room, I saw Claire sitting with a small man. She motioned me over.

'So, Andreas, this is Alex . . .'

'Alexandra,' said the man, my pen-pal.

'Alexandra,' said Claire with a big smile. She fingered the HM Prison Service badge on her lapel. 'So I'm going to leave you to your own devices.' She patted me on the shoulder as she left. 'I'll be in the canteen; ask the way.'

We watched her go. 'A boisterous woman,' said Andreas. I laughed. He rubbed his face.

There was a silence.

'So . . .' I said. 'Thank you for, thank you for having me!' It sounded so stupid that I tried to cough, to swallow the last part of the sentence up.

'Much obliged,' said Andreas, after a pause which felt like a full minute.

I looked at him. You would certainly have put his age in the forties, rather than thirty-three, even though his actual features were delicate and somewhat boyish. 'Careworn' was the word that came to mind; in fact I felt that I'd never wholly understood its meaning until I looked at him. His eyes had deep shadows underneath them, his skin was sallow and his face was washed-out, like someone who had had an enormous shock a few hours before and was feeling it starting to catch up with him. His hair was cropped very short, and the bristles that were left were more grey than black. None of these things alone made him look so much older than the photograph; it wasn't even the combination of them; there was a weariness and blankness about him that seemed thicker than the air between us.

'Well, I've managed to read some of the stuff . . .' I said. 'Stuff' seemed a very weak word. 'Your memoirs, I mean.'

'Thank you,' said Andreas, nodding in a sombre way. There was a pause. The hour could be a long one, I thought.

'I've just got to the bit where . . . well, you've just done the, er . . . the Hitler act . . .'

'Yes, yes,' said Andreas.

'And you have just . . . you are getting to know Rose . . .' I said.

Andreas's face clouded, if it was possible for it to cloud more. He nodded, slowly. 'Rose,' he echoed, so quietly that it was more or less inaudible; just his lips framing the word. He looked at the wall. It was obviously a bad idea to mention Rose, I thought immediately, because wherever she was now, she wasn't here.

I shuffled about in my seat and looked at the other people in the room. Some prisoners were holding hands with their loved ones. Some were in animated conversation with people who might have been their lawyers. One man with a tattoo on each arm was sitting in silence, looking straight ahead; his visitor presumably hadn't turned up. I glanced back at him a few times but he was still there, staring at nothing in particular.

Gradually, things became easier. I began to prattle on about my job and my various petty problems. This seemed to appeal to Andreas. He sat with his head resting on his interlocking hands, looking very hard into my eyes and nodding: very small head movements, like an old man nodding along to a gentle piece of music. Encouraged, I began talking more. I told him about the night of the World Cup match between England and Germany when England lost and my father got drunk and my parents had a screaming argument, whose subject quickly developed from the World Cup to his inadequacies as a provider.

Andreas's eyes darted suddenly to a guard who was patrolling the spaces between the tables. 'They are always watching. They tamper with my mail.'

'Tamper with it?'

'They are allowed to open it and read it. The letters I send you and those you send me. They open everything.'

'Why would they do that?'

He shrugged. 'In case I receive drugs or knives. In case I try to incite a riot.' He looked at me with his lined eyes. 'They do not need a reason.'

The rest of the hour I filled by rambling about Helen, Craig, my brother, Gareth, anything that came to hand. Throughout, Andreas sat with his impassive face and his little nods, as if he were a priest I was confessing to, and as if – I thought – he sort of knew all this already. The time wore on. Someone in uniform came over to see to the man whose visitor hadn't turned up, and took him away. After about three-quarters of an hour I felt I was scraping the bottom of the barrel; I'd started to discuss the recalled doughnuts at work. All this time I knew Andreas must have far, far more to talk about than I did. But it was obvious that he still didn't entirely trust me, and I wasn't sure how to earn that trust. It would help if I knew the whole story, but it would be a long while before

Gareth made that possible – assuming he could even be bothered to keep doing it.

Perhaps it had been stupid for me to come, I thought, as a bell rang, slightly before the hour, and people started to murmur goodbyes. The woman who'd spat gum near me was crying softly as she left her husband. 'Next week . . .' he kept saying. 'Next week, love.'

I glanced back at Andreas when I was near the door and he was still sitting there, as if he was not absolutely sure I had ever been there. I felt disappointed without really knowing what it was I had been hoping for. DEAN winked at me as I passed him.

Claire met me in the canteen and gave me another ferociously strong coffee. As I described the meeting, she hummed and nodded, her head to one side, her eyes very large. 'It is very difficult to find the wavelength of a prisoner,' she said. 'It can be a bit . . . whoof!' She made a noise and waved her hands around her head as if to indicate her brain blowing up. 'But you just have to get past the fact that they have this label, "criminals", and remember they're people like you and me.'

'It wasn't that at all,' I said. 'I don't have a problem with him being a . . . a person. It was more that he seemed to have a hard time relating to *me*.'

'Sure, sure, sure,' Claire agreed.

'Well maybe – you know – maybe you should take it slow where actual visiting is concerned. Maybe it's all a bit too much, too soon.'

She might have been talking sense but there was something about her tone: she was like a teacher gently advising you not to choose her subject at A level. 'I think I will visit again,' I said, mostly to hold my own.

She nodded benignly. 'That's great, babe. Hey – bit of news – I'm pregnant!'

But I hardly know you, I thought. 'Congratulations!' I said.

'We're so chuffed,' she said. 'We've been trying for a while now.'

'Great . . . !' I said.

'Don't worry though, I'll be here until Christmas or thereabouts,' she said, twirling the little red 'WriteToAConvict' badge on her top. 'You won't get rid of me that easily!' Before I could respond to this, her phone sounded its shrill tone and she picked up and greeted some friend effusively. She accepted what were presumably congratulations on the pregnancy, then started probing the friend for problems she could sympathise with. I left her to it. Back out in the car park I cast a look over my shoulder at the wire on the walls and thought about Andreas's pasty face as I waited for a delayed train back to town.

As I was squeezing into the Girl Guide uniform I'd borrowed from Helen, it occurred to me how amazed my thirteen-year-old self would have been to see this; it would have seemed the ultimate climbdown. Dan used to like nothing better than to make fun of my involvement in Guides, which I'd been pushed into to distract me while custody issues were sorted out. Having come late in life to Guides (compared with some of the fanatics it attracted), I had the indignity of being ordered around by younger girls, and I would come home dejected and tired, feeling I'd never amount to much until I could put up a tent. And now this. And all for another party.

Dan's God outfit consisted of an all-white costume with the word 'God' written across his forehead. He spent a lot of time choosing the music to greet the first guests. I suggested a few CDs in vain.

'Gershwin? For the G thing.'

Dan rolled his eyes. 'It's just a theme. It's not a . . . prison sentence.'

'What about this one, then? Yours and Gareth's favourite band.'

'They're not our favourite band,' he said, offended.

'I heard you say it was the greatest album of the past five years,' I said.

'It's all right,' he said impatiently. In the end we put on a suitably ironic free CD from the *Evening Standard* with 'party hits'. Guests began to arrive at eight. At half eight Gareth returned from the wild-goose chase we'd sent him on.

'Surprise!' crowed my brother.

'You bastard!' said Gareth, stunned, as gophers and ghosts began to mob him. My brother glowed with success and I felt affectionate towards him and his silly scheming.

Helen had come as Greta Garbo, with a hat, shawl, ruff, long black dress, and a fake-fur coat over the whole ensemble. I watched her chatting to a young Asian guy who was playing Gandhi, with bare feet and a white robe and round, fake glasses, but a full head of hair. Two of Dan's friends from work had come as 'gays' and were holding hands and making theatrical noises of delight. Another had dressed as Gareth himself, with the hair gelled in the familiar way, and a bit of red crayon on his cheeks. He went around the party quoting arcane facts in a 'clever-clever' voice. The real Gareth smiled frostily each time their paths crossed and turned away to prevent himself from flushing.

As the night went on I drank more than I wanted to; it wasn't as if I could go to bed. Inevitably, news of the party seemed to have spread to people with less and less connection to Gareth. Trixie turned up with about ten friends; she had come as a 'goddess of style': in other words, wearing her usual clothes. Most latecomers turned up without even a pretence of a costume, and looked quizzically at what was becoming a minority of people dressed as golfers or Gary Lineker. I found the birthday boy himself hunched in a doorway inspecting a CD rack worriedly. Someone had spilt guacamole dip over it.

'Thanks for doing all that stuff for me,' I yelled into Gareth's face over the cheesy party anthem coming from the stereo. I intended to keep on going, but to my surprise he got to his feet and leaned against the wall as if we were friends; stranger still he began a conversation.

'It's fine,' he said, 'but I mean, what exactly . . . ? Is it all true?'

It seemed a reasonable question. My head was full and I felt nicely giddy and unfocused.

'I never told you this,' I said, 'but I work in a prison part-time.'

'You work in a prison?' said Gareth. 'What, voluntarily?' His cheeks were reddish, his shirt was partly unbuttoned. 'That's really impressive!'

'So this thing you're translating is the memoirs . . . I mean they are the memoirs . . . um . . .'

'Of a prisoner?' Gareth raised his eyebrows. 'It sounds as if you lied to me. How interesting!'

I can't remember exactly how, but I did some sort of Pinocchio-based joke, pulling my nose or something. Gareth laughed.

'I've nearly finished the next bit,' said Gareth, nowhere near as gruffly as usual. 'What's this guy like? How old?'

'Maybe in his thirties? You know, it's not that long ago he was at university . . .'

'I know, but God, his German is laborious,' said Gareth, screwing up his face. 'He sounds like he's in his sixties. I thought maybe he was a "mature student" or some bollocks. What's he in for?'

'I'm not allowed to ask,' I said.

'I wonder if we'll find out at the end of the story,' said Gareth. 'At the moment he sounds like he wouldn't say boo to a goose.'

'He seems like that in the flesh as well,' I told him.

'Well, we shall see . . .' said Gareth and I tried to think how I could keep this chat going, but too late: Gareth's nickname was being shouted out and a little posse came over to drag him away. 'You're wanted on the other side of the room,' someone told him with a sly grin and Gareth made a gesture to me and sloped away.

There was a lot of noise in the far corner of the room. Dan had hired a stripogram. I watched from a distance, through a lot of other bodies. She was an oldish woman, wearing very little apart from a G-string and carrying a plastic whip, at least I hoped it was plastic. She told Gareth to bend over. Gareth said something which sounded like, 'No, I'm all right, thanks.' People laughed. The woman's eyes, even from this distance, clearly showed what she thought of her job, and I had a sudden picture of her walking through the car park dressed like that, getting in her car and driving God knew where. Maybe Gareth imagined something similar because, with what was almost a sympathetic expression, he got to his knees.

Everyone was clapping and cheering and people were clambering onto chairs to get a better look. I caught sight of

Gareth's face for a second as she began to go through her dominatrix routine. He was very red, his gelled hair was drooping, and for someone enjoying a birthday surprise, he looked fairly unhappy.

As usual after a seemingly important conversation at a party, I soon wondered whether I had imagined it all. Gareth hired a professional cleaning firm to put the flat right and resumed his customary manner, barely acknowledging me around the house. I thought that maybe he was embarrassed about having chatted to me at the party, but it was just as likely he couldn't even remember it at all. The bag of coke in our bathroom cabinet was nearly empty now, but there was a new, largeish brown paper package in the drawer where we kept spare toilet rolls. I decided to pretend it wasn't there.

On Monday morning there was a letter waiting in our pigeon-hole when I left for work. It was a hot day, the sky quite a fierce blue for this time of morning. I ripped it open and read it on my way into the station, getting in the way of all sorts of people, including the man who had once stepped on my trouser leg. This time he gave me a filthy look over his shoulder, which rebounded off me.

Dear Alexandra,

I must start with an apology for what must have seemed my distant manner during your visit. The fact is that I am just not used to talking any more. I hope this is understandable.

I also apologise for sending you my life history in such an odd and sudden way. And for the German! I wrote it, you see, some years ago with no real anticipation that anyone would read it. It is strange to have given it to someone I scarcely know. I felt tempted to do so, but I wonder now if it was an error. This, too, I hope, may account for my abashed behaviour when you were here. Also I am aware of my wretched appearance and so on.

I hope you will be able to oversee these problems and visit me at some future time.

Yours sincerely,

Andreas

I read it three times, thinking about the strange contrasts – the stiff English grammar and the misuse of the word 'oversee'; the fact he seemed so keen to be friends, yet somehow frightened of the idea. Overall, the letter gave me a great feeling of satisfaction and self-justification. Claire might consider me out of my depth but I had achieved something, I was cheering someone up.

The morning was perfectly normal. Helen went out for a cigarette and came back with Dundee cake. As I was preparing for lunch, Jeremy asked me to step into his office.

'Just for the records,' he said. 'What was wrong with you exactly, the other day?'

'Sickness . . . sick, a sickness – stomach bug,' I said, jumbling up my words. I could feel myself getting hot. I glanced at the calendar on Jeremy's desk, with an Eastern European model for each month. This month's was Katya. She was sitting on the bonnet of a car. Her thought was, 'You must be the change you wish to see in the world.'

'Throwing up?' asked Jeremy.

'Yes,' I said, 'three times, and . . . yes.'

Jeremy nodded and made his hands into a cathedral. 'OK. As I say: just for the records. Thanks, Alex.'

I had to wait till after work to discuss it with Helen; she was off looking at one of the prison museums we'd found for the French Revolution shoot. We went to a little café around the corner. 'I can't believe after three years here I get interrogated over one bloody day off!'

'I know,' Helen sympathised.

'I mean, how many days have you had off for no reason?'

'What were you doing?' Helen asked, looking me in the eyes. 'Just out of interest?'

There was nothing to stop me from telling her – she was Helen, after all. I knew pretty much everything that had happened to her from the age of three (dropped on her head by an uncle) to the present day (ogled by museum caretaker who looked about seventy). But something made me want to keep Andreas to myself – well, to myself and Gareth, who hardly counted. It was just the feeling of having some extra dimension to my life; it was like a card I didn't want to play just yet.

'I was, I had to visit an aunt,' I said. 'She's very ill. A form of . . . of cancer.'

'Oh, right,' said Helen, unfazed. 'Terminal?'

'Um,' I said. 'Yes.'

'Definitely?'

'They're not one hundred per cent sure . . .'

'Well,' said Helen, 'if this is how convincing you were the other day, no wonder you got busted.'

I looked at my hands passing my ID card between themselves. 'Look, it's . . . I will tell you, but not yet.'

'Is it a man?'

'If it was a man I would tell you.'

'You know Craig is with someone?' she said, gently.

'I don't care,' I said, sharply.

'OK,' Helen shrugged. 'I thought you might, that's all. I thought better to tell you myself. But OK. We'll just keep our secrets from each other.'

There was nothing much we could say on other subjects now this was in the way. She always had a hard time understanding why someone wouldn't want to disclose every tiny thing on their mind. We finished our drinks and walked to the station making very small talk to fill the silence. We parted to our separate tube lines. I watched her get on an escalator and disappear slowly from sight, her hat still visible for a while after the rest of her. I remembered the time we decided to name our kids after each other, or, if they were boys, Alexander, and Troy instead of Helen.

We'd always had arguments, but it was the arguments we avoided having that I didn't like.

I found it hard to focus on anything that evening. My mother rang and we talked for half an hour. 'Is Dan in?' she asked.

'No, he's out with the girlfriend,' I said. 'Off his face,' I muttered.

'What was that?' she asked. I said it was nothing. She was planning to come to London in a couple of weeks. We made a sketchy plan to go to another musical. The posters for *Singin' in the Rain* and *West Side Story* I'd once had on my wall were enough for her to subject me to a lifetime of all-singing-all-dancing entertainment. I'd never quite got round to explaining that it was only the posters I liked, that I could hardly stand watching the musicals themselves.

During the conversation, my computer gave a little ping to say that I had a new message. I opened it up. There was an email from Jeremy, sent to everyone in the office. The subject was 'Paris'. I scanned the list of names. Helen's was there. Mine wasn't.

A knock on the door jolted me out of the filthy mood that was just about to descend. I opened it halfway. It was Gareth.

He handed me another bundle of paper. I thanked him; he nodded and looked the other way.

'Might not be able to do any more for a bit,' he said, scratching the back of his neck. 'Going to the States for three weeks.'

'A bit of holiday reading?' I said.

'Yeah – I might have better things to do,' he said. 'Sorry. Didn't mean. Just busy.'

'Well,' I said, 'maybe when you come back . . .'

'Yeah,' said Gareth.

'When are you going, anyway?'

'Tomorrow,' he said.

'Tomorrow?' I tried not to sound disappointed.

'It gets a little bit racy at the end,' he added, looking at the door.

'I hope I'll be able to handle the excitement,' I said. Gareth glanced up. Neither of us knew what I'd meant. It never worked when I tried to emulate his dismissive way of talking about everything. Gareth indicated with a tilt of the head that he ought to be going. He shut the door very gently, as if I might be upset by any noise. Five minutes later I heard him go out of the front door, and the sound of the lift along the corridor.

It was hard to settle down to reading with everything brewing in my mind: the fact that he was going, the Paris snub which was presumably connected with the mysterious way they suspected I had bunked off work, the news of Craig having a new woman, and – for some reason it kept pushing into my mind – the thought of Gareth and Dan and Trixie in someone's flat in Shoreditch or Islington, snorting coke off the fittings, talking to people, having a good time. It wasn't that I wished I was there, or that they were here. I didn't know what I wished. The only thought that was somehow comforting was the idea of Andreas in his cell, alone, relying on me in some way.

☞ ANDREAS

It was in April or early May, in Grantchester, under a streaky blue sky filled with birdsong, that I finally took mental delivery of the fabulous change which had occurred in my life; the emotional cycle I seemed to have completed in triumph. I was leaning back against Rose, a picnic basket at my feet and a blanket underneath us. I caressed her thighs, which stretched out grandly on either side of me, and felt her gentle breathing on top of my head. She took a crunching bite out of a green apple and passed it to me.

'You can see King's chapel from here,' Rose said quietly, pointing a thumb back towards Cambridge. I half turned, obediently, and she planted a kiss on my lips. 'Mind you,' she added, 'I can see Paris from here.'

'Stop your joking,' I admonished her.

Quite frequently at a crucial point of a conversation, when we might be about to reach a new level of intimacy, she would either fracture it with a one-liner, or burst into singing some tune or other, maybe 'I Will Survive' or some other irrelevant thing, as if she were the sort of scatterbrained individual who could easily be distracted. I didn't believe that this was consistent with her real personality, but then, who was to say? If everything that was happening was no more substantial than make-believe, I was nonetheless happy to embrace it.

As spring turned to early summer, and Cambridge at last began to live up to its tourist brochures with brilliant multicoloured displays, our affair garnered much attention. We would walk along the Backs with my arm around her waist, defiantly enjoying our conspicuousness, now and again even posing for tourists' photographs. (One pair asked Rose to photograph them, hoping to get an unusual angle.) On the rare occasions I encountered the engineer or Nina, they would greet me with smiles of encouragement as if I were a hamster in an experimental maze, and then share a chuckle when I was gone. I cared very little about this: anyone could say anything but Rose was mine.

'Nice work!' Ralf said over the phone. 'When do I get to meet this chick?'

'Oh, soon,' I said, thinking what it would be like to bring her to Berlin.

'What does she look like, at least?'

'She's . . . very tall,' I said.

'You lucky bastard!' he congratulated me. 'A tall blonde! I can picture her now.'

'I shouldn't think so,' I muttered.

The reality of time began to weigh down on us. I had all but finished my studies and Rose's exams were imminent. We lay in parks and gardens eating strawberries, making vague promises of our future together.

'I don't want to be a bloody lawyer,' she told me one afternoon. 'Not only do I not want to be, it's impossible. Can you imagine it! "All rise . . . except the defence council, who may as well remain sitting." '

'Perhaps you should seek a job that does not pay such attention to your height?' I suggested.

'And where would I find that? Not on this planet.'

'Or perhaps you should be my manager,' I said wryly.

Yes, after the success of my stint as Hitler, I was beginning to consider the unthinkable: might I make the beginnings of a living out of this nonsense? The mysterious party who hired me for Peterborough had already enquired, through Robert, whether I would care to do it again; he had 'numerous potential Hitler clients' as there had been an upsurge in interest in the Führer after a recent comic film. It was so bizarre that it took me some time to say yes, which the giant mistook for sang-froid on my part.

'You should definitely be thinking about an agent,' Robert told me, with what I was beginning to identify as his habitual passive-aggressive manner. 'You'll make more that way. There's three or four that would kill for a Hitler.'

Robert and Rose had a similar hormonal condition; this was how they had first met, at some sort of benefit dinner three years ago. I could imagine the scene: gigantic people everywhere, waiters muttering to one another in the doorways, the chairman delivering his speech from a special extendable lectern.

Where Rose made it the butt of her wit, Robert's approach to his height was to harp on about it with a rather self-righteous air, almost as if it were a lifestyle he had deliberately chosen to pursue.

'We freaks have to stick together,' he said once. I had

certain reservations about such statements. 'I don't think it is a good way to define oneself,' I tried to explain.

'It's his way of coping,' Rose said. 'He calls it reclaiming the idea of freakery. Celebrating it, not mocking it.'

'But he mocks it himself, in his act,' I objected.

She shrugged, wincing at the muscular pain this action cost her. 'It's very hard to explain what it's like to be like this. There's no way you can imagine.'

Whenever she pointed this out, I was forced to concede that I was indeed hard-pressed to conjure in my mind the million niggling discomforts and inconveniences that she and Robert faced each day, and could only remark to myself that I was more fortunate than I had ever comprehended that Nature had elected to give me such a mediocre stature.

A week before exams we went for a long walk along the river, through clumps of flattened nettles which made her nose twitch. There was a summery smell of barbecues in the air. Sometimes we would have to step aside from the narrow path to let past a cyclist. One man practically crashed his transport in his astonishment at the sight of Rose. 'Bloody hell!' he blurted out. Rose laughed and shouted back, 'I know! It's ridiculous!'

We arrived back at college and went to her room. The bedsheets were rumpled and the room chaotic. I fought back the urge to pick at least a few things up and put them away; my tidiness exasperated, as well as charmed, her. Piles of notes lay everywhere, a little city of paper. There were ring binders, books, and case notes everywhere: 'The McKinley Case', 'Shepherd v The Royal British Legion', and so on.

'Christ,' she said suddenly, 'how much crap there is.' She gestured at the reams of names and facts and dates and figures. 'It's not interesting, it's not relevant to what I want to do, but . . .'

'But what?' I asked, in a sudden upsurge of spirit; the afternoon had put me into a heady mood.

'Well, if I fuck the finals up . . .'

'Yes, what?' I challenged her. 'Why are you frightened to flunk your exams, if you don't want to be in the law?'

'My parents,' she sighed.

'They want you to be happy,' I said boldly; of course, this was absolute conjecture.

She had begun toying with a piece of hair, which she wove around her finger, and which she stared at rather than meeting my eyes. 'They want me to be successful first, then happy. I think they're resigned to the fact that a woman of my height is unlikely to have a conventionally happy life.'

I felt that, if true, this was scandalous, and tried to find a way of saying so. Rose had begun to sing some popular song about a baby quietly to herself. 'You should do whatever feels like the right thing,' I said.

'What a lovely thought,' said Rose, impishly, patting me on the head. 'So, what if I "feel like" dumping every one of these notes in the bath?'

'It's a pointless example,' I said, 'because you won't.'

'Do you bet me?' she asked in a low voice.

Our eyes rested on each other for a long moment. I looked into her face, the long nose and flickering brown eyes, the wicked mouth; then down over her broad, powerful shoulders, with the hair bouncing upon them. Rose got up wordlessly from the bed and disappeared into the bathroom. I heard water running.

She emerged and looked at me to say that it was now my move again. Solemnly, I picked up a pile of notes on jurisdiction – the writing was brash, with some smudging and blotches – and carried them into the bathroom. She picked up a stack of ring binders, all dull reds, greens and browns, and, carrying them on her head, added them to the pile. Water sloshed mercilessly into the tub.

We continued taking turns to fetch more notes until the bathroom looked like a warehouse. There was scarcely room for us among the clutter. Rose added a squeeze of bubble bath to the tub. She squatted down painfully on a pile of A4 papers.

'Right,' she said, 'who's bluffing now?'

I eyed the notes nervously. Rose suddenly, in one motion, pulled her T-shirt over her head and looked at me, wild-haired. 'Either we're going to do this,' she said, 'or I'm at least going to have a bath.'

Her mighty, yet somehow delicate chest, the breasts like pears, was a cloud over my judgement. Lifting up a term's worth of lecture notes and balancing them on one hand, I discharged them like a discus-thrower into the water. The block of paper sank as if it were a dead body and there was a silence.

'I didn't give you enough credit,' said Rose thoughtfully, her tongue running slowly over her lip. I felt very anxious about the deed I had worked myself up to: for a second there was a chill like the wearing off of alcohol. 'Well, what the hell!' she said suddenly, and picked up a cargo of paper, tipping it over the side with a jubilant scream. The two of us, like young vandals, dumped one consignment after another into the drink, watching the ink smear and the pages disintegrate, all the knowledge reduced, in minutes, to a messy pulp.

The first time we paused for breath, each of us was a little stunned. The bath was overflowing. Rose peered meditatively over the rim of the tub like a passenger eyeing the sea from a ferry. 'Well,' she said, 'the threat of seeing me naked certainly got you focused.'

I threw myself at her in semi-playful threat and knocked her backwards; she thudded her head against the lavatory.

'So, violent all of a sudden!' she breathed. I started to undo her belt and ease her trousers over her knees. We were folded over each other in the small bathroom, with odd papers still lining the floor. Down the great peaks of her legs, as on her arms, were tiny, almost invisible light-coloured hairs which I began to kiss. She twitched and gasped to herself. I clasped her long, beautiful sides. Her eyes were screwed tight shut and she was whispering through clenched teeth, as if in pain. So much of this seemed fanciful to the point of absurdity, but all I could do was travel with the fantasy as it soared into real life. Then we were just there, looking at each other, and nothing needed saying.

Rose, in spite of her suicidal efforts, scraped a mediocre degree. At the graduation I was to meet her parents and (in her words) 'be assessed as a suitably bland partner'.

At this still-early stage, our love was a compulsion and it had the frenzied, incomprehensible quality of a dream. I wished desperately to bottle the fairy tale, make it everyday. I longed to wake up next to Rose's warm, infinite body, to massage the pain out of her back, to stroke her hair. I wanted to pass my days watching her bending tentatively over a spoonful of soup and swearing as it dripped away before her neck completed the descent; to find the toothpaste absent-mindedly left above my head height; to pick things up for her; to parade proudly everywhere with this eye-grabbing, irresistibly strange woman. And I certainly had reason to believe she wanted the same, though, characteristically, her enthusiasm for future plans came with its smearings of irony.

'I suppose I could stomach moving in with you,' she might say. Or, when I suggested flat-hunting: 'You Germans, so efficient.'

'We'll do it tomorrow' became a sort of joke catchphrase for us. 'We'll sort it out tomorrow.' 'We'll go to the careers office tomorrow.' Once she started singing a song, 'Tomorrow belongs to me . . .', and then stopped abruptly with a guilty grimace as if she might have insulted me, but I was ignorant of its meaning. I was generally poor at pop-cultural references and always tried to blame my country of origin.

Graduation day was a trial for her: she only went to the ceremony to satisfy her parents, who had travelled down from Manchester. She stood in the bizarre regalia, black robes and white apron, sticking out of the neat line of students like an adult in a children's playground. Her costume had had to be specially made from some thick, clinging material. When I kissed her on the forehead at the start of the procession through Cambridge, she backed away in horror of the merest touch; there was a light film of perspiration on her face. I couldn't wait to rip the robes away from her and have her melt away underneath me again. Naturally, it was odd to think of her in these terms while standing with her parents.

Mr Ravenhill was bald, with just a little hair at his temples; Mrs Ravenhill had a lined face and a patient smile. I thought she might be the sort of quiet woman who turns into a psychopath in later life, at least in films. They took us to a restaurant by the river. Rose toyed with the edge of the menu, examined herself in a spoon, played with a salt shaker and in general communicated a desire for it to be over, which, however, she concealed from her parents with patient talk. I ordered some poor fare, out of habit; the second cheapest item on the menu. Rose pushed ribs listlessly around her plate.

The questioning began once the main course was under way.

'So, Andreas, you've just finished an M.Phil. in . . .?'

'American literature,' I said.

'What kind of thing . . .?'

'Well, it's a very wide course,' I said. 'Walt Whitman . . . er, twentieth-century drama and the novel . . . I wrote a dissertation mostly on *Catch-22* and a book called *Slaughterhouse-Five*.' This title suddenly sounded unsuitable for the dinner table, and moreover I had realised halfway through that my answer was too long-winded for what was basically a question asked out of politeness.

Rose's father nodded wisely. 'Whitman. Who wrote . . .' He paused, looking as if he was working up to a quotation, but found his mental storehouse did not contain any words of the nineteenth-century poet. 'And what brought you to England?'

I churned out some standard stuff about the teaching at Cambridge, the marvellous opportunity, the historical setting. Rose glanced appreciatively at me.

'And,' Mrs Ravenhill asked, gently, 'what . . . what might you get up to next?'

My mouth was rather dry.

'I'm thinking of . . . a few angles . . .' I said, haltingly.

'It is difficult, when you've just finished,' said Mrs Ravenhill, rather pityingly.

'The fact is that I was not sure, when I came to Cambridge . . .' I said haltingly. 'That is to say, my ambitions were neither fish nor fowl . . .'

'Rose, of course, has her law,' said Mr Ravenhill with an oily smile.

'I'm giving up law,' Rose said suddenly, and then, 'Andreas and I are setting up a lookalike agency.'

This was as utterly unexpected as if she had read it on her spoon. Nobody knew what to say, and I least of all. As the Ravenhills exchanged a look of baffled dismay, Rose presented me with a crafty wink.

'What do you mean?' asked Mr Ravenhill.

Rose explained. 'You know, lookalikes. Robert knows half a dozen, all looking for better management.'

Mr Ravenhill looked at his daughter as if she had turned into a sea monster. 'Sorry, Rose. Let me get this quite right. On graduation day you inform me that you are going to squander your three years of study—'

'Oh, Frank,' Mrs Ravenhill hissed, 'can't we—'

'Squander it, for God's sake!' Mr Ravenhill yelled. Several people looked round at us, including a couple of parents with an immensely smug-looking son who was obviously an exam champion. 'And begin a ridiculous business venture? I suppose this was your idea?' To my horror he turned to me.

'I suppose it's a mutual thing,' I said faintly. Rose bit her lip to stave off a laugh and Mrs Ravenhill managed to change the subject, but not entirely. I felt desperately uncomfortable and, at the same time, excited almost to the point of sexual arousal by the headstrong way that Rose had forced me to collaborate in this peculiar turn of the conversation. Mr Ravenhill kept moistening his lips with his tongue and Mrs Ravenhill laughed rather wildly a couple of times at less than hilarious things. We did not look at the dessert menu.

Soon, terse goodbyes were exchanged and the Ravenhills trooped dazedly back up to Manchester. This was the second-last time I saw them. I could not have imagined then that the last time would be far more unpleasant.

Some time later Rose and I were lying side by side on her bed, drinking a bottle of champagne her parents had brought as a gift. 'You might as well have this,' her father said as his parting words, 'not that there's anything to celebrate any more.'

'Don't you feel bad about your folks?' I asked.

Rose swivelled onto her side to look directly in my face. Her breath had an alcoholic edge and to kiss her was like drinking.

'My parents,' she said, 'tried to get me adopted as a kid because they didn't think they could raise someone with a medical problem. We all had to go to a therapist together to discuss my "abnormality issues". I mean, I didn't even feel abnormal until the first session. It was really therapy for them.' I rubbed her arm and felt the softness of the tiny hairs against my skin. 'I was in the school netball team because I could just put the ball into the net like someone throwing something in the bin. We won a match 67–nil and the other school complained and I was banned from playing. We forfeited the game, the other girls formed an Anti-Rose Society. My dad said, "What do you want me to do about it?" That was all he said.'

On she went in this vein. Her condition had required expensive treatment which her parents always regarded as something of an indulgence. 'I had to take painkillers – still do – special ones from America. One time when we went to collect them, my dad, for a joke, said, "Right, that's the Christmas budget used up." It wasn't a real joke. I couldn't think of anything at night apart from how much I was costing them. I used to hold cake sales, even though I was fucking useless at making cakes; I even carried smaller kids on my shoulders for a pound a go.' She had turned her face away now; I kissed the back of her neck, where there was a small mole, just above the collar, that made me tingle with desire. 'But it went on and on. My hormones were weird, I had two years of taking pills which made hair grow on my lip. Do you know what it's like to shave with a man's razor?' (I did, but it wasn't what she meant, and shaving was not my favourite topic.) 'I've got a weak heart. I have a seventy per cent chance of arthritis. I have to see an osteopath once a month.' I didn't know what this was, but it sounded discouraging.

There was a long pause.

'So I got into Cambridge,' Rose said eventually, 'and there was an atmosphere of: At last, she can be normal and successful. Of course, people here looked at me just as weirdly. But also, I wasn't interested in law. I would have walked away after six weeks. But I stuck it out. I've worked myself into the ground for three years to make my parents feel I'm worth something. I think they imagined if I got my degree, I would shrink to five foot five.'

We lay in silence for a while. I was clutching her tightly, one arm wrapped around the angular bone of her hip. Her shoulders were tight. I wanted her so desperately it would have been hard enough to say it even in my first language.

'The point is,' she said, 'I've never had the life I wanted.

I'm twenty-one now.' There was another long pause. 'I don't even know what my point is,' she said in the end.

'Are we really going to set up a lookalike agency?' I asked.

THE BEWARE IMITATIONS AGENCY
Top-quality tributes and lookalikes including:

A.H.
A Tribute to Hitler
The UK's number one Führer tribute. Incredibly authentic. Comedy clubs, stag/hen parties, weddings, corporate entertainment. See the evil genius brought to life by a German!

MAJOR MAJOR
The new Tory leader brilliantly parodied by . . . a 'real' Major! Political and military satire in one.

ELVIS LESLIE
All the old classics. The King is dead, long live the King! Weddings a speciality. Voted the South-East's top Elvis Impersonator 1982–5, 1988. Travels anywhere in the UK, own sound system.

JULIAN STATHAM: THE NEW JACK THE RIPPER
As seen in the Great Murderers of the Past exhibition and Jack the Ripper Experience tours. In the streets of Victorian Whitechapel, something evil is stirring . . . bookable for one-off appearances or a whole evening of ghoulish entertainment. Lock up your daughters for this light-hearted look at murder!

NINA FRANCE IS KIM BASINGER
A startlingly accurate lookalike of Hollywood's sexiest star. Parties, commercials, supermarket openings, etc.

MARY-LYNNE MUNRO
Goodbye Norma Jean . . . and hello again! Marilyn herself couldn't have done better. (Can also be hired as Cindy Crawford.)

ROBERT, THE WORLD'S TALLEST MAN!
No, your eyes are not deceiving you. Seven feet two of pure freak! Robert Symons – our unique tribute to the tallest human ever, Robert Wadlow – quite literally looks down on all other acts. The perfect show-stopper! Book early to avoid disappointment.

ALL ENQUIRIES: ROSE RAVENHILL OR ANDREAS HÖNIG.
BEWARE IMITATIONS! LONDON, UK.

Thanks to Rose's knowledge of the field, and her relationship with Robert, it was simple enough to recruit lookalikes.

The small pool of acts we started out with was calculated to make quick returns, rather than necessarily being the most talented people. We had a slightly washed-up Elvis, for example, because he could be guaranteed a regular income, which meant regular commission for us. The same went for our Marilyn Monroe impressionist, who worked on cruise ships and other places with second-rate entertainment.

And we made a phone call to Nina, my old college neighbour. This, a brainwave of mine, caused some discussion. Rose had her doubts. 'I'm not sure we'll be able to get a lot of work for her.'

'I know she is not a spitting image of Basinger . . .'

'That is quite a big part of the lookalike business,' said Rose, 'the looks side of it.'

'But at college,' I said, 'people used to often comment on it.'

'But at college,' Rose replied, 'people didn't know that much about the rest of the world.'

I realised this was true, and mentally savoured a retrospective victory over all those people I once envied for having fun.

However, when it came to it, Rose changed her mind after observing that Basinger's star was so much in the ascendant that even a mediocre tribute act would stand to be in fashion. Basinger was about to make a film called *The Marrying Man* which would come out next year, and the papers were full of talk of her engagement to her co-star, Alec Baldwin.

Nina, as I had surmised, had hopes of being an entertainment star; she had always excelled more in social than academic circles at Cambridge. We found her a couple of jobs working for very little money at a birthday party and a student ball and so on, and received good reports back. Nina was grateful for her opportunity and seemed to have forgotten any ill-feeling she might have had towards me. She had a part-time job in a hospital to keep her going, she said, 'until the performing stuff really takes off'.

Before going any further I should mention how we were sustaining ourselves as we launched the agency. I had scarcely any money and Rose had effectively cut herself off from her parents with this crackpot plan. I hinted once or twice that it might be a pragmatic idea to seek a reconciliation, but she remained defiant, partly, I thought, out of a feeling that she might have upset them more than they deserved. Rose did have some savings, but they would not pay the rent on a place where we could live and set up an office. We looked in depressing areas for low-rent property. We made half a plan to hire an office on a day-to-day basis and secretly sleep in it, although Rose was not someone who could easily squeeze in anywhere.

Then when we were almost on the point of discussing caravans, Rose told me she had some good news. 'Robert's said we can stay for as long as we like. Till we get the agency going and find somewhere to live. He's got a massive place in Finchley. Massive laterally as well as vertically.'

'Tremendous news!' I said, after a pause.

We moved our things in over a very wet weekend. Robert hired a large car and ferried us back and forth, as well as carrying bags and leaving dinner for us to eat (he had gone out to some club; because of his family's wealth he had no job aside from the occasional 'freak show'). We ate, surrounded by our bags, rain pounding on the windows and running down the panes.

'This is so kind of Robert,' said Rose.

'It is,' I agreed, wishing we could talk about something else.

'It's just really good of him.'

'I know it is,' I snapped.

'What's the matter with you?' she asked, surprised, and I did not exactly know.

We saw a lot of Robert in those first few weeks as we set about recruiting, publishing a brochure, advertising and so on. He had a great deal of advice to give. 'Remember to get ARDA-accredited,' he would say, looming suddenly in a doorway, or, 'I've thought of a couple of people you could call,' or, 'I know a half-decent Frank Bruno.' He suggested our agency's name, 'Beware Imitations', and had ideas for a logo; he found us a cheap deal on stationery, he helped to arrange a launch party, and he continued to liaise with the 'contact' who had organised the Peterborough show, and who had, apparently, 'a portfolio of lookalike opportunities'. When he used phrases like this, he and Rose would often meet each other's eyes – at a point well above my head – and I sensed them dwelling on some memory stored from the long days of their acquaintance.

Any time we were sitting together going through plans, he would knock on the door with some new suggestion, and although the house was large, he seemed to be around every corner. Throughout all this, Rose never stopped acknowledging how kind and thoughtful he was being.

I made love to her fiercely, but as quietly as possible, at night, and kept telling myself not to mind that Rose was so grateful to him. Of course, she sensed, and thought it hilarious, that I was winding myself up in this way. 'Jealous of our host!' she whispered one night. 'So, wish you were seven feet tall?'

'I don't know what you are talking about,' I muttered.

'You'd better punish me for being unfaithful in thought,' she said, tickling the back of my neck with her fingers, whose delicacy never failed to surprise me. I let this remark pass and listened to enormous footsteps shaking the floorboards above.

Still, the breathing space afforded us by Robert's generosity allowed us to find a couple of more unusual acts. Perhaps the most intriguing was Julian Statham, or the New Jack the Ripper.

This amiable fellow, who had a round, easy-going sort of face and a way of making rather general, optimistic remarks, earned a living taking a tour of Jack the Ripper's neighbourhood, acting as the Ripper himself. In the course of the tour, the participants – tourists mostly, but also school parties, Ripper 'enthusiasts', and some people whose motives were unclear – were treated to various thrills. Julian would, for example, escort them all to a pub, disappear for a few moments, then suddenly jump from the shadows and drag someone off to be 'murdered'.

For a fee, groups could book him for a private tour and arrange for one of their number (say, a birthday man or future groom) to be the 'murdered' one: they would then have to follow clues to 'save' him. The tour had risen from twice to four times weekly, and was mentioned in many tourist guides.

Julian, who in spite of his happy-go-lucky appearance possessed a good deal of ambition, was seeking to capitalise on this success with more highly paid corporate bookings and, perhaps, television appearances. We interviewed him straight after work – he arrived in his heavy boots, his face concealed by a wide-brimmed hat, and clutching a malevolent-looking kitchen knife. He had walked a quarter of a mile from the station looking like this. 'People always assume I'm going to a party,' he said.

It was in conversation with Julian that we had a stroke of luck in our search for a permanent home. A friend of Julian's, by the name of Charles Steel, worked in a 'Victorian house' museum in Whitechapel. This was the former home of James Oswald, the nineteenth-century writer and socialite, which had been carefully preserved. It stood on Cloth Street, not far from Liverpool Street station. Charles's job was to pose as Oswald, escorting visitors around the house, accompanied by his 'wife', also an actress. Julian and Charles had met at the Pennyfarthing Club, a society for Victoriana enthusiasts, which met once a month in a pub, and whose founder did indeed pedal a pennyfarthing around London.

'Charles actually lives in the Oswald House,' Julian told us. 'He rents a flat at the top of the house, used to be the servants' quarters. It's been in his family for years. Anyway, there's another flat up there which is up for rent. See what you think. Charles is a real eccentric. Mad as a broom. But great fun. Just ignore most of what he says.' 'Mad as a broom' I added to my ever-swelling phrasebook. Rose told me you could use pretty much any noun – mad as a basket of monkeys, mad as a sweet shop – the humour was in the arbitrary comparison. There seemed something very British to me about this.

It was a Wednesday when we visited the James Oswald House and there was a sluggishness about the place. It was one of a cluster of buildings which had suffered no damage in the war, and which now stood together like old men surrounded by struggling textile wholesalers and semi-derelict slums occupied by squatters with ghetto-blasters. Inside, there were quotations from Oswald's writings dotted about on the walls, along with grainy reproductions of photographs showing a jolly, bearded Victorian with his unsmiling family.

There were only three other people on the tour, Americans; they had carrier bags from Madame Tussauds and this seemed to be a sort of bonus expedition for them. 'Mrs Oswald' began proceedings by coming to the door, in period dress and a wig. 'Goodness!' she said. 'So many visitors!' She and Charles had been warned about our visit, and she cast only a fleeting glance at Rose before leading us up a carpeted flight of stairs. On the walls were advertisements of the Victorian era with text written by Oswald.

On the landing we were met by 'Oswald' himself, or Charles – the man we had come to see. He was thin and bony, with a large head, and hair which had been forced into a smooth shape for his role; the beard, though, looked organic. He wore a suit and cravat. He and his actress colleague took us around the ornate house, room by room, re-enacting the real lives that once took place here.

'This is my husband's study,' said the actress, gesturing around a room with thick, almost leathery wallpaper and a writing table. 'He comes up here for hours talking to eminent men like George Bernard Shaw. If only some of Shaw's fame would rub off on him!'

'Fame, my dear, is not to be caught by "rubbing off",' Charles responded. I saw them catch each other's eyes and stifle a momentary laugh; this piece of dialogue had obviously caused jokes between them in the past. The actress had lively brown-green eyes and pale skin; she spoke in a prim-and-proper voice and carried it off very well. There was a chemistry, as they say, between these people playing their endless dressing-up game. I wondered what it was like, doing this every day, indeed several times every day.

'As you have heard,' said Charles, in the dining room, where there was an ostentatious table with horse's hooves for feet, and crockery set for twelve guests who would never arrive, 'my wife wishes me to achieve the fame of Shaw, or Lewis Carroll. I tell her that I am an unheralded genius. She says that she agrees with the first part.'

We all laughed politely. One of the Americans tried to take a photograph and Charles/Oswald stopped him with a genial raise of the hand. 'Please; these new-fangled devices are ruinous to the wallpaper my wife obliges me to buy! But hush, here she comes . . . ah, no, it is the servant girl, Penny.'

In came the actress, minus the wig; her real, blonde, hair

was pinned back and she had effected a quick costume change into a worn cloth dress and apron. She now spoke in a broad cockney accent. 'Sir, Mrs Oswald wishes me to tell you that the visitors are to be shown out now.'

'Couldn't afford a third actor to play the servant?' piped up one of the Americans. The actors, straightfaced, began to improvise.

'I do not know why everyone is forever talking about what we can and cannot afford,' said Charles. 'You are as bad as my wife!' There was again good-humoured laughter all round. When the tour came to an end, there was a little round of applause and the actress came out of character to tell us about the gift shop.

We went into the staff room and thanked them for the entertaining tour. Charles excused himself for a few moments to change. Rachel, his partner, babbled pleasantly to us in the meantime. 'It's quite a fun job, but it's better with more people. Mind you, Charles would do it even if nobody turned up,' she said, carefully hanging the wig in a cupboard and beginning to take the pins out of her hair. 'He's obsessed. It's not just chance that he lives in this place. In his mind, he is Oswald. Or George Bernard Shaw or one of them. One of those beardy men. I mean, half the time I don't know if I'm acting with him or just listening to him give a history lecture.'

'We're thinking of moving into the flat opposite,' Rose said.

'Oh, that'll be fun,' said Rachel. 'Charles is an absolute love. Just don't get him started!'

'Don't get me started on what, might I ask?' said Charles, coming back in. Though he had combed his hair out so that it hung in a red-grey frizz about his head, his 'changing' had not extended to taking off the suit, which, I thought, might be his own clothes. He was, though, one could now see, not so old as his appearance and manner initially suggested; perhaps only a few years older than Rachel.

'Just warning them what an awful bore you are on the subject of Ye Olden Times,' said Rachel with a twinkle. 'Now, better get off, I'm trampolining tonight.' Charles kissed her formally on the cheek and she said something I did not pick up.

I felt a passing yearning to enjoy the same camaraderie of the daily routine with my Rose, which would happen just as soon as I could get us out of Robert's place. I had almost decided we would definitely take the flat whatever it was like.

'The flat is not to everyone's taste,' Charles warned us, 'because it is smaller than . . . well, smaller than a better flat would be.' He gave a short bark of a laugh. 'Besides, not everyone wishes to live above a working museum.' He gave a delicate cough. 'I never expected to end up living here myself. Nor to spend my days pretending to be a long-dead gentleman as a job.'

'What did you do before?' Rose asked.

'Oh, a lot of jobs,' said Charles. 'Carpet-layer. Librarian. Academic. Waste of space. There was a colon between those last two, not a full stop.' There was the bark again. Rose gave me a look. We walked past a vast antique mirror and up a steep flight of stairs. There were two doors side by side, one of them Charles's own flat.

We stopped to look out of the window across the City, with new office buildings and construction work everywhere in the middle of what had once been Oswald's view. A stream of traffic did its best to replicate the air quality of

Victorian London, as I imagined it. The Jack the Ripper tours began just half a mile away, and Charles mentioned that Julian would often drop in on his way to work. 'He is my only friend,' he said with a certain relish, 'other than Rachel, of course.' He snorted with amusement. 'He is a dreadful philistine, obsessed with this "Ripperology" nonsense, and irritatingly jolly, but who is perfect?'

The flat possessed a bedroom, and a main room which would do as a combined office and living area. The bed was a good length, although 'too soft for my poor back,' said Rose, stroking the mattress, which was hard as a sheet of ice.

The only slight difficulty was with the tiny bathroom, whose ceiling was so low that even I had to duck to get inside.

'Some Victorian messed up with the plans here,' said Rose.

'On the contrary,' Charles began, 'servants' rooms were always—'

'Always designed for midgets?' muttered Rose, backing into the miniature room like a vehicle reversing.

Charles creased his forehead. 'Is there a name for it?'

'For?'

'For . . . your condition,' he said.

'Yes,' said Rose, 'it's called being very tall.' Charles spluttered and began to laugh, a different sort of laughter, mixed up with coughing.

On our way out, I asked if he could recommend a café nearby. 'Rachel and I are in the habit of going to a place called Koffee Kompany,' he said, 'with two "k"s. Funny, isn't it?'

'Sorry . . . ?' I said.

'Isn't it funny,' said Charles, 'rather than spelling it with "c"s, they have given it a far more eccentric name.'

'Yes,' said Rose, sportingly, 'it is funny.'

'It is not!' said Charles tartly, making us jump. 'What a nonsense! All right, if one of the words began with a "k", then by all means, change the other – like Keith's Kar Hire. But to change them both! Where is the joke in that?'

We looked at each other.

'However,' said Charles, 'they make a good Earl Grey.'

'He might be an odd neighbour to have . . .' I conceded, as we drank our coffees. On the wall was a large old iron sign dating from the establishment's former existence as the East India Tea Rooms, and a series of photographs of different owners.

'Yes, but so might we,' Rose pointed out. 'How many neighbours run a lookalike agency? Anyway, I think he might be quite fun. I like slightly mad people, being a freak myself . . .'

'Leave that word alone, please,' I said, making as if to rap her on the knuckles.

We discussed what she called the 'pros and cons' of the property. Certainly, it was a ridiculously small place for one of Britain's five tallest women to live. And running our agency from such a strange location might seem, as Rose put it, 'not exactly Hollywood' to prospective clients. On the other hand, it was cheap, and more impressive than showing them through to a spare room in someone else's house. And it would be a place of our own.

Although I tried to be efficient and businesslike about the move, I could, once again, hardly believe my luck. I had never had an easy time being intimate with people; and now this. Perhaps it would all be too much, too quickly, but after what seemed an almost lifelong period of too little, that risk seemed well worth taking.

Our early days in the flat were very successful. I loved waking up with Rose and for that matter going to bed with her. 'I hope we are not disturbing you at all,' I said to Charles, after the first few, exuberant, nights had passed in our new accommodation. 'I mean,' I added hastily, 'in the day as well as the night.' This still sounded awkward. 'Well, at any hour of the clock,' I babbled.

Charles smiled. 'I shall not hesitate to knock on the wall, if I am troubled. At any hour.'

By day, however, we were also productive. We circulated the brochure and were soon making a respectable commission from bookings. Our Elvis impersonator, though only rated as the fifth best in *Ultimate Elvis* magazine's annual round-up, did regular parties and weddings and the like. Nina was in reasonable demand. Julian, our Jack the Ripper, seemed destined for TV appearances. As Rose generated more and more paperwork, I busied myself tidying and cleaning.

As for my 'Hitler act', word had got around, because I was really the only Hitler about, and moreover, authentically German. When I started researching the part, I was amazed what a tradition there was of spoofing Hitler, everywhere but Germany. I watched the video of *The Producers* and listened to the dolled-up cast's bizarre lyrics making free with German history.

'What the hell is this?' I said half to myself.

'It's meant to be a really bad musical, that's the joke,' Rose said; she was whistling along to the score. She stole up behind me and raised my arm in a salute.

A men's magazine paid me for a photo shoot – some silly article or other. I hosted another minor award ceremony. Then came a financial breakthrough when I appeared briefly in a chocolate advertisement for Belgian television. It was filmed in a studio in Soho and I had nothing to do but poke my face briefly into the shot, though it still took almost five hours and I was there for the whole day. During the lengthy hiatuses, I sat in a dressing room, fingering the swastika on my arm, thinking that life truly had dealt me a series of extraordinary cards all at once. I was doing a job that ought not to exist, and I was eating and sleeping and waking up with a woman in whose existence I could only just believe.

'It seems too good to be true,' I confided in Ralf over the telephone.

'Too good to be true, who shat in your brain?' he scoffed. 'Just get on with enjoying it!'

'How is Dad?'

Ralf laughed. 'The old man will be the same when he's a hundred. Same job. Same dinner.'

'Listen, Ralf,' I said. 'I don't know what you will think of this. I have some news for you.'

'You're not ill, are you?' he said. 'Shit.'

'No, no. Listen.' I cleared my throat. 'My act is . . . it's kind of a tribute to Hitler.'

There was a pause, then a crackle of laughter at the other end. 'What, you play Hitler! Brilliant!'

'I mean, the idea in time is to use the jokes to address a serious point . . .' I backtracked.

'Oh, come on!' Ralf said jubilantly. 'You don't have to sell it to me! You, pretending to be Hitler!' He laughed and sighed as if he would never quite get over it. I wanted to tell him to be quieter, in case my father heard.

'Please don't tell him,' I begged. 'I don't know if he'd think it was so funny.'

'Chill, man,' said Ralf, in English. 'We've been dragged through enough shit, haven't we?'

When we drew up our accounts at the end of three months, things were going encouragingly well. We had a file of press cuttings for most of our clients already; the phone was always ringing.

'And I'm sure it will get better,' I said. 'We could take more acts on. And my act is going from strength to strength.' I had just acquired this phrase.

'Yes,' said Rose distractedly, 'it all depends.'

'Depends on what?'

'Oh, you know,' she said. Her mind seemed to be somewhere else altogether. I expected her to start singing any minute.

'What are you thinking about?'

'This will sound odd,' said Rose, 'but how would you feel if I asked you to make love to me in the Hitler uniform?'

>> Alexandra

There it ended, just as it was getting, as Gareth put it, 'racy'. I had to hand it to Gareth: he was really putting an effort in. I had my suspicions that he was quite enjoying himself. Of course, now I wouldn't see him again for some weeks. Maybe by the time he came back, he would have found some other hobby.

The days immediately after he left seemed very long. Andreas and I exchanged another pair of brief letters. Half the office was relieving the dullness of work by chatting about what they were going to get up to in Paris, when out of earshot of Jeremy – the only person who seriously believed that the five days would be spent in solid 'location reconnaissance'. Helen had promised to bring me something nice, but that was the only conversation we had about it; she had the good grace to feel a bit guilty, at least. People from her party had now started using the email list to chat about other things, and someone had mooted a possible 'reunion'.

On Thursday night I had a couple of drinks with Helen after work; she tried to get me to order various bar snacks but I wasn't hungry. We chatted away quite merrily without touching on any of the subjects which had made things awkward recently. Her boyfriend of the moment was an Eastern European guy, called Petr. He was apparently very tall and worked in a haberdashery place on Savile Row; they'd met through someone, I was only half-listening. Helen's relationships rarely lasted much longer than it took to learn someone's name, which was the part of the reason she was always so optimistic about my chances of making a complete recovery from the proposal fiasco.

I had to stop myself from saying, 'If you think he's tall . . .' Soon I was going to tell her about all this, but not quite yet. I had to try to make sense of it for myself first. We parted at the tube station.

I got off at a different stop from the usual one and walked along the river. Near our apartment block, a floating restaurant, aboard a moored steamer, was advertising a Halloween Special menu. We wouldn't get many trick-or-treaters at Bellevue Mansions; not many could be bothered to buzz and go up to the twenty-sixth floor. Pretty soon after that it would be Christmas. This reminded me that our mother was coming for a Sunday visit next weekend. Would Dan be able to stay in his right mind on Saturday night, I wondered. The sun had gone down and the towers of Canary Wharf gave off their cheerless reddish light.

My ID card wouldn't swipe in the slot and I had to ring for the concierge. I sometimes suspected that they disabled the card reader just to give him something to do. He watched me waiting for the lift with what I thought might be a certain pity. It was undeniable that he often saw me come home alone; he probably thought I lived in one of the studio apartments and was a lonely young City worker.

I did go out with several men in quick succession after Craig – later Helen referred to it as my 'plug the gap' period – but I never brought them back here. I'd only just moved in at the time. Plus, most of them were not the sort of people you brought back; they were the sort you went for a drink with, spent a night with, then regretted it and spent a fortnight disentangling yourself by text message. In all honesty I must have been poor company, because the business with Craig had made me so guarded and mistrustful that the simplest conversation could turn to awkwardness. After a bit of this I got sick of it and entered what Helen called my 'I don't need anyone' period. For the past year or whatever it was now, I'd been somewhere in between, theoretically keen to meet someone but not anxious to spend any time actually trying to do it. I had asked Helen not to give a name to this stage.

It was these bits of the day, the mid-evenings, that I found difficult sometimes. Tonight I tried to watch two films, but lost interest in each one about halfway. I gazed out of the enormous window at London, thousands and thousands of little dots. When I first moved here, I used to be quite excited by all the layers of history you could see in a rooftop view of London; the backstreets, the old slums, the jumble of generations of architecture on top of one another. My awe had worn off and I now tended to notice things like the spray-painted graffiti tags on the side of disused warehouses, and the smog clouds.

A re-run of a chat show from the previous weekend came on the TV. Normally this was a pretty good indication that it was time to give up for the night. As my hand reached for the remote control, though, the cameras did a flashy circuit of the studio and came to rest on the next guest. I caught my breath. It was a heavily made-up and eagerly smiling Kim Basinger. I hadn't seen her in years, perhaps not since the time Andreas was managing a lookalike of her. The host mentioned that it was her fiftieth birthday soon; Basinger giggled and made a self-effacing remark and an uneasy laugh went through the studio audience. The host tried to change the subject to his own age. They showed a clip of *Batman*, and another of *LA Confidential*, which came out in the mid-nineties, and a pop video which she'd sung on. The camera cut back to Basinger giving a slightly too bright smile and applauding the little montage with the audience.

'And since then . . .' said the host.

'Since then, well, I have done a lot of things,' said Basinger, with the air of someone dealing with a familiar question. She named half a dozen films which I hadn't heard of. There was an awkwardness so strong you could feel it even sitting at home. The host mentioned her divorce, and the mud-slinging that was still going on between her and Alec Baldwin; she had accused him of abuse, he'd called her an alcoholic, and lots more.

'Was that painful?' he asked.

'Sure, it was painful, it is painful,' Basinger agreed.

A key rattled in the lock and made me jump. I could hear two sets of footsteps. This is early for them, I thought. Then in came Dan, followed by a Chinese-looking man in a hooded sweater. Dan, in turn, flinched at the sight of me.

'What are you doing here?'

'I live here,' I pointed out. 'That's why we sometimes meet.'

'I thought you'd be in bed,' he said.

'It isn't that late,' I said. The Chinese man was surveying the flat with what looked like polite amusement. There was a tense silence. Dan was obviously keen for me to leave. I put him out of his misery. He shut the door very firmly behind him and I heard them begin to talk in very low tones. It was a bit alarming that Dan had begun to do drug deals, if that was what this was, actually in our flat. But, of course, it was not really 'our' flat.

It was hard to get the figure of Kim Basinger out of my head. I looked her up on the internet and got a site with all her old posters, several of which had adorned my various walls at some point over the past ten years. There was one, however, that I struggled to get. It was for *The Marrying Man*, the film Andreas mentioned, her first after *Batman*, which was chiefly noted in the end for hooking her up with her eventually disastrous husband. It might have had a different name when it came out in the UK; a few years ago I would definitely have remembered.

In any case, there had been a giant poster for the film on our walk to school. It was done in a nostalgic style, or what would now be called 'vintage', with swirly writing and Basinger made to look quite a bit like Marilyn Monroe. One evening, having decided it would go nicely with my *Some Like It Hot* print, I spent about half an hour trying to slide my fingernails under it to whisk it away for my room. It had worked for me in the past, but this time it was no use – the glue had hardened like a sheet of glass against the wall. In reality it was no more 'our walk to school' than 'our flat': Dan preferred not to be seen with me and would walk with pretty much anyone else, but on this occasion, as I was staring defeatedly at the poster, I saw him crossing the road with some friends. I hastily went into a shop and let them go past.

Casually, over breakfast the next day, Dan asked, 'What do you want the poster for?'

'What?'

'I saw you trying to get the poster off.'

'Hurry up, please,' said Mum, clearing things away around us. Breakfast had been a perfunctory meal since things started to go seriously wrong between our parents – actually so had most meals.

'I just . . .' I said, defensively. 'Just for my room.'

'I could get it for you,' said Dan, pursing his lips.

'How?' I asked. Of course he wouldn't tell me. But I was twelve or thirteen and still assumed he could do pretty much anything; maybe he had access to a special poster-steamer or something.

'What do you want?' I asked.

'Lunch,' he said.

A deal was struck. I would make him packed lunches for the next week. We'd been more or less left to fend for ourselves of late, and my brother had seen me making sandwiches for myself on more than one morning. But he never asked me to do it for him and I was hardly going to offer; I assumed he was able to sneak into town in his lunch-break, or something. Now, it seemed not. I felt almost sorry for him having to do such a deal with his little sister. I began getting up fifteen minutes early, cutting twice as much bread into twice as many neat little squares, raiding ironically named 'family packs' for crisps. Naturally we did not discuss the arrangement – I left his lunch on the table. The closest we came was that I gave him a meaningful glance one morning when Basinger and Baldwin were on the breakfast news. We didn't tend to see each other much around the house, then as now. We'd spent a lot of our lives ten feet from each other without any actual contact.

Midway through the week I walked past the wall and the poster had gone. There was no other poster there in its place:

just a big, empty slice of brick. My heart speeded up and I almost jogged the rest of the way to school.

I completed the final lunch of the agreement, on the Friday, and spent the school day thinking about it. When I got home he wasn't there. He didn't come home. I was slightly too young to be going out on Friday nights (whereas now, it was already starting to seem as though I was slightly too old). The next morning I opened my door; there was no poster. On Saturday early evening I got a glimpse of him watching the football scores.

'What happened to . . . ?' I said.

He pretended not to hear. 'What?'

'The . . . poster?' I muttered, but it was already obvious he hadn't got it. He gave me a look that was almost pity.

'Did you think I was actually going to get it?'

I thought it would look much worse if I made a scene about it, and anyway, there had been a lot of shouting in our house. I gave him the worst look I could and went back to my room.

The whole thing was never mentioned again. I doubted that he remembered it now, though actually, I doubted he remembered things that had happened yesterday.

Only minutes after reliving this sorry little incident, I heard a tap on my bedroom door. I closed the internet page and called, 'Come in'. For a second I thought it might be Gareth, then I remembered he was in America. Dan poked his head around the door.

'All right?' he said. I said I was fine, thanks.

'Good . . . day?' he asked. It was now pretty clear he had a favour to ask.

'Fine, thanks,' I said. 'A bit boring.'

'Just – about that guy I came in with,' Dan said. 'If anyone asks, you never saw him, OK?'

'OK,' I agreed. 'Is anyone likely to ask? The police?'

'I mean anyone,' said Dan. 'Like Gareth, or . . . or Trixie . . .'

'I'll try and keep it from Trixie next time we're out together,' I said, 'but you know me and Gareth talk about everything . . .'

He looked at me suspiciously.

'I'm joking,' I said with a sigh.

'Thanks, sis,' he said, fingering his fringe. 'Hey, when is Mum coming? Is it this weekend?'

'Next weekend. I'll remind you closer to the time.'

'Cheers, mate,' he said. He nodded and shut the door. By our standards it hadn't been a bad chat.

There was no letter from Andreas that Friday, or Saturday, and then finally nothing on Monday, until it was the time of the week when I normally wrote back. On Monday evening, ignoring the wily grin of the concierge, I checked the pigeon-hole on two separate occasions, before trudging back upstairs in a mood of disappointment which I found hard to justify to myself.

In my lunch-break the next day I went round to see Claire in her Soho office; she'd sent an email suggesting a 'catch-up', which I dug out of my inbox from among the reunion discussions. I told her that I hadn't received a letter this week. She drank tea out of a new mug, with DO THEY EVER GROW UP? spelt out in crying babies' faces around the outside. I wanted to believe that she hadn't bought it for herself.

'Andreas was saying something about how they sometimes open prisoners' letters,' I said, glancing around the room at all the congratulations cards. If I were ever pregnant, I thought, I wouldn't tell people until it was unavoidable. 'Could he have written a letter and had it . . . intercepted?'

'Mmm,' said Claire, nodding, 'it can happen. They might

have suspicions of Andy for whatever reason. He's never sent you anything . . . odd, has he?'

I thought of the bulging envelope which had arrived with his life story in it. 'Not really.'

'It's more likely . . .' Claire said, adding sugar to her tea. 'I really shouldn't be having this. It's more likely that he just didn't manage to write this week for whatever reason. Perhaps he wasn't feeling inspired.'

Again, there was something in her voice I didn't entirely like. I couldn't help feeling that she thought I was a bit too keen on Andreas for my own good, and was making a drama out of nothing. Perhaps she was right. There and then I decided I was going to visit Andreas again as soon as I could. Claire and I chatted for a little while about the fact that she could feel the baby kicking. As I was getting up to leave, she put the word 'CRAVAT' into her crossword with a little a-ha! of satisfaction. Her phone was ringing as I shut the door and walked away with the yawning lion behind me.

Rather than be reassured by Claire, as the evening wore on I turned things over in my head till Andreas's failure to write came to seem more and more important. The usual silence in the flat, the stack of emails in my inbox from people I hardly knew, and a slight headache all contributed to this feeling. The most frustrating thing was not knowing how long it would be until I could read more of Andreas's story. Without knowing what was going to happen, anything I might write to Andreas in a letter, or say to him next time we met, ran the risk of being completely inappropriate. I wondered whether Gareth had taken the manuscript to America and why, rather than asking him properly, I had suggested 'holiday reading' as a weak joke.

Without really thinking through what I was doing, I found myself outside Gareth's door. I had never been in his room, not properly; why would I? I looked both ways down the corridor like a spy. There was virtually no chance of Dan coming home and I was as sure as I ever could be, these days, that Trixie was not in the flat. I pushed open the door.

The room smelt of Gareth's various bottled scents and something else quite pleasant, a bit like the smell you get from a new glossy brochure. It was extremely tidy. The bed was made – it was somehow touching to think of him making it before he left to get his flight – with the pillows propped up like in a hotel room. His desk was bare, with a space where the laptop normally sat. I couldn't see Andreas's papers.

Looking over my shoulder, I advanced further into the room. I wasn't sure why I was doing this. There was one drawer beneath his desk and if he had left the manuscript here, I felt somehow, it would be in there. Taking a fast breath in, I opened the drawer.

There was no sign of the papers. All the drawer contained was his ID badge from work and the one for the block of flats; and a third thing, a card. I took it out. WORLD'S GREATEST, it said, with a cartoon of an Atlas-type figure holding up the globe. Inside there was no name; just a kiss. Was it from the girlfriend I suspected he had, but had never met? It was odd how little we knew about each other. I was reminded of a bit in Andreas's story, early on, when he talked about the Icelander he kept seeing, with whom he somehow never became friends. It was an odd thought that even though we'd lived together for two years now, Gareth could decide to move tomorrow – or when he came back – and we would probably never see each other again.

I didn't know why I was thinking like this. Perhaps it was a hangover from the communal living days, when anything happening to one person might as well have happened to all six. A secret boy- or girlfriend in that environment would have been unthinkable. Of course, there were times when the intimacy was too much, but now with hindsight, I could see its advantages.

I left the room exactly as I found it, assuming a casual face as if I had a perfectly good explanation for having been there.

The parental visit went well, largely thanks to me. I tidied the flat, asked Dan to find a temporary new hiding place for his drugs, reminded him the night before not to die of an overdose if he could help it, and woke him up on the day itself.

Our mother was looking greyer even than when I last saw her, but she seemed in good spirits. She wasn't seeing a new man as far as I could make out, so we could have had a chat about our similar situations if we were that sort of mother and daughter. She kept admiring features of the flat she had admired on previous visits: the view, the 'posh sofas', the 'fancy stereo', the fact that one of her children had spent a lot of money on it all. She mentioned Christmas, tentatively.

'I'm coming home,' said Dan immediately. 'I'll be there.'

'Oh, that'll be lovely, Daniel,' said Mum, her face lighting up. 'I thought you might be off with . . . the girlfriend, or . . .'

'No, no,' said Dan. 'What's Christmas without the family?'

'Oh, I'm really pleased,' said Mum, beaming.

'I'm . . . I'll be home too,' I said.

'Of course, well, that's even better! Two gorgeous children!' said Mum. But it was pretty clear that she hadn't ever expected me to be anywhere else.

There was no prospect of getting a day off work to see Andreas until half the office swanned off to Paris in a couple of weeks.

Then, I hoped things would be slacker, and even if they weren't, I would probably be too fed up to care about getting into trouble.

I was trying to get hold of a copy of the book they were publishing as a spin-off from the series. They were meant to be ready by now. Mum was looking forward to having a copy to show her friends my name in the acknowledgements pages. This had been the biggest thing I could muster to rival Dan's flat, job and girlfriend for her affections. No one in the office seemed to be able to give me an answer, though, or even take the question seriously. I went on the internet during the afternoon to see if I could find a copy online quicker than in the actual office where nearly all the material was collated. It was possible to pre-order one but by the time I'd entered my credit-card details I realised that I was doing it purely out of frustration. I did a search for 'Charles Steel'. Several people came up – a man who had put two hundred pictures of stick insects online, a black American college baseball player, a long-dead architect – but no one who could have been Andreas's former neighbour. Then I looked for 'James Oswald House'.

The museum had an official website but it hadn't been updated since 1998. The phone number had an obsolete area code and there was a picture of a now-disgraced government minister visiting the house. None of the links to other pages worked. By this time I was openly not working, but I was still available to answer the phone and say no to whatever was requested, and there was an air of lassitude about the place, as there always was when a trip was coming up. I tried another page from the search. This was a housing company and the site was bang up to date. It said that the James Oswald House was being redeveloped into 'luxury executive accommodation'. It would be ready in just a few months' time and, the site boasted, almost half of the as-yet-non-existent flats had been sold already. I made a mental note of the address. It was sort of on my way home.

This didn't count as obsessive behaviour, I told myself, weaving through crowds of businessmen at Liverpool Street station. It would just be interesting. All around the station there were cranes and dust, traffic cones and signs redirecting pedestrians. Outside a pub called Dirty Dick's, a man dressed in a black hat and long cloak was giving out leaflets for a Jack the Ripper tour, maybe the contemporary equivalent of Julian's tour. I took one.

'Come one, come all!' croaked the man in the sort of voice you would use to impersonate a pirate. 'Ye'll be in for a night of fun! Ye'll enjoy yerself to death!'

'Excuse me,' I said, leaning in close, and avoiding the eyes of commuters whose path I was blocking. 'I don't suppose your name is Julian?'

He pulled the hat up slightly and looked me in the eyes. I could see now he was far younger than me, probably a drama student or something. 'My name is Jack! Ye might have heard tell of me. I prowl the streets of this town by night. I—'

'Or does anyone called Julian take these tours?' I persisted, realising already this was a bit absurd, it was more than ten years on.

He sighed. 'My actual name's Stephen.'

Someone else took a leaflet from his left hand, which had stayed outstretched throughout our conversation. 'Come one, come all!' he began again. I muttered an apology for bothering him and went on my way, stuffing the curled-up leaflet into my bag.

As I turned onto Cloth Street, where Rose and Andreas had

once lived, a group of Bengali kids roared past in a car with all the windows down. Violent-sounding music shot out of their sound system. I imagined the Victorian, James Oswald, looking down on them in complete incomprehension.

The houses of his neighbours had been converted one by one. One was now a dental practice, one a 'centre for inter-cultural studies', one a block of student accommodation. The Oswald House itself still bore the marks of its life as a museum – a small brass sign in a low window offered discounts for OAPs, students and 'P45s' – but a large banner stretched across the building's midriff gave details of the 'EXECUTIVE HOUSING' it was turning into. There were line drawings of happy-looking workers. There was going to be a multi-gym in what, according to the plans, had once been the Oswalds' wine cellar.

The estate agent had a pinstriped shirt, which had suddenly gone from the least to the most fashionable thing possible. He surveyed the group of six of us. I thought everyone else would be an 'executive', but there were a couple of middle-aged women, maybe property developers, and a bald man who didn't seem to speak much English at all. I supposed there wasn't much to look at yet; it was more about the 'investment opportunity'. I did my best to look as though I was sizing things up, all the time trying to imagine Rose bending to get through the door, and Andreas coming down the main staircase dressed as a Nazi.

'So this will be a foyer area, you'll have a twenty-four-hour concierge, gym – I can show you where that'll be – and valet service etc., etc.,' said the estate agent, who only looked about nineteen. He had cufflinks and very short hair. It seemed to have been part of his training to keep saying, 'You'll have . . .' or 'You'll be able to . . .' as if it were a formality that we would all purchase one of these flats. 'So this staircase will be ripped out,' he said, 'and you'll have two lifts serving the five floors.'

Some of the rooms were now completely empty, but here and there you could still see artefacts from the house as it had been, a picture still hanging on the wall, a writing desk in one of the empty rooms, maybe once Oswald's study, which was going to be a studio flat once they'd knocked down the wall. 'So, all this stuff is being shipped out,' said the estate agent, 'so obviously you won't be running into antique chairs etc.!'

'Where will it go?' I asked.

The estate agent smiled thinly at my non-property-related question. 'It's all been bought by other museums and, um, collectors and people,' he said. 'Now, we can go upstairs and have a look at one of the existing flats. They'll be completely redeveloped but it's just to give you an idea. Unfortunately there's a former employee of the museum still living there but obviously he'll be moving out.'

It was only as we ascended the steep staircase to the top floor – 'bit of a trek, used to be the servants' rooms I think, but as I say, you'll have lifts obviously' – that I thought I could imagine Andreas being here, actually living here. It was more of a stretch to think of a Victorian family going about their business.

The agent knocked hard on the door and said, 'Mr Steel? We'd just like to have a look at the flat.' He gave us a wry face. 'The gentleman who lives here is a bit . . .'

At the name, my mouth dropped slightly open. The estate agent gave me a quizzical look, then turned away again as the door swung heavily and slowly open. There stood an alarming-looking man. Half of his face was smothered by a wild, ragged beard; his mouth was buried in it somewhere. Grey hair stood on top of, and around, his head, something like the mane of a lion. His eyes were green. He looked at the group of us without appearing to see us. Charles Steel, I thought, is still living here.

'As I say, Mr Steel, just like a quick butcher's at the apartment,' said the estate agent.

'Largely unchanged from last week,' mumbled Steel, and he seemed to fade into the air rather than get out of the way as the potential buyers came through.

'So, as I say, this will be knocked through and all the fittings will be brand new of course . . .' said the agent, as one of the women tapped rather critically on the thin wall.

I stared around the place, very disconcerted. I'd been reading Andreas's story like something long gone and done with, but here was one of its characters years on.

The flat was full of books, boxes containing bits of paper, and strange old ornaments: a hatstand, a unicycle. Perhaps they were things he had rescued from elsewhere in the Oswald House. On one shelf there was nothing but six volumes of a biography of Shaw. None of the books in the flat had dust jackets; they could all have been there for a century. There was just one picture on the wall, a framed photo of James Oswald. He was standing outside the house with his family, smiling merrily into the camera. He had whiskers and a beard and looked like someone from a Dickens novel, or, maybe, like a fatter and jollier version of Charles Steel.

The agent thanked Steel and each of us glanced uneasily at him on our way down the stairs; I think everyone felt in some way as if we were personally turfing him out of his home. He returned each look until the other person looked away. At the foot of the steps I stopped to read the remains of a photo display about James Oswald. 'James Oswald was described by his contemporaries as a writer, a wit, a bon vivant, a socialite, an advertising genius, a philanthropist and many more things besides.' The remaining photos in the display had gone already and a sheet of perspex had been bolted to the wall. Outside, I noticed a buzzer with the word STEEL almost faded to nothing. The man in his cloak was still giving out leaflets at the station. I sat on the train thinking about the bizarre sight of Charles Steel, and the fact that he had once lived next door to Andreas.

I had nine new emails. The first eight were from Helen's now unstoppable party list. The ninth said 'ARCHER, Gareth'. There was an attachment.

Dear Alexandra,

It's been a bit slow here so I've done more of the translation. Wanted to see if the pornographic theme might develop. See you soon.

Gareth

I stared at the screen for a while without doing anything. I wasn't sure whether the best thing was to have the new bit of Andreas's memoirs, or the fact that Gareth had bothered to do it. I had several tries at writing an email back, but it was hard to get the tone right. I didn't want to sound ungrateful or, on the other hand, blown away by gratitude. I settled for a brief thank-you, with an 'x' after my name which I deleted, and read the latest instalment off the screen.

☞ANDREAS

The idea of performing sex in my Hitler costume began as a whim and became a fairly regular habit. I had many qualms in the early stages of this new sexual initiative, but, in truth, they were more logistical than moral. The coat was heavy and made me perspire; that was of more concern than the fact that I was sporting a swastika. One must remember that, by this time, I had already, as the English say, burned my bridges as far as impersonating Hitler was concerned: to make love dressed as him was no odder than to stand on a stage and reprise his personality for a laughing audience.

I was not even perturbed when Rose began to introduce role-playing variations. Her taste for punishment in the bedroom was not so unusual, I suspected, and I was just happy that there was something I could do to excite her. It was still odd enough to me to be in bed with Rose at all, and so it required only a little more effort to adjust to slightly odder deeds. Variety in the bedroom, in any case, was a valuable aid to maintaining desire. When I made this observation to Rose one night, she laughed and said that I sounded like *The Joy of Sex*.

Work, however, had become her greatest passion. She sent photographs of me, moustache in place, to entertainment agencies and casting directors and so forth, and even to newspapers, trying to stir up publicity. 'We need to get your face out there,' she said.

'You're my Goebbels.'

She smirked. 'You know how to make a girl feel special.' This remark was all the more enjoyable because, in actuality, it was transpiring that I did.

We had got an old computer through a friend of Robert's and the living space in our flat was now an office by day. As bookings increased, Rose gained both in confidence and in industriousness. She would get up at eight, struggle in and out of the shower and be making phone calls by nine, while I got on with other paperwork. We also began auditioning for new lookalikes, aiming for a pool of about thirty so that we could begin to make a decent profit from commission.

'The hopefuls', as Rose called them, would come to the office in the early evening, after the museum's final tour of the day. Charles would often come back from saying goodnight to Rachel at Koffee Kompany to find a fat man warming up his voice for an impersonation of Luciano Pavarotti, or a spiky-haired youth resembling the child actor Macaulay Culkin, accompanied by an ambitious parent. And then there were our existing clients: Julian, 'Mary-Lynne Munro', or Nina, who became very nervous when receiving her bookings, and would insist with almost fanatical intensity that Rose double-check she would not be required to sing. This was occasionally an issue because Basinger was something of a singer as well as everything else, and some clients would request that Nina do a 'couple of numbers'.

'I'll do anything but sing. I've got a psychological aversion to it,' Nina said once.

'I'm beginning to get a psychological aversion to her,' Rose muttered later. But so long as Basinger remained such a celebrity, it was valuable to the agency to possess an act looking at least something like her.

Some of the aspiring lookalikes were impressive enough to be hired on the spot; for others, I had to rely on Rose, as they resembled British television personalities whom I was not familiar with. Some were doomed to fail from the moment Rose, glancing down at the CV on the table, asked, 'I'm sorry, who do you look like again?' There were a few unlucky people, as well, who were excellent likenesses of persons with practically no commercial appeal, like the man who wished to be taken on as a lookalike of the politician Malcolm Rifkind, or the bewhiskered fellow who looked rather more like Stalin than I like Hitler; sadly this particular villain was far less frequently requested than the Führer.

One or two jobs could sustain a lookalike financially for a while, which, for me, was something of a mixed blessing. Although it was of course sensational good luck to pay my way so easily, I was left with more time than I needed. Rose had quickly established a filing system – along with a system of jargon, phrases like 'corporate potential' and 'career trajectory' creeping into her lexicon like Robert appearing suddenly in a room – and, rather than helping her, I often felt in the way: sometimes literally so, in the cramped 'office space' available. I got into the habit of going for walks around London, visiting historical spots, seeking out the heart of the city in old churches and cobbled streets. I watched videos of Hitler, listened to recordings, practised the walk and the voice. I wrote letters to Ralf as often as twice a week, knowing only the most cursory reply was likely; I began letters to my father but could not get them right. And I spent a lot of time with Charles.

He and Rachel would often be in the middle of a tour when I returned home from some jaunt or other. I would go upstairs with Charles's clipped Oswald-voice in my ears. 'You know, I was lucky enough to attend the last-ever public reading by Mr Charles Dickens . . .' and Rachel retorting, 'Yes, James. What became of the novel you were to write?'

It was amusing to watch the way the two of them kept up their jolly bickering even when out of their historical characters. Charles, as something of a recluse, made it his business to lampoon Rachel's busy programme of social engagements. I remember one occasion when Rachel had signed up to play indoor football.

'Games,' said Charles, setting a cup of tea down with great care in Rachel's hands, 'are for people who can neither read nor think.'

'Let me guess,' she said, rolling her eyes. 'Bernard Shaw?'

'Indeed,' said Charles. 'Why state one's own opinion when one can borrow another's?'

'I suppose Shaw said that as well?'

'No,' said Charles, 'that was a witticism of the great man himself.' He cocked a thumb at the framed picture of James Oswald on his wall.

'Well, "the great man" sounds like a real barrel of laughs,' said Rachel.

'If only you had been here one hundred years ago,' said

Charles, patting her on the arm, 'you could have seen for yourself.'

'I think I'd rather be alive now,' said Rachel. Charles shook his head and tutted despairingly at this misguided thought. Rachel and I exchanged a grin. It was possible to imagine he had been living here since the days of the original owners.

The telephone rang in our flat and we could all hear Rose swearing as she bent painfully to pick it up. The thinness of the walls continued to give me concerns at bedtime, but I was beginning to see that Charles was the last person to take an interest in anyone else's private life; anyone other than James Oswald's, at least.

No London landmark failed to draw some Oswald anecdote or another from him, and sometimes it was rather distracting, as on the evening of the agency's official launch party. Robert had found a wine bar in Camden Town with the apposite name of Twin; all our clients, as well as people from entertainment circles, and miscellaneous friends, were invited. Charles and Rachel were coming along, and the four of us took a taxi across London.

Everyone had made an effort for the occasion. Rose was wearing a long, long split skirt from a West End place specialising in 'the larger or taller lady'. Rachel had got a haircut for the occasion – her hair bobbed on her shoulders. She had also coaxed Charles into some beauty work. 'Your hair needs definition,' she said.

'Poppycock!' Charles snorted. 'Look in a dictionary for definitions.' But he allowed her to apply some gooey gel to his hair and smooth it into shape, and now sat in the car fingering his scalp with a mixture of suspicion and pride. As for me, well, I was dressed as Hitler.

We chugged across town, creeping from the back of one line of cars to another. Rose was rather tense about the party – she had been on the phone for days confirming that such-and-such was coming – and some of her nerves spread to me as I mentally rehearsed my act. The taxi driver kept glancing at Rose next to him in the passenger seat, with her knees pushed up comically high and some part of her leg always in the way of the gearstick; and at me in his mirror. I had not yet donned the moustache, but the Nazi costume was enough to complete the odd atmosphere in the car. It was left to Charles to break the silence. 'London Zoo,' he said as we crawled around Regent's Park, 'where James once rode an elephant with Tessa to celebrate the publication of an article.'

'Do you think everyone will arrive early and go early?' Rose asked me, swivelling around. 'Or come too late and miss the actual lookalikes?'

'She complained of nausea for some time afterwards,' said Charles, 'and James was so worried that he asked a doctor if she might be allergic to elephants. Of course, she was simply pregnant . . .'

'I think it will go according to plan,' I said.

'We're going to be late,' said Rose, shuffling around in her seat. 'That'll look good, won't it? Robert said to take the tube, but no, I actually thought this would be quicker . . .'

'The traffic at this time of day,' said the taxi driver, spreading his hands.

'. . . James later honoured the elephant, Jumbo, by giving its name to the world's largest cheese, which he helped to advertise.'

'Charles,' said Rachel, squeezing his shoulder, 'no one's listening to your story about the elephant and the cheese.'

'Ah, well,' said Charles, 'Julian is coming to the party, so I will have somebody to bore and be bored by.'

Rose knocked her head getting out of the taxi. Charles clucked in amusement and she gave him a quick look with some considerable annoyance in it, to which he was probably oblivious. Julian was the first person we saw in the entrance to the club, dressed in full Jack the Ripper attire, handing out cocktails to new arrivals. He and Charles and Rachel went off for a drink while I went to see to my moustache. Other lookalikes were everywhere; Mary-Lynne Munro with her plastered-on face chatted to the blue-coated Elvis Leslie about the ins and outs of this strange business. The bar was filling up nicely; the lights were low and there was atmospheric music. I had a sudden pang of missing Ralf, for he would really enjoy a night like this; but then, I was a long way behind explaining to him exactly what I was doing at the moment.

In the Gents, our John Major impersonator was mouthing his act into a mirror; he was obliged to keep dodging out of the way as people reached around him for paper towels. I peered into the gap to his right and fastened my moustache to my lip, executing a couple of practice scowls and grimaces. 'Major Major' left, patting me on the shoulder, and when I was satisfied that I had the place to myself I began rehearsing one or two Hitler comments. 'We are strong, and will become stronger!' I had worked out a small piece of humour whereby as I said this, I would stagger slightly to accentuate my character's physical frailty. I tried it in the mirror.

'Very amusing,' said a voice behind me. There stood the telescopic figure of Robert. As ever, he seemed to have come straight through the wall.

'Thank you,' I said, frostily. 'I was just rehearsing.'

'Yes,' said Robert. 'Well, good luck. Do a couple of jokes about killing Jews – that should do the trick.'

He laughed. I looked around furtively in case anyone should hear this rather peculiar conversation, and this amused Robert further. 'Wouldn't worry about people hearing you! They're all going to see you in a moment!'

There was no time to think about the way he always got, as the English say, under my skin; I had to concentrate on my act. I was being kept until last, as the main attraction. Each lookalike was appearing for just a couple of minutes, as a 'taster'. A black sheet had been taped to the ceiling to provide a makeshift back-stage area, and here, Nina was pacing up and down in her Basinger heels, checking herself in a pocket mirror. She was about the third act onto the stage; the microphone squealed as she took it from the stand. She uttered some well-known movie lines, at least I imagined they were well known, in a decent enough American accent. At the end I could hear Rose clapping particularly loudly as she did to compensate for less impressive acts, and Rachel joining in gamely with a couple of whoops. Nina came off looking very relieved.

'That seemed to go well,' I said, in order to be supportive. She gave me a thumbs-up.

'Hopefully it'll bring some, you know, enquiries in,' she said, wiping sweat from her palms onto her dress. I thought how odd it was, her talking in such a professional way – after all, she was scarcely an artiste; she was just a girl from college who looked slightly like Kim Basinger. But then, what was I? So much came down to confidence, or, as Rose put it, 'having the sheer balls'.

Julian enjoyed an excellent reaction with his Jack the

Ripper act. If he was easy-going off the stage, he was something of a menace on it. The spotlight gleamed from his wicked-looking knife as he scoured the faces of the audience, cackling and babbling in a convincingly villainous voice. In the interval afterwards, he stood near the bar with leaflets for his tour, breaking into a menacing laugh each time someone took one, even as he continued to conduct normal conversations.

'It's important to take advantage,' he said to me, 'of these – ha! ha! – opportunities. Spread – ha! ha! – the word.' Such a mixture of professionalism and melodrama was not yet instinctive to me, and I hoped not to be overshadowed.

There was a definite change of atmosphere in the minutes before my arrival. I had the curious sensation that I was about to watch myself, rather than actually performing. The lights were dimmed, I was introduced, and even as I strutted out and began my pantomime German, it was as if I were not quite physically present. I could see Rose sitting on a stool at the back of the room, grinning broadly as I accidentally spat on someone in the front row and then exploited the moment by acting as if it were their fault, to huge laughter. There was a great ovation at the end, and I came off the little stage and Rose clutched my sides and propelled me outside immediately.

'You were brilliant,' she said, her breath coming out in white puffs against the night sky.

'I think those people would have laughed no matter what I said.'

'That's the skill of it!' she said. 'You're amazing. We should have had you hosting the whole thing.'

'Perhaps that would have spoiled the surprise element, though,' said a third party. Rose released her hands from my sides. Robert was leaning with one hand against a wall, surveying us with his sad eyes. Once the shock had receded, I felt, for the first time, rather sorry for him. Hadn't he anything better to do than to wander into others' conversations? I was frustrated as well, however, as Rose fell into talking with him and I was forced to go back into the bar, thinking of what would transpire when we were finally alone together.

Charles and Rachel were at the bar: he sipped at a soda water while she drank a colourful vodka-based cocktail. Rachel was admiring Nina's hair, an amusing sight as her own hair was almost the same colour. 'It looks great!' said Rachel. 'Just like Kim Basinger!'

Nina thanked her. 'I dye it to get it perfect. It costs $25 a bottle.'

'God,' said Rachel, 'you must spend a fortune.'

'Well,' said Nina, 'if you want to make it, you have to make sacrifices.' Rachel nodded her agreement. I turned to let Elvis Leslie past with his pint of lager. 'Still working at the hospital for the time being . . .' I heard Nina say. Then Rachel began to scream, her eyes bulging. Before anyone could work out what had happened, she was laughing. Julian, still wearing his cloak, had stolen up behind her and pressed his cold knife to her neck.

'You bastard!' she said, smiling.

'I'm Julian, the Ripper,' said Julian, extending his non-knife hand. 'I thought, any friend of Charles's is a wench I can rip.'

'This is Julian,' confirmed Charles.

'Your act was excellent,' said Rachel, shaking his hand.

'It may have been,' said Charles, 'but I do wish you would desist from sticking your knife into the necks of people you hardly know.'

‘Good PR thing, this,’ Julian said. ‘Looking to nudge up from seventy-five to a hundred a tour.’

‘A hundred people!’ said Rachel. ‘We sometimes have about five!’

‘By “good PR thing”,’ said Charles drily, ‘I think Julian meant to say that the evening has been a success.’

‘Yes,’ I said, calling a phrase to mind, ‘we are up and running.’

Indeed, the agency was soon far more advanced than that; it quickly became the backbone of our lives, just as the Hitler act went from being a novelty to my stock-in-trade, and our sometimes outlandish exploits in the bedroom had no sooner happened than they were assimilated into the common routine of things.

Rose was rather flushed from the drink and the success of the night, and almost dragged me onto the bed. Her hands, always nimbler than one would have expected, prised the belt away from my trousers. It flashed across my mind that if she were to undress me, it would be something of a relief, as I had no great desire to keep the Hitler outfit on; it stank of smoke, quite apart from anything else. She slipped out of her underwear, tossing it as if contemptuously to the side of the room; I had a momentary wish to pick it up and put it in the linen basket. ‘What do you think we could do with this?’ she asked, dangling the belt like a conjuror in front of me.

For a long moment I was genuinely flummoxed by her enquiry: I could not imagine what answer I was supposed to give. Screwing up her eyes in playful impatience, she made me understand that she wanted me to hit her. She turned her back to me and I complied with her wish, so half-heartedly that she swivelled her head to look at me in big-eyed reproach. ‘Do you not want me?’

I had never yet worked out a way of answering this question except by succumbing to the things she asked for; because after all, I did desire her desperately, and could not bear that she might think otherwise. I brought the belt down on the smooth skin of her lower back, bringing a little gasp out of her. I felt her shudder; her skin was prickly with goosebumps and she gnawed her lip. Her arms, almost comically long and able at times like this, reached around to grab hold of me. After that, things progressed quickly.

When it was over, I put the belt with the rest of the uniform and hung the whole ensemble carefully in the wardrobe, while Rose as usual asked rhetorically why I couldn't leave things until the morning, why I had to be so tidy, and why it was that her toes always poked out of the bed, no matter what angle she lay at. I avoided giving the obvious answer, that she was the fifth tallest woman in Great Britain.

She fell asleep with her head on my chest, but shuffled and grumbled her way across the bed as time went by. Over a period of an hour or more I felt growing, until it was impossible to ignore, the certainty that I was not going to be able to sleep at all. I looked at the ceiling and at the wall behind which Charles could be heard snoring. The bedroom, which had seemed dark before, looked less and less so; the angles and fittings of the room sat there refusing to disappear into my dream, the light from the street was glaring and the silence had an antagonistic quality, it seemed to my tired mind as though everyone in the world knew quite well that I was the only one not asleep.

I tossed many thoughts over and over in my head, thinking, for example, of Ralf in the army base – he had sent a letter the other day, just a few badly spelt lines, but full of little things we alone could understand and enjoy. In the letter, he mocked my father for insisting on going to work despite having both pneumonia and a broken toe. I thought of my father bustling around the building site, checking on idlers, sometimes doing the work for them. Eventually, my thoughts settled on the night just gone. Something was not quite right.

My feeling at the time, that I was only partly responsible for what was coming out of my mouth and indeed for everything I was doing, was reprised now as I tried to relive what was just past; I recalled it like a film rather than an experience. Robert's looming face, his little sceptical expressions. What had he meant by his nasty comment about killing Jews? He was Jewish, certainly, but hadn't he encouraged me to do the Hitler act in the first place – wasn't he indeed the whole reason I had ever done it? I could not get, in the apt English phrase, 'the measure' of him, I could not quite see past my general distaste for him and the way he spoke to Rose.

I thought about the way people had laughed at my take-off of Hitler. I was certainly getting very good at it, and, of course, the more closely I resembled the murderous tyrant, the funnier it was. This equation should not have bothered me by now: I had long since rationalised the fact that I was making entertainment from Hitler. I had all sorts of arguments in favour of it: we all knew it was a joke, and so on. I chased this feeling of vague unease through the night without getting hold of it.

There was no sense in trying to discuss this with Rose, since she would either laugh or be annoyed; so I turned to Charles who always had time and inclination to discuss abstract matters. 'I am worried that, perhaps, I am simply up there getting laughs out of being Hitler,' I said.

'As opposed to . . .?'

'I mean,' I said, haltingly, 'what I mean to say is, I don't want people to laugh thoughtlessly at – at the fact I am pretending to be a killer . . .'

'You would ideally like everyone to consider precisely the context of your impersonation of Hitler, and the ramifications of their decision to laugh,' said Charles with a little smile.

'I suppose. Yes.'

'Well, George Bernard Shaw had something to say on this subject. "The lesson intended by an author is hardly ever the one the world chooses to learn",' quoted Charles. 'He said it in relation to a pamphlet which James Oswald wrote, about Fanny Adams, a little girl who was murdered in 1867.'

'Was he very influential, James Oswald?' I asked.

'He was a marvellous man,' said Charles.

There was a jaunty knock at the door and in came Julian, traces of fake blood still about his face from his Ripper tour earlier that day. 'Afternoon, folks! Hope I'm not butting in?'

'Charles was just telling me about Fanny Adams,' I said.

'That sounds like Charles,' said Julian, with a chuckle. Charles raised his eyebrows sportingly.

'Fanny Adams is nowadays slang for "absolutely nothing",' he explained to me.

'Sweet Fanny Adams, sweet FA, sweet fuck-all,' said Julian jauntily. Charles recoiled playfully at the language.

'How have the tours been?' I asked.

'Very good, thanks,' said Julian. 'Bookings up. And I've had one or two nibbles from TV folk since the launch party.'

'Nibbles! Congratulations,' said Charles, straight-faced.

'Rachel about?' asked Julian.

'Trampolining,' said Charles. 'She asked me along, but I try to limit my gymnastic exercise.' The thought of Charles trampolining was very funny. It is hard here to convey the peculiar emphasis that he placed on some words and the enjoyably bizarre quality this gave to a conversation. Hard as well to do justice to the many happy afternoons and evenings I spent in his company. The word 'company' is not found in the vocabulary of the life I now lead.

Christmas was coming, we had been together for nine dizzying months, and the agency gained in stature as Rose continued to work long hours. I went shopping on a farcically overcrowded Oxford Street, and took nearly four hours to find the three items I wanted for her: a Filofax, a boxed set of moisturising and soothing bath oils for her back which came with a free orthopaedic cushion, and a pretty diamond necklace which she had coveted for some time. We had the money: Christmas season had brought me a lot of bookings, as the offices of Great Britain organised parties galore for workers so drunk that merely to appear dressed as Hitler was enough to satisfy them. At some of these affairs I received all manner of drunken abuse, but even so, the work was hardly taxing.

I presented awards – amazing how every firm, no matter how mundane its business, seemed to dish out prizes. I was photographed, at these functions, with the West London Plumber of the Year and someone who had done well for the *Yellow Pages*. At some of these events, there would be a genuine comedian to host the event, so I did not even have to speak very much, or worry about how well things were proceeding, as I had at Peterborough; I simply had to arrive, 'do a bit of Hitler', and go home to Rose again.

I was Master of Ceremonies a couple of times at a bingo

hall, where I was employed to call the numbers at 'theme nights' designed to attract a younger clientele. ('Just have some fun, do some Nazi jokes,' the man said. 'You know, filthy Hun, forty-one, and that.') I was paid £400 to perform a one-second-long walk-on part in a television sketch show, even though they decided during the day to jettison the sketch I had been meant to film, and I left without doing anything at all for the money.

And this was a job! I continually wondered how many other people got through life with so little real effort. When, as often happened in the afternoons, I took over the office and forced Rose to take some time to lie on her back, and she murmured about how considerate I was, she did not realise that I was partly motivated by a feeling that I was simply getting away with too little; I ought to be more productive. This is not to understate my genuine concern for her health. She was forever scraping her elbows, smacking her head, muttering about her 'dodgy heart'. She had only to sit up in bed at night, or come back from the osteopath with a worried face, to give me the 'heeby-jeebies'.

Perhaps this would fade as the relationship wore on. It must do. And perhaps, I thought, she was less vulnerable than I imagined. To find a balance between being aware of her welfare, and wearisomely motherly, was just another of the many skills I was trying to acquire to prevent this affair from vanishing as inexplicably as it had begun.

I had little desire to spend another sterile Christmas at home in Berlin when I could be with Rose, but I hesitated about the idea of taking her to Germany: it still seemed too soon, I was not quite ready for the various strange situations it would give rise to. There was, though, no prospect of her spending Christmas with her family; she had had no contact with them since graduation, other than letters which they forwarded to her, without a covering note. The best solution was for us to stay where we were: Charles was going to see some ancient relative, and we would have the Oswald House to ourselves. But it was going to be hard to tell my father, and Ralf – and besides, I was longing to see Ralf. I settled on a compromise by scheduling a brief visit home for the days straight after Christmas.

My father, of course, accepted the plan with insouciance. '*So, ach so*,' he said. 'Well, we shall look forward to seeing you on the 29th, then.'

Ralf, too, was philosophical. 'Don't sweat it, man,' he said, or something of the kind. 'Me and some of the guys are going to go out drinking Boxing Day and I'll probably be out of action till you turn up.' Once I had hung up, I pondered a while on how odd it seemed, his being so worldly; because he far outstripped me in gregariousness, the process whereby he went from my kid brother to another adult seemed to have occurred very quickly. But it probably always happened that way.

A Christmas party was to be held jointly in our flat and in Charles's. The 18th was the only night we could find when most of our clients were not performing at other people's parties, which testified to the success of our first few months. Even on the 18th, the quietest day of that period, our John Major and Marilyn acts were in action, at, respectively, a club for British Airways staff and a stationery firm's Christmas 'bash'; while Nina had got a relatively lucrative job, or 'gig' as Rose now tended to say, impersonating Basinger in a nightclub on a boat. This appointment had caused some difficulties. On the day after the first night, Rose took a call from the organiser. I saw her shoulders tense and her jaw set as she listened; she chewed on her lip. I went over to rub her back, but she waved me away and started talking about 'the terms of the contract'.

'They asked her to bloody sing,' she told me, after hanging up. 'It wasn't in the contract. She nearly lost her nerve completely by the sound of it.'

'She has that psychological aversion to singing,' I said.

Rose made a clicking sound with her tongue. 'Basinger sings in *The Marrying Man*, apparently. She plays a singer in it.' She let this hang in the air. I thought what a damning thing it was to be sub-standard even in the modest aim of being like someone else. At least I was a lot like Hitler.

Rose hung a sprig of mistletoe from a light fitting on the ceiling and we had crêpe-paper decorations and a CD playing Christmas favourites, and mince pies and punch. Soon, people had begun to flood into the flat. The noise grew to a hum, the lavatory flushed over and over again and the old pipes gasped and groaned. Elvis Leslie was there, in the blue coat which he seemed unable to take off even when not performing. Someone put a plastic mat on the landing outside the flats, on which Julian and Rachel played a game which necessitated a great deal of twisting and contorting. Charles began by shouting out the moves for them, but was then prevailed upon to join in himself. It was a sight to see: Charles, his shirtsleeves rolled up, on all fours with Rachel beside him, like two Olympic sprinters ready to start a very odd race. I performed a duet of the song 'Hound Dog' with our Elvis man, accepting some mockery for the fact that I had thought the song was called 'Handle'.

Nina arrived later in the evening, wearing a pair of foam

reindeer antlers. She was drunk even when she arrived, and soon cornered me. Apparently, that night she had managed to get away with miming the song she was meant to sing.

'Why is it you cannot sing?' I asked.

'It goes back to when I was at school,' she said. 'I had to sing "Little Donkey" in a Christmas concert but I forgot the words and just ended up singing "donkey, donkey" over and over again. People from that school still call me Donkey.'

'What are you going to do if Basinger becomes more well known as a singer?' I asked.

'You have to make sacrifices,' said Nina, raising her voice over the music. 'I'll do whatever it takes.'

'What are you trying to achieve, ultimately?' I asked, immediately fearing I had been rude and made it sound like a challenge.

'I want to be a star,' said Nina. 'One day I want her to be a lookalike for me.' It was unclear whether she meant this as a bold, rhetorical statement of her ambition, or really believed it could happen.

The party swung on into the night. The place was full of people, about half of whom I recognised. I pulled a cracker with Robert – he won easily, almost wrenching my arm out of its socket – and wished him a happy Christmas.

'I'm Jewish,' he said with his sour smile.

'Ah, of course.' As a joke I said, 'Well, happy . . . birthday, then, whenever it might be.'

'My birthday's two days before Christmas Day,' he said, 'so it tends to get overlooked.'

Charles walked under the mistletoe and there was a clamour for him to find a partner to kiss. He made a great demonstration of looking about the place for a suitable female. Rose, scanning the room like a lighthouse, spied

Nina sitting in a chair talking to no one in particular, nursing a drink. She went over and pulled Nina out of her chair. Nina resisted good-naturedly and tried to push Rose away; it made me momentarily nervous. Eventually Nina allowed herself to be chaperoned over to where Charles was waiting. They surveyed each other without enormous enthusiasm, Nina eyeing Charles's beard, Charles ducking out of the way of one of her fake antlers as she leaned in towards him. Everyone around made a good fist of cheering and whistling, and Elvis Leslie sang a couple of bars of some romantic ditty.

A little later, to my surprise, I came upon Charles and Nina chatting quite animatedly on the landing between our rooms; the awkwardness of the kiss had perhaps fashioned an understanding between them. As I approached, in fact, I thought I saw them start guiltily as if they had been having a rather intimate conversation. What an unlikely pair they would be. Charles wagged his head in greeting. 'We were just talking about this house's fine history of Christmas parties,' he said. 'The Oswalds held splendid gatherings here throughout the 1870s.' I thought, not for the first time, how much like a history book he sounded. 'Little Florrie played the piano downstairs and Lord Tennyson sang "God Rest Ye Merry Gentlemen" . . . Wilkie Collins injured his hip falling down these stairs after mixing drink with the medicines he took for gout.' There was a clamour from our flat; something entertaining had happened.

'How come all these famous people came round here?' asked Nina, distracted by the noise.

'Well, Oswald was a major, er . . .' said Charles. 'Tessa was determined to make the house a social hub for the literati. Of course, ideally she wanted James to write a masterpiece himself. However . . .'

The clapping and cheering flared up again in our flat. Nina took Charles by the arm and used him to steady herself as she stood up. 'Let's go in there!' she said. Charles looked very much younger when talking to women, I observed. He allowed himself to be dragged away. The plastic mat was still lying there. I had the feeling that perhaps our tenure was going to revive this building's long-dead reputation as a party venue.

The hullabaloo in our flat had again been occasioned by the mistletoe. Julian had become the latest to wander under it, and was being cajoled into finding someone to kiss. After a lot of bantering and finger-pointing, Rachel came forward and Julian took her arms rather too easily and kissed her lightly on the lips. There was ribald cheering and applause and the two of them shared a second kiss and a third. 'He has well and truly satisfied the conditions imposed by the mistletoe,' said Charles, with a twitch of his thick eyebrows.

'Yes, professional as ever,' he added, as Julian returned for yet another kiss. There was more hysteria among the spectators and Elvis Leslie thrust his pelvis about in an unattractively suggestive manner.

'It seems I was the only one not to know that those two were in love,' I said to Charles.

'I did not know either,' he remarked.

Extraordinary, I thought, that Charles and Rachel and Julian and all these other people are now a part of my life, when, less than eighteen months ago, I had been nothing but a foreign postgrad student struggling to settle in Cambridge. I looked around the room, at the lookalikes, friends of lookalikes and assorted others crammed beneath the centuries-old ceiling, and last of all, at my mighty girlfriend as she stood with a hand on Julian's shoulder, a hand on

Rachel's, teasing them about their performance under the mistletoe. It made me feel that anything was possible, that no state of affairs was too far-fetched to come into existence. Had I been more sober I would have seen the fearful, as well as the exciting, potential of this principle.

>> Alexandra

They left a copy of the book on everyone's desk. *Revolution and Restoration*, boasted the title in a big vaguely antique-looking font, with a little red flash in the top right-hand corner: '*Accompanies the TV series*'. Our athlete-historian was on the cover, standing with a big grin outside a castle. I flicked straight to the back page, read it, read it again.

'They've left my name out.'

'What?' Helen said through a mouthful of bread. She was mentally already on the Champs-Elysées. She'd been out to buy a Travel Scrabble set for the train, and had pointedly brought back a baguette for lunch.

'My name's not here. Remember I found the thing about Charles II holding his wife's—?'

'Holding his wife's what, I'd like to know?' said Albert the receptionist, dumping a sackload of paper onto a surface. All the neatly addressed envelopes with the hopeful letters of introduction inside.

'So I was meant to be on the list . . .' I said, feebly.

'All this to go?' said Albert.

Helen opened her copy, dropping a crumb immediately between the centre pages. She flicked to the back. 'You're right. Not there.' She shook her head. 'Bastards.'

In the lunch-hour I went off on my own, feeling I could only look petty by staying around and whining about the injustice. In a café rarely visited by people from the office, I sat rereading the letter I'd received from Andreas that morning.

Dear Alexandra,

Thank you for continuing to write to me in spite of my failure, last week, to reciprocate. This lapse was caused by various difficulties which I have had. I very much hope I will see you again at a time in the near future.

'Love letter?'

I jumped and put the letter on my lap.

'It's not a love letter, Helen.' I was getting a bit tired of jokes of this kind. 'How did you know I was here?'

'I trailed you,' she said with a grin. 'You're very unobservant. I'm not just going to let you brood over a shitty book, am I?'

'You're going to Paris tomorrow, then I'll brood as much as I want.'

'So what is it?' She reached into my lap for the paper. I squirmed away from her. We both started to laugh. A man trying to read the *Financial Times* glared at us. I decided it was time to let Helen into this.

'OK, I've been writing to a guy in prison,' I began.

I told her more or less everything, everything from my side

of it, at least; I only gave her sketchy details of Andreas's story, mentioning the Hitler thing, the lookalike agency, but nothing of the increasingly personal details we were starting to get into. 'So I'm thinking of just saying "Fuck it" and going to visit him again later this week,' I said.

'Wow,' said Helen. 'I really thought it was a boyfriend. This is much more interesting.'

'It's much stranger. I don't really know what's going to happen. I don't know why I'm so interested in him.'

'I can't believe you said you had an aunt with cancer,' said Helen, shaking her head in mock disgust. 'Well, you should definitely go and see him again. No one's going to care who's in work for the next week or so.' She thought for a moment. 'Are you sure there's not a sexual frisson?'

'Helen, please. He's hardly seen a woman for ten years.'

'All the better. He'll be hungry for it.'

I tried to imagine Andreas dressed up as Hitler and in bed with Rose. I was on the point of sharing this with Helen, but it would have been disloyal to him, somehow. I could imagine how she would laugh at the idea; how almost anyone would laugh, in fact.

'So how come Gareth is bothering to do all this for you, anyway? Are you paying him?'

'No . . .'

'Are you making it worth his while in some way?'

'No, Helen – believe it or not, he is doing it out of the kindness of his heart.'

'He hasn't got any kindness in his heart. He wants something. Hey . . .' She patted her watch and we got up. The man with the newspaper glared at us and on the way back we laughed at the memory of the man at Spitalfields complaining about the 'love-in'. I put the letter safely in my bag and emailed Claire asking her to make me an appointment for tomorrow.

When I got home, Dan, Trixie and the returned Gareth were all there, watching a comedy show on TV. They were just back from the gym. Trixie was wearing jogging bottoms and one of Dan's T-shirts, and had her elf-feet up on the arm of a sofa and was eating yoghurt off her fingers from a pot propped between her knees, which I had bought the other day. With her other hand she was picking things up from a coffee table, looking at them, discarding them again. Gareth's hair had grown out while he was away; it now sat in unruly little tufts on his head. He glanced up and gave me a half-wave.

'How was America?' I asked, across my brother and his girlfriend.

'Yeah, fine,' said Gareth. Our eyes met and parted.

'What's this?' said Trixie, reading a leaflet and thinking out loud as was her habit. 'Oh, it's about Jack the Ripper? You can do a tour of all the murder sites?'

'That sounds a blast,' said Dan.

'I think we should do it for Halloween?' said Trixie. 'Is this yours?' She turned to me.

'Well, I . . . I brought it home, yes.'

'All right,' said Dan. 'I like a bit of murder.'

'You'll come, won't you, Gareth?' said the relentless Trixie, and then gestured vaguely in my direction. 'The four of us could go.'

'Or what we could do,' said Gareth, as if struck by an idea, 'is not bother.'

'Oh, come on,' said Dan. 'What else have you got planned for Halloween? Or is it just a bit too simplistic for Sir Noddy, American Correspondent?'

Gareth sighed, reddening a little. 'All right. The 31st, right? I'll add it to my diary of shitty things I'm doing after work.'

'Do it for Alex,' said Dan. 'It's her leaflet!'

'It's not my leaflet,' I objected. 'I just brought it home.'

'In a way, it belongs to all of us,' said Gareth, deadpan. The other two laughed and I felt that the joke was somehow at my expense; and, somehow, I had now been made responsible for what could prove to be quite a bad night out.

I went back to my room thinking that I would see if there was an opportunity to corner Gareth and at least exchange words of some kind about the manuscript. Maybe he'd be jet-lagged and go to bed early. But after a couple of hours they went out, and that was the last I heard until the early hours, when I was woken up, not for the first time, by the shrill sound of giggling from our bathroom and the footsteps of my brothers' coked-up friends tottering along the corridor. Once, my door was pushed open by mistake. I lay there and waited for them to go away.

Since Andreas's command of English was obviously so good, I thought, it would have saved me an awful lot of trouble if he could just have written his memoirs in my language instead of his. Perhaps tomorrow I would just cut to the chase, ask him to tell me everything, so we could cut out this frustrating middleman and I could stop feeling I owed Gareth something.

I boarded the train at London Bridge with the same clammy feeling as on the previous occasion I'd been to the prison. This time, my excuse was a 'family emergency' and I had made my claim the day before, late in the day, after a faked phone call which I 'took' out in reception – Albert was asleep over the paper – before returning to the office looking flustered. It was a lot of effort, lying, but I was convinced it was worth it.

The train was littered with fast-food boxes, and again there was the black woman with a loud radio. I picked out the odd phrase: 'There will be terrible weeping and wailing.' It took a long time for the doors to open, as if the driver was deliberating whether it was fair to make people get off here. I walked down the piss-smelling tunnel, along the road and across at the lights to the prison car park.

This time at least, I had an idea what to expect. Among the crowd of visitors, I recognised some of the drawn faces I had seen last time. I'd decided I was not going to seek out Claire afterwards this time, though she did say she would be at St John's today. The gatehouse keeper, Dean, said, 'Lovely to see you again,' as I waited for admission. I thought he was about two visits away from asking for my phone number. Andreas was sitting in the same seat as before, but, I felt, had a healthier look about him; a bit more colour in his face. He took my hand briefly as I sat down opposite him.

'I'm very happy you have returned,' he said.

I asked him how his week had been. Unexpectedly, he began to answer the question in some detail. He'd been keenly watching a series late at night on Channel 4 about people undergoing plastic surgery. The food had been marginally better than usual. And he'd been sleeping better than he was accustomed to, he said, and hadn't been troubled by dreams. I asked him what he normally dreamed of. 'Frightening disasters,' he said. 'And dreams in which the past is still happening and I wake up, and it is very upsetting that it is not.'

We then talked about my week: our mother's visit, the nonsense with the lack of acknowledgement in the book, the return of Gareth and the fact that it was seemingly impossible for me to get him animated. 'In fact,' I said, 'it's only when reading your manuscript that he seems interested in communicating with me.'

I realised, as I was saying this, that this was one of the things stopping me from simply bypassing the manuscript and asking Andreas to tell me the story here and now. It wasn't just a lack of confidence with Andreas; I was also enjoying the process of the translation itself. I tried to resist following this mental strand.

After about half an hour, the conversation had reached a natural lull and, anxious to keep it going, I decided to risk mentioning what I had been up to the other night.

'I went to the James Oswald House,' I said. Andreas looked at me with a furrowed brow as if I had given him a tough proposition to consider.

'Why did you go there?'

'I just wanted to see the place where you lived.'

'And,' he said slowly, 'how did you find it?'

I was already not sure whether I should have got us on to this. It could hardly comfort him to hear that his former home was now being converted into flats.

'I saw Charles Steel,' I said.

Andreas's eyes opened wide. 'What?'

'Well, I think it must have been him,' I said. Andreas stared blankly at me. 'Massive grey beard. Grey hair. And – well, the estate agent called him Mr Steel. He was living in the flat opposite . . . well, opposite the one that must have been . . . must have been . . . yours.'

I tailed off until the final word was almost inaudible, because the change that now took place in Andreas was quite unnerving. He began to swallow violently as if trying to clear an obstruction from his throat. His nose was wrinkled and twitched up and down as if he'd had something horrible waved in front of it. He scraped his chair back slightly from the table.

'Charles is in London?'

'Maybe I shouldn't have—'

'Charles is still in London!' said Andreas, shaking his little head. 'And yet he does not visit! And yet I do not hear from him in all this time!' He thumped on the table. It was a curious, sadly ineffectual little gesture. The people at the next table glanced at us.

'I'm not certain it was—' I said, unconvincingly.

'Julian, that is a different matter,' said Andreas, jabbing his finger at me. 'Julian, I believe, is abroad. Julian and Rachel, yes, they have other things to do, they are in Australia. From Julian I even received a letter not so long ago. From Charles, nothing! I can understand, yes, he was guilty that I ended up here, he thought himself responsible after the court case, but how could I ever bear a grudge! Why in God's name does he not visit?' I looked at Andreas's hands, which had started to shake slightly, and sat there feeling absolutely helpless.

This was what I'd always been afraid of if I tried to be too personal. This was the sort of thing that put sensible people off visiting prisoners they didn't really know. I could feel eyes on us from all over the room, and I suspected that people were looking at me wondering what relation I was to Andreas; and understandably so, because it would have been clear to anyone that I was out of my depth. Across the room, I saw Claire pop her head around the door. She seemed to have an extremely keen sensor for trouble.

'It is my fault for upsetting you,' I said. If anything, my real fault was in trying to poke my nose into something I still wasn't close to fully understanding.

'Ah, it is your fault, is it?' Andreas repeated with a bitter little laugh. 'Not Charles's fault for abandoning me. Not my fault for landing here. Not Rose's fault for—' He stopped dead.

I was poised between asking him any one of a dozen questions, and fearing I had already gone too far. The fact was I didn't really know him; I'd been conned into feeling as if I did by reading his story, like people who think they know a film star personally from having watched them.

'Perhaps,' I said, glancing up like someone in an exam as Claire, the invigilator, wove her way across the room, 'perhaps he hasn't been . . . very well. I mean – perhaps he isn't quite in his right mind.'

'He was never entirely in his right mind,' said Andreas. He let out a long breath through his teeth and we looked at each other in silence.

The bell rang. It occurred to me that the last time I'd heard a bell of that kind, it was school, and it was always good news. On this occasion, as last time, it left me feeling that I'd failed to make the best of the situation. Andreas grabbed my hand again and thanked me for coming. I said he was welcome. Again, the woman to my right began to cry as she got up. I found myself walking backwards for several paces to avoid turning away from Andreas too quickly.

I was in the Ladies trying to collect my thoughts when Claire came in. She was quite short, I had noticed in the visiting room. She went to a sink and began washing her hands, very thoroughly, as people do when they subconsciously feel that other people, however lovely, are likely to be a bit dirty.

'Can't be too careful with this . . . !' she said, nodding down at her stomach. I agreed brightly.

'Anything on this week?' she asked.

'I'm going on, um, a Jack the Ripper tour,' I said.

'Cool,' said Claire. 'Bob and I went to Rome and you can pretty much . . .' the stream of water stopped and she pressed down on the tap again, 'pretty much stand on the exact spot where . . . was it Julius Caesar got bumped off? Such an amazing trip.'

I said it must have been, and inched towards the door.

'So Andreas seemed a bit upset?' she said.

I made a sudden decision to tell her about Charles. I was not doing myself any favours by trying to handle this situation without knowing all the facts. Claire was the one who worked with prisoners all the year round.

'I made the mistake of mentioning one of his old friends,' I said.

Claire listened with the usual hums and nods, scrubbing liquid soap from her hands, as I described how I'd seen Charles Steel at the Oswald House. 'I mean – I think Andreas assumed he'd disappeared years ago,' I said. 'Disappeared years ago,' I was forced to repeat, over a roar of air, as she punched the button on the hand-dryer. Someone else came in and I lowered my tone surreptitiously. 'I was really surprised that he's still there, after . . . well, after all the stuff that must have happened.'

'A bit of a stick-in-the-mud?' said Claire, glancing at herself in the mirror.

'He must be,' I said. A second passed. 'What . . . what did Andreas actually . . . what did he do?'

'Oh, it's confo,' said Claire. 'Completely confo. I'm not allowed to know myself unless he tells me.' She toyed with her hair to no real effect. 'Don't know why I'm fretting over my appearance. I'm going to be big as a whale soon!'

I hesitated.

'Do you think I should approach Charles Steel and – and get him to come in and see Andreas?'

Claire finally gave me her full attention.

'Listen,' she said, 'you know, the thing is, prisoners do get lonely. Anyone would. Without . . . company. They start to lose their perspective. Do you know what I mean?'

I said I did.

'WriteToAConvict,' she said, touching the badge, 'is all about building that bridge between – well, us and them. The community and . . . and them.' She touched me on the hip. 'People like you, absolute stars like you are what it's all about.'

I waited for her to answer the question I'd asked, then there was the sharp sound of her mobile. She began delving in her bag to find the phone. 'What I'm saying, I suppose . . .' she said. 'If you think you can help Andreas, you should . . .' A packet of tissues fell out of her bag as she got the phone out. I bent over and picked them up for her. She gave me a wink and walked out of the toilets with the phone to her ear. On my way back out through the car park, I walked past her little blue Fiat and wondered how long it would be before a BABY ON BOARD sticker appeared on its back window.

At Aldgate East station, a man dressed all in black was holding up a sign which said, simply, 'RIPPER'. Passing commuters, on their way home, looked at us with the vague contempt Londoners feel for tourists. There was no sign of the others. A large party of people were chattering away excitedly in a foreign language. Their tracksuits suggested that they were a Russian sports team – at least I was pretty sure it was Russian – on tour in the UK. Nearly all of them were clutching leaflets.

'In a minute we will start the tour,' said the man, after

slapping his sign to get attention. 'We'll be visiting some of the authentic scenes of the Jack the Ripper story. I warn you,' he added quite aggressively, 'there are some Ripper tours which leave out crucial sites on the way. You can walk round Whitechapel for two, three hours and not even see where some of the horrifically murdered victims lived. There are some very sub-standard tours,' he repeated. Just as he was finishing this little rant, Dan came into view, tugging Trixie by the wrist. She had on a fascinatingly inappropriate pink Barbie dress and a sort of bomber jacket. Behind them traipsed Gareth.

He was wearing a big green coat like Paddington Bear, and had the face of someone about to undergo dental work. I gave him a small, self-conscious wave.

'This tour will not spare you any of the horrors,' the guide said. 'Dare you follow me?'

'Yes,' said Dan, quite loudly. There was laughter from some quarters. The guide, pretending not to hear, turned on his heel and everyone followed.

We trailed along through well-lit streets which, the guide kept reminding us, were once 'dark and sinister'. We turned into Fournier Street, a stone's throw from the Oswald House itself. There was a crane at one end of the street and I thought of Charles Steel waiting for the house to be turned into flats. Where would he go? What was he doing at this moment?

'This was once the Frying Pan public house,' said the guide, as we plodded on, 'which Mary Nichols was seen leaving shortly before she was brutally set upon and mutilated. And we're now coming onto Brick Lane, where you can smell the curry houses which the area is renowned for.'

On and on it went, down cobbled alleys, through nearly invisible archways and passages – the guide certainly knew his stuff. We stopped regularly to peer reverently at brickwork where there had once been famous 'Ripper graffiti', old brewery buildings, office blocks that had been whorehouses which victims had left 'for a last, fateful time' on the nights they died.

By the time we reached Mitre Square, I was getting a bit tired of it. Gareth had his collar up and his hands in his pockets, a resigned look on his face. Dan was keeping up a satirical commentary each time the host's back was turned, while Trixie bounded along like a novelty dog by his side.

'We are now going to follow the route walked by Mary Kelly just before she became the Ripper's final victim,' said the guide, pausing in another passageway, hemmed in by grimy buildings on either side. 'She was skinned, and her breasts cut off.' Trixie checked her reflection in a window. 'It was a murder with the trademark brutality of the Ripper.'

'I didn't realise he'd actually copyrighted it,' Dan muttered. Trixie gave him an affectionate shush.

'Poor Mary,' said the guide as if he knew her, 'was unrecognisable . . .'

It was at this moment that my brother dug his fingers into the back of my neck. I let out a small pig-like squeal. 'Mary! Don't die!' said Dan loudly. Quite a number of people laughed, and one of the Russians shook Dan's hand. The guide had turned his back and was leading us mercilessly towards the spot of Kelly's death. I glanced around furiously at Dan, but he had already begun nuzzling Trixie's neck. I didn't look to see what Gareth was thinking. I avoided looking at anyone until we were in the pub on Brick Lane at the end of the tour.

'Well, that was cracking,' said Dan, on his way to the bar. 'I might go on one of the other ones.' The guide had finished up by giving us leaflets for the Execution Tour and the Madness

Walk, which took in former asylums. Dan put the leaflet down as a coaster for his pint. One of the Russians whom Dan had befriended came up to him and asked for his email address. Soon Dan was being taken to meet the rest of the Russians, who were standing in a huge mass of dark coats in a corner by a quiz machine. Trixie followed behind, watched by dozens of male eyes. I was left sitting next to Gareth, who was elevated well above me on his bar stool, and sipped his beer with a pensive expression.

'Did you want to swap . . . ?' I suggested, looking up at him.

Gareth shrugged. 'It's OK.'

'You know,' I said, 'this wasn't my idea. I just happened to pick up the leaflet while I was . . . while I was looking at the Oswald House.'

'I didn't say it was your idea,' said Gareth mildly, sipping his beer.

'I thought you were looking at me like . . .' I said, then stopped, realising how neurotic I must sound. 'Anyway. I'm sorry you had a boring time.'

'It's just . . .' said Gareth slowly. 'It's just Dan. I'm really finding him tough going.'

This was unexpected. I tried not to smile. 'Really?'

He looked over to the bar. Dan and Trixie were being toasted by their new Russian friends, glasses clinked, heads were tossed back. 'He's just got this inane girlfriend and he goes around cramming himself with this stupidly powerful shit to go one better than everyone. I don't know.' He shook his head.

'I mean,' he added, looking down at the table, the damp leaflet – APPALLING FUN! – with the beer-glass imprint stamped into the middle of it. 'I mean, it's one thing to appreciate that a tour or whatever is a bit dumb. Another thing to not be chipping in the entire bloody time like you think you're Oscar bloody Wilde.'

'Dan's always taken the piss out of things,' I said.

'So,' said Gareth, 'what were you doing at the Oswald House?'

'Oh,' I said. 'I wanted to see, you know, where it all took place. The story.'

'I've, um, I've got a bit more of it,' he muttered. 'Did it on the plane home. Don't want to spoil it for you but it gets weird, well, even weirder.'

My heart quickened slightly. 'Charles Steel is still living there, you know.'

Gareth put his drink down. 'What – you saw him?'

I nodded. 'It's just round the corner from here.' My nerve was hardening. 'D'you . . . did you want to . . . ?'

Gareth ran his fingers through his hair. 'A'right.'

Dan and Trixie didn't notice as we went out into the night. It had started to rain softly; Gareth zipped his coat up. I led the way, hardly looking back to check if he was there. Waiters, brandishing Indian menus, kept stepping into our path to describe special offers; I heard Gareth say, 'No thanks,' politely to each one. Out of a pub came a big group of Halloween revellers all wearing masks like the face in Munch's *Scream*. One dropped hers in a puddle and stooped to pick it up, her short skirt flapping in the wind. We came onto Cloth Street and Gareth was level with me.

The Oswald House was in front of us. It was raining fairly hard. The street was dark, with lamps thinly spread. The house stood tall and silent, with no light from any window, looking like a place which had played its part in things and was now an onlooker.

'Fucking vandals!' said Gareth suddenly. He gestured in

vague anger at the house. 'A hundred and fifty years old – probably older – how old is it?'

I spread my hands helplessly.

'And they're tearing it down,' Gareth went on, 'to make poncy little flats for people like Dan and . . . and me.'

Rain was running down my face. I couldn't think of a thing to say.

'Andreas was very pissed off that Charles had never visited,' I said. 'I wonder what happens at the end of the story.'

'I'm doing it as fast as I can,' Gareth muttered, through the rain, which was getting heavier every second.

'I didn't mean . . .' I said. 'I know. I didn't mean . . .' I thought about explaining what had happened with Andreas, maybe trying to talk him into pressing the buzzer for STEEL and coming up with me to confront the man who should have been Andreas's other friend.

'Should we be going?' said Gareth. 'It's foul out here.'

He turned without waiting for me to pass comment. I felt almost insulted that, once again, the conversation was suddenly being presented as a sort of test I had failed; or was I overreacting? I trudged along half a pace behind him, a little bit indignant in a futile way, shuddering in a sudden wave of chilly air. Unexpectedly, as if he could hear the shudder, he turned.

'I would offer you my coat,' he said, 'but it would be ludicrously big on you.'

A wet strand of hair was clinging to my forehead. I smiled through the rivulets trickling down my face. 'I could do with an umbrella,' I said.

Gareth peered up to the heavens. 'You could take it, and put it over your head.'

'But then you'd be wet. And so would your coat.'

'Well,' he said, 'we're both going to be the losers if we stand here discussing it.' He held out the fold of his coat as if to invite me to shelter under it, but began walking at the same time, and I ended up trailing along in much the same way as before.

Dan was clowning around hyperactively, doing some sort of Cossack dance with the Russians, when we got back; it crossed my mind to wonder whether he'd done a pill in the loos or something. It was hard to remember for sure what he was like before he had a drug habit. One minute he was a few years above me at school, the next it seemed he worked in London and did what our mother called 'London things' – though she'd say it differently if she knew precisely what a lot of those 'things' were.

'We're going to go on somewhere,' said Dan. He named a club.

'A'right,' muttered Gareth. 'I'm up for one more.'

Maybe it was my sodden clothes or the sight of Trixie coming back towards us with a miniature hairdryer in her hand, but it was an easy decision. 'I'll head home,' I said. Gareth met my eyes and looked as if he might make an attempt to change my mind, then he looked away. Dan nodded. I said my goodnights and went out, brushing my wet hair behind my ears.

It had been an odd night, but getting home, I felt somehow invigorated. Maybe all I needed was to go out more, even if the company available wasn't ideal. There was that just-been-raining smell in the air and huge ditches of water by the side of the road as I walked home from the tube station. The river, seen from our flat, looked almost ready to burst its banks. Moonlight came streaming in over the water and, even with all the lights on, there was, once again, a slightly ghostly quality to the apartment. I had a bath and went to bed. All the plodding up and down East End streets had left my limbs heavy and, in the end, I nearly fell asleep in my clothes.

About three o'clock, there was a hammering at the front door. I fell out of a dream and lay there uneasily listening to the sound. It was raining hard outside again, I sensed. I was irritated to be awake and felt momentarily disconcerted, like Andreas waking up after falling asleep at teatime on the comedy night. The hammering continued. I slid out of bed, pulled on some clothes and went to the door.

'Who is it?'

'It's Gareth,' said a mournful voice.

He squelched through the door as soon as I opened it a crack, and immediately stooped to prise off his shoes, which were leaking water; he tossed them contemptuously onto the doormat, where they lay like bath toys. I got a look at him in the harsh hall light. He was so wet that he seemed to squeak with moisture at every step. His face was pink, his teeth were chattering. I had never really seen anyone's teeth chatter other than when Dan did it deliberately to get the central heating turned on when we were kids. Gareth fumbled with the buttons of his coat – his hands were like bricks – and I resisted the urge to help him. His hair was matted over his eyes, and water poured out of it over his face, as if from a sponge.

'You're so wet!' I found myself saying.

Gareth gritted his teeth to ward off any number of sarcastic responses to this. He separated himself from his coat, which was glued to him like another skin, and hung it on a radiator.

'I was knocking on the door,' he said, 'for fifteen fucking minutes.'

'I thought you would have a key . . .'

'Dan has it,' he said very quietly.

'Are you not with him?'

'Jesus Christ,' said Gareth, 'does it look like I'm with him?' He went into the bathroom, trailing water everywhere, and I could hear him, with his frozen hands, struggling even to get a grip on the bath taps.

'I mean,' I said, raising my voice over the water, 'didn't you go off together?'

There was quite a long pause. I thought of going back to bed and leaving him to it. Suddenly the door swung open and he came out, bare-chested with a towel wrapped around his middle. His shoulders were amazingly pink.

'Be careful you don't catch something,' I said. 'I mean, going from cold to hot—'

'Unfortunately,' said Gareth, spitting out the words like acid, 'there was some larking about under the influence of drugs and I fell in the river.'

I tried not to laugh thinking about this, but it was too hard.

'Yes,' said Gareth bitterly, 'it was very very funny. Your brother thought it was fantastic. Of course, he was off his tits, but then he always is.'

He slammed the door so hard, it sprang back open before he could lock it. I went into the kitchen and boiled the kettle.

It was all so childish; these grown men overdoing whatever they were taking, messing around, one of them getting into trouble, the rest of them laughing and running away.

I made tea and stirred honey into it, looking out of the kitchen window. The rain had eased off and left a very shiny, clear night. The moon was nearly full and the rooftops were bathed in silver light; it was lighter than some mornings at this time of year.

Gareth came in, swathed in towels, as I was tapping the spoon on the edge of the cup. 'You really don't have to fuss about,' he mumbled.

'You should probably be in bed,' I said. 'And you should stay there tomorrow.'

'Yes, well,' said Gareth. 'Unfortunately, I have a job.'

I watched his Adam's apple bulge as he gulped down the tea. His tongue peeped out of his mouth and touched his lips. I put my hand briefly against his arm; he was still stone cold.

'Thanks, Alex,' he said. I tried to think whether I'd ever heard him use my name before. I said he was welcome.

A burglar alarm sounded faintly from down the street.

'Did you say . . .' I began. 'Did you say you'd done more of the translation?'

'What? Yeah. I'm getting near the end of it.' He looked the other way and piled sugar into his tea, spilling some on the tabletop, the spoon clinking against the mug in his unsteady hands.

There was a long silence. It was a quarter to four in the morning. In an hour or so, the first people would be getting up for work.

'Well,' he said at last, 'I've never looked such a moron in my life.'

'I'm sure there have been times you looked a bigger moron,' I said.

Gareth looked at me in surprise and then laughed. 'Yes. Perhaps you're right. Well . . .' he added, grimly, 'better get to bed before the landlord drags himself in.'

'Can I have the . . . ?' I asked. 'I'm sorry, I can get it in the morning.'

He rose and went to his room. I followed hesitantly, staying well back.

'Well, are you coming then?' he asked. 'Or do you want me to send it by recorded delivery?'

I came to the door. He handed me a pile of papers, thicker than any of the previous ones.

'There's so much of it!' I said.

He shrugged. 'Plane was delayed on the—' He broke into a ghastly cough. His lungs sounded rusty: I almost expected him to bring up some of the river water.

'You shouldn't go to work tomorrow,' I said. 'I mean it.'

He looked at me for a while and then smiled. 'You're my favourite flatmate,' he said, closing the door gently behind him.

☞ ANDREAS

Our visit to Germany was all booked. Rose disliked travelling by air for the obvious reasons, but we were able to negotiate a special seat for her by offering ten tickets to one of my shows for members of the airline.

'I warn you,' I told my brother on the phone, 'she's quite unusual-looking . . .'

'Unusual?' he asked. 'Tall and blonde, that's what I heard! That's what all women should be like!'

'Well,' I said, 'it's not quite as simple as that . . .'

'Let me guess,' he said, 'does she have a big birthmark or a mole?'

'No—'

'That thing where your eyes look in different directions?'

'No, it's—'

'A stammer?'

'No, she speaks fine, but—'

'Is she black or something?' he suddenly asked.

I was taken aback. 'No, I've told you, she's . . . blonde, and—'

'Just checking,' he said. 'Hey, chill, keep it a secret till I meet her. Is it something that I'll notice straight away?'

'Most probably,' I said.

Although it would not be released in Britain for a while, details of Kim Basinger's latest film – *The Marrying Man* – were now widely known among her fans, not to mention imitators, in this country. Basinger not only played a nightclub singer in the movie, but sang several versions of jazz and swing classics. Rose and I watched a clip of her performance on a film-review programme, along with Charles who had just dropped by; though we suspected that he planned it to coincide with the show, as he made a great pretence of never deliberately watching the TV.

'She sings very well,' I said. 'But the song is rather unrealistic.' Basinger was reeling off a seemingly endless long list of people, animals and insects who might be expected to make love. The audience whistled and twirled smoke from their cigars.

'Unrealistic!' Rose hooted. 'This is a famous song, you idiot! "Let's Do It", by Cole Porter.'

'It does get rather tiresome,' Charles agreed. 'Seventy or so examples would have sufficed.'

'You're both heathens,' said Rose cheerfully. Downstairs, the grandfather clock clunked and struck eleven melancholy chords. Rose played her fingers down my side as if along the keys of a piano.

'That was Kim Basinger, who, of course, actually began her career as a singer . . .' the host said.

Rose ran her tongue over her lip. 'I wonder what Nina thought of that.'

The three of us turned our minds to Nina in her tiny flat. She had reluctantly begun taking singing lessons, from an eccentric old woman in Knightsbridge who did it free in exchange for Nina's feeding her cats. Rose had severe doubts about this woman's credentials, and had once suggested to Nina that it would be advisable to consult a more established tutor.

'Well, if you show me where I can magically find the money to do that . . .' said Nina sharply.

'You've got to speculate to accumulate,' said Rose, and Nina said something about how no one worked harder than her to get to the top. Unfortunately, this was probably true, but it did not change Nina's problem, which was not so much a matter of economy as fear.

'You need to confront her about it,' I said to Rose once. 'Tell her she has to become braver about singing.'

'Yes, well, hmm,' said Rose. 'We'll do it tomorrow.' This continued to serve as our catchphrase for tasks we did not relish, and such was the intensity of Rose's workload that I was always rather relieved to hear it from her.

Early one evening after her self-imposed office hours, and after the last guests had been nudged through the Oswald House's gift shop (in reality just an ante-room with a few postcards), we were in Koffee Kompany – Charles, Julian, Rachel, Rose and I. Julian and Rachel were an official couple by now, and he always made a great show of petting her hand, kissing her on the cheek and so on, and making endearingly gauche expressions to everyone when her back was turned, to show how delighted he was with his catch.

Julian had reason to celebrate on a professional, as well as romantic, front: he had secured a job presenting a four-part series on Jack the Ripper for BBC Radio Four. The producer had come to see the tour, at Rose's invitation. There was speculation that the series would go on to be adapted for television, which, of course, Julian did nothing to discourage. 'This'll be on the small screen!' he said, drawing an imaginary TV set around his face. 'What about that, eh, Charlie!'

'I do not own a television, as well you know,' said Charles wryly, 'and I would advise you not to discuss it with so much enthusiasm if you wish to remain a member of the Pennyfarthing Club. We once expelled someone for owning a radio.'

When the laughter for this remark had subsided, we went on to the pub where the Pennyfarthing people met. We were well known here, which meant that Rose would avoid being stared at – an important consideration when choosing a spot to socialise. She had an arrangement with a swimming pool where a lifeguard let her in half an hour before it opened to the public, and when eating out, we always chose a restaurant where we could get a private booth.

Charles bought a round of drinks, and, highly uncharacteristically, even he was drinking. Indeed he had downed at least a couple of whiskies by the time I made it through my pint of beer, and his beard was twitching up and down as he made a series of bons mots. He and Rachel exchanged their usual badinage.

'Today,' said Charles, pointing at a picture on the wall of what looked like a giant boulder on a plinth, 'is the 110th anniversary of the day Thomas Lipton shipped Jumbo, the 3,000-pound cheese, to London – which was Oswald's idea.'

'Gosh!' said Rachel, patting Charles on the hand. 'I haven't seen you so excited since the 109th anniversary last year.' Everyone laughed but Julian.

'Why such a massive cheese?' I asked.

'It attracted a great crowd,' said Charles. 'Tessa, his wife, brought the children down to see it. They carved slices off and young Theo got one with a sixpence inside.'

'I've heard of Thomas Lipton,' said Rose, gazing at the monolithic cheese in the photo. In another picture, a policeman, helmet under his arm, was dancing triumphantly with a piece of the cheese in his hand and a sixpence in the other, while Oswald, thickly bearded as ever, looked on smilingly. Tessa, his wife, looked by contrast extremely underwhelmed. 'Funny, he's the one who people still remember.'

'Often the way,' said Charles, 'that posterity rewards people who are the best at promoting themselves, rather than promoting the cause of art or—'

'What art did Oswald actually do, though, Charlie?' asked Julian. 'Wasn't he basically a failed writer?' I thought of commenting that Jack the Ripper, Julian's adopted Victorian, was hardly an admirable figure either, but kept quiet. Charles's eyebrows were very low indeed over his eyes, like grey clouds.

'He "did" a great many works,' said Charles, 'by no means all failures. He published three plays, a collection of comic songs—'

'Hey, you should hear Rachel sing,' said Julian suddenly. 'We were watching Kim Basinger the other night and she absolutely cracked me up.'

'Oh, shut up, Julian,' said Rachel, rolling her eyes.

Charles seemed about to remark on the swift curtailment of the previous topic, but kept quiet. Julian took Rachel's protests as an incitement to prove how keen he was to show her off. 'Don't be so modest!' he said, tweaking her nose as if she were a teddy bear.

'Yes, come on, let's hear it,' I said, thinking it would now be very rude not to.

'Really, it's . . .' Rachel muttered.

'Go on, Rach!' said Rose.

Reluctantly, with a look to say she was indulging everyone, Rachel began to sing. 'Let's do it . . .' She ran a hand through her hair and performed a couple of simpering gestures very much like those we had seen from Basinger in the film clip. Julian burst out laughing and thumped the table as if this were completely spontaneous rather than having been orchestrated by him. As the rest of us began to laugh, Rachel gained confidence and began to flutter her eyelashes and pout. Charles, who was used to seeing her acting talents in the Oswald House, rubbed his chin and gave a soft smile.

I looked at Rose, who was studying Rachel intently, and knew straight away what she was thinking. These days we could not cross the road without seeing someone who reminded her rather of some character from *Cheers*, or order a pizza without her remarking after the delivery boy had gone, 'Was it just me, or did he look exactly like . . .?' Once one was in the habit of spotting lookalikes, they were everywhere. And now right in front of us was an apparent solution to one of the agency's major problems. Rachel's hair was naturally rather closer to Basinger colour than Nina's was, her face could easily be done up to make it similar, and here she was singing, and singing unexpectedly well at that.

'Have you thought about doing that properly?' Rose asked, leaning towards Rachel, as she – seemingly quite abashed by all the attention – took a gulp of her drink through a straw.

'You mean . . . as a lookalike?' said Rachel.

'What a brilliant idea!' said Julian at once.

'I don't know,' said Rachel. 'I'm not really a performer, I just mess around with Charles in the museum . . .'

'I never thought of myself as a performer,' I said, 'but once I started doing my Hitler act I managed to be successful.'

'Yes, we've all heard your rags-to-riches tale,' said Rose, patting me on the head.

'Well, we'll have to see . . .' said Rachel evasively, and the subject was changed by Charles, but I knew Rose would not have forgotten it.

I brought it up later, in bed.

'Do you not think,' I asked, 'it is asking for trouble to take on another Basinger act? Isn't it going to cause resentment?'

'You mean, your buddy Nina will be pissed off.'

'She isn't my buddy,' I objected.

'The fact is,' said Rose, 'she's lucky we're representing her, really. She's a stopgap. I mean, she just doesn't look that much like Kim Basinger. And since she also can't sing . . . to be honest, we might just as well send me to do the act, stooped over.'

'So next time a job comes up for Basinger . . .'

'We'll send them both to the audition,' said Rose. 'Let them decide. What's fairer than that?' While I was considering it, she pulled me onto her and began to kiss my neck, and it was beyond me to say what was fairer than that.

Sure enough, Nina and Rachel each went to audition for the same job, posing as Basinger at a night of corporate entertainment perhaps similar to the one I had fallen into that time in Cambridge. Rose booked them in for auditions on different days so their paths ought not to cross, and we (along with Julian and Charles) were the only people who knew about it. Two whole days of auditioning lookalikes of the same woman, I thought. Perhaps as many as fifty young women passing through the waiting room, nervously eyeing reflections of themselves, listening through the wall to other people doing what sounded like impressions of themselves doing impressions of Kim Basinger, who sat at the top of this food chain of identity, not knowing anything about it.

With her arm grasping mine, I could feel Rose's pulse accelerating as the aeroplane soared into the air. London and its environs were beneath us, the patchwork of greens and yellows. Rose stretched as much as possible of her legs into the gangway.

'Are you sure you wouldn't rather be on a ferry?'

'It's fine,' she said, 'much quicker this way. I mean,' she added after a pause, 'I do have a heart condition so any upheaval of this kind could be my last.' She sniggered.

'Please don't make comments like that,' I said.

'Well, you'd better distract me,' she said. 'Tell me about the people I'm going to meet in Germany.'

I told her about my father and brother. Partly, I was also telling myself these stories, trying to convince myself that I had hardly been away from Germany for a moment and that the wild changes in my life had not altered anything. I tried to prepare her for my father's taciturnity.

'There was one occasion where Ralf broke his leg by falling off a climbing frame,' I told her, 'and my father telephoned me at my friend's house and said, "I shall be a little late to pick you up." Only as an afterthought did he say, "I am going to be at the hospital," and then only when I asked did he tell me, "It's because your brother has fractured his leg in two places." '

Rose laughed. 'So Ralf is in the army now?'

'It's compulsory to do that or to work for the community in some way, after school,' I said. 'I don't think he intends to pursue it any further. Although he has grown into it, in some ways. It's funny how quickly one grows into a role.'

'You mean, like you and Hitler?' said Rose with cheerful derision. 'You really must stop finding parallels between your life and everything else.'

'I was not aware that I was becoming boring,' I said a little stiffly. It had not even been in my mind to suggest such a parallel. Anyway, tease me as she might, Rose's entire business strategy depended on my success. I thought of bringing this up, but it would have been petty. We talked some more about Ralf, how he played the guitar and was a champion at tennis, the way he used to pretend to be dead. I talked about the night the Berlin Wall fell, how Ralf and I danced arm in arm with one of our former teachers. These were random snapshots, really; it is rather hard to summarise a lifelong relationship to a third party. We began our descent. When we had landed, Rose was one of the first to get to her feet – her legs were 'killing her' – and thirty eyes went to her and then turned politely downwards. She waved impertinently at those who were still staring.

Ralf was picking us up from the airport, but he was able to walk right up and grab me on the shoulder, so changed was his appearance. His head was completely shaven, the blonde hair all gone. Instead of the colourful American-label surfwear that had always been his style, he wore a drab grey shirt and jeans, and Dr Martens boots. With him was one of his friends from the army, also with a savage haircut.

'So you're Rose!' he said, in English, reaching up to shake her hand. 'Wow! Have you always been so tall?'

'Not when I was a baby,' she said. Ralf laughed, to my relief, and explained the joke to his friend, who evidently spoke no English. He led us to the car. Ralf's friend got into the front seat, despite what would seem to be Rose's greater claim to this spot, and so we had to clamber into the back.

'Dad's not so good,' Ralf announced, over the whine of the engines. Rose, hunched, was peering out at the *Autobahn* whizzing past, getting her first look at Germany. 'He's going to lose his job. They're making him go part-time.'

'What? Why?'

'*Ach*,' Ralf shrugged, impatiently. 'They say he's getting too old. Of course the problem is there's a lot of immigrant labour.'

'There's a lot of fucking Turks coming over for the jobs,' the friend embellished. I left this untranslated.

My father was pastier and fatter than usual, and unevenly shaven. He looked a good deal older than when I had last seen him. If he was cowed by Rose's height, he did not let it show. '*So, so*,' he said. 'Rose. Welcome to Germany.' This was in English. 'How has the weather been?' he added.

'That's it now,' said Ralf, 'he's used up everything he learned at school.' We all laughed and for a while I thought it was going to work.

My father had mustered a selection of unappetising-looking cold meats and breads, which Rose admired as if this was the specific reason she had come so far. Ralf poured pitchers of water and I noticed that he had a tattoo on his arm, looking like a sword or dagger of some kind.

'What's with the tattoo?' I asked.

Ralf glanced at it and shrugged. 'Just got it done.'

'Drunk?' I guessed, hoping an anecdote would come from this.

Ralf shook his head. 'I don't really drink any more.'

'What is it?' asked Rose. 'A sword?'

'Yeah, a burning sword,' said Ralf.

'Cool,' said Rose, and there was silence.

'Played any tennis recently?' I tried.

Ralf shook his head. 'Other things on.' I could hear my father chewing, very slowly and methodically, and I would have liked to be out in the open air.

'So what will you be doing while you're in Berlin?' asked my father in English, just about.

'There's an integrity festival on at the weekend,' Ralf said. 'Just a kind of community thing, bands playing, you know.'

'I'd like to see some of the sights,' said Rose, slowly. '*Die Sehenswürdigkeiten*. You know, the Brandenburg Gate, and where the Wall used to be.'

My father was looking at her in puzzlement, and she thought she had not made herself understood. 'The Wall?' she said again. '*Der Mauer?*'

'Yes, yes,' my father said, 'but why see that?'

'Just . . . historical interest . . .' said Rose awkwardly. Only now was I aware of the difficulty of Rose's discussing this scourge as a tourist attraction. I quickly changed the subject by remarking on the new united German football team. Rose had realised her possible mistake and was concentrating on the food, literally: she peered at a slice of *Bratwurst* so intently that it looked as though she was trying to read it.

There was some harmless chat about my father's friends. I avoided mentioning the fact that he was suddenly going part-time, even though that was by far the most pressing subject we could have discussed. Then, over dessert, my father said, 'So, Rose, you – and now Andreas – are in entertainment?'

'Lookalikes,' Ralf said. There was no German word for it, but between us we tried to explain the idea. Looking for people who resembled stars, booking them for low-quality entertainment nights.

My father nodded slowly; this was quite different from his experience of the working world. 'So,' he asked, 'you might book an Elvis man to sing?'

'Exactly,' said Rose, 'or – well, there's a man who does Jack the Ripper . . .'

'The murderer?' said my father.

'Yes,' said Rose. There was a pause. 'It's quite popular.'

'*So, so,*' my father muttered to himself. He chewed a piece of tart for what almost seemed an endless time.

Ralf seemed also to feel some pressure to lighten the atmosphere, and perhaps this excuses what happened next. 'Andreas is involved in a lookalike act himself,' said Ralf, mischievously.

'Not really, not really . . .' I murmured. But my father, whose interest in this conversation had been so close to disappearing altogether, was intrigued. I cursed Ralf silently.

'And who do you look like?' asked my father. This was particularly uncomfortable because, when I was young, he used to say that I looked like my mother.

'It's nothing,' I said impatiently.

'It is something,' said Ralf with a grin.

'Rose,' my father appealed, 'what is it that Andreas does?'

Rose's tremendous legs were jiggling under the table, and her face had flushed red; it would have been erotic if it had not been such a sticky state of affairs. She swallowed. 'It's based on,' she said, and stopped. 'It's . . .'

'It's to do with a sort of pretend dictator character,' I fudged.

'It's Hitler!' said Ralf, triumphantly.

'Hitler . . .' my father repeated, and I remembered how utterly confounded I was when I first heard about a vacancy for a Hitler lookalike. 'Have you seen it?' he asked Ralf.

'No,' said Ralf, 'but I've heard all about it.'

'It's really a very silly thing,' I said, wishing I could fly out of the window. 'It's really not . . .'

'And people pay money to see this?' my father asked, his brow furrowed.

'Well, it's normally part of a night of entertainment,' Rose tried to explain.

'*Ach so*,' muttered my father, gazing off into the distance as if at a picture of the bizarre scene. 'Dressing up as Adolf Hitler.' Hearing the first name was odd; it reminded me that it was a person, not just an idea, I had been mimicking all this time.

I waited for him to say something, anything, about it, to get angry even, to talk about my grandfather. But after a certain amount of time had passed, with everyone pretending to drink from empty glasses, it was obvious that this conversation, like so many, had been stillborn, and whatever my father thought about his first-born son earning a buck by pretending to be Hitler in a foreign country, all we were going to hear was him whistling 'Lili Marlene'.

After dinner I left Rose and Ralf to get to know each other and went off for a shower. I stood for a long time, trying to think of nothing but the jet of water arcing down over me and sluicing away.

*

At the weekend we went to the 'integrity festival'. It had been organised by a community group of the kind that had sprung up in abundance in the past few years. Ralf described it with a lot of phrases about 'celebrating the true values of Germany' and so on, which he had obviously got from the publicity materials.

A number of Ralf's muscular, short-haired friends accompanied us to the park, where there was a temporary stage, food stalls and blue portable toilet boxes, and people milling about everywhere. A programme of events was handed out by youths in red black and yellow T-shirts. It was a little difficult for me to decide why I did not feel entirely at ease. Perhaps it was simply the fact that this was not quite my home any more, while at the same time I was not completely integrated in England. Or perhaps it was the self-conscious feeling of walking around with someone as conspicuous as Rose, which I imagined was a little like being in the entourage of a celebrity. Fortunately, today she was in a jolly mood and returned the astonished stares of other festival-goers with a relaxed grin.

Quite a few youths were circulating with leaflets but the sight of Rose seemed to deter them from approaching us. After mooching around for a while, we were told that a band was appearing on the stage. 'They play some good shit,' said one of Ralf's friends, 'none of this rapping bullshit.' I translated this limited statement to Rose as best I could. We decided to sit towards the back of the field where she would not obstruct the view of almost everyone else there.

I had my arm around her shoulders; she shuffled to and fro until she was in a half-comfortable reclining position and I had to take the arm away again. The band, all skinheads dressed in muted colours, began to make a grinding noise, the sound system screeching with feedback; a hardcore of people near the front jigged and jumped about obediently. It was a waste of time trying to make out the lyrics but it was noticeable from their splenetic gestures that the band was either very angry or very proud about something.

'What a delightful melody,' said Rose. I kissed her. She had that familiar candy-like taste which always made me want to lick my lips as soon as our mouths separated. I look back on this kiss very often.

A small boy, with enormous curious eyes and a glob of candyfloss on the end of a stick, had been eyeing Rose for some time, peering around the legs of his father, who was nodding his head to the music. The little boy tugged at his parent's trouser leg and conferred with him solemnly. The man glanced in our direction and nodded. With great reticence the boy emerged from the safe haven of his father's legs and addressed me solemnly. 'Excuse me, excuse me,' he said gravely, as if reciting a rehearsed piece. 'Will she lift me up?'

'What does he want?' she asked.

'He wants you to lift him up, so he can see everything,' I told her. Rose laughed in delight.

She straightened up very slowly, brushing blades of stray grass away from her clothes and wiping her hands on her trousers before stretching out to take the bold child. Clutching him like a trophy, she hoisted him up onto her shoulders. The child clung onto her forehead with fierce excitement so that he looked a little like a monkey at the top of a tree. People around us were pointing and smiling at this somehow touching spectacle. The child began to holler wildly in excitement. 'What can you see?' asked Rose in impressive German.

'People, people!' yelled the boy.

'What kind of people?' she asked in English.

'*Was für Leute kannst du sehen?*' I shouted up at him.

'*Keine Schwarze, Keine Jude, nur Deutsche!*' replied the boy, jiggling about in ecstasy.

My stomach had undergone a sliding motion and felt as if it might slip out of me.

'Put him down,' I told her.

'He's loving it!' she said, turning her head so that her hair bobbed about.

'Put him down!' I shouted.

With a mystified shrug Rose lifted the young boy down from her shoulders. He protested shrilly. Placing him on the ground, she patted his head and watched as he went scurrying back to his father.

'What's up with you?' Rose asked me.

I was scanning the park. The sight of the boy had caused me to register the fact that there were comparatively few children around. And this was not the only odd thing. As my eyes roved around the bare heads, the dim barricades of black and grey garments, there were – as the boy had said no Jews, no black people. Also, there was no one from Berlin's large contingent of Turkish immigrants.

'What kind of thing is this?' I asked her.

'I don't know!' Rose said. 'I'm not German, am I?'

'I think it may be a far-right organisation,' I said.

The band finished a song with a long-drawn-out moan of guitars and a shapeless roar from their singer. A huge wave of applause began at the front of the audience and spread back, bottoming out until it was a polite clap by the time it reached us.

'But your brother's not a racist, is he?' Rose asked.

I was silent.

'You know,' said Rose, 'if we had kids they'd probably be freaks like me.'

'It's not the time,' I said irritably.

'How can it not be the time?' she said. 'Doesn't it matter to you?'

'Of course it matters,' I insisted, 'but—'

'Do you think that just because I laugh about things, I don't mind being weird?' she asked. Tears had sprung suddenly into her eyes.

'I don't think anything of the sort!' I said angrily. I trudged away and after a while she followed me.

A couple of people who were lounging lethargically on the grass shuffled out of the way to let us past. One of them had a tattoo on his arm that matched Ralf's. I walked with my head down, not looking at anyone, not responding to the man at the gates who asked us if we wanted to do a survey on our dissatisfaction with the high level of unemployment among whites in our country.

It would be good to say that I sat down with Ralf and had a brotherly chat – he was no idiot, he had presumably been led astray – but in the event we scarcely spoke over the next couple of days. It was not until the airport, on the way home, that we had a genuine conversation.

'Sorry we had kind of a weird time at the festival, man,' he said, as we shook hands, rather awkwardly.

'Ralf,' I said, 'what you do is up to you, but—'

'Hey,' he said, 'let's not have a lecture. Maybe you don't like some of my friends. It doesn't mean we're not brothers any more, does it?'

'It's not about your friends,' I said. Rose was being photographed by a tourist. A security guard told them to move on. 'It's about you becoming a . . . well, a neo-Nazi.'

'Who shat in your brain?' Ralf scoffed. 'I'm not a Nazi! Project Integrity isn't the Nazis! It's just a bunch of people who think that Germany has had enough of being the victims and the villains.'

At this obviously second-hand thought I shrugged, helplessly – at least, I like to think now that I was helpless.

'Hey,' said my brother again, stretching out his arms, 'are we still brothers or what?'

'Does Dad know?' I asked.

'There's nothing to know,' said Ralf, ruffling my hair. 'And anyway I don't think it would shock him more than your Hitler thing!' It was a good parting shot. I embraced him. I wanted more than anything to dig him in the ribs and have him squeal and writhe, and be eight years old.

On the plane home Rose talked enthusiastically about the forthcoming National Lookalike Show, a two-day event heavily attended by entertainment agents, which was the perfect 'showcase' for me and our other 'bankable acts'. Perhaps she was trying to distract me from thinking about my family, but I found this topic no more palatable, and was secretly glad when we hit a patch of turbulence and she fell into an apprehensive silence.

It was four days until I had another appointment as Hitler, in the bingo club. On this occasion they had asked me to perform a camp turn as a 'gay Hitler' because the club was particularly popular with homosexuals. I had refused this request, purely because I felt I would be very poor at it; so all I had to do was read the numbers in the style of Hitler, as usual. Even this was a very unappetising prospect but it was impossible to say that to Rose. She would accuse me, probably fairly, of petulance; she would tell me to 'take the money and forget it', or 'lie back and think of Germany'. It was good money, after all, for doing almost nothing.

Rose continued to set her sights on bigger things. On the day after we got back from Berlin she took herself off to a meeting with a couple of people who were interested in booking me to host a weekly cabaret night in East London, introducing burlesque dancers, circus acts and the like. They were keen on me as a host because they were aiming for 'a seedy, seditious atmosphere in one of London's coolest backwaters'. Having someone dress as Hitler hardly seemed the most breathtaking act of rebellion, but I was constantly being surprised by what passed for high standards in entertainment.

While she was at the meeting it was my job to answer the telephone with the words 'Beware Imitations' and take messages. I fielded a couple of enquiries about myself and heard myself talking as if the Hitler character were a person quite distinct from myself. 'Yes, I think he is available then.' 'I shall have to ask his manager to call you back.'

One caller asked, 'This is just pie-in-the-sky at this stage, but do you think he'd be interested in doing pantomime?'

'I cannot say for sure,' I told him.

Midway through the stint, there was an energetic knocking on the door. Nina stood there. Her hair had been thrown about in the wind and her coat was unbuttoned; she looked, I thought, somewhat like a distressed visitor to Sherlock Holmes.

'Nina!' I said. 'How are things?'

'Haven't you heard?' she asked, wandering past me and sitting down heavily on our sofa. She looked down at the floor, streaky-coloured hair streamed down over her face. 'Haven't you heard congratulations are in order . . . ?'

'Congratulations!' I said.

'. . . to Rachel, your other lookalike,' said Nina bitterly. She was holding the arm of the sofa very hard, in a way which reminded me of my father.

'Ah,' I said uncomfortably, wishing it had not been my fate to be here at this time. 'So she got the job?'

'Yes,' said Nina, clapping her hands sarcastically. 'She got the job. Lots of money for her, lots of commission for you and Rose!'

It was very hard to know what to say.

'I'm sorry,' I said. 'We should have told you there was someone else . . . it really came about quite by accident . . .'

Nina was not really listening to me; she had picked up one of the agency's brochures and was holding it out in front of her with trembling hands. 'Look at this. "Nina France. A startlingly accurate lookalike." What happened to that?'

Again, I was silent. It probably would not help matters if I told her that we wrote that purely as a sales pitch.

'And now this bitch comes along,' said Nina, seemingly taking inspiration from my silence, 'who isn't even a . . . a proper lookalike, and suddenly it's all about her! Where is she? She works in this place, doesn't she?' She looked around the room as if Rachel might be hiding in a cupboard. 'I'm going to find her and tell her congratulations!'

I imagined her walking into the middle of the tour and engaging Mrs Oswald in a fight, the two of them brawling, one on her absurd heels and the other in full Victorian dress, over the right to pretend to be someone else.

'I don't think you better had do such a thing,' I said quietly.

'Is it because you think I'm too fat?'

'What?' I said, off-balance.

'You know what I'm talking about,' she said, and I thought of that night with the comedian, a year ago, but a mental eternity. The memory made me squirm.

'Please forget about that episode,' I said. 'I only laughed because I felt something of an idiot myself at the time. You are not overweight!' I added earnestly, laying a gentle hand on her arm.

The momentary kindness seemed to crack her anger. She began to cry. I held her face against my shoulder. Her own shoulders heaved and shook. I looked out of the window and ran my hand up and down her back.

'Oh, God,' she said, after a while, straightening up. 'I'm an idiot.'

'Not at all,' I said. 'It's . . . the situation is unfortunate.'

She sniffed and wiped her eyes with the back of her hand. 'So I suppose this – Rachel – will be doing all the Basinger stuff from now on?'

'I don't know,' I said, fetching some tissues. 'Rose makes all these decisions.'

'I don't know what I'm going to do,' she said, quietly. 'I've spent all this time trying to look like . . . like Kim, speak, dress, eat like her, stay the same dress size, be the same height even. It's all I've done since university. What am I going to do now you've got someone better?'

I cleared my throat. 'Is there anyone else you might be able to impersonate?'

It was an unhelpful suggestion. Nina looked at me in disbelief. 'Like who? Fucking . . . Winston Churchill?'

The grandfather clock struck heavily downstairs. As if activated by this, the door opened and there stood Rose. Nina met her eyes and looked away.

'I'm sorry, love,' said Rose.

'I'd better be going,' Nina muttered. She brushed past Rose, who stepped out of the way, both of them looking as if they would break if they came into contact with each other.

Nina closed the door and we heard her footsteps as she worked her way down and down through the house, like something it had digested and was now getting rid of.

'So Rachel got the job?' I said in the end.

'She's a star in the making,' said Rose.

'And Nina . . .?'

'A problem in the making,' said Rose, thoughtfully.

Over the next couple of days I began to ruminate on the subject of whether the agency we had created was really worth the trouble it was capable of causing. The problem was that it had all happened so quickly. The relationship Rose and I had was bound up with this business venture we had entered together. Unpick one thing and it felt as if everything else could unravel. And perhaps I was just getting twitchy, to use a word Rose was fond of, because the strangeness of it all was finally catching up with me all at once.

I tried to bring it up with Charles, but he seemed, as they say, slightly 'below par' himself. A couple of days in a row I saw him with his shirt unbuttoned or his beard untidy-looking, which was out of character: chaotic as his appearance always was, it was generally an organised chaos.

'Is Rachel excited about her new career?' I asked.

'I do not think of it as a "new career", more as a pleasant diversion,' said Charles. 'But – to answer your question – yes, she is greatly enjoying her outings as Miss Basinger. Whether,' he coughed, 'whether Nina is so pleased, I wonder very much.'

'I can tell you,' I said, 'she is not.'

'Indeed,' said Charles. 'By "I wonder very much" I actually meant, "I am already certain". I am afraid the English language can be extremely perverse at times.'

'It's difficult . . .' I said. 'The Nina situation, I mean. Clearly, as a business, we must favour whoever is . . . better.'

'Naturally,' said Charles. 'In all aspects of life, we must favour whoever is better. Nature itself does that.' He twitched his beard, or it seemed to twitch itself. 'A quotation from the diaries of Oswald, in 1887, when he abandoned his attempts to get published and applied for work as a secretary.'

'I was not aware he had turned to that,' I said.

'He told his wife he had hired an office to work on his novel. Poor fellow. It is not easy for those who are not in the fortunate position of being "better". For those, a frustrating life and a futile death await. Mint?'

'Pardon?' I said.

'Will you eat a mint?' Charles repeated, producing a packet from his pocket. 'Come on, man. We cannot allow ourselves to become too gloomy. Besides, Rose is one of the winners.'

I took a mint and went on my way, unsure if all this had improved my morale.

'What were you and Charles nattering about?' Rose asked.

'Well . . .' I said, thinking better of giving her the full version, 'he said something about the perversity of language.'

'Old windbag,' said Rose, affectionately.

'Do you mean Charles or me?'

'You are a young and talented windbag, and soon even more people will be listening to you,' she said. 'As well as the cabaret night, the people I spoke to today are interested in promoting you in a theatre show. What do you think of that?'

'A theatre show?'

'Just in a studio theatre like the Soho or something for the time being. Obviously it wouldn't be for a while yet. We'll need to talk about how you are going to expand what you've got at the moment to something that's full length. But I've got a few ideas.'

'Goodness . . .' I said, feeling nothing but misgivings.

'Say, "Thank you, clever Rose,"' she commanded, stooping for me to kiss her.

The sexual momentum we built up over the previous few months had been disrupted by the visit to Germany and my moodiness since. A series of nights ended in botched or unfinished lovemaking with the subsequent recriminations, or pregnant silences, and edgy sleep. This happened the night before my bingo-club gig, and ensured that by the time the evening came round, I wished that the bingo hall and everyone in it were at the bottom of the sea. I looked into the mirror with contempt.

'Come on, Andreas,' said Rose – my first name only really supplanted pet names when I was in some sort of trouble – 'it's money for old rope.'

'I am going off the Hitler shenanigans a little . . .' I muttered.

'Oh, and are you "going off" money?' retorted Rose. She was right. Of course, I could do something else, but what else was I qualified for which would bring in money so easily? I had a degree in literature. I sloped off to the tube station, my Hitler outfit in a carrier bag, on the way passing Robert coming the other way to visit Rose. It was almost worth doing the bingo night just to avoid being there when he visited, I thought. As he passed, he gave me one of his sallow, unfriendly smiles.

A part of me felt that after my filthy mood, the bingo night itself could not possibly be as bad as the anticipation. This was, of course, wrong. There was an atmosphere of almost decadent enjoyment in the room, which was a massive draughty place with balconies and pillars, a former Victorian theatre. Huge groups of people sat around tables with pitchers of drink between them. People were shouting at each other across the room, taking photos, walking into each other with big jugs of beer, wearing flashing devil horns. At a table to the left of the stage a woman had a hat fashioned into the shape of rabbit ears.

The man who ran the event was completely bald and wore a tight white T-shirt. He was not the man who booked me for my first gigs at the bingo hall – it was the sort of job one would get out of as quickly as possible – but had heard, he said, I was 'the business'. 'Just enjoy it,' he said, 'do your Hitler thing.' He spread his hands as if Hitler offered so many possibilities to a bingo caller, it was pointless giving me instructions.

'Very well,' I said, going into my dressing room – which was an office by day, there were work rotas on the walls and posters from men's magazines – shaking my brown uniform out of its bag and staring at it without any thoughts in my head.

By the increasingly familiar method of pretending this was not my life but something I was temporarily overseeing, I got through the minutes. To my annoyance, the start kept being put back. At last the lights were dimmed, though not to as low a level as I would have liked. The bald man appeared on the stage and announced that tonight there was a 'very special guest'. 'Will you please welcome Herr Adolf Hitler!'

There was good-natured booing and hissing. It flashed

through my head that I just wouldn't go on to the stage, I would simply sit here and wait for events to be taken out of my hands. Of course, even as I was thinking this, I was on my way up there. A homosexual couple right at the front were laughing almost hysterically as I appeared, and before long, one of them had to support the other to prevent him from falling off his chair. Not long ago I would have seen this, gay men laughing at Hitler, as the final victory of the liberal world-view. The bald organiser was grinning encouragement at me, his hopeful eyes admitting just an inkling of concern. God knows, I thought, this is just a guy trying to run a club, probably hoping for a promotion and so on. All this was my fault, or Rose's and mine, but in any case, not his.

'One and seven,' I called, 'seventeen.'

There were pockets of excitement, chatter, groans of mock disappointment and so on; it took some time for people to settle down again. This is going to take all night, I thought, miserably. I fished out a couple more numbers: eleven, eighty-eight. The latter was normally symbolised by 'two fat ladies' but I declined to say this. Part of me was dearly wishing that someone would land a full house immediately, that by some fluke the first five numbers would all correspond with some punter's card, though from past experience I knew that even in this eventuality, the game would nonetheless take much longer than that. I could see the bald man giving me a series of Nazi salutes from the side of the stage, his arm jiggling up and down like someone seen on old video reel played at the wrong speed. 'Hitler it up a bit,' he was murmuring, 'Hitler it up.'

I gathered that he wanted me to exaggerate my impersonation in as crass a way as I could. I compromised by making my voice harsher and more clipped as we went through the numbers. We proceeded: forty-nine, eight, sixty-six . . .

'Hitler's dick!' someone shouted. This witticism was very popular. I growled half-heartedly in the general direction of the wag.

'You can go for the jugular if you want,' the bald man was whispering. 'Give him some abuse! He'll love it!' I ignored his tuition and went doggedly on.

Seventy-seven. Thirteen. Forty-five. 'Not one of my favourite years, '45,' I scowled, but hardly anyone laughed. Amazingly, the small speck of professional pride which I still had was moved to annoyance – I considered that I had been witty. I was going to do something regrettable now, there was no doubt about it. It was just a question of when a provocative number would come out of the bag.

'Thirty,' I announced, 'three-zero.' Then, a single digit. 'Six. Six million Jews dead.'

The first thing I saw was the aghast face of the bald organiser; his mouth dropped open like a trapdoor. People everywhere were asking each other for confirmation of what they had heard. There was a lot of head-shaking, a cry of 'Shame!' My hands were trembling with anger. 'Ninety-two,' I called out. 'That's how many people died in Hillsborough.' Any number would do for me, now. Shock was whispering like smoke through the room. 'Seventy-one, the number of people killed by cancer this month.' This was not even a genuine statistic, but it no longer mattered. The bingo players were animated in self-conscious anger and horror; beer was spilt as a fat man leapt up to make a gesture of indignation, and continued to trickle over a tabletop for minutes to come. The organiser was holding his head: the edge of his bare pate was caught by the spill from my spotlight and beamed like a distress signal.

I could not believe I was saying these offensive things, but it seemed no more or less natural than anything else I was doing. I continued to view the situation as if from outside.

'You're sick!' yelled the rabbit-eared woman. 'You're sick!' she screamed again, pointing a finger dramatically. Several people voiced their agreement. The irony was that I almost agreed with her, but not for the reasons in her head. The woman was pleased with her new role as ambassador and gathered the courage for a still more powerful rebuke. 'You,' she said, weaving her way between the tables until I imagined I could smell her beery breath, 'are as bad as Hitler himself.'

'How can it be sick,' I asked, appealing to the whole audience, 'to mention that Hitler murdered six million Jews, yet perfectly all right for you to laugh at me dressed up pretending to be him?'

But nobody seemed very interested in this debate; admittedly, it was a bit late to raise it. In the middle of all the fuss, I could still see some patrons so engrossed in the game that, even now, they were still hunched in concentration over their bingo cards. Not knowing what else to do I rummaged in the bag for another number.

'Twelve,' I called. There was a long pause while everyone waited for me to add some inflammatory remark. 'Sixty-two.' Then, somewhere to my right, a voice piped up, 'House!'

The bald man, seeing his chance, sprang onto the stage and pushed me away from the microphone. 'We have a winner!' he shouted in relief and there was a small cheer from their table. I made good my escape. In the dressing room, I sat holding my head, which had begun to throb.

There was emphatic applause and laughter and I got the impression that something damning had been said about me. I shut my eyes.

Some minutes later, just as I had my shirt over my head, the organiser came in, sweat sliding from his shiny skull. 'What the hell are you doing?' he demanded. 'Trying to ruin me? If you're trying to ruin me, nice work!'

'I wasn't trying to ruin you,' I assured him.

'Listen,' he said, 'I'm going to pay you half the money and you're lucky to get that.' He handed over a bundle of notes. I considered scattering them, then pictured Rose and thought better of it.

'And I'm going to complain to your manager,' he said.

'Go ahead,' I invited him, 'but I will be in bed with my manager in a couple of hours.'

This subdued the man. I left without saying goodbye. Walking home from the tube station, I made a point of looking people in the eye – an old tramp with a scraggy dog, a businessman returning very late from the office – to reassure myself that they did not see Hitler in my face.

Cloth Street was silent in the moonlight. I could feel a tight beat of sexual desire inside me and wanted nothing more than to clutch Rose in the darkness and be away from everything else. When I opened the door, however, there was Robert, lying on the floor of the living room, his immense legs pointing skywards as if he were a part of the ceiling that had fallen down. He must have been there for hours. There was a nearly empty bottle of Scotch on the table, and he and Rose seemed to be in the middle of a game of cards. I asked sarcastically if I was interrupting anything.

'You're sparing Rose further humiliation,' said Robert. 'I've got a hand that she can only dream about.'

'I'm afraid I don't play cards,' I said stiffly.

'That's why I'm here,' Robert said. 'Sometimes it takes a freak to keep a freak happy.'

'Robert, don't use that word,' Rose said. 'Andreas doesn't like it. We're not freaks, just slightly lanky.' This amused them both considerably.

Clearing my throat, I said, 'Well, I made a complete mess of my gig.'

That brought their chatter to a halt. I told them a brief version of the story.

'And what exactly did you achieve?' asked Robert. 'Any of the Jews brought back to life?'

'That's not the point,' I said angrily.

'Excuse me, it is the point,' he said. 'Speaking as a Jew . . .' he added, pompously.

'Robert's right,' said Rose. 'You've got to do a professional job.'

'Oh, Christ!' I said. 'The Nazis were professional!'

'I think you're obsessed with the Nazis,' said Rose. I gritted my teeth and went into the bedroom.

Laid across the bed were copies of our new brochure. There were a few new entries, among them a group of lookalikes of the band Take That, who Rose said were likely to be successful for some time. Other than this, the most obvious change was an entry that read, RACHEL THOMAS IS KIM BASINGER! There was a photo of Rachel looking exactly like Basinger. Further down the page, NINA FRANCE IS KIM BASINGER glared sullenly at its new rival. The centrepiece of the brochure was me, giving a Hitler salute to a smitten audience. It was hard to see what could stop the agency at the moment, unless I did so myself.

I remained in the bedroom until I heard Rose showing

Robert out of the flat, and his footsteps clumping down the stairs in the silence. Rose entered the room and looked at me without saying anything.

'All right,' I said, 'I'm sorry, but I am having a lot of second thoughts about this whole Hitler thing . . .'

Rose sat down slowly on the bed, propping herself against her orthopaedic cushion. I could hear her back click as she straightened her legs out with a tiny sigh.

'You know,' she said, 'all I'm trying to do is be a success.'

She chewed on her lip and looked hard at the bedside table. Her breath smelt of alcohol, but with its residual sweetness; the overall effect was like liqueur chocolates. I was trying to hold back desire.

'I realise that,' I said, in a measured voice. She was singing very quietly to herself. The atmosphere had an odd quality, seemingly content and pregnant with tension at the same time.

'You remember that first day, in Peterborough, talking about how agents depend on acts. Well, I'm depending on you,' said Rose, quietly, after a while. 'I can be as much of a genius as I like at getting you work, publicity, everything, but I can't actually get up there on the stage dressed as Hitler. If I did, it would be very unconvincing.' I acknowledged the half-joke with a raise of my eyebrows. 'And if you think of all the people who would love to be working as regularly as you are . . .'

'I know,' I said, 'but they don't have to do something morally offensive.'

'Oh, for fuck's sake,' she said, casting a weary glance at the low roof, 'I can't be bothered to talk about "morally offensive". You know as well I do, what you're doing means nothing. It's entertainment. Are you walking round Trafalgar

Square with swastikas on your face? Are you preaching anti-Semitism in Hyde Park? There are plenty of people doing things like that.'

'Perhaps I'm being unreasonable,' I conceded, taking her hand and stroking it. 'But then,' I added, 'Charles was telling me that only unreasonable people made progress.'

'Oh, yes, and Charles has made a lot of progress in his life, hasn't he!' said Rose venomously, but she seemed straight away to regret it.

'I'm sorry,' she said, easing into a supine position and laying her head down on my shoulder. 'I've been a bit ratty recently. Robert was talking about how we should be advertising in the *Stage* instead of *Stagecraft* and—'

'Why do you listen to that creep?' I said in disgust. As usual, she found my attempts at indignation comical. 'You're right, he is a creep! He's an absolute rotter!'

But her amusement at my foibles of speech and my inept anger always somehow fired up her affections, rather than dampening them. She lay back and pulled me on top of her with effortless force, like a mechanical arm picking up a toy in one of those seaside attractions. My mind was whirring with competing things: the mixture of satisfaction and revulsion at the night's 'entertainment' and my little revolt; the territorial need to claim her back from the friend who had dominated her evening. I clasped her and wrestled her onto her front. As she began to tighten and shudder in anticipation, I felt like a conductor hearing a piece of music perfectly played after many false starts. I coiled my left arm over the edge of the bed for the belt, which was sitting on the floor, ready for me to take it up.

Not for the first time, as she murmured in happy pain and we whispered obscenties to one another, I subdued the part of my mind that accused me of settling once more for a deferred conversation and for the easy solution of sex or love or whatever this was. Most couples, I told myself, must live like this, in cycles of antagonism and reconciliation; and the habit of using sex as the bridge from the first state to the second was not, as the English say, a 'cop-out', but a natural part of this cycle. It was going to take something really dramatic to shake me out of the complacency, or cowardice, that had quickly made me an expert at this way of living.

» Alexandra

Dear Alexandra,

It seems that, each time I write to you, I am obliged to apologise for my behaviour during your previous visit. This time, I am afraid I was simply startled by the news that a former friend of mine was alive and well and yet had neglected to do me the service of a visit in all this time.

I have thought long and hard about what reasons Charles might have for – as I believe the word is – boycotting me so strangely. Various explanations suggest themselves. But, as I remarked on your first visit, I am not sure that this is the right way to discuss such matters. I fear that my writings are scrutinised. I would ask you to consider making another visit – thankless as your previous endeavours may have been – so that I can tell you whatever of my story you have not yet discovered for yourself, and expound some of my theories on the riddle of Charles's absence.

Gratefully,
as ever,
Andreas

I left the house with Gareth's coughing in my ears; he'd been confined to his bed since the river incident with a mild strain of pneumonia. His laptop was set up on the end of the bed. Once I knocked on the door to see if he wanted anything, but there was no response; when I pushed the door open softly, he was flat on his back, asleep with his mouth slightly open and his cheeks sweaty and red. I had the impulse to go and turn back the covers so he would cool down, but told myself to stop being so silly and maternal.

This morning I'd tried to bring it up with Dan. It was almost the first I had seen of him in the week since the Ripper tour. He was running late for work – that was why our paths crossed, but I soon wished they hadn't. He was rushing about, swearing, knocking things over in an attempt to find his briefcase. The brown package had been torn open and our bathroom cabinet now boasted a bag of coke about the size of a sack of apples from the supermarket.

'Gareth seems in a pretty bad way,' I ventured.

'Well, if you will go playing around by the river . . .' said Dan.

'You were there, weren't you? What actually happened?'

'What do you think happened?' he asked, irritably, grunting as he shoved a sofa forward several inches in case it was hiding the briefcase. 'We were wrecked and someone fell in and, boo hoo, it was your beloved Gareth.'

'Don't be such a wanker,' I said, as he found the briefcase – it was in the shoe cupboard, which was never normally opened – and went out of the door with his laces undone, muttering something I didn't want to hear. It was a safe bet I wouldn't see him again for a while; though as it was rent day, there would be at least be some magical congress between our bank accounts.

I knocked on Gareth's door, then thought better of it, but by that time, he had called me in. I had ten minutes until I ought to be leaving. He was sitting up in bed in his dressing gown with the untranslated pages of Andreas's memoirs on his lap.

'You don't have to do that while you're ill,' I said.

'No, I'm,' he said. 'I'm interested. I want to see what happens.'

'Can I have that in writing?'

He gave me a watery grin. 'OK. You've got my interest. Congratulations.'

He stuck a pale hand out of the bedclothes and I shook it.

'You're incredibly cold,' I said.

'Do you mean my temperature,' he asked, 'or my attitude towards you?'

I smiled. He coughed. 'I don't mean to be, um,' he said.

'It's OK,' I said, 'you're my favourite flatmate.' He acknowledged the joke and shuffled across so I could sit closer. 'I'm swimming with germs, by the way,' he said.

'Still better company than Dan,' I said.

At the mention of Dan, Gareth's face relaxed into unexpected mirth. 'You know that girlfriend?'

'Trixie?'

'Yes – the vacuous, doll-like one. She's left him.'

'Oh,' I said, 'that's . . . that's great.'

'She said she wasn't sure if they were right for each other?' said Gareth, impersonating Trixie's lilting-at-the-end-of-the-sentence tic. I giggled. 'She said she was thinking of going to spend some time in the south of France with her parents?'

'So that's why he's in a bad mood?'

Gareth nodded and reached for a tissue to blow his nose. 'It was the night of . . . after the Jack the Ripper thing. She did it by text after we left the club. Dan couldn't believe it. I made some smart remark and he took the considerable liberty of shoving me in the river. So we've been avoiding each other ever since.'

'Wow,' I said. 'Why didn't you tell me this the other night?'

'I wasn't really in the mood,' said Gareth. 'I had water in my mouth.'

There was a pause. I thought we were both thinking how peaceful it was here without Dan. But it could have been that Gareth was thinking about something completely different.

'He had a massive, incoherent tantrum,' said Gareth, 'talking about how spoiled she was, how she'd gone running off to her rich-bastard parents . . .'

'That's funny coming from him,' I said.

'Well, except . . .' said Gareth.

'Except . . . ?'

'Nothing,' said Gareth, evasively, starting to cough again.

Before the conversation could get awkward, I told him I'd leave him to sleep. 'Let me know when you've finished the, um . . .' I said.

'I will,' said Gareth. 'It's been a strange story, hasn't it?'

'I get the feeling it's not going to end nicely.'

'I've been playing with you a bit,' he said, 'leaving it at the most cliff-hangery moments I could. But there's only about thirty pages of it left, now.'

'Looks like you'll finish it by Christmas, then,' I said.

'Well, forty-five days to go,' said Gareth. 'Mind you,' he added, 'if there is any more sexual content, I may have to withhold the manuscript from you.'

'Yes,' I said, 'when I got you to translate it I didn't realise there'd be . . . all that.' All that, I thought, I sound like an aunt.

'Luckily, I'm a closet pervert,' said Gareth cheerfully. I looked at my watch. The time had sped away. I told him to have a good day and stay in bed. It almost reminded me of when I used to live with a group of friends.

I was twenty minutes late for work, but the Paris party wasn't due back till lunchtime. In their absence, the amount of my time spent answering, and killing off, phone calls had gone up to about seventy per cent. Albert, rustling a week-old newspaper, nodded to me on my way in. I sat in the office, with odd members of staff popping in and out, feeling the weight of everything in my brain.

Andreas's letter had made me want to see him again as soon as possible. It sounded as though he was now ready to tell me everything and save us the effort of translating his memoirs. But then, Gareth had nearly finished it anyway, and I was enjoying the soap-opera element, and so was he now. If I found out everything about Andreas, where did that leave us? Also, it was pretty clear, after what happened at the prison last time, that I should go and talk to Charles Steel and encourage him to visit Andreas, before the housing firm made him move out and he disappeared somewhere. But I didn't fancy that idea when I thought back to the strange, ancient-looking man still prowling around in the closed museum. If he was mad enough back in the days of the lookalike agency, what had the years of – presumably – solitude in that place done for him?

In the end, after reading the letter again, I concluded that I would have to go and see Andreas, and the sooner the better. I wrote an email to Claire asking her if I could visit tomorrow. To judge from past form she should reply within the half-hour.

'All this to go?' said Albert in my ear, just as I was about to send the message. I swivelled around in my chair, surprised.

He glanced at the screen. He seemed to have materialised from nowhere, like Robert the giant. I wondered where Robert was now. You would think such a tall man would find it hard to escape public attention, but then, if you asked anyone who the tallest person in the UK was, who would know? Albert left the new bundle of mail on my work surface and shuffled away, coughing.

In the lunch-hour I went out to a card shop, planning to get a 'welcome home' balloon to put by Helen's computer as a joke. I was in the card shop, standing next to a rack of 'adult humorous' cards, and had just found a suitable balloon, red with white lettering. 'Oh, that's a good one, I like that one,' said a girl behind me, reaching over my shoulder to get at a card which had taken a black-and-white library picture of a smitten couple and added a caption: 'Keith couldn't wait to give her one.' I stepped aside and the girl said thanks; I looked around to acknowledge her and someone said, 'Alex!' It was Craig.

His hair was cut in spikes like a model's and he was wearing an expensive shirt, black, almost invisible white pinstripes. He smelt of something he didn't wear when we were together. His eyes were the same, of course, warm, happy. He hesitated, then kissed me on the cheek. Our noses touched as he went for the other cheek. The feel of him against my face made me flush.

'Alex,' he said, 'this is Kiki. This is Alex, my ex.'

The girl and I said hello. She had dark eyes, strong cheekbones, and hair that fell over her face. She was wearing a purple sarong with jeans, and long earrings.

'What are you up to?' Craig asked.

'Oh. Just . . .' I said. 'Lunch-break. Buying, um, something for Helen.'

'Oh, do you work with Helen?' the girl piped up. 'She's great, isn't she? I love Helen!'

'She is,' I said. 'What about you two . . . ?'

'Buying a congrats card,' said Craig. 'Kiki's brother is being called to the Bar.'

'He's a barrister?'

'He will be.'

'Brilliant,' I said. A pause. 'I'd better get back to . . . !' I said, brightly. I gave them a nice-to-have-seen-you nod and smile and we wrapped up the conversation and I went hurriedly to the exit. I think it's nearly impossible as an individual to talk to two people without going away feeling that the two are discussing you.

At the doors there was a bleep and I was stopped by an assistant with a polite smile; I hadn't paid for the balloon, which was waggling jauntily in the air as I held it aloft. I went back to the checkout with my face the colour of the balloon. Craig and the girl either hadn't noticed, or were pretending they hadn't. I took one look back at them: she was showing him something, their heads touching as he leaned across.

I went back to the office, checked my email, played around on a lookalikes website. It had been some time since I'd given Craig any thought at all, consciously at least. I was already aware that he was with a new woman and that that meant he was winning. All the same it was hard not to keep replaying the conversation. The way he had said 'ex' as if it had been a perfectly natural separation, something no one looked back on with any regret. And her sarong and salon hairstyle, and slightly exotic name, and the way he knew her brother and she knew his housemates and they had a whole world of things to refer to which I had no part in.

The Paris people all came back with professional faces on as if they hadn't been drinking and sightseeing for five days. Jeremy immediately began checking through the mail and making phone calls as if he had only just got back in time to save the whole company from collapse. Helen had bought me a chocolate Eiffel Tower and feigned offence when I didn't eat it straight away.

'I had a big lunch,' I said. Helen punched the balloon gently and watched it sway from side to side.

'No, you didn't,' she said. 'You never eat properly unless I feed you.'

'All right,' I said, 'by a "big lunch" I mean, I saw Craig with . . . Kiki.'

'Ah,' said Helen. She swivelled her chair in a little arc.

'Pretty, isn't she?' I said.

'She is,' said Helen.

Jeremy came in fussing about some letter that hadn't arrived. He looked at me as if I might have hidden it.

'Rich family,' said Helen. 'They've got a huge place in Norfolk where we're . . .' She paused. 'Well, we're invited to go there for New Year.'

'Lovely,' I said.

Helen coughed. 'I mean, not that huge a place,' she said helpfully. 'Like, four bedrooms.'

There was still no email from Claire but events had somehow made my mind up for me. I wasn't coming in to work tomorrow. I was going to see Andreas. I waited until late in the day before cornering Jeremy.

'Listen,' I said, 'I don't know if they told you, but while you were all away, a family emergency came up.'

'I did hear,' said Jeremy.

'So . . .' I said. 'I promise it should all be sorted out after this but I need one more day off, tomorrow.'

'OK,' said Jeremy. For a second I thought that was it: as easy as that. He was twirling a pencil between his fingers. This month's calendar girl, in an unpleasant coincidence, was called Alexa. She was in a treehouse. 'This family emergency. The sickness. Tough time recently.'

'The sickness was just a one-day thing.'

'Yes,' he said. 'They've all been "one-day things".'

He took a deep breath.

'Alex, I know perfectly well that you're lying about this and you've been lying to me for some time.'

My stomach lurched. 'What?'

'You weren't ill, and there is no family emergency.'

I stared at him.

'I know that you've made appointments for the "days off", I know that you've discussed ways to bunk off with colleagues, I know you have some sort of project which is obviously more important to you than doing the job we pay you for.'

I could feel the blood massing in my ears and I felt as though I might cry. Desperately I tried to put up some resistance.

'Who the hell has been lying to you about me?'

Jeremy laughed. 'You're very bad at this, Alexandra. Now. I'm going to recommend that you take a couple of days' unpaid leave, shall we say. I'll speak to a few people, you can have a think, and we'll decide what the best course of action is.'

'Well, maybe the best course of action is for me to leave?' I heard myself say. 'I mean you never give me any responsibility.'

'Perhaps you should ask yourself why.'

'I don't know why. I've got . . . I've got qualifications,' I said, miserably. 'In all this time I've never been properly involved in a project. I just . . . I just answer phones and write letters that a . . . that a trained . . . fucking . . . chimpanzee could write.'

'That's an idea,' said Jeremy, nibbling the end of the pencil.

I turned and went out of his office. Without breaking step I picked up my bag and coat, slung my coat over my shoulder and went out. 'Hey!' said Helen, watching the balloon bobble as I brushed it out of my way. I heard her coming after me and quickened my step. 'Hey,' she yelled, shouting at me from reception, 'you left this!' It was my swipe card for the apartment block. I came back and snatched it from her without looking at her. She restrained me as I tried to turn away. She was very strong; she once won a fight with a bouncer.

'What the hell is the matter with you?'

'I'm leaving,' I said. 'I'm going to be sacked.'

'What?'

'He knew about the days off.'

'He knew you were blagging?'

'Yes,' I said, my face very close to Helen's. 'He had somehow found out that I was lying. I wonder how he could have found out? Who in this office knew?'

Helen's eyes opened wide. 'What? Do you honestly think—?'

'Well, how else could he know? A little group of you piss off to Paris, you get drunk every night . . .'

Helen looked so indignant I thought she might push me back against the wall. 'Can you not separate your real life from your . . . detective games?'

'Who else could know?' I said, again. 'Who else have I talked to about the Andreas thing? Who else have I asked for advice on getting time off?'

'I don't know,' said Helen, angrily. She'd released her grip and was staring at me. Albert had put down his newspaper and was watching us. 'I don't know who you confide in these days but I hope you treat them with a bit more respect than this.'

I couldn't think of a way of replying to that. She turned and went into the office. I thought she was going to come back and say one last thing and we would defuse the situation between us, but after standing there like an idiot for a couple of minutes I saw that wasn't going to happen.

'Nasty business,' Albert observed, picking up the paper and rustling it pointedly. I gave him a sarcastic smile and went out into the cold air.

Yards from the tube station I got a mental picture of Albert, the paper in front of him, held steady in his two hands with the yellow nails. I remembered him skulking around the office when Helen was lecturing me on how to bunk off work. I remembered him sitting there as I came out and pretended to take a phone call about the 'emergency'. I remembered him reading the email on the screen in which I quite clearly asked Claire to arrange a prison visit for tomorrow. I stopped where I was. I remembered Albert's face when I was joking about his daughter's script, and the way he had looked at me for weeks afterwards.

I lay awake looking at the ceiling, which seemed to be throbbing, though it was an illusion – the noise, as ever, was in our own flat. There was laughter, mock arguments, mock fights, two people came into my room and apologised and left without properly shutting the door. Dan was as genial a host as ever; he seemed to have shaken off the Trixie blow. I'd knocked on Gareth's door, but he was somewhere else for the night. I really can't live here for much longer, I thought, but then soon, perhaps I won't be able to afford to.

I felt like getting up and going into the bathroom and snorting a whole line of the stuff off the sink, and letting it go to my head and forgetting everything. I kept thinking about whether Albert had shopped me, and if he had, how stupid I had always been to assume he didn't bear a grudge.

I was up at half past seven, about an hour after the party had died down. There was still no email from Claire, and it was too early to call her office. Gareth didn't return – maybe he had stayed the night with that girlfriend who gave him the card. It was drizzling over London. I felt I could see the worst side of everything. Dan was still buzzing; I watched him wolf down a bowl of cornflakes in less than a minute. His tie was slung over his shoulder, his hair stood up, his shirt trailed like a naughty schoolboy's, his right eye was bloodshot. It was unbelievable that someone could do any sort of job in the condition he was always in. He blew me a kiss on his way out. I cleared away his cornflakes bowl and washed it up, without really realising I was doing it.

I think it was nine o'clock before I realised I was definitely going to the prison. I knew it was a visiting day, same hours as usual; and I didn't, suddenly, have anything else to do.

I trudged across the car park, with just about enough composure left to work out what I was going to do. I would turn up, flirt with Dean the gatehouse keeper, say I didn't have an appointment but I would be awfully grateful if he could let me see Andreas as a surprise. To hell with it – maybe I would go out with him. Who cared? What did I have to lose? It was almost exhilarating being in this frame of mind. I had never seen myself as someone who would get in trouble at work, storm out maybe never to return, and now this. I walked with some confidence into the prison.

Straight away my plan faltered. Dean wasn't on duty. Maybe I hadn't been here on a Friday before; I wasn't sure. The new guy, black and with the build of an ex-military man, looked at me sceptically. I thought about pretending I did have an appointment and there had been a mistake, then decided lying hadn't done me very much good recently. 'I'm not on the list,' I said, 'but I know Andreas would be very happy to see me. Please.'

'Andreas . . .?'

'Honig. H-O-N . . .'

The man shook his head. 'Nah.' He had his finger on the list of Hs.

'He is there somewhere.' I bent my neck so I could see the same as him. It was true; no Andreas. Perhaps he was looking at the wrong list. I wasn't sure how to suggest this. 'I've visited him quite a few times.'

'You going to be fannying about all day?' asked a woman, tapping me on the shoulder. I moved out of her way. She had her hair tied back and was carrying a tiny child, like a parcel, in a baby harness. I waited while she was searched.

'Don't think he is here,' said the guard, once she'd gone.

'Look,' I said, 'is Claire here? Claire Taylor. Welfare. Maybe I could speak to her.'

The man fiddled with his radio and muttered a few inaudible things. 'She's coming,' he said. I felt brighter. He asked me to take a seat. I sat, looking at the coffee machine – it was the last thing I needed – and at a golf magazine which I couldn't even get past the front cover of. After a couple of minutes the guard got a buzz from his radio. 'She wants you to go to her office,' he said. He issued me an ID badge. He spelt my name ALEXANDER.

Claire was temporarily using an office which belonged to

'C. Fullman, Senior Administrator'. The filing cabinet, bare desk and functional intrays looked almost frighteningly austere compared with the gaudy Soho office, I thought, though there was the ELEVENSES mug – at least, it looked like the same one, maybe she kept one everywere she was likely to go – and in front of her, a crossword and a single 'congratulations!' card from someone a bit slow off the mark.

'On hold,' she mouthed. I sat down and passed the 'Alexander' badge, in its plastic cover, from one hand to another. 'All right, can you get them to call me back?' said Claire. 'Claire Taylor. I'm running out of patience, I'm afraid; it should have been delivered over a week ago. All right. Bye.'

'Alex!' she said. 'I would come and hug you, but . . .' She gestured as if she had grown to an enormous, unwieldy size, though there was no visible difference from last time we were together. I nodded understandingly.

'So,' she said, 'I'm sorry I haven't replied to your email.'

'It's all right,' I said, 'I've come anyway. But they don't seem to . . .'

'Yes,' said Claire thoughtfully. 'Listen, honey. I was going to give you a call today. Andreas has been resettled.'

'Resettled?'

'Moved.'

'Why?'

Claire did her official face. 'It can be at his request, or at the decision of the prison authorities. It happens quite a lot. The exact reasons are confo.'

'But where is he?' 'Resettled', I thought, it sounds like he's a refugee.

She gave me an apologetic and, I thought, slightly guilty

look. 'That is confo as well for the time being. Apart from family.'

'But *you* must know!' I said. 'You must know where he is!'

'It's not one of my five,' she said, 'so it's . . .' She shrugged helplessly.

'But don't you care?'

She smiled. 'The thing is, Alex, I have a lot of prisoners to look after, we have a couple of new chaps here – there are other welfare officers wherever Andreas has gone . . .'

'So,' I said, slowly, 'how the hell am I meant to find out?'

It might have been my mental state, but I thought she was on the verge of laughing. 'Well,' she said, 'as soon as he's settled, Andreas will contact you.' She sipped her drink. 'Mmm. That's – assuming he does decide to . . . to do that.'

Her phone was ringing.

'Why wouldn't he?' I challenged her. 'Do you mean, unless someone stops Andreas from getting in touch with me?'

'The thing is,' Claire said, glancing at her phone, 'the thing is, this is why we recommend pen pals to go through us, because otherwise relationships do become a bit over-close, sometimes, and a bit . . .'

'What do you mean?' I demanded. Claire, with a raise of her eyebrows as if she was making a great sacrifice for me, pressed a button to reject the call.

'I know you've really enjoyed writing to Andy . . .' she said.

'But what?'

'I didn't say but.'

'But what? But you think he didn't want to write any more? He gave me his life story!' I was leaning across the desk. Claire had scraped her chair back slightly to be clear of me. My hand knocked over a card. I was sick of greeting cards.

'Listen, Alex,' she said. 'I will do my best to find out where he is for you. Or if – if you want to try another pen pal . . .'

'I don't want *another* one!' I almost shouted. 'I want you to tell me where the fuck Andreas is!'

She looked at me and put a hand to her stomach, whether consciously or not I couldn't tell; either way, the effect was to imply that, with her being pregnant and all, I was really treading on thin ice speaking to her like this. I apologised.

'That's quite all right,' she said in a not-jolly-any-more voice. She had always been somehow like a teacher; she now reminded me of the popular one who is forced to end the fun and games because some pupils have taken advantage. I hated her for conveying this, I hated the whole situation.

Her phone rang again, and, this time, it was clear she was going to answer it. I made to leave.

'I'll let you know . . .' she said, already not looking at me. I stood there looking across the desk, waiting for inspiration, some final thing I could say that would really throw her, then turned and shoved through the door which, rather than slamming behind me, remained patronisingly ajar for a few seconds.

It was raining when I got out to the car park, flinging the 'Alexander' badge into a bin on the way. I walked past Claire's little blue Fiat, the cute, immaculate interior, the easy-listening CDs, the little square box of tissues on the dashboard, the lovely little car Bob had bought her as a runaround. I would have liked to smash my fist through the windscreen.

I sat on a cold red bench on the station platform watching empty fast-food packaging drifting across the tracks. An announcement apologising for a delayed train was repeated five times. I realised I was probably going to cry if anyone so much as asked me the time. I took my phone out of my bag and played with it aimlessly to deter them. Before I could stop myself I had called Gareth. It was voicemail. I got as far as 'It's me . . .' and then hung up. It was stupid; what did I mean, 'me' – I had never called him before.

I sat, passing the phone from one hand to another. The little kiosk on the platform was closed, the serving hatch covered by a big sign. The announcement was repeated a couple more times. The train was going to be thirty-eight, said the toneless voice, I repeat, thirty-eight, three-eight, minutes late. The wind caught the stray raindrops on the back of my neck and howled around my shoulders.

All along the Thames, Christmas lights had started to appear. Strings of coloured lights rigged up across the decks of moored boats; white or blue lights nestling in trees; tacky neon Santas. It was just under a month away. The lights would get more and more profuse and burn for longer and longer as the days wore on and it was dark almost all of the time.

What have I done? I wondered. The sentence kept coming into my head, along with, What am I going to do?

Helen wasn't returning my calls. I didn't want to go home. I possibly didn't have my job any more, and if I did, it was now clear that I had no status at work. And the person all this was about – I didn't know where he was or whether he wanted to see me. None of this could be dressed up as anything other than a series of stupid decisions which I had made. Arguably, everything since (and including) the proposal I had got wrong. These past two years had been a long denial.

Of course I could get another job, working in another office. It wouldn't be any different. And I could live in a studio flat. That would be different, but it was unlikely to be a lot better.

The floating restaurant had its Christmas menu proudly handwritten on a huge board. Turkey, chipolatas, seasonal vegetables, punch. BOOK NOW!! I had a vision of a future in which I was the sort of person who dined alone in a pub on Christmas Day.

In less than a month – again, this reminded me of Andreas – I would be at home fielding the questions from relatives: What are you up to exactly? So, have you been in any of these television programmes? And now, a new one: So, any idea what you might do now you've . . . left? Dan, meanwhile, smirking and agreeing as Mum enumerated the many expensive things he had, and described what a 'snazzy' area she'd read the Docklands was in the *Guardian*. And why not? Why – I was as smart as Dan, smarter – why had I never gone out to make lots of money and have that kind of life? Why had I settled for this? What was I supposed to say as an end-of-year progress report: Well, I frittered half of the year away following the story of a prisoner who then vanished?

By the time I got home it was clear that the long walk had made me churn myself up much more, rather than smoothing things out. Dan, thank God, was out. I knocked on Gareth's door; silence. It was already quite late; I'd been wandering for hours.

I sank onto my bed and lay there without a proper thought in my head. The walk and the day had, at least, knocked all the energy out of me; plus I had hardly slept last night. Remembering this, I was suddenly exhausted. I lay for maybe half an hour in semi-sleep, too sluggish to make any proper moves towards going to bed. I got up, tried to call Helen; no luck. This finished me off. I threw my clothes in a heap and fell onto the bed, this time for good.

There was a knock at the door, tentative, then more forceful. It could have been a few minutes later or a few hours. I had an unpleasant sensation of not knowing whether this was a dream memory, or reality. I stretched an arm out and struck the wall. The door opened a crack. 'Hang on, hang on,' I said. I couldn't find the light; or I tried and it had gone. I was on my knees on the floor rummaging among my discarded clothes for something to wear. I grabbed an old, far from attractive jumper and pulled it down over my knees and sat on the bed thinking it just wasn't worth caring. 'Come in.'

Gareth came in and put the light on. I squinted and cowered from the light like someone who'd been in a windowless room for a week.

'Christ!' he said. 'You look . . . !'

'I know!' I said. 'I look like shit. Please don't say anything! I know already!'

Gareth frowned in surprise. He was carrying cartons of takeaway food; the smell filled my room. 'D'you want . . . ?'

'What?'

'I've finished the translation,' he said. 'If you want to read it. And I've got some food.'

As my eyes got used to the light I could see his concerned face. 'What's wrong?'

I took a deep breath. 'What's not wrong?'

'Well,' said Gareth, 'you aren't dead. But you look . . . you don't look like shit, but you look like you've had an ordeal. You look shaken. Haggard.'

He was now looming over the bed. I shuffled across and he sat down. He opened his briefcase and brought out the papers.

'So what happened?'

There were clothes all over the floor. I glanced in the mirror. It was an awful sight. I looked like a middle-aged woman who had got drunk at a wedding and woken up in someone else's house.

'Don't worry about that,' said Gareth, impatiently. 'You look fine.'

He went to the kitchen, came back with plates and started doling out the food. The smell was almost overpowering and my stomach wouldn't shut up. I began eating. Gareth came back and sank back down next to me. After a while he picked a book off the shelf and the two of us sat there, reading.

☞ ANDREAS

After all the tensions aroused in our office by Basinger's new film, not to mention the real-life romantic drama to which it had given rise, it seemed appropriate that it had been released, in Britain, under the name *Too Hot to Handle*. However, the movie had, ironically, proved less than hot with cinema-goers. It was a rather bland romantic comedy with only Basinger's singing and some fleetingly amusing chat to recommend it. 'Well! What was all the fuss about!' said Rose, as we left the cinema, where we had had to sit on the end of the back row.

But we both knew that the Basinger phenomenon had now swollen too large to be deflated by the mere question of her actual film output. Her love affair with Alec Baldwin continued to be in the news, a poster had appeared on our street advertising the soundtrack album of the film, and she had even provided the vocals for a dance music hit which found its way to number four in the British charts. This continued broadening of her appeal made competition, in the world of the shadow Basingers, all the more ferocious.

Things came, as they say, to a head in our office when a major job came up, working as a Basinger impersonator on a cruise ship in the Caribbean for a month. Nina came in to collect the paperwork for the audition. Rose managed to be absent. We both had a sinking feeling just looking at Nina these days.

'You're looking great,' I said, hoping to do some good, 'very . . . slim.'

'Do you think so?' she said, looking worried. 'I was exactly Kim's weight last week.'

She was fiddly and nervous now all the time. Just when I thought she was about to go, she picked up one of our new brochures from the kitchen table, featuring Rachel and herself, in that order, as dual Basingers. 'Seen this?'

'Yes,' I said, uncomfortably. I cleared my throat. 'I think it's purely alphabetical order.'

'But my name comes before hers,' said Nina. 'Both my names.'

I conceded this in silence.

'Why does your girlfriend hate me?' asked Nina, matter-of-factly.

'She doesn't hate anyone,' I said. 'She is just quite business-minded.'

Nina laughed bitterly. 'And she thinks I'm bad business. Well, hopefully when I'm earning . . .' she consulted the audition sheet, '$500 a night in the Caribbean, she might think differently.'

'Yes,' I said uncomfortably, 'well, good luck.'

'It's not really a question of luck,' said Nina. 'It's how much you want it.'

As often when Nina talked about her ambitions, I thought she was really addressing herself, not me. Sadly, it was becoming obvious how misleading a mantra this was, this 'How much you want it': while no one could want success more than Nina, scarcely anyone could be more separated from it by circumstances. As she was leaving, I wanted to say something; I suppose I wanted to tell her to give the whole thing up and find some more substantial ambition to give herself to, as if I had some great master plan for myself.

I gazed out of our window and, after a while, could see Nina walking slowly away from the house, past the enormous billboard from which Basinger's face gazed benignly down, her lips frozen in the act of cooing a velvety note.

'Rachel is sure to get the job on the boat,' Charles predicted. 'And after that, more, no doubt. She has had Basinger-ship thrust upon her – no maritime pun intended.' He gazed up at one of Oswald's old chandeliers. 'Perhaps before long she will consider this place more trouble than it is worth.'

'I'm sure they can find someone else to play Mrs Oswald,' I said, consolingly.

'Yes,' said Charles, gruffly, 'well, for that matter, they could find someone else to play Mr Oswald, but that is not quite the point.'

As sometimes happened with Charles, I did not really know what 'the point' was meant to be.

'What would the real James Oswald have thought of all this, I wonder?' I mused, to fill the silence.

'He would have been very surprised that people were still talking about him,' said Charles. 'Posterity does offer these odd consolations. Only if the house ever shuts down will he finally be, as it were, defeated.' His eyebrows lowered forbiddingly at this prospect. 'As for poor Nina – at the moment, it seems unlikely there will be a house dedicated to her memory.'

'Well,' I said, brightly, 'we don't know. Life is long.'

'It is,' Charles agreed, 'and it can feel it. Open a window, Andreas; it is awfully hot in here.'

The summer was full of stifling afternoons which reminded me of the uncomfortable occasion we spent with the Ravenhills in Cambridge. The hopefuls kept coming to audition and Rose kept recruiting; we now had almost thirty clients on our books. One time she announced that she had taken on a 'lookalike' of the cartoon character Homer Simpson who could emulate the voice and knew all the relevant catchphrases. (The show was at the time very popular and still seems to be, to judge from the limited choice of television channels in my present home.) We went to see him performing at a fan club convention. It was 10 August: I will never forget the date.

This man – Roger – used for his impersonation a yellow food-colouring-based dye which was nearly impossible to eradicate from the skin, and so he walked around everywhere looking like someone adversely affected by radioactivity. But Roger, like most lookalikes, had plans for bigger things. 'I see this as a platform,' he told us. 'I'm looking to be doing the big Shakespeare roles, ultimately. The Hamlets and the Macbeths; perhaps not the Romeos because I don't have a romantic face.' I laughed, but he was serious.

'He's a bit pompous,' Rose said, when our yellowish client had gone to the bar, 'but it's good for us to have someone we can use in the kids' market. I don't think Hitler or Jack the Ripper go down well at children's parties.'

'Most of my shows might as well be children's parties,' I grumbled. Rose patted me on the head.

'Poor little Andy, not being taken seriously enough again!'

'Stop it . . .' I said.

'Perhaps you should try your hand at opera?' she suggested.

Roger had come back to the table. He wiped his forehead; a lurid residue was left on the back of his hand. 'I'm very glad to have joined the agency,' he said. 'Are you a business partner?' he asked me.

I was startled by the question. 'I am in fact a lookalike myself,' I said, probably rather snootily.

'Andreas does Hitler,' Rose explained. I waited for Roger to register this and say, 'Oh yes, I've heard of you,' and suddenly behave in an obsequious manner, as happened to me fairly often, but he blinked and said, 'That sounds rather a niche market.'

'So is Homer Simpson!' I retorted, with a show of good humour.

'Well, *The Simpsons* has an enormous following . . .' said Roger.

'Hitler had a following of thirty-nine million!' I said, still straining not to sound petulant.

'Now then, Andreas,' said Rose, patting my hand, 'it's not a pissing contest.' Roger laughed in a fawning way at the phrase which, being new to my ears, put me at still more of a disadvantage. I went out of the room to try to compose myself next time there was a break in conversation, and felt a new type of disappointment with myself, stemming from the fact I had been so quick and heated in the defence of something I was rapidly coming to think of as idiotic.

When I returned, they were talking about Robert, whom

Roger knew well, which should not have been a surprise: Robert seemed to have a link to every variety act, 'freak' and eccentric in London. I sat irritably on my bar stool, not relishing the discussion of what a great guy Robert was, what a fine sense of humour he possessed and how bravely he brought it to bear on his physical disability. As time wore on, I made territorial attempts to stake a claim to Rose by slinging an arm around her and playing with the little hairs on her arms, but she brushed me off, muttering, 'Not now.' The sting of possessiveness swelled in the usual way and by the time we got home, I was longing to tear her clothes off.

Our bed was covered in paperwork relating to the forthcoming National Lookalike Show; I swept it off the bed with one hand and took her in my arms, collapsing onto the mattress and breaking her fall with my body. The breath was knocked out of me as she landed on top. Her face fell into mine.

'Punish me,' she whispered.

'Can't we just . . .' I said. 'Can't we just make love?'

'What do you call this?' she whispered. I was breathing heavily as I tried to drag her further up the bed, so that her toes did not catch the wall behind her.

'I mean – love,' I said, 'rather than, you know, punishment.'

'Do you want me or don't you?' she asked.

'I do, I do,' I protested, 'but I don't want to . . . play games.'

Rose sighed. 'Well, can we get on with it, then? I'm getting a bit chilly here.'

'What do you mean, "Get on with it"?' I asked, as angrily as I could, given that I was still clutching her knickers. 'Can't you get interested in me unless we do all this . . . nonsense?'

'Don't call it nonsense!' said Rose angrily, flipping herself away from me and snatching her underwear with unlikely dignity. I began to apologise.

She had already slung a bedsheet around herself. 'I'm sorry if you think my tastes are nonsensical,' she said, her eyes flashing. 'I suppose that's what you get if you make love to a freak.'

'Will you leave that fucking word alone!' I yelled. Both of us were momentarily silenced by the outburst. 'It's just an excuse,' I said in a more measured tone, 'for you to pity yourself and feel that you will never be a normal person.'

'Have you even got a clue what it's like to be this tall?' Rose asked.

'I have more than a clue,' I said unkindly, 'because you talk about it all the time.'

Rose went into the living room. I was about to follow her when the phone began to ring, its tone rather contemptuous. I waited to see if Rose was going to answer it. There was no sound of her shifting, and after a few rings I heard her begin to sing some wretched song from the Basinger movie. I waited for the telephone to stop. This went on for at least a minute. Swearing as I grazed my elbow on the door, I went to answer it.

It was Ralf. The sound of his voice was both a pleasant and an uneasy surprise. We had scarcely spoken in the last three months; it had just been easier not to.

'It's Dad,' he said.

Since losing his job, my father had been working on a semi-voluntary basis at a development site just outside Berlin. This morning, he had begun to have chest pains. When the foreman suggested that he stop early to catch his breath, my father only redoubled his efforts. He lifted and moved a huge pile of breeze blocks to which two men had been assigned. They only realised how much he had done when he fell over and a colleague, who had crouched down to help him up, instead ran screaming for help towards the foreman's hut. By the time paramedics had arrived, my father was dead.

'I don't believe it,' I kept saying. 'Are you serious?'

'Does it sound like a joke?' Ralf asked.

We discussed practicalities. He was being buried in five days. I was going to have to fly back. Ralf, helped by one of our uncles, was taking care of the arrangements and expenses. All this was completely incomprehensible. My father was only fifty-eight. We had not had a proper conversation in several weeks, and, arguably, rather longer than that. I had all kinds of loose ends which he was meant to tie up when we were older. I said goodbye in a daze. There were no feelings at all.

I sat down on the bed where a few minutes ago we had been in the middle of a naked argument. My limbs were heavy and I had 'pins and needles'. I began trying to phrase the sentence, in vain, but in any case, she had heard enough of the conversation to understand.

'Is he . . . is he dead?'

She took my hand and began to stroke it gently.

'My God,' she murmured. 'Are you all right?'

'Yes, yes, I am all right,' I said.

The hours wore on. We had always been so formal in our dealings, my father and I, that my brain seemed to feel any immediate display of grief would be excessive. Rose, half-asleep, whispered comfortingly to me through the grainy darkness. I felt her long arm wrap around my back and tried to let her soothe the sadness I was desperate to feel.

*

I flew from Gatwick on a misty Tuesday morning. Rose had decided not to accompany me. 'You don't want people gawping at me,' she said. 'I'll overshadow . . . you know.'

Much as I disliked encouraging this kind of statement, I felt a certain relief. For one thing, it was true she would stand out sorely, and moreover I needed a little time to myself. I was hoping that this bleak enforced trip would serve as a jolt of some kind to me. So Rose stayed at home, completing our preparations for the National Lookalike Show, where I was going to be one of the main attractions.

I ate tasteless chicken and looked at my former hometown from above. It seemed optimistic and orderly. A couple sunbathed naked in the Tiergarten as I went past in the taxi. Near the Brandenburg Gate there were red, black, and yellow posters mounted by groups like the one my brother had got caught up in. Some had been partially torn down.

Through all the readings, the reminiscences about how brave he had been when our mother died, and in boyhood when he had 'lost' his father in the war, I sat dry-eyed. 'Despite all this he managed to raise two fine boys,' someone concluded, and I looked at Ralf, shaven-headed in his dark suit. We were no longer boys and I wasn't sure how fine either of us was.

In the church hall, groups of older relatives sat around discussing my father's father, and his death in the war. 'It was such a blow to Klaus,' someone said, 'the way he went. After that, Klaus was like a snail going into his shell.' For some reason this image affected me more than all the conventional tributes of the funeral service. I remembered how my father always used to grip the arms of his favourite chair very hard, and the way he looked out of the window, and the tunes he whistled. What made me feel empty and sad was not the memories themselves but the hopeless slimness of them.

'Well, he played his part,' said a man with bushy eyebrows, referring to my grandfather's death.

There were wise nods. I felt a sudden bitterness towards this man, who I gathered, from others' conversations, had been a middle-ranking government official in the war, and had gone, as someone said, 'under the radar' for a long time afterwards by going to the United States until the sixties when it was safe to return. In his tiny way he had allowed the fuse to be lit for the destruction of a whole generation, and had therefore cooperated in the driving of my father into that shell. And here he was still, this man with his silly eyebrows, his double chins, eating a piece of pork at the funeral. Of course it might be ridiculously arbitrary to accuse him even in my head, but was it, really? Everything affected everything else.

I went outside, where it had started to rain softly as my father began his long residency under the earth, and toured the churchyard, feeling very old as my shoes sank into the soft turf.

In spite of everything, I naturally thought about Rose, and in general about what was waiting when I went back. All I could be sure of was that the present, alone, mattered now. How I had come to be impersonating Hitler, how Ralf had ended up this way, how Rose and I had gone quite swiftly from sexual perfection to loggerheads was unimportant. It was the status quo that had to be dealt with.

In the church hall, another one of the older men was denouncing the present state of Germany, in particular the way that the lowering of the Wall had allowed 'all kinds of people' to take their places in our society.

Ralf was nodding solemnly. 'The trouble is,' he said, 'nationalism has become a dirty word. National pride has to be restored.'

'Klaus might still be alive now,' said the man with the eyebrows, 'if he hadn't lost his job . . .'

I went outside again, to a telephone box.

'Beware Imitations,' said Rose's voice.

'It's me,' I said.

'How was the funeral?'

I took a breath. 'Rose, I think it is time for me to give up the Hitler act. I don't ever want to do it again. I want you to cancel the theatre show and so on. I'll do whatever else you want. I could just help to run the business, or I could get another job.'

The pause was very much longer over the telephone. 'It's extremely bad timing,' she said, 'with the Lookalike Show coming up.'

'I've definitely made my mind up,' I said. 'It's finished.'

'Right,' said Rose quietly. 'I'd better start telling people, then.'

I knew that if we discussed it for any length of time, I would relent. 'Is there any other news?' I asked.

'Rachel got the Kim Basinger job,' said Rose, distantly.

'That's great!' I said. 'Is she pleased?'

'Of course she's pleased.'

The time was already beginning to run out. We said goodbye. I put the receiver back into its slot and leaned against the glass. Surely, now, I had taken a positive step. If only I had the Hitler costume with me, I thought, I would burn it. In reality, though, I probably would not have done any such thing.

*

Back in London, I hesitated over going home. I had probably imagined that breaking the news of my resignation over the phone would make it easier; on the contrary, it meant that I felt I now had to do it all over again. She would expect me to apologise, say it was the emotion of the funeral, and so on. I was attracted by the window of a job centre and went in to ask if they had any temporary positions, unsure of how serious I was. I gave them a brief summary of my life up to, but not including, Hitler.

'And what have you been doing for the past year?' asked the man behind the desk, who seemed weary of the conversation almost before it had started.

'I've been involved in a cabaret act.'

He looked at me as grimly as if I had confessed to a career in grave-robbing. 'And are you a British citizen?'

'Not yet,' I said, 'but I am cohabiting with one. She represents several lookalikes,' I added, hoping to strengthen my position.

The man pushed a blue file at me. 'This is all the unskilled stuff we've got at the moment.'

'I've got a degree from Cambridge,' I said desperately.

The man pursed his lips. 'In what?'

'American literature,' I said, 'especially . . .' I, like the man, was now wishing this had never begun, 'especially the twentieth century.'

The employment expert now seemed to believe I was deliberately wasting his time. 'Listen,' he said, 'I don't know if you have noticed, but Germans aren't exactly flavour of the month round here.'

I was shaken by the virulence of this remark and felt tempted for a moment to attempt to get him into trouble of some sort, but weakness overcame this instinct. I went out and stood numbly on the street. A red bus rattled past, belching smoke. I felt very much on my own.

Rose got up to kiss me when I arrived, but with little enthusiasm. I slung my suit listlessly onto the bed and without comment she salvaged it and folded it up. She smelt strongly of a new perfume. After very little chat about my flight, she went back to her desk. 'I'm up to my eyes in it,' she said, 'even my eyes.' On the desk was a pile of newly taken photos of Rachel as Kim Basinger, each one stapled to a glossy CV.

'Now Rachel's about to really take off, it's the time to push her everywhere we can,' said Rose, half to herself. Pinned to her word-processor was a request for our Take That band to sing at a benefit evening for retired midwives. And everywhere was documentation about the National Lookalike Show. Outside, I could hear Charles's 'Oswald' voice floating up the stairs. 'I keep telling you, I am an unheralded genius!' And Rachel: 'I agree with the first part.'

Experiencing a pressing desire to get out of this office and away from the feeling of having betrayed Rose, I thought it might be amusing to join the tour and give the two of them a surprise. As the tour group drifted from one room to another, I melded myself with them like a ghost, slipping between a doddery couple of Americans, one of whom had an expensive camera around his neck and kept crouching over tables and ornaments as if to eat them.

'On the last day of September 1888,' Charles informed the group gravely, talking like a book more than ever, 'Oswald came home drunk from a party at Linley Sambourne's house to find the house cold and empty. Tessa was nowhere to be found. Convinced that the drink was deceiving him, he shouted her name in every room of the house, and the names of his children.

'During that evening Tessa, having polished each item for a final time, had collected up her valises and, with one confused child on each arm, had departed for her sister's in Scarborough, where she would be staying, she wrote to James Oswald, "indefinitely, for the good of everybody".

'She was tired of living with a man who did not give her the things she most craved, she said; tired of making do with less money than other people's wives, of lying to her friends about what exactly James did. Tired of his lower-deck accent and of their house in the wrong part of London.'

I could see Rachel hovering in the corner, smiling to herself at Charles's loquaciousness. It was 'touch and go' how long Charles would talk for when he chose to come out of the character and become a history lecturer. Today he was on particularly verbose form. One or two of his audience were shuffling, or leaning back against antiques.

'James Oswald went to find Penny,' Charles went on, relentlessly. '"She's gone, she's gone, she's gone," he told her, in a tremendous frenzy. "I shall have to go to Yorkshire and bring her back!"

'And off he went, the next day. There was nobody at home: Tessa and the children had gone with her sister to see some other relatives. Not knowing what to do, James Oswald sat on the doorstep and waited as the night wore on. His hat, from A. Gold, was blown off his head, into a mound of cow dung in a neighbouring field; his jacket became heavy in the drizzle. It was colder in Yorkshire than he was used to, and there was nobody to look after him. He felt sure that when Tessa returned, his wretched state would force her to relent.

'But when at last they came back, at about noon the next day, Oswald was asleep on the doorstep, looking, in his own account, "like the lowliest vagrant, like a fat will-o'-the-wisp", and Tessa's sister had to be dissuaded from summoning the constabulary. He went back to London, a humiliated man.

'Here you can see the word "ABANDONED" has been scratched into the desk,' said Charles, and his listeners leaned in one at a time like dominoes to study the minute inscription. The voracious American next to me fiddled with his camera lens and poised himself to snap the desk, but Charles stopped him with a polite raise of the hand.

'I am very sorry for your loss, sir,' said Rachel now, rejoining the fray as Penny.

'Ah, Penny,' said Charles, drawing himself up to his full tragic height and, in his own mind, I thought, delivering a soliloquy of Shakespeare. 'This separation is a cruel thing. I am not designed to survive on my own. I am like one of the plants Mr Darwin describes which rely on symbiosis, which may seem strong and self-reliant, but—'

'Excuse me,' chipped in one of the tour group, 'how much longer will the tour go on for? I have an appointment.'

'Ah! abandoned again!' said Charles immediately, tapping the desk. There was general, rather relieved, laughter.

The tour went on along the corridor, past a marble bust of Tiberius, and a framed copy of one of Oswald's advertisements: 'Children holler and wail for Johnson's Ginger Ale'. As Charles began his discourse again, I slipped away and back up to the office, where Rose was still half-buried in a mountain of Lookalike Show paperwork. I made tea – recently there had been fewer trips to Koffee Kompany – and persuaded her to take a break.

Over the next couple of days I managed to make myself useful, largely by doing the day-to-day work of chasing up money and organising auditions and jobs and so on, while Rose continued her preparations for the show. Our agency was going to have a stall, where potential clients could see our acts and read information about them. At the same time Rose would be circulating among the lookalikes who were present, to see if there were any she might try to 'poach' for us. And there would be a number of temporary stages set up on which, throughout the weekend, individual lookalikes and tribute acts would perform. Lesser acts might get two or three minutes, with hardly anyone watching, but in the prime slots on the Friday and Saturday nights, there would be considerable crowds. I flicked through the itinerary in the event's programme: the word CANCELLED was written across my face on the Friday-night line-up.

It could not help but occur to someone reading the programme as an outsider, as I tried to do now, that this whole thing was rather funny and odd – a whole trade fair given to advertising people who played the songs of the Rolling Stones or looked like Madonna. Perhaps any job was similarly absurd if one looked cold-headedly at its pretensions and paraphernalia. But for Rose, this was really serious. The Lookalike Show was the most important event of the year for businesses of our kind. Robert, who had been to the past three or four, seemed to have filled her head with the idea that this event would be, as she said, 'make-or-break'.

In the run-up to the big occasion, I settled nicely into the role of personal assistant to Rose. I took phone calls while she was on the other line, sealed envelopes, made sure everyone knew what time they were meant to be there, printed out CVs – all this sort of thing. It was a harmonious couple of days, and it gave me a glimpse of how the future might possibly be. I was never meant to be up on a stage doing something uncomfortable – I was not one of those people who felt drawn to the attention and the acclaim, and I would happily be the one who held the fort while bigger battles were being fought. I massaged her back, made sure that she took lunch-breaks at respectable times, and went shopping for camomile tea and bath oils to relax her.

'Is there anything else I can do?' I asked, on the eve of the show, as we packed everything up for the next morning.

'There is one thing you could do which would be great,' said Rose, putting a pencil between her teeth as she turned her attention to a second pile of envelopes.

'Yes, anything,' I said eagerly.

'Do you think you could find me someone exactly like you who could do Hitler over the weekend and for the rest of the time and save me from looking like an idiot and save the company from collapsing?'

'I'm sorry,' I said, after a silence. There was nothing else to say.

'I'm sorry,' she said. 'It's your decision. It's not as if I only love you for your Hitler impression.' Whether this was a coded reference to our bedroom exploits, I was not sure, but there was none of that tonight, in any case; Rose was asleep almost before I got between the sheets.

We left the house for Kensington at about half past seven in the morning; I carried files, made telephone calls, helped to set up a table, fetched her coffee, knowing all the time that no help I could give would cancel out the trouble I had already caused. Our acts assembled at half past eight, in time for the nine o'clock start. Rachel and Nina stood, not looking at each other, in identical dresses, Rachel's brown eyes matched by Nina's coloured contact lenses. Elvis Leslie had been applying his make-up since cock-crow. Robert was unsettling other agencies by peering over the tops of their stalls as they tried to get ready. Julian, clad in his overcoat, would occasionally squeeze Rachel's elbow or stroke her arm, his fake knife brushing against her dress as he did so. Everyone kept looking at me.

Rose had got up several times in the night. I tried to ask if she was all right more than once, but each enquiry was brushed off quite sharply. She gave all the lookalikes their instructions for the rest of the day. Julian was to sneak up behind people and put his hands over their eyes, and other such pantomime antics; patrons had been warned in the programme, 'Watch out for a certain Victorian gentleman making his rounds – you'll have a ripping time if he gets to grips with you!' Elvis Leslie was 'busking' in the foyer, along with a cacophony of other tribute acts whose competing warbles provided a ghastly welcome to ticket-holders. For Robert, it was enough simply to strut about everywhere being tall. Everyone was useful, except me.

Important people wore name badges, which meant that every conversation began with a mutual glance at the lapels. 'But the ones to watch out for,' Rose told me as she drank her third cup of coffee, 'are the ones who are too important to bother wearing name badges at all.'

'Like who?'

'Like her, she's from the BBC,' she said, indicating a woman of Caribbean origin who wore a business suit and was smiling at everyone. 'Or him,' pointing across the hall to a grey-suited man with short salt-and-pepper hair who was deep in conversation with another agent, while a low-quality Marilyn Monroe lookalike tried in vain to catch his eye. 'He's head of entertainment for a TV company. He's interested in . . . in the Hitler thing. Was interested.'

I gripped her hand, but she withdrew it. 'Not here.'

'Look,' I said, 'I'm sorry. I should have said something a long time ago.'

'What you should have done,' said Rose, 'is not got my hopes up by being so good in the first place.'

'It wasn't just a whim . . .' I began.

'Excuse me,' someone said, jogging her elbow, 'can I ask which agency represents you?'

Rose looked up to see the woman from the BBC. 'Oh, I'm not an act,' she said, 'I'm an agent. Rose Ravenhill, Beware Imitations.' She extended her hand. The woman took it and seemed to weigh it in her own hand, as if she had been invited to guess whether Rose was a real person.

'But I thought I saw you talking to the other . . . giant,' said the woman.

'Yes,' said Rose, reddening, 'he's a freak act, but I just run the agency.'

'You are extremely tall, though,' the woman observed.

'Yes,' Rose conceded. 'I mean, if you're interested in a freak act,' she went on hopefully, 'Robert would more than fit the bill.'

'Thank you for your help,' said the woman with a brilliant smile. She headed off to the next stall like the Queen meeting ballboys at Wimbledon.

'I thought she was someone important,' I said in a surprised whisper.

'Important isn't the same as intelligent,' Rose said with a sigh.

'You are tall, though, she had a point.' I risked joking. Rose gave me a reluctant laugh and there was a palpable warming of the air between us.

The day seemed to drag on for so long that, by the end, to

remember breakfast time was almost an act of nostalgia. Finally, with some stalls already beginning to pack up for the night, Rose secured an audience with the grey-suited man she had been eyeing up in the afternoon.

'You're Rose Ravenhill,' he said, arching his neck gamely to look her in the eye. 'I spoke to you on the phone about my current project.'

'About murderers . . .' she said.

The man nodded. 'It's basically a look at some of the worst murderers ever. We're looking to be controversial, a little bit challenging, which is why I thought of you. Tell me, you have a Hitler on your books, don't you?'

Rose hesitated for a long moment. 'Unfortunately, he's retiring.'

'Retiring!' said the executive. 'He must have been successful!'

'Too successful for his own good,' Rose said, with a slow smile.

'Well, what a shame,' the grey man said. 'I guess we'll have to rule that out, then.'

'But if it's a murderer you're looking for,' Rose said, 'then Julian really is good.'

'Yes. Hmm.' The grey man pondered. 'Jack the Ripper. It's just a bit old hat. Whereas Hitler: new. Modern.'

Rose's smile was now like a car accident. 'I suppose you're right,' she said. 'Well, if he comes out of retirement, I'll let you know.'

The grey man smiled kindly. The number of smiles that had been exchanged that day was almost painful to consider.

Rose was so tired that she could hardly walk. Thinking about the crowds at the station, the rattled glares of other passengers, I offered to pay for a taxi.

'It's a waste of money,' she said faintly.

'I've been a waste of money,' I said. She gave a wintry smile and squeezed my hand gently. She fell asleep on my shoulder in the car, and I strained my spine to sit up as straight as possible. West to east we went, the taxi inching forward along what seemed one endless black column of cars stretching all the way along the river. When we pulled up on Cloth Street – the driver pulling on the handbrake with touching gentleness – I wished I could lift her out of the car and sling her over my shoulder like a baby.

'Don't do any more work,' I pleaded with her, as she picked up the phone and began listening for messages. 'You need to sleep.' Ignoring my advice, she sat motionless for some time, the receiver pressed against her ear. When she replaced it, it was with a frown of disappointment. 'No enquiries. Nothing.'

'You wouldn't expect it so soon,' I said, 'the event's only half-over.'

'You'd expect something,' Rose insisted.

'You need to relax,' I said. 'You can't afford to be thinking about work non-stop.'

'Oh, I'm sorry for being so professional,' said Rose bitingly. 'I'm sorry for trying to take this seriously rather than just toying with success and dropping it.'

I was sick of this sort of argument. 'Can't you stop hammering me over this Hitler thing!' I said in a rising voice. 'I'm doing what I think is best!'

'And I'm doing what I think is best,' Rose protested, 'trying to make something of myself, for once in my life, instead of just some giant—'

'Always the tall thing!' I yelled, viciously. 'Always feeling sorry for yourself!'

'You'll never understand,' she said, with a bitter smile. 'You pretend to be all compassionate.'

'Let me guess,' I sneered, 'only Robert can ever understand you, no matter how much anyone else loves you.'

'Don't mention Robert!' she shrieked.

'Ah, the holy cow . . .' I began, sarcastically. She started laughing wildly. 'Shut up, shut up!' she said. Tears were suddenly clustering in her eyes and making a mess of her face.

'Stop it,' I said, 'don't cry.' This only had the effect of making her weep more violently. She covered her face, her shoulders were wrenching and I almost thought she might be sick. It was alarming.

'Look,' I said, 'this is a stupid argument . . .'

'No, it's not,' she gasped, with a phlegmy cough. 'No, it's not, I slept with Robert, I slept with him, I'm so sorry.'

My first impulse was simply incredulity, not of the theatrical kind that leads people to shout, 'I don't believe it!' but a blank refusal to engage with the facts. It seemed ridiculous.

'How?' was the first thing I asked. 'When I was in Germany?' She nodded. Tears had forced themselves back down her throat and were causing a coughing fit, which made her wince and put a hand to her left breast. Far downstairs, the Oswalds' old grandfather clock struck.

'But he wasn't even around when I went to Germany!' I objected. 'He was doing the audition for Freaks USA!'

'It was cancelled,' she muttered, a tear making it all the way down her chin to slip into her lap. 'The guy had flu,' she added. At this last, bathetic detail, wordless feelings finally began to flare up in me. I laughed, amazed. Rose, snuffling, left the room and came back with a wad of tissues pressed against her nose.

There was a terrible hollow sensation as if the memories of all our happy days had been physically removed from my insides like so many strands of DNA; and I felt a desire to find Robert straight away and kill him. And ladled on top of the stew of feeling was the element of sheer farce, her with her moist mountain of tissues towering above me, describing how I had been cuckolded by two of the tallest people in the country.

'Please,' she said, 'please forgive me.'

I shrugged. 'I forgive you.'

'But as if you mean it,' she said, in a crushed voice. 'What can I do?'

I spread my hands helplessly. There was a giant feeling of nothingness in the room. Soon, light would begin to break outside. There were some shouts from drunks on the street below. Rose went to blow her nose again; water gurgled in pipes above us. With every silent minute that passed, the mundane nature of reality was robbing the situation of its gravity. She walked back in from the bathroom and sat down slowly, slowly. Each action seemed to suck something from the moment.

'I'm tired,' she said in a small voice. 'I'll sleep here on the floor.'

'Don't be stupid,' I said, walking around behind her and touching her neck. I felt her stiffen with desire and, instinctively, bent to kiss her. She whirled around and grabbed me, and suddenly we were wrestling on the floor. Thought did not come into it. Thought had failed me, action was all that spoke now, and this was the only action that seemed equal to everything. As the excitement built, I shouted at her, 'Wasn't I good enough?'

'Of course you were,' she said, her eyes closed. 'Please don't . . .'

'Wasn't I good enough?' I asked again, and slapped her in the face. Her eyes sprang open in amazement.

'I didn't want that,' she said.

I was speechless. Her cheek was a little red. We eyed each other. Neither of us knew what it meant. A second later it was over anyway, and we crawled apart, tired and confused beyond discussion. Two minutes later she was asleep, sprawled naked across the bed on her back, her head thrown back with honey hair all over the place, as strange and beautiful as ever before.

On top of everything else, we were meant to be staging a party on the Saturday night, when the Lookalike Show was over. We were up early dusting and cleaning, smartening things up. Neither of us mentioned the previous night, any part of it. There was a tacit understanding between us that I would not go to the show today, because Robert would be there, and she would put him off coming to the party because I would be there. This was exactly the kind of half-baked solution that had got me into half the trouble I was in, but the habit was proving hard to shake off.

I had lunch with Charles in Koffee Kompany. 'At the risk of seeming nosy,' he observed, 'I thought I heard something like a very loud series of shouts from your flat last night.'

'Ah,' I said, embarrassed. 'There was an argument.'

Charles nodded. 'Regarding your decision not to go on as Hitler?'

It was easier than explaining everything. 'Yes,' I said. 'I feel guilty.'

'It is never wrong to stick to principles when those principles are sound,' said Charles.

I felt a lot better after this reassurance, fairly banal as it may have been – perhaps it came from George Bernard Shaw, or somewhere of the kind – and was moved to shake his hand.

'Please,' said Charles, 'do not be tempted to go back on your decision. You will never forgive yourself.'

I nodded, feeling the truth of this. 'And I would be very disappointed if you put yourself in that situation,' he added.

All day, I thought about Rose and Robert at the Lookalike Show. He was clocking up minute after minute after minute in the little book of her time he had stolen from me. My mind was finding every possible path to jealousy. What I should have been pondering was, of course, what in God's name I was going to do with my life if I wasn't going to be Hitler, but there were no obvious answers.

It kept coming into my head to call home, and it would be some moments before I remembered that my father was dead and that things were no longer the same between my brother and me.

I turned myself to the distraction of finishing the cleaning and tidying job we had begun for the party. Rose was of course fond of making fun of my orderliness, and at first it was even painful to think of this, because my mental picture of her teasing me came packaged with another one, of her with Robert. It was as if everything I could feasibly think or feel about Rose would, from now on, be contaminated by traces of this phantom memory. Gradually, as I scrubbed the bath, polished the surface of our coffee table, worked a cloth around the rim of a tumbler, applied a glass cleaner to the face of our bedside alarm clock and vacuumed the place until everything looked new and processed, my mood began to lift. It was not as if I had discovered a long infidelity, or as if she had been unapologetic. It had been an aberration. This kind of thing occurred very often without doing severe damage to the health of a relationship: not if there was real love at the bottom of it.

And, I thought, ironing a pile of Rose's clothes – the oversize T-shirts from a factory reject shop, the leggings a friend made her by sewing together material from two normal pairs – if I were man enough, I would admit to myself that it was essential for someone like her, with such a physical peculiarity, to have a confidant in a similar predicament. A shame that it had to be Robert – a shame it had to be someone so smarmy and unsettling and, yes, someone who would sleep with her right under my nose, but with a strenuous effort I could see that it was only natural she would be tempted. How could I really tell her how to behave unless I had sampled all the inconveniences she lived with, unless I had gone through life knowing each day I would be stared at everywhere I went?

I ironed her nightgown, a dark blue satin thing made in Morocco, hung it on the door, considered putting it out of the way because we would soon be overrun by guests, then decided to leave it. Some time later I came back into the room and thought for a moment there was a person hanging there.

At about nine, the sound of high-pitched laughter on the stairs announced the beginning of the party. About fifteen people came clattering up towards our flat. Someone tripped over on the final, lethal flight of stairs and there were cheers.

Rose was very much more relaxed, now it was all over. She kissed me on the mouth and I put my arms around her waist; I could feel the long, smooth curve of her buttocks.

'Anyone would think you hadn't seen each other for years!' said Rachel, as the kiss went on.

'Where's Julian?' I asked.

'He's coming, bless him,' said Rachel.

'Rachel's got good news,' said Rose, lifting Rachel off her feet; Rachel screamed.

'It's nothing that big,' she said.

'One of the TV people wants Rachel for *Stars and Their Doppelgangers*!' Rose said.

'That's wonderful,' I said, grabbing them both by the arm. We had an ungainly embrace there on the step outside the flat. Charles's door opened.

'Good evening,' he said to everyone with a little bow. He seemed to avoid looking anyone directly in the eye as he went into our flat to join the party. I hoped he would find someone to talk to, at least until his friend Julian arrived. I had laid out snacks in little bowls, at Rose's direction, and these were already being passed around and dropped onto our carpet. Laughter and general noise began to wrap itself around everything.

The hours raced away. The delusion that I had 'earned' a drink soon fooled me into carrying a bottle of red wine around and swigging from it almost constantly, licking my lips as it stung the inside of my throat. A lot more people arrived and I remember being a little alarmed that some of them might spill downstairs into the off-limits parts of the museum. Cannabis clouds were in the air. A Jesus lookalike showed us a plate-spinning trick. People were going from our flat to Charles's and back again. It all spun around me.

Deep in the haze I had brought down over myself, someone tapped my elbow. I spun around; it was Nina. 'Hello, stranger,' she said. She had not only removed her coloured lenses, but she was also wearing spectacles; she had tied her hair back to bare her forehead; and she had discarded the high heels she nearly always wore to bring her up to 'Kim's height'. She looked very much like she always used to at college. It would have been delightful to draw the moral that she looked far more beautiful as herself than as a copy of the star, but that was, in fact, not true.

'How's the weekend been for you?' I shouted, over the music.

She gave a thumbs-up. 'Fine.'

'When are you working next?' I risked asking.

She put her arm around my shoulders, drunkenly; I saw Rose glance at us across the room. Nina shouted into my ear, 'Not actually got any work in my diary now. But you've got to keep going!'

I think it was after midnight when I became hazily aware of a number of people pointing at me and murmuring. Rachel was standing on our coffee table singing along to a song on our stereo; one of our Take That lookalikes was accompanying her in the duet and Julian, next to Rachel, was thumping the beat on a biscuit tin. I couldn't see Nina or Charles. I spun to look behind me; Rose was standing there. 'I'll ask him,' she yelled at the people around the table. 'That's all I can do!'

'What seems to be the problem?' I asked, good-naturedly.

Rose rolled her eyes. 'You can say no, please feel free to say no, but they all want you to do you-know-what.'

Several guests nearby began to chant, 'Hitler! Hitler!' The two syllables seemed to lend each other weight until it was hard to hear anything else. I looked around at the expectant faces.

I tell myself now that it was the drink, or the need to reclaim Rose's respect, in fact I have tried all sorts of justifications, but the fact is that – bolstered on all sides by frenetic whooping and clapping – I allowed myself to be hoisted up onto the table. A hush fell over the room. I think every part of my brain had gone to sleep except the part which craved love.

'People of Germany!' I said, in German. 'Our hour has come.'

All the different laughs became one huge talon, plucking me from the table and lifting me over all the heads, even Rose's, and holding me suspended in power over everyone assembled. I gabbled on, in German, German–English, anything went. After a while I was conscious of Charles's face towards the back of the room, his arms folded as he watched the Hitler act being beaten like a carpet in front of this mob, with everything that had been good or valuable escaping in great clouds. But it was easy enough to squeeze him out of my mind, along with the hundred other reasons I ought not to have been up there.

It was a great deal of time later – and a lot of wine and who knows what else – that I emerged from this sad spectacle, and the dizzy haze that followed, to find myself supine and dull-headed, Rose beside me on our bed. The first weak rays peered accusingly through our windows; we had not drawn the curtains before lying down, indeed, I could not remember having lain down in the first place. I had been into a deep, brief sleep only to wake rather abruptly: it was five-fifteen. I spent some time stumbling in and out of consciousness: five-thirty, five-fifty. At the time, though, I experienced things as one long sequence: it was only later, when I tried to piece our conversations and actions together, that I realised how much was missing from my memory. My main recollection is of the unusually powerful headache my drinking had got me. I felt as if something heavy had been transplanted into my skull and was sitting there malignantly.

I went to the bathroom and, through the wall, heard Charles muttering in his sleep as I lifted the lavatory seat only for my unsteady hands to drop it with what seemed a deafening clatter. When I returned, Rose had stirred and woken, and we lay simply looking at each other for a while. She, too, was worse off from alcohol. 'Silly cow,' she moaned at herself. 'Drank enough for ten people.'

'You have been like ten people recently,' I said, meaning it as a tribute to her workload of the past few weeks; but it sounded peculiar and rather missed the mark.

Rather than lapsing back into the drunken sleep one would have expected, each of us gradually became more alert, though it was an unpleasant sort of alertness. Light from outside was now shining through the windows, rather too strongly for comfort; neither of us could quite raise the energy to get up and draw the curtains. As it became brighter, I could see that our bedroom was a tremendous mess. Empty beer cans were everywhere, spillages had been amateurishly mopped up with crumpled clods of tissue paper left at the scene. Cigarette butts lay in, and around, ashtrays. All this augured badly for the rest of the flat, where there had been far more revellers.

I felt her hands run gently over my chest, down into my groin; I shut my eyes.

'The place is a pig-hole,' I said, confusedly.

'We'll do it tomorrow,' she murmured.

I played my fingers along her neck and shoulders and we began to kiss. Even in this inglorious moment, her breath retained a certain sweetness which I felt fairly sure was not matched by my own. At the time, I remember feeling as if the heaviness of the hangover was melting away in the rising heat of the moment, though a third party would probably have noted how clumsy my movements still were. Looking back, I am unable to remember the whole thing in much detail, and, God knows, I have tried many, many times.

Individual moments I do recall with a little clarity. She began to hark back to her infidelity. 'You know I'm sorry, don't you? You know I'm sorry?' I was not in the mood for talking or thinking about her and Robert.

'There's no point in any more apologies,' I replied, or something to that effect, and then realised what she wanted was not forgiveness, but on the contrary, punishment.

She gnawed on her lip and reached behind her head to grip the headboard as, stiffening all the way through my body, I pushed her backwards and clambered onto her, making the first contact as hard as it could be: at the feeling of me she let out a yell. The blood was rushing through my head.

'Hit me, come on,' she whispered, wrenching herself out of my grasp and rolling away onto her side, then onto her stomach. The sheets beneath us were slipping off the bed. I straddled her, pressing into her back. I ran my hands through the softness, the richness of her hair and she moaned with impatience. Her long, smooth back, the way it cleft into buttocks which in turn gave way to the longest legs anyone could ever imagine. What I wanted was to kiss each tiny hair on each leg. But I raised my hand and brought it down on her, hard enough to leave a mark, harder, over and over again.

'That's it . . .' she groaned.

You might say it was disgust with myself that gave me the energy to do it. Or maybe there was still some voice in my head claiming that, if I kept on succeeding in these little missions, other problems would disappear. She had buried her head in the blankets, her mighty back was rising and falling ecstatically, and her hands had knotted themselves together on the headboard.

Shuffling off the bed and turning my back on her with an unbecoming combination of sexual fervour and clumsiness, I took down her dressing gown from the door, removed the cord and secured it around her wrists. I could feel her breath, fast and hot. She muttered directions; she was never quite out of control of things. I picked up the belt which had become such a familiar tool.

After that, God help me, my memories are – perhaps wilfully – dim again. Everything was patchy and blurred enough even at the time. Certainly we seem to have acted with an abandon that surpassed anything that had gone before. All the emotions that had been gathering like smoke in the air, the week's strains, the ongoing tensions between us, the headiness of things, all these had coalesced into a potent atmosphere. I think I can remember her mockery of my efforts – 'Is that the best you can manage? Are you even trying?' – and my frenetic efforts to knock the contempt out of her. And, yes, of course, in some atavistic and semi-conscious way, I wished to hurt her and to hurt Robert. I whipped and whacked her until she begged for mercy, and more after that. She climaxed with a dramatic double movement, a lurch and slump, like a giraffe, I thought dotingly, that had been tranquillised.

When it was over, I think that we lay, panting, in silence for a good long time, looking blankly at each other, as if it had not happened, much as if we were complete strangers who could not work out how they had ended up in the same room.

Then all at once she was sitting up straight in bed. I thought she was moving away from the damp area on the sheets, and began to protest in a jovial way. But she clutched her chest and I sat up as well. By a strip of orange light from the street I could see fear on her face. The climax of sex seemed to have receded an hour in the past minute and in its place there was cold.

'I don't feel well,' she said.

I reached out to comfort her, but she swatted my arm away. I felt frighteningly sober now, though, again, it was probably only relative sobriety. Her hands were clammy and she was still breathing very rapidly. She had slid off the bed and was standing on the floor, taking long, solemn breaths, her hands behind her head.

She reached for the dressing gown and wrapped it with brave grandeur around herself, fastening the cord as if it had never had, nor would ever have, any other possible use. 'I'm going to go and get some fresh air.'

'Shall I come?'

'No, no,' she said, 'stay here, I'll be back in a minute. I'm fine.'

Then there were her heavy footsteps outside, and then, a confusion of noises, the order of which I cannot exactly recall because I have made so many hundreds of attempts to reconstruct it in my mind that what remains is really, as it were, the memory of other memories. I thought I could hear her half-singing, half-muttering to herself. My concern for her welfare was competing with a post-coital sentimentality at the distinctive, creaking tread of her large feet. But the only important sound was a great discordant crash and thud, and – almost at the same time, but not quite – a short cry. It was not until I heard the opening of doors and raised panicky voices that I fully understood something was terribly wrong. Hurrying outside, I was comforted by my old favourite idea that nothing could in reality be as bad as the noise had seemed to portend. This idea lasted one or two seconds, then I looked down to see Charles crouching on the stairs, and next to him, the figure of Rose.

The Ravenhills, who had effectively disowned Rose for the past couple of years, suddenly became very interested in her again. They quickly released a statement which included the phrases 'our daughter was stolen from us' and lamented the tragedy 'that she ever became involved with this man'. It strongly implied that Rose had been an innocent victim of some sort of sexual predator, who had 'coerced her into becoming a business partner'. It stopped a few degrees short of calling me a murderer.

Her father had a great many contacts in legal and medical fields, and several of them became involved in the case, some publicly, some rather more subtly. In advance of the hearing in court, they managed to get a statement from a cardiologist confirming that, although Rose had had a congenital heart defect, such a spontaneous overloading of her heart as had caused her collapse could hardly have occurred without 'considerable violence'.

In a piece of sleight of hand, the same testimony also remarked that, given her 'remarkable dimensions', she had always been unusually physically vulnerable and I should have been 'far more circumspect' before using 'sadomasochistic sexual techniques' upon her. In other words, her heart was weak enough to make me guilty of mishandling her, yet not weak enough to mitigate my guilt in the slightest. It was ingenious.

My defence, a recently qualified barrister named Alan Bath, began the process as a youngish, energetic, ruddy sort of person. Very soon, he had the face of a fifty-year-old and had taken to muttering aggrievedly about 'the establishment' and 'best practice'. He told me that the maximum sentence for manslaughter was life, although 'of course it would not really mean life'. He kept saying he was still optimistic. I soon realised he only said this when he was feeling very worried.

But all of this had virtually no effect upon me, because from the moment I knew she was gone – which was even before paramedics had arrived at Cloth Street – I ceased to take an interest in what happened to me. That sporadic feeling I have previously described, of being in some way not wholly a participant in my own life, now became, as the English say, the norm. I did not taste food, I did not acknowledge things as belonging to me, I did not remember conversations held just minutes previously. I endured the first of a still ongoing series of dreams in which Rose arrived in the office, clutching some files, and, for example, bent to remove her great black boots, or flung herself wearily onto the bed on her back. The waking up from these dreams was such a bitter disappointment that I became even less inclined to try to differentiate between reality and memory, or nothingness.

The theatre of the court case only increased my unfamiliarity with my own story. I did not recognise this 'sadomasochism' I was forced to describe, while the black-clad Ravenhills (the father now completely bald, the mother in shaded glasses throughout) refused to look at me, and the jurors fiddled awkwardly with their papers. I did not recall having 'imposed' myself upon Rose. I might have 'exacerbated the strain upon her' by my withdrawal from the Hitler role, but it hardly seemed fair to present this, as the prosecution did, as another act of aggression on my part.

Yet, perhaps it was all true. Perhaps I had conveniently misremembered things. Maybe she had always submitted to, rather than initiating, what we did. Besides, as everyone kept implying or saying outright, a person who would not only impersonate Hitler professionally, but carry over the impersonation into what was called (with pitiless irony) his 'private life', had somewhat forfeited his right to that old British institution, the benefit of the doubt.

The only aspect of the court case that affected me was the interrogation of Charles, who was called as a witness. He had bought a black suit which looked as odd on him as if he had appeared in fancy dress. His hair and general appearance were as slapdash as ever, and there were some snickers when he came into the box. He was repeatedly asked to testify whether he had heard me 'making threats' and 'bullying' Rose. The fact that such 'threats' were all meant in play, and often specially commissioned by Rose, was of course part of my defence, but somehow, this made less of an impression than Alan Bath had been hoping. Charles met my eyes across the room as he mumbled that, yes, our exploits had been noisy and violent-sounding on occasion. He looked guilty and miserable. Of course, I would have liked to say that I did not blame him a bit, but I was not allowed to speak to him at all.

After all this – I am not sure how long the case went on – I was sentenced to six years. When asked if I wished to say anything, I stated that I would not care if I were sentenced to decapitation. The Ravenhills said to the press that it was very lenient. They then asked the media to leave the story alone because of the 'distress caused to the family'. Alan Bath shook my hand sweatily. He seemed very glad the whole thing was over. I was really neither glad, nor upset, nor anything.

I have been in jail – in a total of three different jails – since 1992. The fact that my sentence has proved to be longer than the one originally dealt to me is owing to a man named Peter Nicol, who moved into a cell along the corridor from mine around four years into my sentence, and just at the point where I might have been considered for early release. This Nicol was a thug, but also an excellent sportsman who preened himself and held court during all exercise sessions. During a game of football one afternoon, he began to address me as 'Adolf'. At this time, Germany had just beaten England in another big game and someone told me later that this had been a factor in his hostility. But in truth, Nicol was the sort of person who would probably attack an animal if he heard it came from another country.

A few weeks later, I irritated him by taking the last boiled potatoes at lunch and he returned to the Nazi theme. Again, I allowed this to pass. I received no support from any of the prison officials, most of whom were afraid of Nicol.

Some weeks later there was another game of football and Nicol again addressed me as 'Adolf' and 'Hitler' throughout. After perhaps half an hour of this, my patience failed. 'Will you stop saying that fucking name!' I said, angrily. Nicol and some of his cronies laughed at my indignation, and this stirred a painful half-memory of the woman I had spent the past couple of years trying not to think of.

The next thing I knew was that one of Nicol's friends muttered something to him and he turned to me during a break in play. The supervising officer was elsewhere on the field. 'So, I hear you used to dress up as Hitler and beat your woman!' said Nicol, with the veins throbbing in his big, flat head, his mouth turned up in a hideous grin. I ran away with their laughs and whistles behind me. My hands were shaking.

I did not, contrary to accusations levelled at me, premeditate what followed. It happened that the ball came towards me; Nicol challenged another player, the two of them fell in a heap almost next to me. To my own surprise as much as anyone's, I went up to Nicol and stamped on his face, several times. I was wearing an old, heavy pair of football boots I had found in the prison's equipment store. I caused considerable damage to Nicol's eye. A judiciary procedure took place. I was charged with grevious bodily harm and made no attempt to defend myself; indeed I indicated that, given the opportunity, I would put my foot through his other eye. This weakened my position. I was given an eight-year sentence on top of what I had already accrued, and transferred to another jail, in Norfolk.

If I sound casual in the reporting of these incidents, I was equally casual in experiencing them. Once, I would have been appalled to find myself committing such violence, but after what had already happened to me, it was as nothing. And the prospect of further incarceration was of course irrelevant; in fact, I almost courted it. In truth, I had been looking ahead to my release with something like trepidation. I could see absolutely no use in being, as they say, a free man.

After all, what would this 'freedom' consist of? There was nothing waiting for me outside. I had lost or alienated everyone of importance. Admittedly, there is still my brother – and indeed, I have recently begun communicating with him again – but, unlike many of the prisoners who have served shorter sentences than me for graver crimes, I have never had any ambition of 'beginning again'. There is nothing to begin.

» Alexandra

By the time I finished, Gareth was asleep, propped at an odd angle against the wall. I sat there for a while with the final page, passing it from one hand to the other. He was breathing so quietly that for a second I could almost believe he might have stopped. I tried to sit him up slightly for the sake of his back, but at the touch of my hand he shot up straight and opened his eyes. For a few moments he looked around, confused and incredulous to be in my room. Then he remembered.

'So,' he said, flexing his toes. 'Sorry – pins and needles. So you've read it.'

'Yes.' I looked at him. 'So Andreas . . . murdered . . . well, manslaughtered her.'

'She died, yes,' said Gareth.

There was silence.

'The two of you will have a bit more to talk about now,' said Gareth.

I realised I hadn't told him what had happened. 'I don't know where he's gone,' I said, and described all the events: the bust-up at work, going to the jail, finding no Andreas there. Gareth listened attentively.

'So that's why you looked as if you'd had a difficult day,' he muttered.

'But . . .' I said. 'I mean, thanks for doing so much. Going to so much effort.'

'But what you are going to do?' he asked.

'Well . . .' I tried to sound businesslike. 'There are a few options. I've already emailed the prison service. I'll find out soon enough where he is.'

'What about Steel?'

'Yes . . .' I admitted. 'It might be worth talking to him.'

'Of course it would be,' said Gareth, looking at me for a second in the old way, as if I were a moron. 'He's the one person with any link to Andreas.'

'But I think he might be a bit mad,' I reminded him. 'He never visits Andreas. And he looks – well, he looked pretty crazy. I wouldn't fancy . . .'

'But if I went with you . . .' Gareth murmured, looking the other way.

We heard a key clattering about in the lock and, eventually, the door swinging open. Gareth shuffled off the bed and stood up. I tried to conceal my disappointment.

'No offence,' he said, 'but we'd better not . . . I'd better not, um.'

'You'd better not be seen with me,' I said for him.

'Not with you,' said Gareth, reddening. 'It's not that. It's . . .' He scratched his nose. 'I'll see you tomorrow, right? After work.'

I heard him greet Dan in a guarded tone. Not long

afterwards, Gareth's bedroom door shut, along the corridor. I lay in bed rereading the end of Andreas's story. I remembered the first time I had seen his picture, in the WriteToAConvict brochure: 'a series of events too freakish to mention', it had said. True enough. My sleep was full of very strange dreams, none of which I could remember properly when I woke up.

Officially, I was suspended from work for another two days, I left a couple of messages for Helen during the day, after getting up very late. It was hard to kill the time until six, when Gareth had said he'd meet me in front of the Oswald House. Whatever else was wrong with my job, it was certainly a time-killer. I played around on the internet, doing searches on 'Rose Ravenhill death' and 'Andreas Hönig imprisonment' and so on. Even now, with all this information about the story, there was little to be found on the net; there was a paragraph about Rose on the Tall Club of Great Britain's website, but even that glossed over the details of her death. For Andreas, there was nothing at all. Perhaps he had changed his name. Perhaps he had made the whole thing up, the lookalike agency, all of it, and was a delusional maniac who was really banged up for fraud. It wasn't impossible.

Helen called me in her lunch-break, her voice muffled by a mouthful of Swiss roll. Very quickly it began to feel like a make-up conversation between lovers who have fallen out. We laughed eagerly at each other's jokes. She said that things were boring without me. I told her I was very sorry for having accused her of shopping me; it was a relief to have her, rather than her voicemail, hear it. She said she was pondering punching Albert. I said it might not improve the situation, and we laughed.

'When are you coming back?' she asked after a pause. 'Are you coming back?'

'I don't know . . .' I said.

'I think I'm going to leave,' Helen said.

'Really?'

'I can't do this for ever. You've sort of made me realise that we're underestimated. Or . . . if you leave, I'll hate it. Or . . . well, something.' I thought Helen was as taken aback by her own solemnity as I was, but then there was a chewing sound and I realised she was just finishing off the Swiss roll. Even so, I was touched.

It was at that moment I knew I was definitely not going back to my job, and that whatever I did next was likely to be more satisfying.

'Shall we get another job together?' Helen suggested, as if reading my mind.

'OK,' I said. 'I think it's my turn to find it this time, isn't it?'

'Yes, get on to it,' said Helen. 'No proposals this time, OK, and no letters. Ideally, no paper at all. Maybe a florist. One that doesn't wrap flowers in paper.'

We said goodbye and I walked about with a smile on my face. Well before four o'clock, I left for the Oswald House.

Cloth Street was quiet as ever, with the exception of Andreas's former home. What had been the Oswald House was a cloud of dust, hard hats, tape and warning signs. Loud pop music was playing on a stereo and a builder whistled along to a tune as he wheeled a cement mixer past me. The banner stretched across the building now boasted that the flats were '85% SOLD'. The sky was overcast, but although it wasn't a clear night, there was an early-December chill in the air. It occurred to me that we could easily be too late; Charles might have vanished now, in which case I would feel very stupid for not having spoken to him before. On the other hand, he would surely cling on to the house as long as he possibly could.

I saw Gareth's gangly frame, briefcase in one hand, gliding towards me through the dusk. He was still in work clothes and had a takeaway coffee in one hand. 'A'right,' he said. 'Well, here we are.'

We both looked at the house.

'What've you been doing?' he asked.

'On the internet,' I said. 'Trying to find out more about it. There isn't a lot, though.'

'Her parents might have managed to put an embargo on press coverage or something,' said Gareth. 'They were lawyers, weren't they?'

'Why would they have done that, rather than let Andreas get as much abuse as possible?'

'Well, no one particularly wants the world to read about their dead daughter liking a bit of a beating in the bedroom,' said Gareth matter-of-factly, gazing off into the distance. 'Whereas, with the official version in place, everyone would think it was just Andreas being a pervert or something.' He paused. 'As if a bloke like him could just command a woman like her. As if any man can just . . . make a woman go along with sex games and . . . punishment.'

'You know what you're on about, do you?' I asked. He flushed. I looked the other way.

'Well, anyway,' I said. 'There's not much trace of the story left. If I hadn't written to Andreas and you hadn't translated it . . .'

'Yes,' said Gareth sardonically, 'how awfully clever we both are.'

As if independently of each other, we walked up to the Oswald House. There, in the faded writing, was the word Steel. We looked at each other. He pressed the buzzer.

'It's like being in the Famous Five,' Gareth muttered. 'Or those ones, who were they? The ones who solved mysteries.'

I couldn't help him.

'The Five Find-Outers,' he said impatiently.

He buzzed again, shivering in the wind.

'You'll get ill all over again,' I said.

'Yes?' said a faint voice suddenly, making us both jump.

'This is, we are,' said Gareth, slightly red and flustered, 'we would like to talk to you.'

Steel said something fuzzy and inaudible.

'What's that, sorry?' Gareth shouted.

'I said,' said Steel's voice on the intercom, 'I am not contracted to move out of this place for another three days, and I shall not be going anywhere one minute earlier than that time.'

'No, it's not about the house,' said Gareth. 'It's about . . . we need your help.'

As I was about to remark on how unlikely it seemed that Charles might want to help us, the door clicked and yielded to Gareth's push.

We walked slowly up the series of staircases through the middle of the building. Here on the inside, there was no work going on; the drilling and hammering outside sounded far off. There was now nothing left of the former museum: the pictures, ornaments, curiosities that Charles once pointed out to visitors had all gone. Our footsteps sounded very loud. Gareth led, but kept glancing back, either in a protective spirit or just to check I hadn't disappeared. We got to the foot of the staircase leading to Charles's flat and what had been Andreas's; the staircase where Rose had died. Gareth seemed to be thinking the same as I was.

'This is freaky,' he muttered.

'Well, obviously you'll have lifts serving the floors,' I said, as a joke, but he looked at me oddly and I remembered that he hadn't been here last time. We were on the landing. Random scenes from Andreas's story came to mind: the Twister mat with Julian and Rachel playing on it, Andreas fussing about, the parties they used to have. You would have thought there had been no parties here for a century. I was wondering which of us was going to knock when Gareth did, twice. I rubbed my hand against my wrist and could feel the frantic rhythm of my pulse. The door opened, so slowly that I had time, three or four times over, to think, Perhaps we shouldn't be here. My hand stretched out for Gareth's, then went back to my side.

'Yes?' said Charles Steel.

He was wearing a shirt, tie and suit jacket. His beard swarmed over his face like shrubs. He had on a thick pair of glasses, which he removed.

'May . . . can we come in?' said Gareth, with a very slight quaver in his voice.

'Well, you might,' said Charles Steel, after a short silence. 'But there is very little to see.' He stepped aside, allowing us to see into the room. Its contents had been packed into a bunch of cardboard boxes. 'Bare!'

We nodded, hoping to humour him, if that was the word.

'Bare!' said Steel again. 'I cannot even offer you tea or coffee! Every last thing is in a box. I am about to leave and I shall not come back, you see. There is, however, a café just around the corner. I forget its name these days.'

'We are here in relation to – concerning Andreas,' said Gareth stiffly.

'Andreas Honig,' I said.

'Or Hönig,' Gareth said, correcting the pronunciation.

'Andreas,' Steel repeated. Some emotion twitched his

eyebrows and his mouth curled upwards for a second with what looked like nostalgia, or at least sentimentality of some kind. For a second I felt I could see through everything that was disquieting or weird about him. I could imagine him chatting to Rachel, all dressed up as his character.

'Can you tell us where he is?' I asked, boldly.

Charles Steel looked me up and down. 'Certainly,' he said. A momentary pause. 'He is in prison!'

'Yes, we know . . .'

'He is incarcerated!' said Steel with a stifled bark that sounded like laughter crossed with indignation. 'For the death of Rose Ravenhill, which occurred just yards from where you are standing.'

'We know the story,' said Gareth again.

'I'm a voluntary, I do visits to a prison, I met Andreas and he told me his – well, he gave me his memoirs,' I said, trying to rush the words out before I could hear them. 'And Gareth translated them.'

'Gareth,' said Charles Steel sardonically, 'must be quite the polyglot.' I could see the sunset of Gareth's face in my peripheral vision.

'Well!' said Steel, brightly. 'It seems curious to me that you should come here asking a question which you are already so well equipped to answer – especially the erudite Gareth.' He seemed to be taking a perverse pleasure in repeating Gareth's name as if it were ridiculous.

'He's been moved,' said Gareth. 'We wondered if you knew anything about where to.'

'Again, I can oblige you,' said Steel. 'I can answer your question easily. I do not know anything of Andreas. I have not seen him in some years.'

'Why not?' I asked.

'Why not?' Steel repeated as if he had not understood.

'Yes, you were Andreas's best friend. Why—?'

'Why not!' yelled Steel with a sudden, bizarre gesture, thrusting his arms into the air as if he was trying to part some invisible cloud in front of him. 'Why did I not make more of everything! Why do I not move out of this place and let the "executives" take over! Why in this day and age would a man wish to live on his own, to be left in peace! No, no . . .' He gestured at us as if to say he was impersonating us. '"We have to come and hunt him down and tell him all about Andreas and ask why he did not do this and that!"'

Gareth and I glanced at each other. His hand was tight on the banister. 'We're sorry for disturbing you,' I said. Gareth turned to go. He got as far as the second step before Steel gave another yell, this time with a completely different note, quavering, pleading – like a grandfather calling back his children. 'Don't go!'

We turned. Steel broke out into coughs. 'I am sorry for my manner,' he said. 'I would not wish to disappoint my first visitors, other than that infernal estate agent, in so long.' I met his eyes and wondered if he remembered me from my previous visit. It seemed not. 'Let me . . . what do you want to know? Ask me something else.'

'What happened to Julian and Rachel?' asked Gareth promptly. I was impressed; I couldn't think of anything to say. Steel gave a rueful laugh.

'They are still together, and now reside in Australia,' he said. After his little outburst he seemed perfectly calm, and his tone was conversational. 'I hear it is very pleasant at this time of year – almost too hot – you know, it is their summer.' He gave a laugh so short, he might have just been clearing his throat. 'Every year he writes to me. Julian. And never fails to say, "You know, it is actually summer here at Christmas time . . ." Every year! He takes me for an idiot to this day.'

'Are they still lookalikes and . . . Ripper . . . ?'

Charles grunted. 'Heavens. No, of course not. Nobody in their senses does that for longer than they have to. They own a farm.'

Gareth and I stood there. It seemed the story was receding before our eyes. I had to keep glancing around and remembering that everything had happened here, and all so recently, even though, pretty soon, there would be even less trace of the lookalike agency here, of Rose and Andreas, than ever.

'What about Nina . . .' I began to say, but Charles had started talking again.

'You can imagine how odd it was when Rachel came along,' he said, as if addressing a larger group. 'I had been conducting the tours on my own. Dress up as Oswald, get a clap at the end, do it again, so on. Uneventful. Left me plenty of time. Suddenly here was this very charming girl. And we were colleagues. Trying to make each other laugh and the like. Putting on idiotic voices. Spouting a load of baloney which the tourists took as fact. Some of the things she came out with would make me snort. She is the only person ever to have made me laugh in public, I think.'

'Did you . . . ?' Gareth began, but again, the question was cut off dead. Charles Steel was now talking at a fair pace and seemed, if not oblivious, certainly indifferent to us.

'It was a good time,' he said, gazing at the staircase. 'You know, I had done a great many jobs. A great many. All, in one way or another, idiotic. Dropped out of the army as a young man. Tried and failed to write this and that. Did research nobody needed. I was drifting through my life. And suddenly here is this job, and soon afterwards, here is this girl. We had a good deal of fun. Trampolining. Her, of course! Not I! You should have seen her bouncing. Her hair all spread out. She was very clever at haircare. One time – some party. She rubbed all this nonsense into my hair to give me a 'style'. Her hands, so very delicate . . .' His hands traced a route over his scalp, through his now straggly locks. It was uncomfortable viewing.

'And the coffee. Many, many visits to the café. I could not really stand coffee or any such drink. I swilled down hundreds of cups of the stuff to be in her company. And zipping up her dress in the morning. She couldn't reach it . . . the zip. Fastening it all. Getting ready together. A good couple of years, it was. I never introduced her to Julian. Never brought her to the Pennyfarthing. Wanted to keep her to myself.'

He paused for breath, but this time, neither of us tried to say anything. 'Rose never took to me,' he said. 'When the lookalike agency came, I remember her looking at me askance behind my back, the first time they came here; I could see her in the mirror. Quite a cheek! Being as tall as she was. An extraordinary spectacle. Bending under that ceiling beam there, inspecting the bathroom, all the time making a lot of little sniping comments about the Victorians. And, later, about James Oswald. And about everything. Oh, well, I thought. Let us be a good neighbour. She is awfully tall. It must be difficult.

'Andreas was a decent sort. I wished them all the best with – with all of it.' He waved his arms again, it looked as though he was indicating a specific patch of the wooden floor in front of him. 'Here, they would wait, all these odd folk. People who thought they looked like – Eddie Murphy. Or Frank Sinatra. And seriously thought that that, alone, would make them famous; or popular, or whatever they wanted to be.

'Rose was very good at making them feel important,' said

Charles Steel. 'The successful ones.' Gareth had crept along the wall so that he was standing, in his usual manner, at the angle of two walls, his body sloping lazily; but his eyes were riveted on Steel. I could feel the cold metal of the banister against my back. I was still standing bolt upright. It must be an extremely strange scene, the three of us out here. I could hear very faint drilling. The internal walls may have been thin, but something about the house choked off most of the sound from the rest of the world, to this day.

'Yes,' Steel repeated, 'she loved successful people. She was obsessed with it. Success. She pursued it like a madwoman. What she wanted, she normally got. Oh, yes, I knew that all too well from trying to get to sleep next to their interminable noisy copulation! Him saying this and her saying that and then the noises of hitting and wailing and God knows what. Extraordinary. Extraordinary lack of consideration for the neighbour, a bachelor who was still trying to . . . to work up the . . . what-have-you to make a formal proposition to Rachel. I once said if they ever annoyed me, I should bang on the wall. Of course I never meant to do this really. If I had hit the wall every time they kept me awake with their shenanigans, my hands would have been red raw! No, no; good old Charlie plays along with everything and pretends to be quite deaf. As a matter of fact I did buy a, a . . . what? what?' He snapped his fingers at us.

'A Walkman?' Gareth blurted out, startled.

'A Walkman!' Charles Steel repeated, approvingly. 'Beethoven's 7th would come on each time I wanted to get away from them.' He hummed a couple of bars. 'Beethoven, of course, was deaf – the lucky bastard.'

Gareth sniggered at this.

'Yes, Charlie always plays along,' said Charles Steel, his

monologue showing no sign of running out of steam. 'That was Julian's attitude. He thought I was a very strange sort for not being as ambitious as he. With his epic tours. Leading three thousand people across Brick Lane. Parting the Red Sea. Julian, always such a good-natured fellow. And boyish. Charming. No one had a bad word. No wonder that Rachel fell for him! As James Oswald once said . . .' he began. 'Well, what's the use?'

'So you . . .' my mouth was very dry, 'you were in love with . . .?'

'With Rachel, good Lord, yes,' said Charles. 'Yes, but of course old Julian landed the prize. Watched them . . . kissing like a couple of . . . at the Christmas party. I'd been under the mistletoe trying to catch her eye, but no, good old Rose pushed me at Nina, this hapless girl with some nonsense on her head – antlers! Well, never mind, I still had Rachel as a workmate. But – wait a tick! What's this? That's right, Julian and Rose put their heads together and, well, what do you think, Rachel turns out to be a dead ringer for some old cow or other from the films. So suddenly she is a lookalike! Suddenly every Tom, Dick and Harry is a lookalike, except me! Who the hell was I going to look like?' He grabbed his shirt as if he was going to tear it. It reminded me of something like *King Lear*, this old man raving away, one minute almost genial, the next alarming.

'Well, that was that!' said Steel. He coughed and cleared his throat. I thought, though it had to be my imagination, that I could hear the Oswalds' grandfather clock tolling downstairs. 'Rachel had a glamorous job, much more glamorous than the museum. Matter of time before she quit this and swanned off to perform on boats and all that. With Julian on her arm. Naturally. The two of them were more and more polite in my company, going to great pains not to mention one another. A sorry thing, to have people sorry for you.

'Casual slurs,' said Steel, more than ever now talking as if to himself. 'Rose: "Charles, that old windbag! Charles, prattling on about sweet FA!"'

'I thought that was—' Gareth tried to interrupt, but in vain. The tirade about Rose was in full swing.

'"Charles is just the old codger next door; no talent there, no 'earning potential'. No 'bankable commodity'. Charles is the tedious fellow rattling on in the taxi about cheese and elephants, while I, Rose, have serious business on my ever-so-serious mind." Oh, that got on my . . . on my wick, when she bashed her head on the car door, and I tried to make a sympathetic noise, and she glared at me as if I were grinning like a Cheshire cat. And it was always like this. This farce of bumping into her in the corridor, or going round to call upon Andreas, and having to smile and be all polite and friendly, when it was as plain as the nose on her face – that great long face of hers – that she had no respect for me! God knows, for a woman who thought she was so clever, it seemed beyond her to realise that I could hear every last thing they said and did in that flat!

'Or perhaps she was aware, and she simply never cared. She was a great one for not caring, Rose. It was the only way she could manage, you see, with the terrible misfortune of being a "freak", as she was at pains to remind Andreas almost every night of her life. No, she did not care what anyone thought of her. She did not care if Andreas suffered while she allowed that other monster . . . Robert, into bed with her. And then made Andreas enter into ever greater . . . sexual efforts to gratify her. It was all right with her that he had to keep doing the Hitler act long after he had realised the whole thing was not really for him, and was, perhaps, dangerous. It was all right if that poor deluded girl Nina watched her ambitions being made a mockery of. If the whole world went to hell, never mind, Rose was all right, and who could criticise her? It was so hard for her! So very, very tall!'

He stuck out a long finger at Gareth. 'How tall is Gareth? The angular Gareth?'

'Six two,' Gareth muttered.

'There we are,' said Steel, 'an estimable height! Yet, does Gareth seek special allowances?'

'I'm not quite as tall as—' he said.

'Well, but what height must one reach before one is given special dispensation to meddle with others' lives?' Charles asked with a rhetorical gesture as if he had been rehearsing this for years. 'Six and a half feet? Six feet eight inches? Or did one have to be "the fifth tallest woman in Great Britain" or whatever absurd boast it was she made?'

He took a couple of steps towards us. I backed away as far as I could. I met Gareth's eyes and we silently agreed that we could still run away at any point.

'Those parties,' said Steel. He paused for a long time.

'Those parties,' said Steel again, 'noisy, crowded, smoky, and full of people who thought they were the cleverest thing ever to set foot in London. But where were the geniuses of Oswald's time? The great men, the artists? No, no one of real calibre. Andreas was the only one of them worth anything. And Rachel. And Rachel was disappearing from my sight.

'He wished to die in this house,' said Steel.

'Andreas?' I said. Steel snorted derisively. 'Oswald,' he said. 'But he could not, of course, afford the upkeep. He moved out five years after Tessa left. Lived on his own for twenty years in places of declining salubriousness. Ended up back in Devon;

died before his fiftieth birthday. Drunk.' Charles ruffled his beard. 'Theo Oswald bought the house back in middle age, for reasons no one has ever understood. Passed it down. Leonard Oswald had it during the two wars. His daughter tried to turn it into some sort of hippy-commune atrocity. Then, the Victorian Trust made it a museum. It was a museum for thirty years. Oswald lived on.'

He cleared his throat. 'But that is that.'

The silence was thick again. I could hear myself breathing, or it might have been Gareth.

Steel jerked his bony wrist to check his watch with elaborate care. 'It is rather late,' he said pointedly.

I felt I would be happy enough to leave now. But Gareth spoke up.

'Do you remember the night she died?' he asked. 'Rose.'

Charles Steel stood there for some time as if he had not heard the question, but by now we were accustomed to the rhythm of his reminiscences.

'You probably imagine that I took some satisfaction,' he said. 'That I was happy!' Another long pause. He shook his head slowly. 'It was a night like this. Rainy. Not that that was of much consequence to me. I spent it indoors, as I have tonight.' Once more there was that throaty bark of his, which I was coming to think of as not really a laugh at all.

'It was loud as ever,' he said. 'So loud they might as well have had the party in here!' He tapped his head with two fingers. 'In my skull!' Then as we watched he took a few steps across the landing, to what had once been Andreas and Rose's front door. With a swift shove of his hand he sent the door swinging open. Gareth and I leaned forward to look.

'Well, come on!' said Steel. 'Come and have a look inside! Come and have a butcher's!' he added, venomously.

I glanced at Gareth and the two of us edged forward until we were standing on the threshold. There was nothing at all in the room: no furniture, no carpet, no light bulbs; just a bald window through which an eerie orangey light shone in from the street. Neither of us wanted to go any further. I tried to remember whether the estate agent had said this flat and Charles Steel's were going to be knocked together into one. Someone would move in here with no idea what had once happened.

'They were everywhere,' said Steel, 'those people.' He came back out of the room towards Gareth and me, and the two of us retreated, quite thankful to be back where we were. 'Andreas standing on a table, performing as Hitler,' he said, folding his arms across his chest. 'I told him not to.'

Another pause. I wondered how long we were going to be here. I was feeling very tired; the atmosphere of the house seemed to be moving in on all sides. 'Finally, when it was over,' Steel said, 'I tried to get some sleep.' It seemed a long time since I had slept really well. I tried to push these thoughts away. 'But easier said than done,' said Steel bitterly, 'with those two up to their usual tricks once more!' He gave a deep sigh. 'The loudest, most obscene assault on the ears the two of them had ever presented. For the first time, I took action – yes, for me, decisive action! I rapped on the wall.' With his fist, he knocked on the wall above his front door. The sound was oddly loud and, in this place with no one but us, somehow very lonely.

'But on it went,' he said, 'and even when it was over, more disturbances. Muttering, footsteps out on the landing. Then the creaking of the stairs. Rose, padding about – but a woman of those dimensions could hardly "pad". I heard the plod of her great feet. To the devil with this, I thought!

'I came out onto the landing. Stood at the top of the stairs. There she was, with a hand on her heart.' He pointed at me. 'Go on – go and stand over there!'

'Don't . . .' Gareth began to object.

'Stand there!' said Steel in a frightening voice. I took a couple of very tentative steps around the corner, so that I was standing on the stairs, clutching the banister very hard. Gareth took a step towards me as if to shield me from Steel. 'Here I came, in my woollen dressing gown,' said Steel. 'The look that passed between us! Two people in dressing gowns have never looked so hostile!'

Steel walked towards me, brushing past Gareth. He was a couple of steps above me. I wished we weren't here. My stomach was slipping around. Gareth's eyes were boring into Steel and his mouth had dropped slightly open.

'"Are we disturbing you, Charles?" she asked. I thought perhaps he was going to make me say this line, since he was already using me as a body double for Rose, but on he went.

'"You are rather," I said.

'"Well I'm sorry," she said, tetchily, "I am feeling ill."

'"Could it be," I said, "because of all the drinking, partying and masochistic sex acts?" She was taken by surprise, but not for long; give her credit, she was a fast talker. "I'd say you are the masochist, Charles, pining over Rachel so pathetically."

'Well,' said Steel, looking down at me, 'I did not like that. I pushed her.'

He motioned with his hands the act of pushing me down the stairs.

There was silence. Gareth and I looked at each other. Gareth was pale.

Steel seemed very pleased by our expressions. With a

mixture of gravity and a raconteur's pride, he let it soak in before continuing. 'Of course, straight away I knew it was a terrible thing. A terrible . . . I did not wish to harm her! Let alone to kill her! Let alone to kill her!'

His voice rebounded around the house.

'It was quite obvious straight away,' said Charles, 'that she was . . . I mean to say, she was an awful shape. Just there!' He gestured at a spot behind me. I turned, shuddering, feeling certain that I was going to see Rose's body lying there. Charles's melodramatic behaviour was making it hard to focus on the things he was saying. Gareth had screwed up his eyes as if he was having trouble seeing. My mind was spinning. 'I came and knelt by her,' said Steel, but he was not, thankfully, going to act this out. He had taken up a position on the landing again. 'I heard a noise and came out! That is what I said to Andreas. And at the trial. And for ever, when anyone asked me.'

Perhaps a couple of minutes passed in silence. It might not have been as long as that; it certainly felt like it.

'Why . . . ?' Gareth was staring at Steel with what almost looked like awe. 'Why did you let Andreas . . . ?'

'Why let him take the blame?' Steel said. He seemed genuinely to weigh it up, as if he had never even asked himself the question. 'Andreas was convinced that he had killed her,' said Steel at last. 'He was resigned to punishment – well, in fact he wished for it. I did not wish for punishment. I could not live in a prison, with people all around. I would not last. In the trial, I simply went along with all the questions, allowed them to reach the conclusions they seemed to be after. Did Andreas mistreat her? Well, perhaps he did on occasion, for all I knew. Might he have done various things against her will? I supposed he might. Yes, I supposed he might, if it was my neck or his on the block. Having convinced people I was innocent – very easily, as I was not suspected in the first place! – I began to convince myself. And months became years.

'Well, perhaps you understand now,' Steel concluded, with the ghost of a smile, 'why I could never visit Andreas.'

'Unbelievable coward,' muttered Gareth. Both of us looked at him.

'I'm sorry?' said Steel, blinking at him.

'Gareth . . .' I said.

'You're an unbelievable coward,' said Gareth, 'if this is all true.' My stomach felt as if it wanted to escape. 'You've let an innocent man rot in jail!' said Gareth.

'Ah, the fiercely moral Gareth!' said Steel, spluttering with laughter.

'How can you . . . ?' Gareth asked, shaking his head. 'How can you just . . . ?'

Steel again produced his watch and examined it theatrically. 'I think perhaps we have talked for long enough, don't you?'

Gareth and I looked at each other.

'I mean,' said Gareth, 'with what you've told us, we could—'

'I would get out!' Steel roared, so loudly that it made us both jump. A globule of spittle which had leapt out of his mouth landed in a gleam on the banister. He shouted again. 'I think you ought to leave!'

Gareth began to say something else. I grabbed his sleeve. 'Let's go.'

'Yes,' said Steel, 'I think it is time you went! And I do not think I shall have the pleasure of your acquaintance again. But I thank you for listening to this funny little tale.'

'I—' said Gareth.

'Get out!' said Charles, motioning as if to push us away. 'Goodbye!' He took a last look at us and slipped inside, allowing the door to slam behind him.

I was on my way down the stairs almost at a jog, over the spot where Rose Ravenhill died and around the corner. I heard Gareth's footsteps behind me and glanced back to make sure it wasn't Steel. I slowed to allow Gareth to catch up with me. By the time we reached the ground floor, it already seemed impossible that Steel had really been there, that everything had happened.

Gareth leaned over me to pull open the heavy old door. Outside, rain was coming down in sheets illuminated by the orange glare of the lights. The workmen had packed up for the night. The air was cold and sharp. My mind felt as if it had been through an exam, or something similar. I had a strange sense of things not being solid, or real, which I remembered from the night of the botched proposal. I was still breathing very quickly.

After a few moments I noticed I wasn't getting wet. 'Budge up a bit,' muttered Gareth, holding an umbrella over our two heads. We stood together, looking at what had been the Oswald House.

Although we were walking together, Gareth led the way; I was still in a daze. So I couldn't be sure if it was a coincidence that the café we ended up in had once been Koffee Kompany, or whether he somehow knew. Anyway, there on the wall was a little photo of the shopfront as it had been in the nineties, with the garish orange words whose big Ks had so annoyed Charles. There were other photos of various incarnations of the café: Reilly's, Oak and Sons, all the way to the East India

Tea Rooms, with a fierce-looking man in white overalls staring at the camera. Now, it was part of the largest coffee chain in the world.

'Completes the tour nicely, doesn't it,' said Gareth. 'What are you having?' I was still trying to clear my head. Someone in a wet coat came past and made the table wobble. I looked at Gareth dumbly. 'I said, what are you having? Apart from a nervous breakdown.'

He went away and came back with two huge white mugs. Some sort of African percussion music was playing. Gareth set the mugs down and peered at me over them.

'Hard to take it all in, isn't it?'

I wrapped my hands around the mug and began passing it from one to the other. 'Why do you always do that?' he asked.

I looked down at my hands. 'Sorry . . .'

'No,' said Gareth, 'it's, er, I like it.' He looked away, then back at me. 'You'd be a good juggler.'

'What are we going to do?' I said.

'About Steel?' Gareth rubbed his nose. 'Well, we could tell the police everything we know. We could try and get Andreas a retrial or something. I somehow think, though, that Steel might be reluctant to repeat that performance.'

I was thinking furiously, as furiously as I could, anyway; my brain still felt foggy and overloaded. 'At least, if I can find Andreas, I could tell him.'

'We'll find him,' said Gareth.

His phone started to ring. He got it out of his pocket, looked at it sternly like a misbehaving child and pressed a button to shut it up. As he began to speak again, my phone went off; I ignored it. Gareth's began again. He inspected it with a sigh. 'It's Dan. I just can't be . . . he'll be wanting to tell me about some woman he met today or, Christ knows, panicking because he thinks a police horse looked at him weirdly, or . . .'

My phone was going again. This time I looked at it. 'That's odd; Dan as well.'

'It's not odd,' said Gareth logically, 'he's obviously trying to get hold of one or other of us. If it was Kim Basinger – now, that would be odd.'

'But why would he want to get hold of me?' I objected. 'We don't usually talk when we're in the same room.' Gareth shrugged and looked at the phone, which continued to bleep away. I picked up.

'Where the hell are you?' asked Dan, as if he called me about this time every day.

'I'm out.'

'Listen,' he said, 'I've been trying to get hold of Gareth, but he's fuck knows where . . .'

'He's with me,' I said.

'Of course he is,' said Dan grimly. 'Listen, sis, I need you to . . . are you far from home? I need you to go home. There's a bust on. There's about four grand's worth of stuff in our bathroom. I need you to get there as quick as you can, flush it down the toilet, or better still . . .'

'Dan, I don't want to be involved in this,' I said. 'Why can't you do it?'

'They won't let us go anywhere,' he said in a voice between a whine and a sneer. 'They've got a warrant. Allie, I really need you to do this. The coke isn't even mine.'

I hesitated. Gareth seemed to have guessed what this was about.

'I'll do anything,' said Dan.

'You won't,' I found myself saying. 'You'll just go back to normal.'

There was a strange, breathy noise at the other end and I realised he was crying.

'Traffic at this time of day . . . !' said the driver, tapping on the steering wheel. My hands were shaking slightly; I wedged them between my knees. 'A'right?' Gareth muttered. I nodded, looking out of the window. His fingers brushed against mine.

'You two up to anything nice tonight?' asked the driver.

'We're just off home,' said Gareth, 'in the hope of thwarting a massive drug raid.'

'Right you are!' said the driver cheerily.

'I don't understand . . .' I said, feeling as though, at the moment, I didn't seem to understand most of what happened. 'Why has Dan got all that stuff?'

'It's a long story,' said Gareth. 'The short version is that Dan is a fucking idiot. The long version is that he's still a fucking idiot, but with some circumstantial detail. He got into debt, basically, to a dealer. A Chinese fellow; you may have seen him around. The one with the sharkish grin.'

'I did see him once . . .'

'Nice man,' said Gareth quietly, playing with the strap of his seat belt. 'And a very accomplished dealer. One of the best in his field.'

'So Dan had to keep this stuff in our bathroom?'

'Yes, well spotted,' said Gareth. 'He was forced to deal on the dealer's behalf. Half the time when we went out, I was just keeping an eye on him.' He shook his head.

'Is it going to be all right?' I asked, timidly. It had been a very long day.

We were slowly breaking out of the bottleneck of traffic, and in the distance the clump of apartment blocks where we lived could be seen. Along the river, the coloured lights bobbed and twinkled.

'It depends what you call all right,' said Gareth. 'He's not going to be killed. On the other hand, he's not going to have the nicest Christmas.' I thought of Mum.

'Isn't there anything we can do?' I asked.

Gareth patted my knee. 'If the police are already there, then no. We're going back so we can rest easy that we tried. I mean – we could have done things in the past, obviously. We could have forced him to stop. We could have just told him he was being a prick. But I've never been much good at . . .' He let a long breath out through his teeth. 'Like Andreas.'

I thought of the scene we had left, Charles Steel there at the top of the old house.

'I'm going to miss the translation work,' said Gareth quietly.

We pulled into the car park. A police car was sitting right by the main doors, as if they'd been thinking about driving straight up into our flat.

'They might not have found it,' said Gareth. 'In the movies, cops are always very stupid.' I was fumbling in my bag for money, but he leaned past me and handed a twenty-pound note to the driver. We got out. He waved away my efforts to give him some cash. We could see the breath in front of our faces. Gareth led me past the concierge, who gave me a raised-eyebrows look. I looked at the two of us reflected infinitely in the two walls of the lift.

» Epilogue

The first few days of 2004 were fine and cold, no rain; there wasn't a single opportunity to use either of the umbrellas I got for Christmas, the sleek dark green one from Gareth, or the transparent one shaped like a cow from Helen. The two of them brightened up what was a pretty strained Christmas Day at home; I think it would have been better if Dan had been there, in all honesty.

On about the 2nd or 3rd of January, as the holiday season began to die on its feet, *Too Hot to Handle* was on TV. The meagre decorations in our flat had been cleared away by now; we got rid of them on New Year's Day. We spent most of that day cleaning, scrubbing and spraying, and rearranging the place. It was one of Gareth's New Year resolutions not to allow anyone to touch or even allude to drugs in our flat again; not for now, at least. 'Admittedly,' he said, 'the horse has bolted about five miles away, but then no one ever makes a resolution before something bad happens.'

With mugs of hot chocolate, we lay on Dan's vast sofa watching *Too Hot to Handle.* We paid extra attention to the credits. On New Year's Day, we'd been half-watching the festive special episode of an urban drama on TV and Gareth's sharp eyes picked out the name Nina Francisca at the end. She played the junkie mother who shouts 'Christmas is ruined!' and throws her new necklace across the room. We'd looked on the internet. Nina Francisca was thirty-three and had been educated in Cambridge. It had to be the same woman who used to be Nina France. Her CV was almost all bit parts: 'woman number two', 'female priest' in an advert for deodorant. But to look on the bright side, over the past couple of years she had probably done more acting than Kim Basinger.

There were no interesting names in the credits of *Too Hot to Handle*. 'I wonder what happened to that poor bastard who painted himself yellow and did Homer Simpson,' said Gareth. 'He's probably a teacher or something.'

'Or in a mental instititui on,' I said.

'Now, speaking of institutions,' said Gareth. 'Big day tomorrow.'

I went to check my email on his laptop while he got ready for bed. There was one from Claire, sent to two hundred people: it was a list of jokes about being pregnant. There were a couple of late Happy New Year wishes from Helen's party guests. Helen had sent me a link to the website jobsinthefloristindustry.co.uk.

We sat on a near-empty train looking at bleak, wintry countryside. Gareth spotted two tiny birds hopping about at the base of a bare hedgerow. We stopped at some tiny place where no one got on or off and he told me it was the birthplace of some

Victorian who was, presumably, a contemporary of James Oswald's, but I wasn't brave enough to ask.

The letter from Andreas had been waiting there in our pigeon-hole when I got back to London on 29 December. I gave a little cry of excitement when the handwriting, and the HMP stamp, registered. It was short, but everything I needed was there. He said he had never sought a transfer, but they'd told him it was because of a 'security risk'. He agreed that it was probably Claire's interference. As well as the address, there was a map to his new jail.

This prison was a lot bigger than St John's, and the car park was as big as one you'd get at an out-of-town shopping complex. It also looked, as Andreas had said, less like a prison. The main buildings looked more like a health centre, I remarked to Gareth. 'Yeah, well,' he said. 'In a way it is a health centre, isn't it.'

'Are you OK? You seem nervous.'

'Not nervous . . .' he said. 'I've never been to a jail.'

'Don't worry,' I said, 'I have.'

I was the one they frisked more thoroughly, for some reason. Gareth watched with a smirk as they patted my pockets, went through my bag, made me turn around and ran the little truncheon-like metal detector up and down my legs.

Andreas got to his feet when we came in. He embraced me and shook Gareth by the hand. 'So this is Gareth!' said Andreas. He was wearing a red and green knitted sweater which a seventy-year-old might have worn, and his hair, longer now than when I had first visited him, had been carefully combed, though little bits stuck up on both sides to give him a slightly bird-like appearance. His hands were very cold to the touch.

'I must thank you for struggling with my sentences,' said

Andreas to Gareth. Gareth grinned and said something in German which made Andreas laugh.

'So, er,' I said.

'The two of you, then, are now cohabiting?' asked Andreas, looking between us. We both muttered various things. 'We're looking after the flat, while . . .' I said.

'Temporary arrangement until . . .' Gareth murmured. Andreas enjoyed our discomfort.

'It seems like a cohabitation to me,' he said merrily. 'Is this the same Gareth who, in your first letter, you described—'

'Well, things have changed,' I said hastily.

' "Supercilious, an intellectual snob, an arsehole"?' Andreas quoted with relish. I looked at the floor. Gareth laughed. There was a pause.

Then we began to talk about Charles Steel. Andreas said he had been thinking about it all over Christmas, and he had read the letter one hundred times or more, and shown it to a friend on his corridor with legal training, who was in for illegal jewellery trading. The friend said that without being able to prove what Steel had said, it would be extremely difficult to get a retrial or even get anyone interested in the case.

'But anyway, I have only three years to go,' said Andreas, 'I can imagine life now. My brother is getting married,' he added. 'He sent a photograph. I will not be able to attend, but all the same.'

We looked at him and he at us for a while. 'Even with your excellent German,' he said to Gareth, 'and your empathy,' to me, 'I doubt I can begin to thank you for your . . . contribution. You have – well, as the English say, you have brought me back from the dead.'

'The first thing I shall do when I get out,' he said, 'is visit her grave.'

'Where is it?' asked Gareth nearly inaudibly.

'In Manchester,' said Andreas. 'Her parents . . . they forgave her in the end.'

This time, the hour went by very quickly. Before it was over, we had promised to come back as often as we could. I told him that I didn't yet have a new job, so there was lots of time. Gareth said he was going to take more time off; it was another of his resolutions. Andreas shook us both by the hand and held on to mine for so long I thought he would never let go of it. Gareth again made some remark in German.

'What was that you said?' I asked him as we trudged back across the giant car park. There was just the hint of raw winter rain in the air. I got the green umbrella out and proudly unfastened the popper.

'Just warning him off you,' said Gareth, looking at the ground. We reached the station and he bent to study the timetable. Twenty minutes until the train back down into London, where we would stop off to visit Dan before going home.

Acknowledgements

I'd like to thank these people, in alphabetical order, for essential help with this book:

A lot of common sense: Juliet Brooke
Early inroads: Rebecca Carter
Second wave of editing: Clara Farmer
Insights into entertainment: Rebecca Fox
Factual background: Hosanna's aunt Elaine
Saving the entire project from collapse: Ed Jaspers
General inspiration: Matthew Sweet, 'Inventing the Victorians'
Agenting: Patrick Walsh
Wifely excellence: Emily Watson Howes